The GAMES WE PLAY

CASSANDRA DIVIAK

Copyright ©2024 by Cassandra Diviak

All rights reserved.

No part of this publication may be reproduced, distributed, or transmitted in any form or by any means, including photocopying, recording, or other electronic or mechanical methods, without the prior written permission of the publisher, except as permitted by U.S. copyright law. For permission requests, contact Cassandra Diviak through her website, social media, or email (cdiviakauthor@yahoo.com).

The story, all names, characters, and incidents portrayed in this production are fictitious. No identification with actual persons (living or deceased), places, buildings, and products is intended or should be inferred.

No AI tool was utilized in the writing of this novel and its contents.

Without in any way limiting the author's [and publisher's] exclusive rights under copyright, any use of this publication to "train" generative artificial intelligence (AI) technologies to generate text is expressly prohibited. The author reserves all rights to license uses of this work for generative AI training and development of machine learning language models.

Book Cover by Melody Jeffries Design (Whim and Joy)

Editing by Cassidy Hudspeth and Sophie Fitzpatrick

First edition 2024

Content Warnings	VII
The Dicktionary	IX
Playlist	XI
1. Daisy	1
2. Jensen	14
3. Daisy	25
4. Jensen	41
5. Daisy	55
6. Jensen	68
7. Daisy	80
8. Jensen	91
9. Daisy	105
10. Jensen	117
11. Daisy	129
12. Jensen	145
13. Daisy	157
14. Jensen	169
15. Daisy	183
16. Jensen	199

17. Daisy	211
18. Jensen	222
19. Daisy	235
20. Jensen	249
21. Daisy	265
22. Jensen	277
23. Daisy	293
24. Jensen	305
Epilogue	317
The Story Continues	323
Afterword	325
Acknowledgements	327
About the Author	329
Also By Cassandra Diviak	331

For all the girls labeled as "difficult" or "too ambitious." Shoot for the stars, baby, and ***never*** let anyone dull how brightly you shine.

Content Warnings

Dearest readers,

Welcome back to the Love at Royal Ridge series for Book 2! Please enjoy your stay in the California sunshine with a side of romance. *The Games We Play* is underneath the contemporary romance / romantic comedy umbrella; the overtones of the book are meant to be more humorous and sexy. However, the following themes included in the narrative may be triggering for some readers.

- Infidelity (happens to the main characters)

- Medical emergencies (Ch 21)

- Workplace sexism

- Parental abandonment

If these themes relate to personal triggers you might have, please proceed with caution. Your mental health matters to me, and I'd rather you put the book down or DNF than expose yourself to any harm. I've worked hard to handle these topics as sensitively as possible.

This book will also be reserved for the 18+ crowd as there is sexual content consistent with the adult romance genre. For a full breakdown of the scenes or kinks/acts, please proceed to the dicktionary on the next page ;)

The Dicktionary

For those parties interested in either skipping, skimming, or searching for any smut scenes or tropes used, I've listed all of them below:

Smut Scenes and Kinks (by Chapter):

Chapter 5 contains semi-public drunk make outs, dirty talk/banter, blowjob, fingering, tipsy sex, penetration (girl on top)

Chapter 8 contains sexting, oral (female receiving), spitting, mirror sex, penetrative sex (from behind), dirty talk/banter, and jealousy

Chapter 11 contains face-sitting, dirty talk/banter, masturbation, and praise

Chapter 15 contains exhibitionism, dirty talk/banter, praise, hand necklaces, oral (female receiving), work desk sex, fingering, and penetration (from behind + girl on top)

Chapter 22: spitting, lingerie tearing, praise/worship, fingering, intimate/romantic sex, and penetrative missionary

Playlist

Each chapter had a different song I listened to while writing the scenes, befitting the vibes of the chapter or the characters at that point of the story.

    1: Coincidence by Rosse
    2: I Know What You Did Last Summer by Shawn Mendes
    3: Sweet & Sour by Amelia Moore
    4: Deja Vu by VOILA
    5: Can't Remember to Forget You by Shakira
    6: Switch by Mike Taveira
    7: cake & iced coffee by Leyla Blue
    8: Make You Mine by Madison Beer
    9: Aphrodite by RINI
    10: Sweet Relief by Madison Beer
    11: American Money by BØRNS
    12: Bad for Me by VOILA
    13: Maybe You're the Problem by Ava Max
    14: Unlikely by Leyla Blue
    15: Motivate by Little Mix
    16: I Feel It Coming by The Weeknd
    17: ESOEMOEHOED by Leanna Firestone
    18: Homesick by Madison Beer
    19: redbull by Leyla Blue
    20: bad idea, right? by Olivia Rodrigo
    21: Break My Own by Taylor Bickett
    22: Moonlight by Ariana Grande
    23: making the bed by Olivia Rodrigo

24: Shameless by Camila Cabello
Epilogue: Iris by the Goo Goo Dolls

Chapter 1
Daisy

DAISY RIGGS PARTED THE sea of strangers around her with graceful strides. Every step of her heels against the smoothed pavement brought her closer to the towering skyscraper she called "work." Eyes swept across the faces in the crowd in a cursory glance, but the few eyes hers met flickered away.

May sunshine and warm winds blessed the Beverly Hills streets she walked down, nipping at the shimmering second skin of her pantyhose stretched over her mile-long legs. Despite her hands being packed with a purse and morning coffee, she picked at her dark pencil skirt until every wrinkle smoothed out.

Nothing short of perfection would suit her... Daisy Riggs didn't do anything half-assed.

She tightened the angle of her earbuds while the upbeat, irresistible melody of her morning playlist ushered her up the stairs outside her office. She waved to the security guards before ducking into the rotating door.

Stepping into the lobby of Hidden Oasis Hotel & Resort Group headquarters, Daisy marched through the hustle. Like the strangers on the street, people moved out of her way as she approached. But here, they knew her.

Her position as Vice President of Project Development ensured that people knew her face, name, and reputation no matter their position in the office—a reputation she had so rightly earned over her nearly ten years working there.

If anyone asked her years ago if she imagined herself in a high-powered position at a multimillion-dollar company, complete with a personal office and the promise of a life-changing promotion, she would've said no.

But there she was, living the life of a corporate girl and loving every moment. The salary helped, without a doubt.

"Hold the elevator!" Daisy exclaimed, earbuds still in when she approached the nearly full carriage. Several hands reached forward to stop the door from closing on her, letting Daisy squeeze into the space. "Thank you. Good morning, everyone."

She studied the smiling faces of people she used to work alongside before her promotion. Many of them had been with Hidden Oasis since her start at the company years ago.

Hell, they had watched her grow up.

Daisy leaned over and pressed the button for her floor, shining several rows above the others. The V-suite offices were two floors beneath the CEO's personal space at the top of the building, which became a perfect metaphor for her sprint up the corporate ladder.

Most of it came from her dedication to succeed, impressing people by working herself harder than everyone around her. However, her boss refused to let her efforts go unnoticed, and his attention made her a rising star in the company.

She counted each floor they passed under her breath. More people filtered out of the carriage at every stop until Daisy stood alone.

Once the last person stepped off, she let loose. The bubbly, infectious pop music blasting in her headphones inspired the slow swiveling of her hips and the mouthing of the lyrics, eventually breaking into a small performance in the empty elevator.

No one would ever know that Daisy loved bubblegum pop or spent her mornings getting excited by pretending she was throwing a concert for her adoring fans, complete with choreography. That was her secret to keep.

Midway through her rendition of *Genie in a Bottle*, her music cut out, replaced with the buzz of an incoming call. Despite her busy hands, she dug around the deep pockets of her leather jacket, yanking her phone out by the cord of her earbuds.

"This is Daisy Riggs speaking. How can I help you?" Daisy answered, switching into her clipped, professional voice before she checked the caller ID. She never checked it during business hours, already in the zone.

"Hey, beautiful," Easton's raspy drawl greeted her. "Are you at the office already?"

"You know me, I like to start the day early. I assume you'll be here soon to review the Alpine project invoices," Daisy said, leaning against the elevator's back wall.

"Right. Almost forgot about that meeting... You know we could've finished the files if you stayed at my place last night."

"It's cute that you think we would've gotten any work done if I came over. You're always complaining I spend too much of my off-time busy with work."

"Yeah, but you're the workaholic between us," Easton's voice faded underneath the hushed noises in the background. Daisy pressed the earbud harder into her ear, overhearing muffled noises like the movement of bedsheets. A noticeable *shhh* blanketed the other side before Easton's voice returned. "Is it a crime for a man to want to spend time with his girlfriend?"

Girlfriend. The word tasted foreign on Daisy's tongue, echoing around her head louder than the silence falling over the call.

Hearing Easton call her his girlfriend felt... weird. The two had met in her final year at UCLA, sharing two classes in the spring semester. They had hooked up a few times back then. It was strictly casual while Daisy graduated with her bachelor's and Easton crawled through a master's degree in finance. The two bounced between on-and-off in the last several years until Easton ended up at Hidden Oasis. Over the previous few months, the two had been firmly and exclusively on.

And yet, 'girlfriend' hardly felt right to Daisy.

Absently, she looped the earbuds cord around her fingers. "Sounds like you haven't rolled out of bed despite our meeting in an hour."

"Uh, yeah," Easton paused, but the doors to the elevator opened at her stop. Daisy's hands adjusted the dark brown leather of her jacket when Easton sighed. "Look, I promise I'll be there on time."

"Good, because my calendar is booked through Friday, and I can't reschedule our meeting for the third time. I'll talk to you when you get here. Drive safely." Daisy cleared her throat before ending the call. One of these days, Easton needed to realize his successes would come when he actually applied himself instead of making her his keeper. *Some days, she acted more like his manager than his girlfriend.*

She walked ahead until she rounded the corner to her office, almost colliding with another body. Daisy lurched to a stop, coming face-to-face with her least favorite person on the planet.

"You're later than usual." With a resting scowl on his lips and the ever-present glint of trouble promised in narrowed gray-blue eyes, Jensen Ramsey burst the last bit of Daisy's good mood with a simple scoff.

Daisy swept her eyes down his pressed gray blazer, layered over his favorite white henley and dark brown slacks. Clearly, he got up early to run through his pretty boy routine, down to the brushed-back hair and perfect skin. She recalled her close friend Giselle's first impressions of Jensen as "a marble statue that came to life and escaped from the museum." She couldn't disagree. Jensen's angular, strong features looked chiseled from stone, and he never shied away from basking in people's admiring stares.

"If by 'later than usual', you mean I'm still ahead of ninety percent of our coworkers and here before we open for business, then yes. Despite how hard it might seem, I can still have a life outside of this office and be better than you. Try to keep up." Daisy smirked.

Her voice dripped with annoyance so sweet it became saccharine, spoken in a tone reserved for Jensen's usual antics. For someone so smart, he loved to start fights with her that he'd never win.

"Says the woman who fell asleep at her desk at least three times in the past month. You'd never catch me sleeping on the job," Jensen replied coolly as he pushed off the wall, standing just above eye level with her.

"You've never fallen asleep because your job is the easiest of the V-Suite. I'm the one who creates the moneymakers that generate millions in revenue. All you do is go to fancy lunches and stroke the egos of other rich people until they throw extra money at *my* vision."

"I'd love to see you do my job. You'd have to be nice to people for over an hour. Your head might legitimately explode if you couldn't make a snarky comment."

Ugh, she couldn't believe he was the biggest obstacle between her and her next promotion.

"Please, I could do your job *and* mine with my eyes closed. Don't act like you're special for being addicted to hearing yourself talk," Daisy snorted. She stashed her earbuds into her pocket and marched around Jensen, ready to ignore him for the remainder of the workday.

But within seconds, Jensen walked in perfect sync with her strides. The two passed the walls of glass cubicles, finding them all dim and empty with their colleagues not in yet. The thin hallway barely had enough room for them to stand together without their shoulders brushing the glass walls or each other.

"Excuse you, but I'm very special," said Jensen, and Daisy caught the tail-end of his eyes rolling in her peripheral vision. "You can't pretend that it isn't true."

"See, we have a word for the reason why. Eight letters, three syllables, starts with an 'N'... Tell me if you need help figuring it out, big boy."

"We both went to UCLA, Your Highness. I know what subtext is."

"Huh, could've fooled me."

"Drink more of your coffee. You're more tolerable when you've got your mouth full."

The hand Daisy had wrapped around her coffee nearly crumpled the metal from how hard she squeezed, imagining it was Jensen's neck instead. The urge to shove Jensen against the nearest cubicle with her arm pressing down on his throat until he squirmed flashed through her head, growing harder to ignore with every passing day.

She refrained from enjoying her coffee as the two approached the end of the hallway, where the break room and file storage closet took up the remaining space. Their offices sat across from one another at the furthest end of the hall. Daisy and Jensen spent every day in each other's line of sight.

None of their fellow V-suite members agreed to switch offices with Daisy no matter how hard she tried. She assumed Jensen asked around as well but got the same response as not to offend either.

Daisy stopped outside her office, fingers curled around the door handle. "Another morning spent in your sparkling wit. One of these days, I'll finally figure out how Delaney stands it."

"Don't worry about Delaney. Our happy relationship is none of your business," Jensen hissed, facing his office door instead of her. His shoulders tensed like a string pulled too tight, on the verge of snapping.

"I almost feel sorry for her. Imagine how much emotional labor she expends putting up with yo—" Daisy hadn't finished her sentence before Kendall, the CEO's secretary, sprinted into the hallway.

She spotted her first by Kendall's short but tight chestnut curls, her favorite pair of small golden hoops, and the mountain of folders stacked in her arms. Kendall, a part-time college student at a nearby junior college, worked at Hidden Oasis to pay for tuition. Daisy liked and respected her hustle around the office, bouncing between evening classes and her job.

"Sorry to interrupt, but Mr. Ramsey wants to see you both," Kendall panted behind the stack of folders in her arms. "He says it's urgent."

Daisy turned to Jensen, confused. She hadn't seen any meeting on the calendar. Forgetting something with the big boss would demolish her career in the blink of an eye, but Jensen's raised brows and parted lips told her he didn't know either.

"We're coming." Jensen yanked open his office door enough to toss something inside, landing with a thud on his desk. Not one to be left behind, Daisy ducked into her office to drop off her coffee and purse. She rushed back out, almost running into Jensen for the second time since arriving at the office.

With silent glares at one another, Daisy and Jensen followed Kendall to the elevator. Jensen held open the door for them. Daisy, however, considered shutting it on him to watch him scowl. The little fantasies of him spilling coffee on his designer clothes or dropping a stapler on his foot kept her amused during the long work hours.

The elevator shuttered as the three rode up to the top floor. Jensen and Daisy leaned against opposite walls while Kendall stood in front of the door, shifting in her cream satin pumps. The tight space thrummed with a collective tension pressed up against every nook and cranny.

Daisy said nothing as her and Jensen's eyes locked. Their stares simmered with mutual malice, heating up the metal walls of the elevator around them. Daisy refused to back down first or look away.

He didn't intimidate her, and she wanted him to know that. Keep trying, loser.

The chime of the elevator sounded, and Kendall sped out without wasting a second. Daisy and Jensen, however, lingered in their silent staring contest.

Jensen broke first, striding past the open doors. Daisy caught up to him within seconds. The two moved past Kendall's desk, where she retreated behind her monitor.

"He's expecting you. Please go in," Kendall murmured, more a plea for them to leave with the tension hanging over the room than a suggestion.

Daisy and Jensen reached for the doors at the same time and pushed one open, announcing their presence to the man seated at the ornate desk with a perfect view of Beverly Hills stretched out below.

"Jensen. Daisy. Make yourselves comfortable." Harrison rose from his chair, offering a warm smile to them. "This won't take too long, but I wanted to speak with you before the day began."

Harrison Ramsey, CEO of Hidden Oasis, commanded the presence of every room he stood in. Brown hair peppered with gray strands and smile lines crinkling around his blue eyes accentuated the friendly, confident reputation Harrison enjoyed with all who made his acquaintance. Daisy once said that he was well on his way to full silver fox status, making Harrison nearly fall out of his chair from how hard he laughed.

In the story of Daisy's life, Harrison Ramsey became her mentor and the closest thing she ever had to a father figure. As much as she wanted to strangle his son every time they made eye contact, Harrison stood worlds apart as her favorite person in the office.

Daisy grasped one of the chairs, and Jensen took the other, but neither sat down. She watched Jensen in her peripheral vision, but his eyes stayed on Harrison.

"Kendall said it was important."

"Yes. Important is underselling it."

"Mr. Ramsey." Daisy cleared her throat, earning the attention of Jensen and Harrison. "Is it an emergency?"

"Not quite. Please take a seat and relax. The matter is serious, but I need you to be calm." Harrison gestured to the empty chairs that Jensen and Daisy gripped in their hands.

So, as he requested, Daisy and Jensen sat down. The plush seat cushion dipped underneath Daisy, causing her to sink into the chair. She crossed her legs and straightened her posture to be as present as possible.

Harrison followed their lead and sat back down. His hands laced on his desk, and his otherwise calm expression gave way to tired eyes. As of late, Daisy knew their properties were flourishing, so lawsuits or financial issues seemed unlikely.

But *something* ate at her boss.

He sighed. "What I'm about to say hasn't been shared with anyone outside this office—not yet. I didn't want you to hear it from anyone else or through office gossip. I can trust you two to be discreet for a few days, right?"

"Absolutely." Daisy nodded.

"Of course, Dad," Jensen replied.

"As you know, our annual shareholder meeting this December has several seats up for re-election, and my CEO spot is one of them. However, I'm not running for re-election. I've decided that, after this fiscal year, I will be stepping down as the head of Hidden Oasis."

Daisy's heart fell into her stomach, suddenly losing the steady thump of her pulse through the aftermath of her boss's words. The world muted like someone hit the wrong button in her head, leaving her alone with her rationality and emotions at war.

The thought of a promotion streaked through her thoughts, but faster than she could dwell on it, guilt sliced through the idea. *Not now, Daisy.*

Beside her, Jensen appeared as still as a statue. The shock turned his face ashen gray, sapped free of all its color. His hands gripped the arms of his chair with his knuckles the same shade of ghastly as his face.

"Sir, are you okay?" Daisy asked Harrison while nudging Jensen hard, knocking him from his stupor.

"What do you mean?"

"Physically. Is there something motivating this, like a health issue?"

"Nothing like that, Daisy. I appreciate your concern, but I'm perfectly healthy. That's not the reason I'm stepping down as CEO."

"Then why?" she *and* Jensen chorused, head snapping to acknowledge the other before facing Harrison again.

"Honestly, I'm tired. Eileen and I have been planning our next moves for some time. We miss traveling, and the job's demands have cut into our time together. Besides, I'm in my early fifties. I never planned to work until forced retirement, not if I could help it," Harrison explained.

Jensen sighed. "Mom has been talking about travel more lately, hasn't she?"

"She has." Harrison nodded as a fond smile brightened his otherwise tired features. "I know this company is in good hands. I have a luncheon with the shareholders today, and I'll be sharing this news with them there. You two deserve to know before them, considering what comes next."

Daisy turned toward Jensen, finding him already staring at her, and said, "We knew this day would come, but I didn't expect it to be so soon. I know you'll always do what's best for the company."

The new CEO of Hidden Oasis sat in that very room, about to be crowned. Daisy Riggs, CEO extraordinaire, had a nice ring to it.

"Of course he will," Jensen agreed, sensible for once. Daisy fought against a smirk. Had he finally conceded to the realization that she was the better replacement for CEO than him? It must be a cold day in Hell.

"I already prepared the press release and announcement to the shareholders, other directors, and the general public. Since we have three other seats up for the election, my seat will be determined between the eight remaining board members. You two will be the only candidates on the proxy materials for CEO," Harrison remarked.

Daisy's quiet celebration of her imminent victory collapsed in a crashing halt. Still, she held her composure together with an iron fist. Chewing on her cheek, she snuck a glance toward Jensen to find his face painted in a different shade of betrayal, not too unlike her own.

"Wait, you aren't picking one of us?" Jensen gawked, rising from his seat. "Come on, your endorsement should be behind me. You promised me the company when the time came, and I've been one of the best-performing workers in the entire company."

"But not *the* best. That title belongs to me. You don't get to snap your fingers and demand my years of service become obsolete," Daisy gasped. She rocketed out of her chair with the grace of a panther about to pounce. "We all remember you've tried before."

She faced Jensen with an accusatory finger leveled to his chest while his eyes met hers, stinging with resentment. He hated her? *Tough shit.*

She earned her rightful place behind that desk more than he did by being a Ramsey.

"Both of you, sit down!" Harrison's voice boomed off the walls, eclipsing her and Jensen's squabbling effortlessly. He pointed to their chairs with a stern, disappointed stare that only a father could muster.

Reluctantly, Daisy and Jensen inched away from one another and took their seats.

Harrison pinched the bridge of his nose. "Look, you two have worked equally hard for this company since the start of your careers. Daisy, you have seniority. People deeply respect you and your work ethic. Jensen, you are a Ramsey. People know being CEO is in your blood and trust you to honor my vision. However, the issue is that neither of you has a clear majority among the shareholders, and the directors will be split without one. I can't pick."

"You don't want the shareholders to think you've taken away their power," Daisy remarked.

"Yes. A substantial amount of stock is dispersed across the family, except for Jensen. So, some shareholders will defer to my wishes. That's why you two are running alone." Harrison slumped back in his chair. "I can't let an outsider taint the legacy I built. You two will keep my work alive. Do you understand?"

"I understand," Jensen agreed without hesitation, prompting Daisy's eyes on him. She didn't escape his notice, and the cutthroat glare aimed at her screamed his intentions. *If he wanted a fight, she had one ready for him.*

"I understand." Daisy knew war arrived at her cubicle door, but she had spent the last five years laying the groundwork for when that came. The race for CEO was on. "We will keep your legacy thriving, sir."

"Good. I knew you would understand. You have six months to impress the Board. You're both capable of doing so. We'll talk more about it later. Don't forget, we have the annual retreat for the corporate officers in less than two weeks, so you won't start competing until after we leave The Ridge."

"Yes, sir," Daisy and Jensen chorused, shooting each other a glare.

"You two can head out for the day. Thank you for your time." Harrison's dismissal awakened a dull buzzing in Daisy's ears. She walked out of his office with Jensen beside her, striding past Kendall in total silence.

She didn't hear a breath pass between either of them while they stood in the waiting room. Instead, she watched the numbers on the display climb into the teens, itching to head to her office and plot her next moves.

Anything to get a leg up on Jensen meant she moved one day closer to being CEO.

As the doors revealed an empty elevator, the doors to Harrison's office swung open. Harrison's voice echoed from inside the office. "Jensen, stay back for a moment? We need to talk about family dinner at the end of the week."

"Of course." Jensen stuffed his hands into the pockets of his slacks. "Be right there."

Daisy huffed when she stepped into the elevator, pressing the button to her floor. She raked her eyes over Jensen. "Have fun with that. I'll use the extra time to secure my voters."

"I can't wait to put you in your place." Jensen's jaw clenched when Daisy leaned against the wall, comfortably slouched in her leather jacket and pencil skirt.

"And where would that be? You won't talk such a big game when I'm the new boss, Jensen."

"Keep dreaming, Your Highness. The only future CEO in this room is me."

Jensen's once grouchy scowl morphed into the smug smirk Daisy associated with his stupid face, becoming the last thing she saw before the elevator doors shut.

Chapter 2
Jensen

"And she wouldn't stop making snarky comments under her breath the whole meeting. I should've asked Miranda to switch spots with me. The chocolate éclair wasn't worth the torture of dealing with Daisy," Jensen shouted over the wind rushing past his convertible.

It hadn't been two days since his dad announced his intended retirement at the end of the fiscal year. Yet, his impatience jumped several steps ahead, counting the days. Jensen went to bed each night, wishing to wake up in December instead of May.

No matter what happened in the next several months, he would defeat Daisy for good. She spent too long as the unwanted thorn in his side, standing between him and what belonged to him since his dad promised.

Jensen pulled into the turn pocket at the intersection, underneath midnight-painted skies and the streaks of pink from the sun below the horizon. The air stayed warm with the summer months right around the corner, more balmy than the scorching of a true California day. *He loved summers in LA.*

His eyes wandered to the passenger seat, where his girlfriend, Delaney, curled into the leather upholstery. She sat with knees tucked to her chest and her face buried in her phone. She'd been entranced by it since he picked her up for dinner.

"Delaney? Earth to Delaney?" Jensen asked, waving his hand in front of her face. Despite the noise of the city enveloping them in its embrace, Delaney pressed her phone to her chest like he scared her.

Delaney Malone was a quiet beauty. Her jet-black hair glowed silkily underneath the neon lights they passed on their drive, framing her slender cheekbones. Behind dramatic lashes, her round, hazel eyes gleamed. She wore the same preppy clothes as their high school days when she ran the drama class, and Jensen reigned as class president.

"I'm sorry that work's been stressful for you, babe," Delaney sighed, sounding more irate than sympathetic. The slight curl of her top lip pulled together an expression of annoyance, darkening her eyes. "But I think you're being nearsighted again."

'Nearsighted' was a term used between them when Jensen became fixated on work, or more specifically when Daisy got under his skin with her attitude.

Jensen's shoulders hunched over. He didn't want to spend all day frustrated and come home to fight with his girlfriend again. "Del, please."

"I'm serious, Jensen. You've been obsessed with the promotion, and her, for the last two days. I'm tired of hearing about her. I know this promotion or whatever is important, but tell my boyfriend that there's more to life than his dumb job."

"I understand that it's a lot—"

"Do you? Because you've been ranting about it for the last thirty minutes, and I don't know what else to say. It's bad enough that no one will switch offices with you, so you're stuck in close quarters with that bitch every day," Delaney spat.

"Don't call her that—"

"Oh, so you're defending her now? I'm your girlfriend and on your side, Jensen."

"That's not what I'm doing. Look, I understand you're frustrated with me because work has taken over. Believe me, I know I get wrapped up in it too much. But I'm not comfortable calling anyone a 'bitch,' even Daisy," Jensen murmured while making the turn as the light flashed green. He caught sight of

Delaney's narrowed eyes, harsher than before. "We've talked about this before. It crosses a line I'm not comfortable with."

He sped down the side street, lined by gated properties in the opulent designs of The Flats. Wealth radiated from the sidewalk like the streets were paved with gold, but the novelty still burned bright. Living in a neighborhood like this for most of his life could've turned Jensen jaded and unimpressed.

It hadn't.

The car slowed to a roll as he approached the gate outside his family's home, its spotless white walls and black metallic accents framed by bright greenery. With all the lights on, the glow trickled through the open windows to the gradually dimming skies.

Jensen reached for his gate remote, but his hand brushed against Delaney's. Her mouth twisted into a grimace, neither angry nor guilt-ridden, while she leaned forward in her seat. "Sorry. I know you don't like me calling her that. It's just frustrating to see you stressed out because of her. I don't know what else you want me to do. I'm trying to be supportive."

"I'm not mad at you," Jensen sighed. "The situation isn't ideal, but we're almost at the end. I'm sorry for being nearsighted and ranting about work again. Let's put it behind us for the night and enjoy dinner."

"Good. Office rivalries should stay there once working hours are over." Delaney clicked her tongue. Jensen parked his car behind his sisters' shared SUV, basking in the night's warmth.

Office rivalries *should* stay there. But the reality meant extra baggage came home, especially with change in the air. Jensen hoped that, with some time, Delaney might understand his perspective. She was to be the partner of the CEO, after all.

Jensen jumped out of his seat and ran to open Delaney's door for her. Grabbing her hand, he spun her close to him. Del's soft hum barely preceded his mouth brushing against hers. His hands slipped to grab her waist, but Delaney backed from the chaste kiss in the same breath.

"We should head inside," Jensen suggested. Delaney hovered next to him as the two headed inside, greeted by the smell of something chocolatey and the excited screeches of his sisters.

Jensen peered over the couch to find Piper and Hayley sitting on the floor with several bottles of nail polish stacked on the glass coffee table. The two giggled like conspirators and held up their hands, gleaming with fresh polish on their nails.

"What are you two losers doing down there?" Jensen asked, leaning over the couch. He grinned as his younger sisters nearly jumped out of their skin, screaming and scrambling away from him.

"Jensen!" Piper, the youngest of the Ramsey clan, quickly launched to her feet and barreled straight for Jensen. He, like a good older brother, caught her in his arms. "You made it!"

Piper was the only one of the three Ramsey kids who looked like the happy medium between their parents. Her tousled brunette hair, cut into a shoulder-length shag, matched his and their dad's, but her eyes were stormy like Hayley and their mom. A rogue smattering of freckles dusted across her nose and round cheeks, stopping right above her lips, which glowed in shimmery pink lipstick.

"You think I'd miss dinner with my favorite people? Not a chance." Pulling her into a bear hug, Jensen lifted Piper clear off the ground, careful not to smudge her newly painted nails against his nice shirt.

"Mmm. Hayley said you might've been glued to your desk since the Dad's CEO announcement went down."

"Hales has an interesting sense of humor. Ignore her."

"I heard that," Hayley popped up from behind the couch like a meerkat, hands lifted with her fingers splayed wide open. "You could use some of my humor. The shareholders love me, which you need right now."

In stark contrast to Piper, Hayley shook out her dirty blonde ponytail, done by the skilled hands of a former cheer captain. A lean, athletic frame sported a nice pair of jeans and a silk top in a rich, woodsy brown. Her eyes gleamed like gathering storm clouds over the ocean while she climbed off the floor, hands incapacitated by powder blue nail polish.

She wandered over with arms wide open, and Jensen welcomed her into the Ramsey sibling sandwich. He peered over Hayley's high ponytail to Delaney, ready to envelop her in the hug; his family considered her one of their own after seven years.

Yet, Delaney's eyes stayed glued to her phone as her fingers whipped out a rapid response. The phone chimed, and she cringed, switching the ringer off. She didn't notice her boyfriend's quiet stare.

He had to wonder. For the last few months, Delaney rarely went a moment without her phone in hand, always busy with something.

Sensing his distraction, Piper and Hayley relinquished him from their bone-crushing hug. All three turned to Delaney, still occupied by her phone, until Hayley cleared her throat, "Delaney!"

Delaney nearly dropped her phone with how quickly she shoved it into her purse, emotions flashing across her face in a dizzying array. Yet, they vanished behind a polite smile. "Hales! So good to see you!"

The two embraced, sharing air kisses and holding each other at arm's length to squeal about each other's outfits. Piper hung back at Jensen's side and waved to Delaney from there, who waved back.

Something metallic clattered against the granite countertops in the kitchen. The chocolate aroma from before intensified, filling every inch of the room with its presence.

"They're perfect!" His mom's victorious yelling followed a brief silence, drawing a smile out of him. "Is that Jensen I hear?"

"He *and* Delaney are in the living room with us!" Piper shouted back before Jensen announced his arrival. "So, you'll need an extra chocolate lava cake!"

"It's fine. I don't need the carbs," Delaney interjected, but her voice faded with more clattering from the kitchen. Seconds later, Jensen's mom sped through the doorway, a flower-patterned apron thrown over her shoulders in her haste.

"My last baby has returned!" his mom exclaimed, racing toward him with a wide smile. She piled her light brown hair high into a bun and dressed in a sensible but classic black dress. Eileen Ramsey glowed, defying aging because she didn't look a day over thirty-five.

"Hi, Mom." Jensen stepped forward to catch her like he had with Piper, curling up in her arms. Some of the best memories of his childhood involved his mom and hugs. "You look lovely tonight."

"I've missed you, sweetheart. You need to come over for dinner more often. I know you're busy with work, but our family lives too close not to see each other."

"You're right. How about we plan for dinner once a month, just the five of us?"

"Yes. We'll give Chef Shiloh some much-needed time off. Piper has taken a real shine to cooking, and I'm sure she and I can manage dinner and dessert for one night."

"Is that so?"

Hayley groaned. "You have no idea. I'm eating Michelin-star meals at home because Piper loves me," she gushed, draping herself over Piper dramatically.

Jensen watched Piper pull a face, prompting the two to flash middle fingers at one another once their mom's back had turned. Hard to believe they were eighteen and twenty-two.

He turned when feeling a hand on his bicep, seeing Delaney beside him again. The far-off, glazed-over look in her eyes wavered when their gazes locked. Delaney murmured, "I'm going to wash up. Be right back."

"Sounds good. I'll be here," Jensen whispered. He buried a hurried kiss into her hair before Delaney left the room. She knew her way around the Ramsey home after all the years she visited for holidays, Jensen's birthday, and the occasional work party.

Jensen's eyes followed her trail long after she left his sight, only broken from his staring contest with the empty archway when something pressed into his palm. His eyes snapped toward his mom, whose smile deepened as she pushed a velvet box into his hand. Understanding passed between them, silent but precise.

His mom always had his back.

Footsteps echoed against the spiral stairs across the room, where all eyes landed on his dad as he entered. A tumbler filled with dark liquid sloshed along the glass's rounded edges, rattling the ice lost in the sea of liquor. His dad raked his fingers through his hair, mousing the strands loose from the rest slicked back with pomade.

His eyes scanned the living room, brightening at the sight of his kids. "Welcome home, everyone. I'm happy to see you all here... especially you, Jensen."

"Me?" Jensen rammed the velvet box into the pocket of his slacks, walking toward the stairs. "You see me at the office every day. Besides, I promised I'd come."

"Good. Could I borrow you for a few moments? Alone?"

"Of course."

"We'll be back shortly."

Jensen jogged up the stairs, meeting his dad halfway. A look passed between them. *So much for leaving the office for work hours.*

The two men climbed the stairs to the second story and quickly ducked into his dad's personal office, the first door on the left. Unlike the modern feel of the rest of the home, his dad's study exuded old money with dark stained walls and matching leather furniture surrounding the hand-carved wooden desk.

His dad walked halfway around the table before he leaned against it, setting down his partially finished drink. He sighed, "Are you doing alright?"

"Why wouldn't I be alright?" Jensen replied instantly. The frown on his dad's face made him want to kick himself in the shin. *Nice lie, idiot.*

"Well, when you've been "too busy" to have lunch with your old man for the last two days, I caught the impression that you might be angry with me," his dad said. "So, want to try that again?"

Jensen stared at his dad, caught off-guard. He tried to keep his distance while processing his dad's resignation, racked with the competing urges to demolish Daisy's entire career and the lurking fear that he might lose the job that was supposed to be his.

"Why didn't you pick me, Dad? You know how much I care about the company. You don't want an outsider acquiring your legacy. Daisy is the definition of an outsider," Jensen questioned, arms crossing over his chest.

Was he mad? Kind of.

He needed to understand how his dad couldn't see him as the obvious choice for the promotion. Yes, Jensen hoped that his dad might honor the promise he made to him years ago, but Jensen never sat around when it came to the company either. Arguably, he worked just as hard as Daisy in his position, even as the boss's son. He loved Hidden Oasis more than he got credit for.

His dad's shoulders dropped. The tension woven into his body softened. Jensen turned his face, not interested in witnessing his dad's disappointment in him. So rarely did they clash, but he couldn't back down.

"Jensen," his dad remarked. Jensen heard his voice become kinder than he would be if the roles were reversed. "There was a time that you didn't want to run the company when I retired. You vehemently rejected the thought, and I didn't push you to change your mind. Instead, I found someone else to take over in case you left the company."

"Found. You say you 'found' Daisy like she wasn't already working at Hidden Oasis."

"Jensen, you're focusing on the wrong things."

"She's not made for the position!"

"I disagree. Daisy is more than capable of being the CEO. You disliking her doesn't change that fact."

Jensen's nose flared, stricken by frustration. His dad should be in his corner, not pulling for his rival. He spoke through clenched teeth, "I have every reason to dislike her."

"It's been seven years since you two first met. Have either of you apologized for getting off on the wrong foot?" his dad asked.

"I'm stubborn. I get it from you. Daisy's petty and likes to make it her mission to remind me how much better she thinks she is. You know what she told me?"

"She said you're like all rich people: pretty but with no substance. You thought the best reply would be accusing her of being intimidated by your good looks since she called you pretty. She doubled down by calling you vain, and the rest is history. Jensen, you two have both ranted about how you met so many times to me that I have it memorized."

Jensen paused, lips parted open in a failed retort and closed his mouth. His gaze wandered away from his dad, who stared at him with that annoyingly knowing glint. Daisy's closeness with his dad shouldn't bother him as much as it did, but sharing him with her never became easier. "Well, I suggested eliminating this issue back then."

"You came into my office and suggested I drop her as my protege. You apparently changed your mind about being CEO overnight after swearing you needed more time. I knew what you actually wanted," his dad reminded, still calm even in the face of Jensen's mounting annoyance. "I didn't stop mentoring Daisy because I needed a backup CEO. I'm not surprised she still holds onto a grudge after you asked me to dismiss her because she 'wasn't needed'."

In Daisy's shoes, Jensen would latch onto that grudge like his life depended on it. But he would never admit it to his dad.

Before he spoke another word, a knock on the door derailed the conversation. Piper poked her head in without Jensen or his dad calling for her to enter. She offered a shy smile.

"Mom says dinner's ready. She doesn't want it going cold." Piper blinked, glancing between Jensen and their dad. She held onto the door, so all the tension raced out of the room.

"We'll be there in a moment," Jensen promised and gently eased Piper's grip off the door. She jogged down the hall in a ball of soft pink fabric.

His dad grabbed his drink off the desk, stopping at Jensen's side to loop his arm around Jensen's shoulder. "Son, I don't want this to come between us. I love you. I want you to succeed."

"I know," Jensen replied. "I'm sorry for avoiding you and being petty. You have my word that I'll prove I can be a great CEO. You can trust me with the company."

"Jensen, you don't have to prove it to me. I've long overcome the indecision, but many shareholders haven't. Show them that you've matured enough to have a whole company on your shoulders. Daisy may not be my blood, but she gets things done. That's why our shareholders trust her." His dad clapped his shoulder, bringing the conversation to a close.

Jensen stared at him. His dad might've not said it explicitly, but he uncovered a gem of advice in those words. Maybe his dad couldn't play favorites, but Jensen knew how to move forward.

He could still win... if he erased the mark on his record and became the decisive, confident CEO that Hidden Oasis needed.

The two men headed into the kitchen, finding the table set with plates full and their family waiting for them. Jensen slid into his chair next to Delaney, who shoved her phone into her purse without a word.

Jensen raised his brow, choosing to say nothing. She had been jumpy, but everyone had their off days. When she was ready to lean on him, Jensen trusted her to come clean.

Chapter 3

Daisy

THE SILKEN FEEL OF champagne-colored satin gripped her curves as Daisy walked through the double doors of The Hollywood Topaz Hotel. Under the refurbished lights and the architecture preserved from the twenties, she felt like a star on the Walk of Fame, glittering for all to see.

The late May evening brushed its warm kiss along her skin, over the sleeveless gown with its plunging front and back, as she entered one of her favorite properties owned by Hidden Oasis.

The dress would turn every head in the room, bringing everyone's attention to her and the conversation around the next CEO.

Attached to her side, Easton cleaned up nicely. He traded in his favorite polo shirt for a crisp brown suit. Pomade slicked his sandy brown hair into a trendy quaff. He even trimmed his beard, framing his oval-shaped face nicely. Beyond the distinguished aura exuding from the perfect fit of his tailored suit, excitement sparkled in his dark, mahogany-colored eyes.

He looked very handsome. Daisy told him as much before they left his apartment, lodged between their work-centered conversations. He said... *something* back before networking dominated the conversation again.

"You're the secret weapon that'll take my career to the next level. Investors love you. If they love you, they'll love me with the right push." Easton's sharp inhale dragged Daisy from her thoughts and tossed her headfirst into the endless circle of networking talk.

"Sure thing, babe," Daisy said, burdened by the expectant weight of his eyes on her. She nodded along, but realistically, why did he need her help? Easton grew up in the same wealth and social brackets as those in attendance that evening. "I don't think you need me to network, though. Making the shareholders feel good about themselves always works for me."

"Well, you make it look easy. Do this one thing for me and help me network."

"One thing? I've never done anything else for you before tonight?"

"You know what I mean."

Daisy's eyes threatened to roll, unsure why Easton hid behind her like a shield. They occupied the same level of responsibility and power with their jobs; her association with him didn't raise his marketability.

However, she held her tongue, refraining from an argument. If Easton wanted her help, he had her attention for as long as she could spare.

Daisy's eyes scanned the room on the hunt for shareholders, sifting through the faces of familiar colleagues and their plus-ones. Everyone was dressed in full glamor, taking the evening's high spirits in stride. Through the sea of jewel tones and neutral fabrics, clusters of shareholders emerged like beacons of light.

Daisy tugged Easton's arm to guide him through the crowd of people. She nodded and mouthed greetings to faces as they passed. Heads swiveled with wide-eyed stares and slack jaws whenever people caught sight of her.

She lifted her chin high, plastering on a dazzling smile when she whispered to Easton, "Follow my lead. These are some of the closest shareholders to Mr. Ramsey."

Daisy brought him outside the nearest cluster, but the circle opened with immediate greetings of her name and pleasantries. Her hand grasped those outstretched toward her and Easton, still smiling. As she identified the faces, the notable lack of Kenneth Malone and several other shareholders inspired a wave of relief. Tonight would already be a challenge with Jensen due to arrive at any moment. The last thing she needed was old men with bad attitudes to stand in her way.

"Miss Riggs, you never fail to captivate a room," Tristan Merritt, one of her favorite shareholders, remarked as he grasped her hands in his. "Isn't she radiant, folks?"

"You flatter me, Tristan. How's the family? I assume you've been tearing up the green links in your free time." She laughed, head tipped back to shake out a few loose, wispy strands from her updo.

The shareholders joined in the laughter, but little did they know they were eating out of the palm of her hand. *She could be charming, contrary to Jensen's assumption.*

Since day one, Daisy had assembled a mental dossier of everyone she had met. She collected their likes, dislikes, information from their past conversations, and their relevance to her career. Some might think it manipulative of her, but the corporate world demanded survival. So, she rose to the challenge.

"Shea and the girls are wonderful. They don't mind my golfing habit while they're hitting the shops with a mimosa brunch afterward."

"That sounds amazing. Up at the Ridge, right?"

"Of course. You do a great job with the upkeep of the properties, so I'm never disappointed when I visit. We moved into Del Mesa a few months ago—it's so nice to get out of the city."

Daisy nodded, all smiles for the shareholders. Frequent trips down to Del Mesa existed as a perk of the job, but she would never leave the city. The hustle and bustle spoke to her soul, a perfect reminder of how far she succeeded.

The loud, borderline-annoyed clear of a throat from Easton jostled through the pleasant flow of the conversation. Daisy noticed several shareholders glancing toward him. All too aware of how bad it looked, she nudged Easton forward.

"Has everyone here met Easton? He's my date for the evening," Daisy said, quick to salvage the conversation from a potential snafu.

Several shareholders extended their hands toward Easton, who greeted them with wordless handshakes. But Daisy's chest twitched while staring at the almost flat expression painted over Easton's face. *Would it kill him to smile a little? Women in corporate do it all the time.*

Tristan grasped Easton's hand first, giving a hearty shake while smiling. "Ah, are you part of Daisy's department? I appreciate how she knows her people like the back of her hand."

"I'm in the financial department," Easton replied, voice cracking awkwardly at the end. "I'm the VP of Financials and Accounting. So, I'm responsible for all the auditing and ensuring Daisy's department stays within budget."

Easton gave a dry chuckle before he paused, almost like he waited for acknowledgment from the crowd. But no one responded, not with laughter, neither pitying nor genuine. Instead, the shareholders turned to Daisy, who stayed perfectly still.

Even with her thoughts racing a mile a minute to spin some damage control, she hummed, "Lucky for us all, I'm persuasive. Easton's known me since my UCLA days; he's probably exhausted by my refusal to lose."

That response garnered laughter from the crowd, soothing the anxiety coursing through Daisy's veins harder than the shot of Pink Whitney she downed before leaving the apartment. Damage control could be her middle name.

"That sounds like something Harrison would say."

"She's an honorary Ramsey at this point. Everyone knows it."

"Daisy, any chance you'd be looking for a protégé if you promote? My daughter is attending UCLA in the fall."

The conversation fractured, but all the attention centered on her with every comment and question. Daisy held her smile firmly, calculating answers to each one when the gathered shareholders bristled quietly.

Daisy didn't need to turn to understand the shift in the air or the quiet wariness spreading across the shareholders. *Jensen had arrived.*

"Good evening. I'm glad to see all of you made it to tonight's events." Jensen held his composure for long enough to greet the shareholders, chiming in from Daisy's right. "Daisy, I didn't expect to see you so early."

"I never miss an opportunity to attend to our best shareholders," Daisy remarked with a wink, eliciting a few rogue laughs from the shareholders she knew best. Her eyes flitted towards Jensen, finding him in a classic black suit with Delaney clinging to his arm in a matching cocktail dress. "I take client relations seriously."

"Seeing as it's *my* department, I'll happily take over from here."

"No need. I'm capable of holding my own."

"I'm sure you are. Del, would you mind grabbing some drinks for us? Take my card." Jensen kissed Delaney's forehead and slid his wallet into her hands, smiling hard enough for his eyes to crinkle in the corners. In those moments, an image of a younger Harrison emerged.

Daisy knew what he was doing. He sent Delaney away to limit his distractions so he could dive full-force into the evening of schmoozing, making promises they might not always keep, and supplying their voting body with liquor. *Two could play that game.*

Daisy released Easton from her hold, patting his chest, "I'll meet up with you soon. Go talk to people, hang out with your friends."

She spoke to Easton, but her eyes caught Jensen's. Delaney hovered at his side still, yet Daisy held Jensen's attention on a tight leash.

"Daisy," Easton said, sounding far from pleased with her suggestion. "I don't think that's a good idea. We should stick together tonight."

"I have some business to conduct first, but I'll find you later. You said you wanted to network, and I'll only get in your way. There are plenty of people who you should speak to."

"Fine. I'll see you later."

Easton huffed quietly, loud enough for Daisy to hear him, before he marched into the crowd like a man on a mission. Daisy's eyes darted between Jensen and Delaney, who lingered at his side. Jensen's hand on her shoulder finally turned Delaney away, and she stalked into the crowd without protest.

Everyone in the circle faced Daisy and Jensen while closing the gap left in Easton and Delaney's departure. The space between Daisy and Jensen shrank as their bodies shuffled closer together, sparing a hair's breadth between their hands resting at their sides. Daisy could smell Jensen's cologne bathing him in cedar and sandalwood, close enough to feel his knuckles hovering over her skin.

Every infuriating piece of Jensen Ramsey amplified the deeper he invaded her personal space, whether intentionally or not. Daisy imagined going home to cleanse herself of his presence, sticking to her like secondhand smoke.

Neither broke the silence, but an understanding switched on as easily as a light. *Let the games begin.*

When another shareholder, Gladys Beck, clasped her hands together, the clang of her rings signaled the shift from banter to business. Much like the bell before a fight, Daisy prepared to start swinging.

Gladys hummed, "I speak for many of us when I say Harrison's announcement of his impending retirement took us all for a surprise, but I feel optimistic. We are fortunate to have such accomplished candidates to lead us into the future."

Jensen politely cleared his throat. "Of course, ma'am. I never expected the day to come so soon. Still, I look forward to representing Hidden Oasis in the best possible light. I watched my dad build this company into the giant it is. Nothing will change its trajectory to success, not on my watch."

"Whoever becomes the next CEO will be what the company needs to thrive. The greatness of Hidden Oasis is only beginning," Daisy remarked, fine-tuning her interjection into a weapon. Jensen hadn't received the promotion yet. "I want this company to succeed beyond our wildest imaginations. I look forward to my role in shaping its course."

There was a time and place for her to puff up her accomplishments, but that evening wasn't it. Instead, Daisy played Miss Congeniality, the poster child for the employee almost everyone loved.

Almost.

Jensen's hand brushed against her shoulder. Electricity from his fingers leaped up her neck until all the hairs stood up straight, sending thoughts of smacking his hand away too tempting to ignore. Yet, she stayed so perfectly still.

"It seems Daisy and I share your optimism, Gladys. But tonight isn't about either of us. We should focus on my dad's long service to the company, shareholders, and community." Jensen's hand dropped from Daisy's body fast, which was better for both.

"Exactly. Which is why we should toast." Daisy peered around until she caught sight of a server carrying a tray of champagne. She leaned over, plucking two flutes filled to the brim. She offered one to Jensen before lifting hers. "To Harrison Ramsey, the best among us."

"Whoever fills his shoes will be the right fit."

"Those are big shoes to fill, but it'll be done."

Daisy and Jensen held their flutes high, watching as the champagne caught the light to turn into liquid gold. The company's future stood between them like the world's longest game of tug-a-war, swiftly speeding toward its end.

The shareholders applauded, garnering attention from the neighboring clusters to all the fuss. Their newfound focus meant more people to greet, charm, and please. Lucky for them, Daisy developed a taste for the charade.

She sipped on her champagne. Jensen did the same, taking slow and steady tastes while their eyes glared the other down from behind the rim.

Daisy hummed, "It's been lovely to speak with you all. I need to make my rounds and welcome everyone else who's arrived. But I will stop by later." She prefaced her exit, ready to get ahead of Jensen.

As she turned, she heard Jensen speak, "Have a fantastic evening. Thank you for supporting Hidden Oasis for another year."

Daisy snuck a glance over her shoulder, finding Jensen staring at her back with those narrowed eyes he reserved for her. They stalked in opposite directions, ready to show the other who deserved the promotion.

Time blended together in a blur of faces and conversations Daisy could barely slot into her dossier for later. Nevertheless, she endured the fatigue until her face ached from smiling too much.

Sipping on her champagne got her through every conversation, often drier than the fucking desert. When she hit her limit, she used her drained glass as an excuse to move on. No one seemed the wiser.

In every conversation, Daisy became a perfect reflection of what they wanted from her, racking up congratulations and boisterous professions of support. Yet, those meant nothing while the liquor flowed. She couldn't rest on her laurels too early; she wasn't Jensen, the promised heir.

Daisy wandered through the crowd, her gaze always moving, picking through the faces for Easton. She hadn't seen him since Jensen arrived, and she owed him a drink. Call her many things, but she prided herself on following through.

She caught sight of the catering table, where a few finance department guys lounged with their drinks from the bar, jackets draped over their arms. The room pulsed with warmth from all the bodies packed into it, even with the doors flung open to invite fresh air in.

Sauntering over, Daisy dropped her empty champagne onto a passing tray, no longer needing its services. Her hands straightened the gorgeous golden body chain she layered over her dress, which twinkled with every move she made.

The guys in Easton's department snapped to attention when she entered their vision, stumbling over themselves. Daisy raised her brow; she barely knew most of them except for Nelson, the vice president of sales.

Daisy liked Nelson. She appreciated his dry wit and uncanny knowledge of the best Mexican food places within a five-block radius. During their meetings, he brought a voice of reason to the V-Suite, making him her favorite referee when she and Jensen bickered.

"Hello," she greeted, hands tucked behind her back. Her eyes swept across the faces of her nameless coworkers. "Have any of you seen Easton recently? We're supposed to have a drink."

"No, ma'am."

"Can't say I have."

"Not since the beginning of the night."

Daisy took each denial in stride, not daunted by her search. Easton wouldn't have left without finding her since she drove them there. He should be somewhere among the masses congregated on the first floor, stretched between the Art Deco walls.

Nelson waved, finishing his cocktail from the bar. "I don't know if he's still there, but I overheard him mentioning needing fresh air. One of the guys suggested he check out the private pool deck. Floor seventeen, if I remember correctly."

"This is why you're my favorite. Have a great night, gentlemen." Daisy saluted, spinning around on her heel. Her dress's train kicked up slightly in her wake, drawing the eyes of nearby shareholders.

Daisy nodded to every person who met her stare, focused on a route to the elevator through all the bodies. She slipped past conversations whose snippets beckoned her to stay a while and chime in, but she needed to find Easton.

She emerged from the crowd, showing the golden wristband snugly wrapped around her arm to the two guards flanking the elevator. One of them kindly hit the button for her. She beamed, choosing a thankful, closed-lipped smile to rest her sore cheeks.

The doors parted open to an empty elevator, but Daisy heard a shout ring out from behind her. "Hold the door!"

She spun around, stepping through the doors, as Jensen raced over. He lifted his sleeve to flash the same golden wristband Daisy wore when passing the guards.

With great reluctance, Daisy pressed her hand over the door until Jensen slid into the elevator. She sighed, clicking the button for the seventeenth floor. "What floor?"

"I don't know. I've been looking for Delaney for the past thirty minutes. No one has a clue where she's gone."

"What a coincidence. I've been looking for Easton... Have you seen him?"

"Not since earlier. I assume you haven't seen Delaney either."

"Afraid not." Daisy poked the 'close door' button until the doors shut, comforted by the ambient metallic hum. She leaned against the nearest wall and sank into the cold metal caressing her back. The body chain branded its shape into her skin, jingling as the elevator ascended.

Her eyes wandered to Jensen, standing in the center of the elevator with his brows furrowed together. He stared at his phone, perfectly agitated for a man whose girlfriend was missing.

"Is that Delaney?" asked Daisy.

Jensen's head snapped up. "Uh, no. It's my sister, Piper. I haven't seen her since earlier tonight, but Dad said she wasn't doing well. Something about feeling insecure in her dress," he mumbled, returning to the screen.

Daisy closed her eyes, leaning deeper against the wall. "This might not mean much, but tell her that she looks lovely. The darker pinks suited her coloring. Plus, A-lines are perfect for a young woman and complement her curves. She's easily one of the best-dressed women here."

"I'll pass on the message. My mom and Hayley tried to say the same, but she might take it better from someone who isn't related to her and who... yeah."

"Good. I'm infinitely cooler than you are anyways."

Daisy half-expected Jensen to retort with some snarky comment or a huff, but another few incoming texts chimed. She opened her eyes again, seeing Jensen's frown deepen.

He leaned over to press one of the buttons, fingers stopping short at the seventeenth. He double-checked his phone in silence and stepped back. However, the shift in his posture became undeniable. *Something had him worried.*

The numbers switched into the double digits and soon arrived on the seventeenth floor. Besides the dimmed rooms for pool equipment, two glass doors led to the glowing pool deck overlooking West Hollywood.

Jensen dug into his pocket, cursing under his breath, until he revealed a key card. The almost neon shade of aqua illuminated the dark glint in his eyes, which had been downright haunted since the elevator.

When he opened the doors, Daisy stumbled onto the pool deck behind him, hit with the hot air of the evening. The dark skies and sparkling skyline held her attention for a moment, standing brighter than the manicured hedges and the still waters of the pool among the wooden deck.

Daisy's eyes raked over the deck chairs laid out until she spotted a dark purse discarded on the white cushion. "Isn't that Delaney's?"

"Yeah, it—" Jensen replied, but Daisy shushed him with a finger to his lips.

"Then, she's probably here," she whispered, removing her hand from his face. Daisy stepped forward on the ball of her foot instead of her heel, careful not to make the wood creak into the empty night.

She and Jensen walked down the length of the pool, tucked close together. But neither could prepare for when they approached one of the hedges at the end of the row.

In the alcove created between the wall, the hedge, and the glass railing stretched around the deck, they found Delaney... with Easton. Delaney's dark cocktail dress puddled above her hips, but the sight of lace panties hanging around one ankle painted an unexpected twist. Easton's body pinned her against the wall, but her mouth against his left no room for doubt.

"Are you fucking kidding me?" Jensen snarled, causing the two unsuspecting lovers to freeze. Within seconds, they scrambled to let go of one another and frantically pulled at their clothes. Yet no "fixing" would undo the red bleeding into Daisy's vision.

She knew they weren't worth losing her job but lunged anyway. Only a pair of firm, muscular arms wrapping around her waist held her back from a fearful Easton and Delaney, derailing the first punch.

"Let go of me!" Daisy hissed at Jensen, twitching in his arms. Seeing Easton and Delaney with their rumpled clothes and the lipstick smeared between their mouths—she wanted to throw them in the pool. "Jensen, I'm serious!"

"I can't do that." Jensen's hot breath panted into her ear while he kept her from swinging. She thought she knew the depths of his anger, but the venomous edge to his voice superseded anything he leveled at her.

His arms curled around her and tightened their coil until she stopped thrashing. Once the kicking and wrestling ceased, Jensen's grip loosened enough for her to stand on her own.

Daisy pointed between Delaney and Easton, who hadn't moved since they were caught. "Explain. Now. Or I will be leaving the venue in handcuffs."

"Have you two ever wondered how exhausting it is to date you? All you two care about is work. You put your relationships on the back burner," Delaney blurted out, and the guilty expression on Easton's face injected a new rush of anger into Daisy's veins. "Easton and I aren't sorry—we're in love."

"In love?" Jensen spat. If his arms loosened any more on Daisy, she might escape and tackle Easton and Delaney off the roof. Jensen could have the promotion because she wasn't one to accept disrespect.

"It's true! Jensen, we haven't been in love for years. Ever since you graduated college, you've become *obsessed* with Daisy. You always talk about her; I couldn't take it anymore. I don't understand why she has you wrapped around her every move. But I know it's mutual... You two are preoccupied with one-upping each other."

"I started talking with Delaney about how isolating it is to be involved with Harrison's favorite. After so many months of neglect, one thing led to another," Easton finally spoke up, not looking at Daisy or Jensen.

"How long has this been going on?" Jensen asked.

"It only happened once. Tonight. We reached our boiling point and had a moment of weakness. The rest of the time was talking only," Delaney remarked, chewing on her lower lip. Her eyes flitted over to Easton, who closed his mouth.

"You're lying," Daisy hissed.

Jensen whispered, voice lilted in a warning, "Daisy."

"No, they're lying. I'm far from stupid. You two are already in deep shit, so you might as well embrace the rest of the storm coming your way."

Easton and Delaney glanced at one another before Easton sighed, "Fine. We've been seeing each other for months. Happy now?"

"Yeah, I'm so fucking happy to learn that you were sleeping with her and me at the same time, you absolute jackass." Daisy's sarcasm left every word punchy on her tongue, hoping she carved his heart out. He only used her to advance himself.

"You know what, Daisy? You brought this on yourself." Easton shook his head, wrapping a protective arm around Delaney like she was the victim.

"Oh, I can't wait to hear this one!"

"Earlier, you were supposed to help me network, but you didn't. I've had to put up with you being a frigid bitch in the bedroom for weeks because you're too busy with work. Tonight was the last straw."

"Hey, don't fucking call her that," Jensen snapped, sending Daisy's heart into pure silence. The frantic rush from her anger ceased so abruptly that she almost worried her heart gave out.

But when his arms dropped from her waist, she heard it start again. "Your weakness as a man isn't her fault."

"You got this job because I gave you a good referral. So, watch your mouth... And you have two days to collect your stuff from my place before I burn it." Daisy bared her teeth. She readied a slap so loud the greater Los Angeles area would hear it if he came any closer.

Easton didn't argue back or say a word when Jensen stepped forward. Daisy's eyes studied the pain as it seeped out of every feature while he stared at Delaney.

She had lost a bum who mooched off her for months, but he lost his high school sweetheart. *Fuck.*

"We're done too," Jensen snapped at Delaney, who hid behind Easton like he was a human shield. "You can move out of the townhouse with your things. You're also uninvited from the corporate retreat. Don't call me, apologize, or ask for a second chance."

At that moment, Daisy's heart almost wept for Jensen. She didn't hurt, not when she gained more than she lost. But he looked ready to break at any second.

"You should leave, lovebirds... before I decide to forfeit my job by wringing your necks," Daisy snapped, breaking the tension with her threat. Easton and Delaney sprinted toward the elevator without hesitation, running off into the night as new lovers.

She watched them vanish but froze as Jensen wandered to the nearest deck chair. He staggered as he sat, burying his head between his knees and curling into himself, closed off from the world.

Daisy didn't need to see him cry.

Daisy wandered over, standing in front of him to no response. She touched his shoulder. "I'll grab Piper or Hayley, okay? You need someone who doesn't remind you of the shitshow we just participated in. Stay here."

Jensen said nothing but reached over and laid his hand on hers for a beat. Then, he pulled back, and Daisy headed for the elevators. A truce fell over them for the moment while their relationships crumbled into rubble around them.

Chapter 4
Jensen

No amount of Californian sunshine beating down on Jensen's face would alleviate the scowl he'd worn for the past three days. The week since that fateful night at the Topaz blurred together, closing the end of May with an unforgettable implosion of life as he knew it.

Those five days crawled by too slowly, leaving a bitter taste in his mouth to wash away with the itch to drink. Luckily for him, the Royal Ridge had his promised salvation at the bottom of a bottle.

What a great fucking start to June.

The sea breeze buffeted against his cheeks, racing along the stretch of road winding past the cresting waves of the Pacific Ocean. Sunlight and wind flitted freely with the convertible top of Jensen's car rolled down. The clusters of palm trees lined the road into the Royal Ridge, his summer vacation since the company developed the property almost fifteen years ago.

"Jensen?" Beside him, Piper scrunched up in the passenger seat. Although her eyes hid behind pink cat-eye sunglasses, he sensed the weight of her gaze on him. "I'm really sorry about Delaney."

"Pipes, please don't apologize again. Nothing about this situation is your fault," Jensen sighed, trying to be gentle. She had seen Delaney riding the elevator to the pool deck during the party, which led to Jensen's finding her with Easton. Somehow, Piper convinced herself that she had done something wrong.

After finding out about the cheating, Jensen filled his family in and asked for some space to process. They all agreed, but Piper suggested she stay with him until they left for the corporate retreat in Del Mesa.

Jensen couldn't say no to her. He gave his little sister the bedroom and took the couch, refusing to use the bed he and Delaney shared. He couldn't bring himself to change the sheets, knowing what the smell of her lavender perfume would do to him.

Piper, however, didn't take his dismissal. She rubbed over her sleeved arms, forgoing a tank top despite the sweltering weather. Her throat bobbed as she said, "But my text was why you found her with that guy! You wouldn't have seen that, and now you don't get to enjoy your favorite trip."

"It would've ruined the trip more if I proposed to her and found out later on that she was cheating. You saved me months of heartbreak."

"I guess so."

"You're my hero, Pipes." Jensen ruffled her hair, ignoring her squealing and the playful smacking against his wrist while driving up to the entrance of the Ridge. His little sister's text worked like divine intervention, so he owed her a little gratitude. She opened his eyes to what his lovestruck brain refused to see.

The cheating... The lies about how much she loved him... And the fact that Piper and her never got along. The last one came as a raging shock to him, but Piper's sniffly confession about how Delaney treated her differently than Hayley because of her weight had doused his rage in a truckload of gasoline.

He should've seen the signs, but he hadn't. No one else played a role in the tragedy of his romantic life besides him and Delaney.

Jensen swiped them in, speeding through the shining gates for the roundabout. Knowing the roads like the back of his hand, he brought them to the semi-packed parking lot. Yet, his luck found them a parking spot in the closest row to the main building.

Jensen switched the top closed and leaned over the center console to wrap Piper in his arms, squeezing her tight. "Don't worry about me, okay? It'll make me happy if you have a good time for the next month."

"But—" Piper tried to protest.

"Do it for me? Please?"

"Okay. I'll have fun for the both of us."

"Thank you. Now, let me grab our bags." Jensen helped Piper out of the car, hustling to grab their bags from the backseat. He slung his duffle over his shoulder with ease. Piper snatched the handle from him playfully when he tried to take both suitcases.

Jensen and his little sister walked side-by-side over the simmering asphalt and the paved roads lined by swaying palm trees. Piper stuck to his side when groups of people passed them on the narrow footpath, but Jensen didn't mind.

The two ducked under the archway of the main building, greeted by the loud whirring from the air conditioner working overtime whenever the automatic doors slid open. Faint touches of tropical spa oils scented the air inside, leaving Jensen's head a little fuzzy as he inhaled.

A few feet from the door, the rest of the Ramsey clan waited in the lounge with its burnt orange leather chairs and glass tables hosting a mountain of brochures from the local businesses. His mom and dad's heads pressed together, exchanging hushed conversation behind their hands. Conversely, Hayley glared at the nearest wall, fiddling with her lime green earbuds.

Piper rushed forward, tugging her suitcase behind her. Her eager beeline caught the attention of his parents and Hayley, whose eyes jumped over her to Jensen standing by the door.

He planned to join them, ready to put on a brave face instead of being angry, but Hayley abandoned her three bags at their parents' feet and sprinted to Jensen. She hugged him tighter than she had in years.

"I hate her," Hayley mumbled into his shoulder. Jensen didn't have the energy to defend Delaney. "How are you holding up?"

"I'm managing. Piper's been keeping me occupied with movie marathons and making my favorite dishes." Jensen rubbed Hayley's back, feeling the tension melt from his sister's shoulders.

Unlike Piper, Hayley and Delaney used to be close. Endless conversations about how the two would be sisters-in-law rattled in Jensen's head, but the anger in Hayley's eyes promised the death of those dreams. All the unspoken slights and ill feelings came out in light of her betrayal. No one in the Ramsey clan mourned for Delaney; she betrayed them as much as she stuck a knife into Jensen's chest.

Hayley kept an arm looped around his waist when the two wandered over to the rest of the family. She passed Jensen into the arms of their mom, who crushed him in the tightest hug of all.

Jensen's chin rested on her shoulder. "You should have the ring back. I don't want it near me right now."

"Of course." His mom pulled back and cupped her hands together. "Did you bring it with you?"

"I did. Didn't feel comfortable leaving it in my place."

"I understand."

Jensen passed the ring box to his mom's accepting hands, watching her fingers curl over the dark velvet to shield it from his eyes. He turned to his dad but found himself buried in a hug instead. Yeah, he needed a dad hug.

"Do you want to talk about it?" his dad asked.

Jensen shook his head. "I'd rather not. I feel talked out."

"Alright. I'm always happy to lend an ear if you change your mind. You should check in and get some rest before dinner. You look exhausted."

Not wanting to admit that he hadn't slept more than five hours a night, Jensen headed for the front desk with his bags in tow. He approached the nearly empty line, save for the lone worker and a tall, leggy blonde standing with her back facing him.

But as he drew closer, the voice smacked him with recognition. "I'm here for the Hidden Oasis corporate retreat."

"Can I get your name, Miss?"

"Daisy. Daisy Riggs."

Jensen hung back, digging his sweaty hands into the pockets of his linen shorts. He and Daisy hadn't spoken a word to one another since that night. Several people commented on the quiet around the office, earning a few glares from colleagues for their lack of tact.

The girl behind the counter, wearing a name tag with 'Maisie' written in neat font, typed a few things into the computer. Clearing her throat, she said, "The computer says you're booked with another guest who hasn't checked in yet."

"That shouldn't be," Daisy replied. From how fast she responded, Jensen swore he overheard a little terror in her voice. Daisy never panicked. "I called several days ago to detach my rooming assignment from Easton Keller. He and I can't be in the same room."

"Yes, that's reflected in the notes here. No, you're roomed with someone else... A Jensen Ramsey," Maisie read aloud to Daisy.

But Jensen choked on his damn tongue, announcing his presence to Daisy and Maisie. "You've got to be kidding me!"

"For once, I agree with him," Daisy's voice shook when she turned around. Her face drained of all its color when her eyes landed on him. "We need to be separated."

"I'm afraid that's not possible, Miss. You and Mr. Ramsey have missed the twenty-four-hour period for any room changes. The Ridge is also at full capacity for the next few weeks, so no replacement rooms are available." Maisie frowned, eyes jumping between Daisy and Jensen.

Daisy whipped around, stepping forward to protest, but Jensen blocked her with a hand across her stomach. "Daisy, we can't fight this."

"You really want to room together?" Daisy hissed under her breath.

"No, but what other choice do we have? You know I'm right—"

"I hate this. I hate everything about this."

"That makes two of us," Jensen mumbled under his breath, dodging a wicked glare from Daisy as he stepped to the counter. He slid over his ID to check in. "Can you tell us if our rooming arrangements have space for two beds?"

"Absolutely, Mr. Ramsey! You and Miss Riggs are staying in the Bluff Building in one of the Villas. It'll be a two-bedroom suite with an ensuite bathroom, a connected living room, and a full kitchen area. The Villas face the ocean and have balcony access in each room. They're our most luxurious accommodations."

"Alright. Consider us checked in."

"Here are your keys and spare copies for you and Miss Riggs. Do you need someone to help you with your bags?"

"We'll manage," Daisy grumbled, snatching up her key and the extra copies. She flipped her sunglasses down, grabbing her suitcase. Jensen knew from the smoke escaping her ears and the hellfire blazing in her dark eyes that she was pissed.

"Have a good day." He nodded to Maisie before he grabbed his things and walked alongside Daisy. Neither of them said a word when passing by his family, who witnessed the latest blow to Jensen's pride.

The trip kept getting worse by the minute. Surviving for a month in close quarters with Daisy sounded borderline impossible.

The two escaped from the prying eyes of those in the lobby, trading air conditioning and too much noise for stuffy summer heat and silence. Jensen trailed behind Daisy, who stomped down the pavement in her wedge sandals. The breeze kicked up the long coral skirt of her summer dress, fabric tangling around her ankles to slow her down.

Jensen caught up to her, managing to keep pace. He and Daisy remained together for the short walk to the Bluff Building. They ducked inside and followed the terracotta tiled floors, counting the brass numbers on the white walls.

Eventually, they found the lucky number 707 toward the end of the hall. Jensen and Daisy paused outside the door. Neither moved to open the suite, and they stood with their bags and the keys to the room.

"We should go inside," Jensen said, breaking the silence first. His dad's suggestion that he should get some rest sounded all too tempting after this morning's shitshow and the remaining fallout with Delaney.

"Yeah," Daisy whispered. She swiped the key to the mechanical chirp and the green light across the keypad. "Let's go."

Jensen pushed the door open and let Daisy in first with her bags, squinting at how bright the room glowed. With sunlight filtering through the glass doors to the balcony, the white and tan palette of the room glittered in the daylight. Pops of blue in the room tied everything together with the sight of the ocean over the nearby bluffs.

His eyes flitted between the two sliding doors on opposite sides of the room, past the kitchenette and driftwood dining table, with their opaque and smudged glass. Each revealed a king-sized bed, a private balcony, and an ensuite door. As promised, the suite's layout left enough room for his and Daisy's personal space.

Daisy marched toward the left bedroom, dropping her bags in the doorway. "Unless you have any reservations, I'm taking this room."

"None," Jensen replied, his voice slipping back into the usual irritation Daisy invoked. "Whatever Your Highness wants."

"Shut up. I don't have the energy to deal with you today. How about we agree to stay out of each other's way for the next month?" Daisy scoffed when Jensen passed with his bags. He dropped them at the foot of his bed in the other bedroom, staring at Daisy in her doorway.

"Fine by me."

"Good. Don't go through my shit while I'm at the spa."

Jensen watched Daisy stuff a few items in the loose tote dangling over her forearm and close her bedroom's sliding door. She marched toward the front door, but Jensen had already turned his back when the door slammed shut.

He kicked off his sneakers by the foot of the bed, climbing into the plush mattress, content to sink in face first. Daisy could blow off steam at the spa because he would be too busy catching up on sleep to care.

Life seemed less bleak with a full stomach.

Rising from his place at the dinner table, Jensen straightened the lapels of his suit jacket, smiling at his family. As his dad suggested, sleeping the afternoon away until the heat dwindled helped his mood. He hadn't stirred from the embrace of his bed until his phone buzzed with a call from his mom, reminding him of their dinner plans.

If Daisy returned after her spa visit, she left him alone as promised. They might survive the month stuck together after all.

"Thanks for dinner," Jensen leaned against his chair. He soaked in the swaying overhead lights and the sea breeze waltzing through the open doors of Abalone, the most popular fine dining spot at the Ridge. "I had a good time."

"We're glad. It's nice to see that smile again." His mom grasped his hand with hers, sitting next to him. The implication cut deep, yet Jensen hung onto that smile for his family's sake.

Several days of endless shit beat him down, but things should start looking up. Piper said something that stuck with him during dinner, lodging between his ribs. *Make the retreat a fresh start.*

Jensen clung to the idea like a promise. A month should put the whole cheating scandal behind him. With nothing but the sunshine, the pool, and good food demanding his attention, he had his choice of distractions. He didn't have to worry about the shareholder vote either, able to enjoy some much-needed peace.

Jensen sighed. "It's nice to have a reason to smile again. I should head in for the night."

"We'll see you for breakfast tomorrow at Bayside, right?" Piper stared expectantly. Jensen leaned over to ruffle her hair.

"I wouldn't miss it for the world," Jensen promised softly, making his way around the table for hugs. His parents and sisters split two rooms in one of the other buildings, so he walked back to Bluff alone. "If I suddenly go missing, my roommate did it."

Hayley and his mom gasped, struck by the nonchalance. Jensen exchanged a look with his dad, the last one on his walk around the table, who chuckled. "Try not to murder my protégé."

"She's more likely to get me while I'm sleeping," Jensen snorted, but the gentle slap of his dad's hand against his chest sent him on his way. He wandered into the summer evening, greeted by ink-colored skies and the faintly visible stars. Palms swayed in the distance to the ocean's soft crashing against the rocks below the Ridge. The lack of people allowed peace to spread its presence across the resort.

Jensen walked down the pavement alone, burying his fingers into the tight knot of his tie around his neck. He loosened it while he moved away from the Waves Building, passing by the occasional group or a car curving around the roundabout.

His hands slipped into the pockets of his slacks, leaving the undone tie to hang around his neck limply. Up ahead, the rippling and neon blue waters from the four pools between the Palm and Bluff Buildings illuminated the path to his room.

Jensen paused on the road, staring into the water where several dark silhouettes frolicked in the shallow end. Laughter carried across the roundabout, loud enough to echo over any cars, and the knife stuck in Jensen's chest twisted a little deeper.

Thoughts of a night swim left as quickly as they came. At the risk of what-ifs haunting him until he couldn't sleep, he watched the strangers swim for another moment. Then, he continued on his way.

Jensen almost made it to the Bluff Building before something new caught his eye, stopping him in his tracks. That time, however, it was the amber light trickling through the open doors of the Sunset Vermouth Bar.

Next to the Bluff Building, Sunset Vermouth shared the same architectural styles as the rest of the Ridge. Yet, the inside exuded classic speakeasy vibes—soft jazz streamed through the open doors, luring each passersby into the hardwood flooring and the smokey lighting straight out of the twenties.

Jensen stared through the open doors when his wandering eyes spotted her alone at the bar. Wrapped up in a classic black dress, Daisy leaned forward while staring at the shelves behind the bar.

She ran her finger along the rim of what appeared to be whiskey, not drinking or nursing it to her chest. She sat there, unmoving.

With nothing better to do and a newfound urge for a drink, Jensen ducked into Sunset Vermouth, strode over, and claimed the seat beside Daisy. "You're supposed to drink it, not poke at it like it's Brussels sprouts."

"I don't mind Brussels sprouts," Daisy spoke without glancing his way until he climbed onto the stool. She turned her face, adorned with her sharp eyeliner and a frown painted cherry red. "I lost my appetite. So, I shouldn't be drinking at all."

"Oh? I'll have what she's having." Jensen waved to the bartender, an older gentleman dapperly dressed like he and Daisy. Beside him, Daisy huffed in unabashed amusement.

"Guess that means you'll have to start with the Pink Whitney shots topped off with edible glitter."

"Not what I meant, but I'm never too good for glitter. Bring it on."

"Hilarious." Daisy picked up her whiskey for a drawn-out sip. "Put my companion here on my tab. Whiskey, neat."

"So, should I ask why you're drinking your sorrows away with... three fingers of whiskey at ten at night? Rooming with me isn't that unbearable already," Jensen asked, leaning an elbow on the bar to get a better view of Daisy's face.

Strands of her blonde hair framed her face in loose waves while the rest piled onto her head in a neat bun, casting shadows over her face. Her eyes became the same shade as the whiskey sitting in her glass in the dim lighting.

For lack of a better word, she looked haunted.

"Unless you want your night ruined, I'd advise against it," Daisy hummed, lifting the glass and holding it to her lips without drinking. But when Jensen didn't contradict, she sighed. "I had a dinner reservation tonight but couldn't bring myself to eat after seeing Delaney there."

"Delaney's here? By herself?"

"No. With Easton. The two looked cozy at dinner, feeding one another from their plates and playing barely-concealed footsie under the table. It killed my appetite, which is a shame because

I had planned to enjoy the restaurant's tiramisu for the last three weeks. Another thing Easton ruined for me."

Jensen's head spun hard like he downed those shots Daisy joked about, enough to induce an upset stomach. He might've uninvited Delaney, but she scored another plus-one slot on the trip.

Fuck all his other plans. He should drink his sorrows away, too.

"They came together? I need that drink now." Jensen's jaw clenched. He graciously accepted the whiskey from the bartender, watching him scuttle back to polishing glasses in the corner. They had the bar to themselves for their pity party.

"And to think I felt bad for her dating you. It's the other way around now," Daisy snorted into her glass. Jensen might've been offended another time, but that sounded damn close to a compliment.

"I'll take it." Jensen poured some whiskey down his throat. The burning blossomed, but the warmth stoked his battered ego. He nursed the glass close to his chest.

"I'm sure there's a silver lining in here somewhere."

"And what would that be?"

"Neither of us will be distracted by relationships, so we can invest all our attention into the promotion." Jensen's eyes abandoned the sight of his glass for Daisy, whose eyes lifted from giving the wall the thousand-yard stare.

"You have a point there. Still, it sucks to be cheated on, especially by someone below your league." Daisy took another tentative sip, hesitant compared to Jensen's chase of a whiskey buzz.

He stopped mid-sip, swallowing. "You think Delaney is below my league?"

Daisy's eyes caught his. She arched a slender brow at him, face painted in curiosity. "I was talking about Easton and me. When I said I helped him get the job at the company, I meant that. His lackluster personality helped him score no offers while barely scraping the bottom ten percent of his graduating class at UCLA. I built him up and let him treat me like his manager."

Her eyes never broke his, not even as the two drank in unison. Her slow sips were wiser than him, racing to the bottom of the glass, searching for some relief. The thought of Delaney running around the Ridge with another man punched a hole through his bravado.

Jensen finished his glass, not realizing he tipped the rest of the liquor down his throat until the heat shot straight to his head. The world numbed around the edges, fuzzy and tingling with warmth like the sun rose back over the horizon to shine on him.

Daisy leaned toward him, sliding his glass out from his hand. "Do you want another one?"

"I shouldn't, but yes. Are you getting another?"

"Probably not. This is number two for me. If I drink more than this, I might as well let the tipsiness take me on a trip."

"Okay, one for me, and we'll close the tab?" Jensen offered to Daisy, who nodded, signaling the bartender for another. While the bartender poured him another glass, he watched Daisy abstain from her drink.

Jensen's right pocket burned before he instinctively slipped his hand into it, searching the space for something that wasn't there. Days with the ring box hidden in there imprinted its shape. Without it, he felt lighter.

He glanced over at Daisy when the bartender slid him a new glass of whiskey, seeing her eyes on him. Her stare became hard to ignore, much like the whiskey in their glasses. Such an intoxicating shade of brown... Had they always brightened so brilliantly, swirling into a new shade with kaleidoscopic ease?

His thoughts blurred together, yet Jensen could barely blame the liquor. He lifted his drink into the air, still holding Daisy's gaze. "How about a fuck you to Delaney and Easton?"

"Hah, sure." Daisy lifted her glass, too. "Fuck you, Delaney and Easton... It's too late to cry over cheaters, so I hope their relationship is a flaming trainwreck."

"Amen." Jensen nodded. Their glasses clinked together, filling the bar with more than their commiseration. The two stilled while simmering in the silence of the summer night, sharing a whiskey where they usually swapped bitter words and snark. Their eyes held firm in their linked gaze, allowing an understanding to pass through.

And again, they drank.

Chapter 5
Daisy

Daisy didn't know exactly where she went wrong, but it probably started with the liquor on an empty stomach. After finishing their second glass of whiskey, she and Jensen closed their shared tab, walking back to their suite in silence.

She had noticed the loaded stares throughout their exchange, but those happened often. She and Jensen got into staring contests and shouting matches with such regular frequency at work that one might assume they were part of her job description. Yet, Daisy slipped up somewhere in the amber haze of Sunset Vermouth.

The next thing she knew, she was kissing Jensen's stupid face in the hallway outside their room.

Daisy's back collided with the nearest wall, panting hard when Jensen's hands gripped her waist. His body pinned hers, trapping her between the cold exterior of the building and the delicious heat lapping off his skin.

Jensen's eyes darkened like midnight waters when tracing over her body, drinking in every inch of her. His tongue swiped over his lips, taking a moment to breathe.

Daisy chewed on her inner cheek when his thumbs traced a loose shape over her stomach. Wherever his fingers touched, heat followed in the wake of his path. Her thoughts swam through whiskey, ignoring the last shred of her rationality screaming above the dull thudding between her legs.

Jensen leaned in, pausing when his lips hovered over hers as he murmured, "You started this."

"You continued it," Daisy replied, and her cheeky tone caused Jensen's mouth to crash back to hers.

Her hands slid up his buttoned shirt, fingering at the second button. A moan escaped her when Jensen's tongue slid along her lower lip, brushing against hers while he mapped out her mouth.

Ugh, him being a good kisser sucked. Daisy would be annoyed about it later. For now, she chose to enjoy Jensen's attention.

Jensen's mouth trailed away to skim her jaw, peppering heated kisses to her skin until she pawed at his back. When Daisy's nails dug in and pushed him closer, he chuckled.

"It's not funny!" Daisy gasped, betrayed by how her hips arched upward at Jensen's wandering mouth.

"It kind of is," Jensen's hot breath caressed the column of her neck seconds before his mouth returned to its ministrations. He sucked against her neck, and Daisy's breath held in her throat, leaving her lightheaded. He'd leave a mark for the morning if he kept kissing that hard. "Never pegged you for the needy type."

"I'm not needy! My vibrator and I haven't gotten enough alone time lately," Daisy grumbled, trying her best to ignore Jensen as he added to the growing constellation of hickeys.

When Easton blamed her for the dry spell in their sex life, he hadn't been entirely wrong. But he shouldered half the blame for when he acted coldly mid-sex. It didn't matter anymore, not when she could have whoever she wanted.

Right then, she saw an opportunity in Jensen.

Daisy braced further against the wall as she tipped her head to the side, offering him more of her neck. Jensen hummed in appreciation right before he traced over one of the hickeys with his tongue. *Fucker.*

"If you keep this up, we're going to get caught in an indecent position. The two potential CEOs fraternizing during the company's retreat wouldn't be good for our reputations. And I don't even want to think about HR," Daisy hissed, yet her warning fell flat on its face when Jensen laughed.

"Maybe," Jensen's voice muffled against the skin of her neck, but its warmth sent a wave of goosebumps across her body. Daisy shivered quietly, squeezing her eyes shut. "What would people think seeing me pressing you against the wall? You wouldn't be able to hold onto that ice princess act if they witnessed you moaning and writhing for me, hmm?"

"Shut up!" Daisy's eyes met Jensen's when he pulled his face from the crook of her neck, losing herself in those stormy eyes. So transfixed, she barely registered the sensation of his fingers sliding up to cradle the back of her neck. When his mouth returned to hers, she sank into him.

Daisy always gave as good as she got; her lips chased pleasure, and she found a gold mine in Jensen's sharp inhales when she pushed against him.

She dragged her fingers down his back while her head buzzed with the growing chant to take Jensen to her bed. He got on her nerves, under her skin, and maybe into her pants if she didn't stop there.

The metal clattering of a belt startled her eyes open, bringing Daisy's gaze down to his waistband. Jensen still had one hand tucked behind her neck, but his other hand unbuckled his belt without breaking the kiss.

Oh. God.

Daisy's breath strangled as Jensen pulled back, eyes opening. But he followed her gaze to his newly unbuckled belt, smirking, "Like my party trick?"

"You're a slut," Daisy teased, but her voice faded when Jensen's face lit up. His smugness radiated off him, and she swallowed the urge to throttle him with her bare hands.

The whiskey inside her, however, disagreed. *Keep going, Jensen.*

As if he heard the little voice inside her head beg, Jensen grabbed one of her thighs. Daisy stilled while his fingers caressed her skin, gliding toward her ass. She couldn't think, not when their hips flushed together, and she felt the firm bulge through his slacks.

Jensen's eyes bore into hers, demanding her attention. "Is that a complaint, Your Highness?" he whispered against her lips, still holding her gaze hostage between half-lidded eyes.

"No," Daisy replied, folding too quickly. Apparently, she left her common sense at the bar, circling the bottom of her whiskey glass.

Her admission was the correct answer because Jensen wrapped her thigh around his hip. Space became nonexistent between them, sucking all the air from the hallway into the dry heat of a California night.

Jensen opened his mouth to say more, maybe to tease her for her loss of words, but the nearby clatter of feet against metal stairs broke the immersion.

His eyes dropped from hers, shaking his head. "C'mon."

Daisy buried a yelp in Jensen's neck when he, without warning, scooped up her other thigh. She molded her body against his, and her legs tightened around his hips.

One of Jensen's hands gripped under her ass while he raced for their room several doors down. As he rifled for a room key, Daisy swore the hem of her dress inched higher. She posed a serious risk of flashing the empty hallway an eyeful of the dark, lace thong underneath her skirt.

Jensen quickly swiped them in, and the two tumbled into the darkened room. Daisy heard the door click shut, but Jensen didn't wait to carry her to the nearest bedroom. *Her bedroom.*

Moonlight filtered through the open curtains, but no one could see them from outside. Daisy heard Jensen's knees bump into the mattress at the foot of her bed before he gently lowered her into the sheets—not the rough toss and manhandling she expected from him.

Jensen's silhouette raced to the bedside table. Within seconds, the room filled with the sickly yellow light from a lamp, washing over the walls. Grimacing until her eyes adjusted to the brightness, Daisy peered over her shoulder, watching Jensen turn to find her staring.

Daisy raked her eyes over him. "I might be too much for you to handle. You should head back to your room."

"Is that right?" Jensen yanked the loose tie from around his neck, tossing it toward the door. He stalked closer. "And what if *you're* the one who can't handle me?"

"Trust me. I can handle you easily. All that in the hallway was foreplay."

"You talk a big game, Riggs."

"No 'Your Highness'? Now, I know it's getting serious... I won't hold it against you if you can't live up to expectations." Daisy smirked, taking in Jensen's darkened eyes while he inched closer. The tension pulled her taut like a bowstring someone twisted too tight, helping little to calm the friction sparking between her thighs.

If things continued to heat up, the Ridge might burn down around them from the tension.

Jensen leaned forward to rest his knuckles on the edge of the bed. His posture boxed her in. Their eyes connected somewhere in the middle as the rest of the world went to hell.

Daisy's hands held his face as Jensen bridged the gap between their mouths to shut her up. He kissed her until she saw stars, tumbling helplessly into his gravity. The aroma of cedar, sandalwood, and whiskey on his skin threatened to rewire her brain, immersing her in all of him while aimless hands explored over pesky clothes.

When they broke for breath, their hands raced to strip. Daisy's hands slipped behind her head for the clasp of her dress, stuck right out of reach. While she fought to free herself, Jensen shed the layers of his suit.

The quiet click at the nape of her neck preceded the slump of her dress down her shoulders, but Daisy didn't wait around or brag. Her fingers tucked into the hem and yanked the dress clear over her head, taking her strapless bra with it.

The cool sting of the room's air against her hardened nipples quelled the fever enveloping Daisy's body. She panted, reaching up to yank the bobby pins from her hair.

Jensen stilled. Daisy caught his eyes running up her exposed skin, dousing her ego in gasoline and striking the match. He stood there with his suit jacket crumpled on the floor and his belt undone from earlier, but his shirt was still on.

"You should close your mouth before the drool drips down your chin." Daisy stretched across the bed, rolled onto her stomach, and kicked her feet up like a classic pin-up girl. She propped herself onto elbows, running a finger up Jensen's still-buttoned shirt. "I told you I might be too much for you."

"Hilarious," Jensen tried to scoff, but the heaviness of his breathing wasn't lost on Daisy. His chest heaved while his fingers fumbled down each button. He missed the hole a few times, but Daisy silently counted each miss while hiding a smirk. "Don't laugh at me."

His exasperation pulled at the last of Daisy's resolve. She finally let the smirk out fully. "How'd you know I was laughing at you in my head?"

"You're the worst."

Jensen nearly tore the last button off, but he peeled off his undershirt in the same move. Daisy stared at her rival's sculpted abs and broad, defined chest, glistening in the light. Okay, Giselle wasn't too far off in her assessment, but Daisy knew better than to tell Jensen he looked like an Adonis.

She stared at him through her lashes, smirking when she wrapped her arms around his hips. Jensen's brow raised, but he moaned when Daisy yanked him toward the bed by the belt loops. Her mouth brushed against his lower abdomen, running along the sparse hairs of his happy trail.

Daisy's lipstick left behind smudged red stains as she moved closer to the waistband. Her eyes held Jensen's, taking in his breathless expression and how his cheeks reduced to a delicious shade of pink.

Daisy pressed her lips against his naval until the rumple of fabric filled the room. She pulled back enough to see Jensen's pants discarded, his cock in his hand.

For all the times Daisy sneered that Jensen's obnoxious attitude overcompensated for other *shortcomings*, the sight of his dick tossed all of those assumptions out of the window. A few notable veins ran down the length of his cock, on the longer side of average, but it was the girth that awakened something feral in her.

Jensen stroked a hand up his length, panting a little when he smirked. "Now who's drooling?"

Maybe she was, but Daisy would deny it until the day she died. She rolled her eyes. "You're so full of yourself."

"But you like it. Now, if you're still sure you can take me, tongue out," Jensen demanded. Looming over her with such a cocky glint in his eyes infuriated Daisy, but the whiskey in her veins softened it.

Despite her glare, she stuck her tongue out. A noise of approval left Jensen's lips as he tipped her chin upward.

He tapped the head of his cock against her tongue. Daisy hated how her thighs clenched at the sloppy echo when Jensen repeated the motion.

Jensen groaned loudly, uninhibited in the safety of their suite. "If you keep looking at me like that…"

"What? You'll finish too fast?" Daisy laughed at the blush spreading down Jensen's neck, running her tongue along the underside of his cock. She swirled it around the head, licking pre-cum off his slit.

Jensen grimaced, jaw clenched. "Yeah, right. I'm not in high school anymore. I have self-control."

"That self-control's about to go out the window. You'll be begging me to keep going," Daisy whispered as she wrapped her lips around the tip, suckling a little. Her hands guided his hips, taking his cock fully into her mouth.

Jensen moaned, breath shuddering when Daisy bobbed her head slowly. His hair fell into his eyes while he struggled to keep them open.

The sight of Jensen thoroughly debased because of her filled Daisy's chest with pride. She took more of his cock, but its weight made her head go empty. Pleasure buzzed hollowly, drowning out any thoughts of anything but the man in front of her.

"Shit." Jensen panted hard, breathing interrupted by the occasional moan whenever Daisy's tongue brushed the underside of his cock. Each time, his hips weakly bucked, and he pushed himself further down her throat. "I can almost stand you when you're behaving yourself instead of pushing all my buttons."

With her fingers curled into the belt loops, Daisy eased Jensen's cock from her mouth. She admired the lipstick marks littered along his length in her signature red. The urge to send a picture to Delaney and Easton sounded almost too good to ignore.

Daisy licked her lips as her hand wrapped around his rock-hard length, smirking when Jensen's scowl morphed into a lip bite. Still holding his gaze, she dropped a bead of spit against the tip before she ran her hand up his shaft.

"Mmm, it's cute that you think you're in control here. If you assume you're going to boss me around, you have another thing coming," Daisy chided, albeit more playful than bitchy. "You're enjoying this, or else you wouldn't be bucking your hips down my throat."

"Okay, I'm enjoying it." Jensen's hands slid from her face and threaded into her waves. Before she knew it, one of his hands gathered her hair into a ponytail, wrapping it around his palm. He angled her face so the tip of his cock smeared against her lips. "But you like it *just* as much."

Daisy blinked up at him wordlessly. She opened her mouth for Jensen's cock to slide back in. That time, Jensen controlled the pace, using his grip on her ponytail and slow yet deep thrusts.

Daisy shifted on the bed until her knees bent and her thighs parted wider, pressing her hips flush to the mattress. Each shudder of his hips teased the friction between her legs. The low, dull throbbing of her clit screamed to be touched, but she'd rather die than beg Jensen for some attention. She wasn't that desperate.

She started to rock her hips into the duvet, matching Jensen's pace. Yet, his eyes lazily traced down her arched back and hummed, "Keep your eyes on me. I'll take care of you."

Daisy's eyes narrowed, downright indignant, until Jensen's fingers walked down her back. He traced around the lace of her panties and over the supple curve of her ass.

She cried out when two of his fingers slid underneath the thin string to rub at her clit, muffled by his cock. Jensen's lips twisted into a smirk, rubbing two fingers between her clit to the slick entrance of her pussy.

Jensen repeated the motion but paused long enough to time his hips thrusting as his fingers pushed inside her. Daisy moaned hard, and her eyes fluttered heavily.

Jensen let out a low groan at the sloppy sound his fingers made sliding in and out of her pussy. "You're clenching so hard, Your Highness. Are you that eager for me to touch you?"

Daisy couldn't speak, not with her mouth full. Her eyes narrowed further, hoping to convey that he should stop talking. Her glare elicited a chuckle from Jensen, who slowed his hips.

He stepped back, but his eyes widened when seeing the saliva trail strung between Daisy's mouth and his cock. He swallowed hard, lips parted open and blushing. "Oh."

Daisy wiped her mouth, careful not to smudge her lipstick more than blowing Jensen already had. She admired the glistening of her slick on his fingers, sighing.

"What now, hotshot? Too much?" Daisy teased, rolling to sit upright at the foot of the bed. Her heels clattered on the ground harmlessly.

She didn't expect Jensen to hold her gaze while he sucked her slick off his fingers, nice and slow. Jensen hummed, "Nope. You're going to lose that pathetic excuse for panties."

Daisy raised a brow, smirking as she hooked her fingers through the thin elastic of her thong. "You mean this?"

"If you worried about panty lines, you should've gone commando."

"I never like to make things easy for you."

Daisy slid the panties down her legs, tossing them toward the bathroom. She gestured to his slacks and boxers puddled around his ankles. Those needed to go.

Jensen never moved faster than to ditch them in a puddle of fabric. He glanced toward the living room. "I need a condom. I might have one in my suitcase—"

"I brought some." Daisy stretched toward the bedside table to grab the small makeup bag tucked underneath it. She found a foil and tossed it to Jensen, hearing the rumpling of the packaging. "Don't ask."

"Wasn't going to," Jensen mumbled.

After a moment, Jensen climbed onto the bed while Daisy met him in the middle. She opened her mouth, but only a moan came out when Jensen slid her onto his lap. His stiff cock rubbed against her pussy, throbbing from the slightest contact.

Jensen flashed her a wolfish grin when rutting his hips against hers, eliciting a small gasp out of her. "Feels good?"

"Maybe." Daisy sniffed, but her body trembled traitorously when Jensen's hand dipped between her thighs, straddling his hips. He guided himself to rest just shy of her entrance. "Stop teasing me."

"I will... but you need to ask me to fuck you."

"Fine. Please, *Jensen*... fuck me?"

Jensen's eyes widened, but he pushed up, sinking Daisy onto his cock with his hands at her hips. With each inch of him she took, the knot of arousal tightened in her abdomen until her body quivered all over.

"There we go," Jensen's voice shook when Daisy's hips based, flushed to his. His stormy eyes glazed over until Daisy's hand threaded into his hair. He panted, "Rock those hips for me."

Daisy's head tipped back after the first bounce of her hips, grabbing Jensen's shoulders like an anchor. "Fuck."

"For someone who hates me so much, you're loving every inch of me inside of you," Jensen whispered, broken up by shaky breaths and the slapping of skin while Daisy rode him.

"I still hate you."

"Feeling's mutual."

Neither said another word. Not when Jensen's hips matched Daisy's pace or his hands helped her ride, causing her thighs to shake. Jensen's face buried into the crook of her neck while Daisy faced the ceiling.

Sensations blurred together for Daisy, embarrassingly close to orgasm. She sped up her rocking when Jensen's breathing grew heavier, mirroring her pants.

Jensen's arms coiled around her waist, holding her still while he bucked his hips a few more times. He came with a weak moan. The drip of some cum from the condom slid down Daisy's thigh, coaxing her to finish.

She stilled in Jensen's lap while she embraced the high. Jensen's arms hadn't relinquished their hold on her, but his voice cut through the moment. "Oh, fuck."

"Huh?" Daisy leaned back enough to see Jensen's face, which flushed red with embarrassment.

"Daisy, we hooked up."

"I know. You're still inside me."

"We're still reeling from Delaney and Easton, but it would be wrong to stoop to their level. Not to mention, we're in competition for the same promotion. This was a mistake, one that can't happen again," Jensen said.

"I'm not a mistake. This wasn't a mistake either," Daisy remarked, shushing him with a finger to his lips. "As for Delaney and Easton, those idiots decided to ruin our vacation. When you were pushing me against the wall or with your hands on me, did you even think about either of them? Admit it, I had your full attention, and not your ex-girlfriend dating my ex."

"You... aren't wrong." Jensen frowned. Daisy dropped her hand to her side, squirming in his lap.

"Look, Easton and I were never going to be long-term. I'm well aware I'm not the dream girl who comes home to meet the family. You, on the other hand? Have you been with anyone outside of Delaney?"

Jensen said nothing, eyes averted to the side in shame. Daisy reached out, tipping his face back to hers.

"You're trying to be loyal to her and your commitment to the happy life you dreamed up. She cheated on you." Daisy shook her head. "Maybe you were going to marry this girl, but she threw it away because of her insecurity. She created a self-fulfilling prophecy that led to tonight."

"You knew about my proposal?" Jensen's brows knit together.

"Jensen, I think everyone knew you planned to propose with how often you checked your pocket. But that doesn't matter."

"Then, what does matter?"

"You and I might be at odds on everything else, but we have good sex. We had an itch needing to be scratched, so we found a mutual solution. We're still rivals, but I'm smart enough to know that closeness doesn't help tension. I won't say never to becoming rivals with a little something more involved," Daisy reasoned, studying the pensiveness slipping over Jensen's face.

"So, if we hypothetically became rivals... with benefits, then we'd need some ground rules," Jensen said, finally meeting her eyes. "That or it can never happen again."

Daisy wrinkled her nose. "I won't argue about ground rules. Starting with the fact no one else can know."

"Fine." Jensen nodded. "If we do this, we shouldn't cross a certain line with aftercare. No spending the night, no cuddles, no pillow talk."

"Okay. Neither of us expects a relationship as a benefit, and it should probably resolve before we return to work. What happens in paradise should stay here."

"Fine. Neither of us can sleep with anyone else without letting the other person know first, out of courtesy."

"Last thing, we'll have to sit down and talk about things that are acceptable and hard limits in the bedroom tomorrow morning... or when we're fully sober."

"Fine," Jensen remarked.

"Fine." With the last word, Daisy climbed off Jensen's lap. She slid to the edge of the bed, glancing over her shoulder at Jensen, who slumped back into the pillows. "I'm going to shower. You should probably do the same... in your room."

Chapter 6
Jensen

THE MIDDAY SUN BORE down on Del Mesa without a cloud in sight, greeting Jensen as he stepped from under the red-tiled roofs. The weather struck a perfect chord for the early June afternoon and his packed schedule.

Beyond a few meetings and group meals peppered throughout the week, everyone was encouraged to fill their days with whatever floated their boat. With the Ridge's four pools, golf course, local excursions into town, hiking trails, and other relevant activities, the world was Jensen's oyster.

He had rearranged his schedule before arriving at the Ridge, finding himself inundated with more free time than he initially expected. His family, however, eagerly volunteered to include him in all their plans throughout the month. He appreciated the thought, accepting a few offers from the bunch.

Crossing the plaza between the Waves and Shore Buildings, Jensen kept his head down with his hands in his pockets and a baseball cap pulled low over his eyes. Every excursion out of his room ran the risk of encountering Delaney and her new boy toy. While he no longer loved her, the anger hadn't resolved yet.

He avoided her since their relationship fell apart, and he stayed out of the townhouse when she came to collect her things, supervised by Piper and Hayley.

Undeterred, Delaney called him half a dozen times and texted him plenty more. He blocked her everywhere; he didn't want her excuses or explanations—it wouldn't fix what she broke.

So, the less Jensen saw of her out and about, the more of the retreat he would enjoy. *Out of sight, out of mind.*

"Stop thinking about her," Jensen grumbled under his breath, approaching the wooden posts marking the entrance to a hiking trail along the beach. A winding but less steep walkway to the sandy beaches adjacent to the Ridge offered a good view and the quickest route to meet his family. "If you don't see her, she doesn't exist."

Before Jensen managed to escape the plaza, a hand on his shoulder stopped him cold. From behind him, a familiar voice called his name.

"Jensen! Glad I caught you." While not the person he intended to avoid, Kenneth Malone was close enough in Jensen's eyes. Delaney and he met through Kenneth, Delaney's grandfather, so Jensen considered him Delaney-adjacent. "Could we borrow you for a moment?"

Sweat gathered along the nape of Jensen's neck, but not from the heat hanging in the air. *We?* He swallowed hard, still facing away from Kenneth, before clearing his throat. "Sure. What can I help you with?"

He spun on his heel, expecting Delaney to be with her grandfather. Instead, luck sided with him—he spotted the faces of shareholders like Tristan Merritt and several members of the Board of directors. *Thank fucking God.*

The shareholders weren't technically invited to the retreat on behalf of the company. Yet, their presence on the Ridge wasn't unexpected since many paid for personal memberships.

"It'll be quick. The fellas and I planned to find you this morning but didn't see you at the breakfast hall," Kenneth said while leaning onto his cane. His stark white hair hung shaggily around his face. His floral Tommy Bahama shirt fit with the other guests milling around the plaza. His dark eyes gleamed coolly while looking at Jensen.

"I grabbed breakfast earlier in the morning. I hit the gym while it was still dark out."

"Ah, to be young again. I remember what it's like to have endless energy to do things, not getting winded after walking up the stairs."

"It's why elevators are man's greatest creation." Jensen shrugged to laughter from the directors and shareholders. His lips fought a smile; he should make corny comments more often if they'll elicit *that* reaction. He would joke his way into the CEO position if necessary. "I'd love to spend all day shooting the breeze with you, but my family's expecting me down at the water. If I'm late, my sisters will never let me hear the end of it."

Tristan clapped a hand on Kenneth's shoulder, stepping forward to stand beside him. "We won't monopolize your time for much longer. Several of us thought scheduling lunch for this week would be a good idea, and you're invited. Six months might seem like a long time, but it'll be here in the blink of an eye."

"Oh, I understand. Is this off-the-record or in an official capacity?" asked Jensen. Part of him hoped he could leave the CEO talk in the city and enjoy his vacation along the coast, but Kenneth had other ideas.

"Your dad knows we've got some tentative plans set, but he excused himself from the lunch. Something about plans with your mom. We understood," Tristan replied. If his dad knew, then Daisy would know.

"When's this lunch supposed to be?"

"Two days from now. Is that a date that works for you?"

"Yeah, it works great. Do you need me to tell Daisy about lunch, or is she next on your list?"

"We'll tell her," Kenneth interjected before Tristan, fanning at his ruddy cheeks. Underneath the heat, his slumped posture and sweaty face looked like the early stages of melted ice cream on the sizzling sidewalk. "Don't worry about it."

Jensen nodded. "Sounds good. Thank you for the invitation, gentlemen." He and Daisy hadn't said more than a passing "hello" when they occasionally ran into each other in their shared space, but he would've tracked her down. He didn't need to play dirty to win.

Besides, the other night replayed in his head on a loop. He had left Daisy's room before her shower finished, laid up in his bed with the feel of her hands lingering like phantom pleasure. The space between their rooms shrank with the knowledge that a simple knock on her door might pull Jensen back into Daisy's bed.

"Of course. We'll see you in two days. One of our assistants will forward you the information." Tristan waved, and the shareholders and directors headed to the Shore Building with him.

Well, almost all of them.

Kenneth dabbed at his face with a handkerchief, which he slid quickly into his pocket. His eyes met Jensen's as he beckoned him closer. "I know things are awkward right now, but thank you for working with such grace under pressure."

Jensen couldn't be sure if he meant with the CEO promotion or things with Delaney... or both. His lips pulled taut, hoping the expression leaned more toward a smile than a grimace. "It's my job to be professional, no matter the circumstances."

"It's why you'll make a fine leader for the company, young man. I've always admired that about your father, and now it shows in you. I'm proud to be in your corner. I'm sorry things didn't work out with you and Del," Kenneth sighed.

"Didn't work out" sounded a much kinder phrasing for "getting cheated on by the girl he thought he'd marry" in Jensen's mind. Yet, he knew better than to be surprised.

He never disclosed the reason behind his and Delaney's break-up to Kenneth. A year ago, Kenneth experienced serious cardiac issues where stress nearly put him in the hospital. Although Delaney deserved some serious karma, her grandfather having a heart attack because of him wasn't on Jensen's to-do list.

"Sometimes things don't work out. That's life."

"I hope the break from the office does you some good. I'm glad to see you two in relatively good spirits."

"It's the Ridge." Jensen almost twitched hearing about Delaney's happiness but held his shaking composure with a vice grip. "Spending time with my family in sunshine and fresh air helps me keep my head on straight."

Kenneth nodded, stepping back. "Speaking of which, I won't hold you any longer. It was good to see you, Jensen."

"You too, sir." Jensen's smile held long enough for him to turn around. He jogged onto the hiking trail, dropping his smile into the dirt. He stayed silent for Delaney's benefit, and her bullshit bit him in the ass again. Being the bigger person sucked harder than it was worth.

Despite the soreness in his legs after his early morning in the gym, Jensen's jog sped up to the dull thud of his sneakers. He descended the cliffs until the path spat him out at the golden sands and the tall grass growing in patches along the bike path.

He spotted his parents and sisters dressed in summery clothes at the wooden dock big enough for boats and jet skis to rest. His dad stood beside a speedboat with Piper glued to his hip, speaking with a stranger dressed in a Royal Ridge uniform polo.

Jensen cut across the sand while jogging over to the dock, but the creak of the wood under his feet announced his presence the moment he stepped onto the pier. Hayley's and his mom's attention snapped up from their side conversation. Jensen quickly found himself sandwiched between them.

"Mom... Hales... Can't breathe—" Jensen coughed until they released him, brushing off his untucked white tee and the unbuttoned half-sleeve shirt layered over it.

"We started to worry that you weren't coming because you decided to mope in your room," Hayley remarked, earning a pinch to her bicep from their mom. She yelped while rubbing her arm, eyes narrowed and pouting.

Their mom shook her head. "Ignore your sister. She's cranky because I told her no alcohol on the boat."

"I was promised mimosas!"

"I'll take you to get a drink later, Hales." Jensen fumbled into his pockets for his sunglasses. Sunlight glinted off the waves; the serene Pacific waters of that morning made for perfect boating conditions.

Hayley crossed her arms, face scrunching up as she smiled. "Have I told you that you're my favorite brother?"

"I sure hope so, seeing as I'm your only brother." Jensen and their mom shook their heads in perfect unison. He might look like the spitting image of his dad, but the mannerisms belonged to his mom. "Now, are we going to stand here all day?"

"Nope. Everyone get your asses on the boat!" his dad interrupted at the perfect moment, holding the keys up. Piper eagerly climbed on first, beelining for the helm.

Jensen and his dad helped the rest of the Ramsey ladies onto the boat, climbing after them. While his dad started the engine to the raucous cough from the motor, Jensen slid to the padded bench in the back.

Hayley handed him a basket of snacks, likely packed by their mom. Jensen pillaged around until he grabbed some extra granola bars. He fixed his sunglasses but lost the baseball cap, ready to hit the waves.

"You know, you've been looking better these days!" his mom shouted over the engine when the speedboat left the dock. She, Hayley, and Jensen smushed together while the boat navigated further into the water. "Hayley and I were talking about that before you arrived."

"Really?"

"Yeah! Mom mentioned it, and I said that you looked way better. Like you've got this post-breakup glow after the first night."

If the boat hadn't bounced too hard on the waves, Jensen choking on his saliva would be an out-of-character reaction. His mom and sister weren't the only people who mentioned his changed attitude. Several coworkers commented over meals about how his frown appeared nowhere in sight.

Of course, the reason for his improvement usually sat across the table from him, enjoying her meal so much she needed to lick her lips clean between every bite.

The other night with Daisy, with the vague promise of "if it happens again," pushed Delaney out of his mind for a while. He needed the break from overthinking every moment of the break-up.

Jensen rubbed the back of his neck as the boat glided onto calmer waters. "It's the pool. It's been helping me keep busy."

He should feel bad about lying outright, but he and Daisy agreed. No one could know about their indiscretion, not even his family.

Two days passed, bringing the first week at the Ridge to its promised end. Although Jensen tried to embrace the relaxing vibes, work found a way to shred his peace.

His hands adjusted the tuck of his crisp, white polo into the waistband of his linen pants for the tenth time since leaving his room. Jensen woke up that morning with an undeniable case of nerves. Unfortunately, his escape to the gym didn't cure him of its presence.

Jensen approached the open deck seating of Pearl & Port, the newest restaurant on the Ridge, which was ironically one of Daisy's suggestions for expansion. He admired the driftwood arches and the canopies hanging off the overhead beams, drawn to the almost rustic vibe radiating off the outdoor deck.

As much as he clashed with Daisy, she possessed an exacting eye for aesthetics and décor, evident by the pleased patrons when entering the open-air deck.

Jensen jogged up the sandstone staircase, sweeping his slightly sweaty hand to knock away any specks of lint or sand. He spotted the packed table with Kenneth and a few of the directors before anyone noticed him first. Yet, he also noticed the missing presence of the greatest thorn in his side.

Where was Daisy?

He pulled out the chair at the head of the table, managing a grin despite his confusion. "Afternoon, gentleman. I see you're enjoying our newest addition to the Ridge."

"Jensen! Order whatever you'd like. Your dad approved company funds for this luncheon." Kenneth's laugh bellowed with its heartiness while he eagerly slapped Jensen's shoulder in that familial affection. *Old habits die hard, huh?*

"My dad's generosity knows no limits," Jensen mused, earning a round of glasses raised, toasting to his dad in his absence. "So, is this a more informal lunch, or should I be prepared to campaign?"

"No need. Today is to celebrate you and how we're close to celebrating the second generation of the Ramseys being such influential men in the Los Angeles business sphere," Kenneth said.

Jensen held back his smile when his breathing eased, signaling for one of the waiters. "So, have you been enjoying your stay at the Ridge, gentleman? It's my job to ensure our clients' satisfaction."

Several directors chimed in with their comments, overlapping but overwhelmingly positive from what Jensen picked up. He accepted a glass of ice water from a waitress, still smiling.

His eyes swept across the table, searching every chair for a still-missing Daisy. It wasn't like her to skip any meeting or corporate event, no matter how dull and dry.

In her own words, many years ago, she made it her mission to show him how much more she liked the company. Ever since, Jensen attended every meeting open to him but always saw her there.

No one else matched her unswerving dedication to pissing him off.

Jensen sank lower into his chair while the directors chatted amongst themselves, off on a side conversation he knew better than to interrupt. Instead, he ran his eyes across the faces of nearby tables out of sheer curiosity but stopped at the flash of sandy blonde hair and red beside the deck.

Standing with two women he didn't recognize, Daisy lounged in the sun without a care. Her mouth moved in rapid-fire conversation, adorned with lipstick the same shade as the wide-legged jumpsuit she wore. However, her demeanor shifted when her eyes landed on him, narrowing into thin slits.

Being at the receiving end of her glare wasn't unusual for Jensen. After their tipsy hook-up, they agreed that neither should act out of character. Within the public eye, they were to trade their usual snarky remarks and detest one another's company.

Daisy seemingly possessed no issue in playing her part.

Jensen excused himself, not waiting for permission before rising from his chair. He walked across the deck, making a beeline toward Daisy as her expression changed from pure disdain to confusion.

He kept his eyes on her face, having already swept his gaze down the plunging v of her jumpsuit's neckline while seated at the table. He scowled. "You're late."

"First of all, were you raised in a barn? It's rude to interrupt someone's conversation," Daisy replied, raising an accusatory finger at him. Her companions exchanged glances, stepping back from the conversation when Daisy moved forward. "Second and more importantly, what the fuck do you mean I'm late?"

"I don't have the time to argue with you. Either you'll keep the directors waiting, or I'll take the opportunity myself."

Daisy said nothing more, but Jensen watched her face flash with several indistinguishable emotions. She appeared torn between a flush several shades lighter than her dress and the paleness of shock.

Instead of speaking, Daisy grabbed his wrist to drag him toward the stairs. She marched ahead with purpose while Jensen stumbled after her, righting himself in a few strides and yanking his hand from her grip.

The two approached the table as a chorus of "Hello, Daisy" rang out from the directors. They smiled with the same politeness they gave Jensen at his arrival—all except Kenneth, whose face slid into a quiet pensiveness while he drank.

Jensen pulled out his chair but gestured to Daisy. "Take my chair. I'll grab another one."

"That's unnecessary," she started, but Jensen had already grabbed another chair from an empty table nearby. He slotted the new chair between Daisy's and Kenneth's, leaving the rest of the table to shift and accommodate the late arrival. "Thank you."

"Sure. Now, we can get started with lunch. Most of us at the table aren't pretty enough to get away with being fashionably late," Jensen hummed. When several members of the table broke into laughter, he fought a smirk.

Jensen sat down when Daisy slid into her chair. In his peripheral vision, Jensen noticed the tight twist of her lips, which quickly vanished when she reached for her place settings still wrapped in the napkin.

"Perhaps, but some of us are late because of massive news that's too important to wait," Daisy said, tone dancing along the edge of coy. Jensen witnessed as half of the directors leaned closer to her, captivated by their curiosity. "I'll keep it brief, but I was late because I secured assurances from Gryphon Capital Group and Xie Zhihao. They have agreed to add their financial backing to the Big Bear developments."

Immediately, the table clamored with a slew of questions. The shocked but delighted faces of the directors ripped the spotlight from Jensen. Making them laugh earned him a small splash, so Daisy decided to cannonball without remorse.

Stealing his thunder was a habit of hers.

"I was in talks with Gryphon and Zhihao. They never voiced their final decisions on the matter." Jensen cleared his throat. That didn't make sense; client acquisition fell under his purview.

"Oh! They contacted me directly to ask for my opinion. It seems they trust my judgment and honesty on the venture." Daisy smiled at the table, but her words stabbed Jensen through the chest. *Investors trusted her more than him.*

Easily pleased, the directors erupted into half a dozen fractured conversations and calls for celebratory champagne. In their distraction, Jensen scooted closer to Daisy, jaw clenched.

He whispered in her ear, "I thought you secured their support before we left for the retreat. I recall you mentioning this same feat during our last debrief with my dad."

"I did," Daisy smirked, turning to face him. Their closeness should've set off sirens in Jensen's head, but Daisy's whiskey eyes hooked him in. "But since that knowledge isn't public, it makes for a good alibi when you try to ruin my reputation."

"Me? You were the one who almost didn't show up for lunch. If anything, you're ruining your reputation by not taking this CEO thing seriously."

"You have no idea how seriously I regard that promotion. Take your head out of your self-centered ass for two minutes, and you'll realize I've always taken it more seriously than you'll ever understand."

Beyond their usual sassiness, Daisy's words hit him hard. Those damn eyes glowed with such intensity that Jensen couldn't look away from them, no matter how his head screamed for him to act normal. As if he knew what normal was when it came to Daisy anymore.

People are watching. Stop staring at her.
Look away.

Daisy's gaze held Jensen's with the same look she chose on the night they drank too much whiskey and blurred their already shaky boundaries. Jensen's lips parted, but he swallowed every comeback on the tip of his tongue, choosing to avert his eyes instead.

Chapter 7
Daisy

"It's official. I need a pool back home," Daisy mused to herself, keeping her voice at a whisper while approaching the crowded deck chairs. Sweltering heat with an occasional reprieve from the ocean breeze continued into the second week of June, making for perfect poolside weather.

To Daisy, however, unspoken tension intensified the heat. After the confrontation at lunch, she and Jensen stayed out of each other's way. She spent her hours between the spa, shopping on Boutique Block, visiting Giselle while she visited her boyfriend's family, and going on stupid hikes for peace of mind. She spent most of her time anywhere but in their room.

Unfortunately for her, she enjoyed a dozen Delaney and Easton sightings while trying to mind her business. So, if she kept encountering the two idiots, she deserved an ice-cold cocktail and relaxation time by the pool.

Daisy fixed her sunglasses on the bridge of her nose until the world tinted in a sepia hue. She hoisted her pool bag higher on her shoulder, bouncing against her hip with every stride. Her thin, blue cover-up fluttered in the weak breeze.

Daisy's path wound her past the bigger pools for the kids and families to the adult-only pool. She spotted the volleyball net strung up toward the shallow end and all the alcoves for the swimmers with fresh cocktails filled with people.

Daisy sought out her favorite cluster of deck chairs, enveloped in the shade of a large umbrella. Her spot sat a perfect distance between the full-service bar and the jacuzzi attached to the pool. She got a prime view of the pool while being at the center of the action.

Tossing her bag to her right, Daisy shook her hair from a loose ponytail before reaching for the strings of her cover-up. A simple tug at the loop sitting along the nape of her neck caused the dress to melt off her body.

She picked out her favorite bikini—white with thick blue accents around the edges and silver chains around the hips and between her boobs—for that day. It covered everything for nearby children and families but didn't shield much else.

As a newly single woman, she deserved a pick-me-up to remind her how hot she was. Vacation should be fun; Daisy's idea of fun included breaking a few necks from how hard people turned to stare.

She bent down to grab her dress from the floor and set up her chair for lounging, but she paused midway when she noticed the jacuzzi.

Easton and two strangers sat in the frothing jacuzzi waters, transfixed on her bent-over figure. Their gazes raked over her exposed body with little remorse, even from her unfaithful ex. *Wonder what Delaney would think if she saw Easton gawking like a horny teenager.*

Daisy tipped her face away, pretending she hadn't seen them. Ignoring Easton felt like the right thing to do, especially if she wanted to enjoy her afternoon of poolside fun.

She stuffed her dress away and spruced up her deck chair with her items before someone whistled from behind her. "Look who it is."

Daisy glanced over her shoulder, finding Jensen wading through the shallow waters of the pool. Behind him, three colleagues—Nelson, Miranda from Marketing, and Holden from Acquisitions—waved from different spots around the volleyball net. "Can I help you with something?"

"We have an uneven number of players for volleyball teams. Any chance you'd want to play?" Miranda held the pink volleyball over her head, all toothy grins and perfectly tan skin under the California sun. Her dark hair glimmered like spilled ink.

"Which one of you is without a teammate?" Daisy raked her eyes over the group curiously. She counted four of them unless Easton planned to waltz his way over and dive in.

"Iris!" Nelson pointed. Halfway across the pool, Iris from Human Resources and Employee Relations flashed a comfortable peace sign from her position in a turtle-shaped pool raft. Her ginger curls barely fit into her messy topknot, and her freckled skin shone from the sunscreen she slathered herself in.

Daisy considered it but shook her head. "Sorry, Iris. I'm going to sit this one out."

"All good. I'm kind of stuck anyway." Iris rattled her half-filled Mai Tai glass. She lounged back, drifting further into the deep end.

Daisy turned back, seeing Holden and Jensen setting up on one side of the net and Miranda and Nelson treading toward the other. She stretched out, careful not to let her bikini rise too much.

Miranda held the ball up. "Well, if you're going to spectate on the sidelines, would you mind keeping score for us? We're playing until one side scores five before we shuffle up the teams."

"I don't—" Daisy paused when greeted with the pleading of Miranda and Nelson and the quirked brow from Jensen. She liked Miranda and Nelson a lot, so she could spare some time to help. She exhaled, "I can do it. I can still enjoy my music and relaxation from the referee chair."

"You're the best!" Miranda exclaimed, tossing the ball neatly into Daisy's arms. She cradled the volleyball to her chest and nodded.

Her body fought against a laugh when she overheard Holden's mumbling, "Great. Whichever of us is on Jensen's team will be an automatic loser."

"Not unless you don't carry your weight." Jensen scowled and sank toward the water. Holden's cheeks burned. His longer, dirty blond hair hung around his face, hiding more of his embarrassment from Daisy. "I'm always a winner."

Daisy snorted. "Debatable. As a gesture of goodwill and my commitment to playing fair, you two will serve first."

Her eyes met Jensen's as she handed off the ball to Holden, the closer of the two to her side of the pool. Daisy moved the umbrella over before flopping onto her chair, stretched out with her arms draped over the top.

She watched Miranda, Nelson, Jensen, and Holden huddle in their respective teams, giving them time to talk strategy or whatever. While waiting, she reached into her bag for sunscreen, tanning lotion, and her earbuds.

Daisy arranged them into a neat pile on the glass table between her deck chair and the occupied one beside her, clad with one of the standard issue towels of the resort.

As she reached for her sunscreen, she heard Jensen clear his throat. "Could I borrow some of that? I forgot mine back at the suite."

"Sure," Daisy huffed and grabbed the sunscreen. She spotted Jensen standing at the pool's edge, resting his elbows against the damp walkway. He must've splashed some water over the ground, or else he would've been burning. "Come get some."

The words barely left her mouth before Jensen pushed himself out of the pool. His bare torso glittered with water rivulets streaming over his toned figure. From his shoulders to the peak of his defined v-line, his muscles rippled harder than the waves as he rose onto dry land.

Daisy slumped back in her deck chair as Jensen hovered in front of her, shielding his eyes from the sun with a hand. Daisy's eyes ran over his body, almost getting stuck on his low-riding, navy blue swim trunks.

Shit, it should be illegal for him to look *that* good wet. Yes, she experienced it before, but that hardly mattered when his skin glistened so brightly.

Jensen being ridiculously attractive, a good lay and a know-it-all pain in the ass would always bother her. No matter what way she spun it, he existed as pure torture.

"Thanks," Jensen remarked, still dripping onto the stony tiles. His eyes darted between her face and her hand, but when his gaze wandered below her chin, Daisy sat forward. Instantly, his eyes snapped upward, and the bob of his throat elicited a snort from her.

"You might want to dry off first. The sunscreen won't stay if you're still wet."

"You're right."

"I usually am."

"No one can twist a compliment quite like you," Jensen sighed loudly. Daisy watched their colleagues in the water return to conversations amongst themselves. With a simple jab, they fell back into their normal routine. Emphasis on normal.

"Mind if I sit on your chair?"

Daisy shook her head. "Knock yourself out."

She scooted to the side as Jensen dried himself off, using the towel on the chair beside her. After a moment, he plopped on the deck chair beside her, palm held out.

Daisy doused her hand in sunscreen, all gloopy and cold compared to the heat outside. She ran her palm over his, splitting the massive blob of sunscreen right down the middle.

Wordlessly, the two began to coat their bodies in the cream, rubbing it into their skin until the stark white faded. Although she refrained from conversation, Daisy observed Jensen in her peripheral vision. Her eyes followed his movements—running his hands across his chest and torso, head rolled back, and eyes closed.

Daisy sped up, squirting a hefty amount onto her sticky fingers to get her back. She tested a few angles, and none felt suitable to apply the lotion. Forget about the tanning oil.

"Need some help getting your back, Your Highness?" Jensen asked, leaning into her view with his elbows perched on his knees. Daisy suspected a trick of the light when his eyes glowed with softness while looking at her.

Daisy clicked her tongue, speaking dryly, "Are you offering?"

Jensen nodded. Not having another option, Daisy smeared the extra sunscreen onto his palm before turning her back to him. She shifted onto her knees, tucking them underneath her ass, while Jensen scooted closer to her on the chair.

"Bold move, Jensen," Daisy whispered, facing forward to the rows of deck chairs behind them. Jensen's hands pressed into the curve of her spine. The act of him touching her skin awakened every nerve in her body with a violent shiver. "This isn't very 'I hate your guts' of us. The others might notice."

She bit down on her lower lip when Jensen's hands trailed downward. He started by her shoulders, coating them in sunscreen with a firm hand, but his path wound down her spine. Every inch his hands dropped, Daisy's thighs clenched together to stop the treason of her body.

"Maybe they will." Jensen's breath skimmed along the nape of her neck. Daisy swore her throat tightened and rasped for air when Jensen murmured, "But someone else's watching us."

Daisy didn't need to ask who Jensen meant. She glanced toward the jacuzzi in her peripheral vision, where Easton, now joined by Delaney, studied them. *Oh, right. Jensen wouldn't be nice to her without a reason.*

From his seat, Easton sat up taller. His arm around Delaney's shoulders dropped into the water, abandoning his lover. Lucky for him, Delaney seemed newly preoccupied with conversation and the fruity umbrella cocktail in her hand. Easton's jaw twitched a few times while his eyes narrowed, always timed when Jensen's hands dipped close to Daisy's hips or the imaginary bikini line.

Little did he know, she and Jensen observed his reaction in return.

Daisy leaned forward as Jensen's hands ran along her sides, wiping off the last bit of sunscreen. He said, "I covered everything. You're good to go."

"Your turn." Daisy grabbed her sunscreen for the last time and coated her hand in the lotion. Jensen, knowing better than to argue, flipped to face the pool. "Sunscreen is no big deal. But I know he's mentally fuming."

"Oh, without a doubt. I'm the guy he felt second place to in your relationship, remember?" Jensen stayed perfectly still while Daisy ran her hands over his sculpted body. She covered his back in sunscreen and quickly turned his face toward her. He had a point.

Daisy painted her fingers over his nose and cheeks, rubbing the lotion in despite Jensen's face scrunching up. As soon as she applied the last bit, she cleaned her hand on his towel. "Try not to lose or get burned, dimwit."

"If you talk to me any nicer, I might start thinking you care about me," Jensen smirked, rising from the deck chair. He stretched in the sun, forcing Daisy to focus her eyes on a distant point past Jensen. They were supposed to act like they hadn't explored each other's bodies before.

Daisy rolled her eyes, waving Jensen away from her sanctuary. By the time she grabbed something to clean off her sticky palms, Jensen vanished into the crystal blue waters of the pool.

His head emerged from the deep end. He shook out his damp hair, pushing toward the volleyball net where Miranda, Holden, and Nelson waited. Daisy leaned back into her deck chair as Jensen served the volleyball, starting the first game of many.

As the official scorekeeper, Daisy held her hands like her scoreboard while she drowned out the shouting, laughter, and general noise with her favorite playlist. Spice Girls and Britney Spears's earliest albums became the soundtrack for the summer afternoon, vibrant and adding some much-needed entertainment between the competitive volleyball game unfolding before her.

Like Jensen promised Holden, he wasn't about to lose simply because Daisy sat as referee. Poor Miranda and Holden barely survived volleys from Jensen, who cranked the athleticism to a superhuman degree.

Daisy rolled her eyes each time Jensen scored a point, more so when he turned to her and gestured for his victory to be added to the tally. Three back-to-back scores by Jensen against one from Miranda had him playfully flexing for the captive audience of other swimmers.

When Jensen's back faced her, Daisy lowered her sunglasses and observed his peacocking every so often. With the slight sheen from the sunscreen, his skin gleamed under the sunshine.

Yet, when Jensen spotted her eyes on him and her sunglasses perched lower, he didn't call out her stare. Somehow, the smirk and subtle wink he shot in her direction shamed Daisy more when she glanced away.

As fast as the game started, Jensen dominated and scored five points to switch teams. Daisy scanned their moving lips to decipher their conversations, too buried in the comfort of her playlist to listen.

"Switch teams," Daisy remarked while flagging down one of the rotating bar staff. "I'm getting a drink in case anyone else wants one."

She slid out an earbud as the smiling face of a waitress entered her vision, hearing a small chorus of "No thanks!" or "I've got water" from Miranda, Holden, Nelson, and Jensen amongst all the splashing.

"Can I have your specials for today?"

"Of course, ma'am. Today, we have a blueberry and ginger spritzer, which is alcohol-free. Please let me know if you're interested in our classic cocktails or our regular drink menu."

"The spritzer would be excellent, actually. Thank you," Daisy said. She gave the waitress her room key, lounging back into her deck chair. She fixed her glasses over her eyes, prepared to slip back into her comfortable state.

But two shadows stretching across her sunlight startled her eyes open, finding the smiling faces of Sandra Foley and Kagami Hirayama. Not one, but two members of the C-suite standing before her forced her to sit up straight.

Sandra and Kagami had been with Hidden Oasis long before Daisy joined the company, but both women's careers paved the way for Daisy's meteoric rise. Sandra started as the Chief Operations Officer during the early years of Hidden Oasis. Kagami replaced the former general counsel close to fifteen years back.

"Mind if we sit with you?" Kagami gestured to Jensen's chair. Daisy couldn't yank her earbuds out fast enough; she might have some sway, but when the top women of the C-Suite asked her for anything, Daisy would bend over backward to accommodate.

"Of course! Please sit." Daisy kept her voice from cracking as Sandra and Kagami perched on Jensen's unoccupied chair. The two exchanged a quiet glance before Sandra cleared her throat.

"We won't bother you for too long." Sandra adjusted the brim of her floppy sun hat over her newly trimmed, brunette pixie cut, still sporting the ghost of a smile. "Kagami and I have been talking, but we want you to know we're fully behind you for this CEO thing."

"Me? I have your endorsement for CEO?" Daisy choked on her tongue but smoothed it over with a cough.

"Absolutely. Sandra and I know our reach is limited on the formal outcome since we don't vote. Still, we hope our endorsement and a verbal campaign on your behalf is a good showing of our support," Kagami assured, brushing sleek strands of dark hair from her face to the jangling of the bangles stacked down her slender wrist.

"And we've got a good feeling about you winning it all." Sandra leaned in more. "We don't dislike Jensen. He's a bright young man with great potential, but we see even greater potential in you."

"There's been a noticeable shift in morale among our female and non-binary employees at the news of your potential appointment as CEO. Someone as young as you and as outspoken about promoting equity across Hidden Oasis has an impact on people's confidence.

"So, we want to keep the momentum going. Whatever you need from Kagami and me—a more involved endorsement, our knowledge of how to win over certain holdouts, moral support as two women who have fought the same uphill battle—it's yours."

Daisy stared at Sandra and Kagami, at a loss for what to say. For the first time, she realized that she wasn't alone in the fight. Her throat tightened while searching for the words to thank them, to lay herself in their hands and let them help her. She never liked asking, not even when life tried to pull her under.

"I will take everything and anything you give me," Daisy whispered, arms wrapped around her stomach like a cover. "I will win this. I'll win this for the company and for us. How much harder have we worked to reach the positions we're in, and how much easier can we make it for those who come behind us?"

"That's what we like to he—" Kagami's voice cut out when a pink blur shot past them, bouncing to a stop against the leg of the table. Daisy leaned over, scooping up the damp volleyball.

Her gaze trailed over to the pool, finding the eyes of Nelson, Holden, Miranda, and Jensen on her. Although the first three looked, Jensen's eyes crackled. The traces of his smirking and showboating vanished behind an unbridled glint of distrust, long gone. His focus jumped between her, Sandra, and Kagami, visibly struggling to fit the puzzle pieces together.

So, Daisy whistled, "Miranda, heads up!" She tossed the volleyball back to Miranda, quick to avert her eyes from Jensen's. She overheard the splash of the ball into the water, but that became the last of her concerns.

Sandra and Kagami nodded. They vacated their spots on Jensen's chair, likely sensing the shift in the air. Daisy waved goodbye as her drink arrived, stricken by the swiftness of their departure.

With her spritzer, Daisy sprawled back out on her chair, soaking in the summer breeze and the sparkling fizz of her drink. Her eyes avoided Jensen's gaze until she fixed her sunglasses to block him from seeing her.

It wasn't personal. Jensen had his last name doing the heavy lifting in his campaign. Therefore, she needed power behind her nomination. She finally found a place to start investing her efforts.

Chapter 8
Jensen

As the retreat slipped into the third week of June, Jensen knew two things: he wanted more time in paradise, and Daisy had been avoiding him ever since the volleyball game.

The sunscreen move might've been too much for such a public setting. Maybe his vindictive streak went too far in wanting to show Easton and Delaney what they lost.

Maybe it was all speculation, and Daisy avoided him because of whatever she, Kagami, and Sandra whispered about with him a few feet away. His role at the company never kept him out of the room where things happened. He didn't like to be left out.

Without a moment alone to corner Daisy for some much-needed clarity, Jensen waited in the dark, stuck with guessing to fill the uncertainty.

Despite his murky thoughts, Jensen mustered a polite smile for the gaggle of older ladies holding the door to the Bluff Building and grabbed the door from them. "Thank you, ladies. Have a lovely evening."

"You too, young man." One of them, old enough to be his grandmother, flashed him a toothy smile and fluttered her dark lashes. Her companions giggled like schoolgirls as they shuffled down the ramp, but their whispers were a little loud. "If I were twenty years younger, I'd make him my fourth husband."

Jensen swallowed a laugh at the affronted gasps and a lone, "Frances behave," from her gaggle of friends. *Never change, Frances.*

He strolled down the empty hallway toward the suite, comforted by the quiet after spending all day in Hayley and Piper's clutches. Yes, he loved his sisters with all his heart, but not when Hayley suggested that he ask out every cute girl they spotted while in town.

Piper diverted the conversation by letting Hayley pick a few outfits for her. Piper *hated* trying on clothes. So, Jensen bought the charm bracelet she'd been eyeing at one of the stores afterward, his way of thanking her for throwing herself onto the grenade. He appreciated Hayley's intentions, but jumping into the dating pool would be premature.

Hooking up with a certain blonde, on the other hand, felt different.

As he entered the suite, he paused in the doorway when confronted by the kitchen light. His gaze wandered over to the kitchenette's counter, and there, dressed in a pair of denim shorts and a tank top, Daisy stood.

Daisy's back faced him, utterly unaware of his presence. While Jensen's eyes first landed on her ass, awestruck with how the shorts molded to her figure like someone painted the fabric straight onto her skin, his attention moved upward. The tangled cord of her earbuds swayed whenever she shifted her stance, mimicking her high ponytail doing the same. Her hands frantically scribbled something onto a legal notepad, occupied so entirely by it.

Jensen shut the door behind him. Even with the loud click of the lock, Daisy's focus never wavered.

Jensen took another step forward, testing the waters. Despite each step bringing him closer to her personal space, Daisy hadn't noticed his arrival. How could she when her music played loud enough to slip from her earbuds?

Jensen strained to look at the legal pad from over her shoulder but found himself at the mercy of Daisy's shorthand. The gentle slopes of her printed letters jumped out at him. Yet, the meaning of the sentences strung together meant nothing, with symbols tossed between every few words.

So, he hooked a finger around the earbuds, pulling one out. "We need to talk."

"Fuck!" Daisy yelped. Jensen watched her clear the ground, nearly jumping out of her skin. Her hands flipped the notepad face down and slapped on top of it, shielding what she wrote from view. She yanked out the other earbud, breathing hard. "Don't sneak up on me like that! You're lucky I didn't hit you."

"Oh, please. You screamed like a little girl," Jensen snorted, craning his neck to look past her. His hand skimmed along her hip, reaching for the tiled counter where the legal pad remained face down. "What's got you so distracted?"

"None of your business."

"Mmm, feisty today. Is this 'none of my business' why you've been avoiding me? Or why you, Sandra, and Kagami were gossiping by the pool the other day?"

Jensen's hand splayed across the legal pad, watching Daisy's eyes catch fire under the kitchen lights. She gritted her teeth. "We weren't gossiping."

"Conspiring, then? Regardless, that's why you've been dodging me. Or maybe seeing me win so much at volleyball reminded you too much of what awaits you when we get back to work. I didn't mean to scare you." Jensen scrunched his fingers while Daisy tightened her grip on the notepad.

"Scare me?" Daisy scoffed. The harsh sound echoed off their suite's walls, but the venom got Jensen's heart racing. After that afternoon, he craved something bittersweet, and Daisy knew how to give him what he wanted. "You don't scare me."

"Is that so?" Jensen clicked his tongue, falling into a smirk. "Then, what's this?"

Without giving her a second to breathe, Jensen jerked his hand back. Daisy's grip on the legal pad slackened. With enough pull, Jensen snatched the notepad into his hands. He angled away from her and tried to read.

Daisy gasped right before she lunged for the notepad in his hands. "Give it back, you asshole! You wouldn't be able to read it anyway."

"Tell me what it is, then." Jensen hardly moved out of Daisy's way while she tried to grab the paper, holding her back with a forearm settled against her chest. He turned his head away to read, confronted by more shorthand. "It's that simple."

"In your dreams. Give it."

"Aww, you're cute when you're pissed off."

"Jensen," Daisy snarled.

"Daisy," Jensen echoed. "See, I can play the name game too."

By then, Jensen angled his arm backward to hold the legal pad above their heads. Jensen stood barely two inches taller than her, but he intended to use those two inches to his advantage.

He attempted to read her notes a few more times, constantly interrupted by the flash of her hands over the paper. Jensen's head turned toward Daisy's with a grin, finding himself on the receiving end of her razor-sharp glare. *If looks could kill...*

However, something dark and almost sinister flashed across Daisy's eyes, turning them into that tempting shade of whiskey. Jensen kept the legal pad over his head, but the rest of him froze under her gaze.

It made it all too easy for Daisy to cross into his personal space and crash her lips to his, bringing all his thoughts to a grinding halt. Her hands slithered up his chest, agonizingly slow compared to the heated rush from last time.

When Daisy broke the kiss, Jensen's throat bobbed hard, finding himself at a loss for everything. Her hand snatched the legal pad from him. Her once-angry face brightened as victory crowned her triumphant.

She slapped the legal pad onto the counter, face down again. She laid her hand on top of it, breathing hard as she laughed. "I haven't used that trick since I was fourteen. Aren't you special?"

Daisy's eyes flicked over him with a newfound curiosity swirling in those rich, whiskey-colored irises. Her tongue darted over her lower lip to swipe over the newly smudged lipstick, a dark berry shade instead of her trademark red.

That cracked Jensen's resolve.

One of Jensen's hands curled around Daisy's throat, pulling her back into him until their mouths met. Her kiss danced along a playful edge and caught him off-guard, intended to confuse. His kiss strove to bring the room down around them, filled with every curious thought haunting him since they last touched. He sought clarity in her.

His tongue swiped along her lower lip, begging for entrance. Daisy's mouth parted wider for him, but the pathetic, pleading moan following it electrified Jensen's ego. His fingers didn't let her go too far when his mouth broke the embrace.

"God, you're insufferable," he murmured into her mouth, beginning and ending the exasperated statement with a searing, hungry kiss. Oh, how badly she made him crave her.

"You say that," Daisy half-laughed, half-panted against Jensen's lips, but her voice trembled when Jensen's free hand dipped into the waistband of her shorts. "But I knew you'd come back for more."

"Oh yeah?"

"Everyone does. I'm irresistible."

"You could've asked me if you wanted me so bad."

"Please. I don't beg men for their attention. That's beneath me."

Jensen would've rolled his eyes if Daisy's mouth hadn't tucked into the crook of his neck, leaving a feisty little bite against his pulse point. He was in for a world of trouble if she kept at it, but his hands forgot everything except how to hold Daisy.

They finally reached their breaking point.

Jensen's hands kept Daisy unbearably close, restraining himself from kissing every snarky comment off her tongue while his fingers slid the button to her shorts open. A quiet moan of his name slid out from her.

"How about we forget about the paper for the rest of the night? We can fight about it in the morning," Jensen murmured. When he glanced down, he found Daisy's darkened gaze peering up at him.

"You drive a hard bargain," Daisy replied, but the tremble of her voice told Jensen where she stood. Without sparing a glance, Daisy shoved the legal pad across the kitchenette's counter before Jensen settled her in its place. "I'll give you hell in the morning."

"Deal." Jensen's mouth collided with hers; his hands found ways to stay busy while Daisy kissed him back. The hem of her tank top rode up, exposing a flash of Daisy's toned midriff and giving Jensen all the flashbacks to the bikini that haunted his waking moments.

Jensen broke away from the kiss first. Although Daisy's lips chased after his for a split second, she relaxed as his mouth peppered sloppy kisses along her neck and the tiny sliver of her collarbone.

Jensen had been tangled in Daisy's embrace once before and in her presence numerous times, swearing he knew every piece of her. However, that evening, her body smelled of her favorite perfume, stronger than he could ever remember. He caught small whiffs of the scent before, but nothing like how it radiated off her.

Basking in the dark and seductive aroma, Daisy smelled of black cherries on a heady spice and floral base, too good not to taste. The image of Daisy laid across his sheets, naked and legs spread wide for him, flashed across his head, threatening to get him drunk faster than knocking back several shots.

Jensen's hands roamed down her back with a mission, but as he dipped right below her waist, where the hemline of her tank top rode up, insistent knocking against the front door interrupted the heated moment.

He glanced toward the door but stayed silent, not calling out to whoever stood on the other side. Daisy's hands sliding along his shoulders almost pulled his attention back to her, and he chalked the knocking up to a mistaken room or something.

"Were you expecting someone?" Jensen asked.

"No. Were you?" Daisy cleared her throat. She tried to slide off the counter, but Jensen's hands held her firm, waiting for the knocking to either stop or the knocker to identify themselves.

"Jensen? Are you in there?" Delaney's voice shouted from the other side of the door, followed by several loud slams of her fist. In not his proudest moment, Jensen froze like a teenager caught red-handed while the knocking continued. "Look, I know you're mad at me. But I need to talk with you!"

A gentle hand tipped his face away from the door, dragging his focus away from Delaney outside. Jensen peered up at Daisy, whose face flickered between warring emotions. Her eyes darkened from anger's looming shadow, but her mouth pulled into a taut, teasing smirk.

"Ignore her," Daisy commanded.

Jensen nodded; he shuffled closer to the counter, fully prepared to dive back into Daisy. Yet, the third round of knocking from Delaney interrupted him each time he leaned closer.

His jaw clenched. "Go to my room. I'll be there as soon as I handle Delaney."

Daisy sighed, sounding as exasperated as he felt, but she slid from the counter. She snatched her phone and raced across the suite in a blur of sandy blonde hair. Jensen waited for the sliding door to his bedroom to close with Daisy hidden inside before heading toward the door.

Jensen yanked the front door open, leaning in the frame to Delaney's startled expression. His scowl must've been evident from how she shrunk away from him, smart enough to look sheepish.

"What do you want, Del?"

"No 'hello, how've you been'?"

"Where's your boyfriend? Heard you and Easton have been joined at the hip since the start of the month."

Delaney's brows knit at his hardened tone, shuffling in her spot. "Jensen, come on. This is already really hard for me."

"Then say what you came to say and leave me alone," Jensen snapped. Delaney winced at his harshness, but Jensen refused to feel guilty. *Why should he?*

"I'm here to say sorry for cheating and for how you found out. I didn't give you a good explanation, and I—" Delaney said, but Jensen couldn't bring himself to let her finish.

"Oh, now you want to explain yourself and apologize?" Jensen scoffed, pushing himself off the door frame. "Wasn't the time for that over a month ago? You know, when I caught you screwing some other guy. If I remember correctly, you used your chance to say that you loved him, and the cheating was essentially my fault."

As his voice carried down the hallway, loud enough for the neighbors to hear, Delaney's 'apologetic' expression faded under a red flush. She shushed him. "Hear me out, please. I'm begging here."

"Fine. Talk," Jensen barked, but his phone buzzing inside his pocket diverted his attention. At first, one chime seemed like a message he could attend to once he cooled off.

But then, two more followed in rapid succession.

"I'm so sorry that I hurt you. I'm so sorry that I cheated on you, especially with someone at the company. That reflects badly on you as much as me, and that was messed up," Delaney said. Somehow, every word sounded like a poorly written Notes app apology or the kind of reluctant statement a guilty elementary schooler would write as a punishment.

Instead of a response, Jensen grunted for her to continue. He pulled out his phone and opened his messages, finding several from Daisy. He clicked their chat, not sure what to expect.

> DAISY: Let's play a game.

> DAISY: *1 attachment*

> DAISY: Each minute you entertain her pathetic sob story, I lose a piece of clothing. Maybe the fun will be over by the time she finishes.

The picture of Daisy showed her reflection in his bedroom mirror, but she held her newly discarded tank top above her head. A thin, strappy bra with barely enough fabric to hide her hardened nipples, and her shorts remained on.

Jensen's throat swelled from the lump of desire pressing down on him. He heard Delaney sniffle behind his phone, so he glanced up enough to see her eyes watering, lips trembling and all.

He held back a grimace while Delaney wrapped her arms around herself, performing for an imaginary audience. Meanwhile, Jensen swore his hands clenched into fists so hard when his phone buzzed again. *A minute already?*

> DAISY: *1 attachment*

As Daisy promised, her second picture showed those damn shorts puddled on the floor with the tank top, leaving her progressively more naked. She posed for the camera in her bra and panties, bending over his bed with her back arched.

> **JENSEN: You're killing me.**

Despite his phone in his hand and his attention clearly elsewhere, Delaney continued to blubber in circles. Jensen swore he heard "I'm sorry" at least three times in a single breath, but maybe it was more after tuning out the rest.

The old him would feel bad, but at that moment, fighting the insatiable urge to pounce on Daisy in the other room, shoved any guilt far away from him.

Jensen dropped the phone enough while Delaney dabbed at her eyes, still light on the waterworks despite the cry in her voice. He tried to inch back, but when Delaney moved closer, he stopped.

"I know you deserved to be broken up with first, but I felt so trapped. The way Daisy managed to invade every aspect of our lives pushed me too far. Still, I messed up." Delaney paused, looking at him expectantly. Jensen stammered, but any reply died when his phone buzzed again.

He abandoned any illusion of decorum to check the chat, finding himself at the mercy of another Daisy image. That time, however, he saw her loosened bra falling just short of flashing him.

> **DAISY: *1 attachment***

> **DAISY: If you're busy, I can look for someone else to pay undivided attention to me.**

God, her mouth would be the death of his patience.

"I don't want your apology anymore, Del. You should move on and leave me alone. I already have," Jensen said, grabbing the door in his hands. Before Delaney could protest or stop him, he shut the door and switched over the lock.

Like fire nipped at his heels, Jensen sprinted for his bedroom. Along the way, he yanked his shirt over his head and discarded it somewhere as he threw the doors open, finding Daisy waiting for him.

Her bra, tank top, and short shorts sat in a pile by the mirror while she lounged in front of it. Her fingers toyed with the elastic band of her dark blue panties, even as she caught Jensen's eyes in the glass's reflection.

"What took you so long?" she teased, striking a seductive pop of her hip while peeling the panties away from her body. Daisy's fingers didn't discard them, waiting for him. Jensen dragged the door closed, chest heaving.

"Bed. Now," Jensen demanded, but Daisy stayed in her spot. Still smirking like the devil of his dreams, her posture and the gleam in her eyes screamed for him to give her one good reason to obey.

"Aw, that's cute," Daisy laughed, which didn't help the throb in his pants. If he popped an erection every time she mouthed off to him, he would be in some serious trouble when they returned to work. "Make me."

Jensen strode toward her, grabbing her face between his hands. He backed her into the mirror until her bare skin pressed against the cold glass, eliciting a gasp out of her right before he cut her off with his mouth.

His kiss devoured any resistance from Daisy. His touch made her body malleable, but Jensen refused to ease up.

She wanted to be mouthy with him? He'd turn that snarky commentary into begging for him to pound her into the mattress.

Daisy kissed him back. Yet, unlike their first time, she didn't wrestle for control; Jensen had her wrapped around his finger.

His hands slid down her neck, caressing her breasts, and traveled to her hips.

He lifted her off the ground, and Daisy's legs wrapped around his waist; she caught the memo he whispered when his tongue brushed against her lower lip. The two ambled toward his bed, where Jensen laid her flat out.

Daisy propped up on her elbows, wiping her mouth and panting hard. She ran her eyes over his bare chest when Jensen approached, hands running up her thighs.

He hummed, hooking his fingers into her panties. "Hips up," Jensen rasped. Daisy's hips arched off the bed, helping ease her panties off her body. Jensen tossed the panties to the side. "So, you *can* follow instructions."

Daisy pulled a scowl, but it dropped when Jensen nudged her higher on the bed, pressing his stomach onto the edge of the bed. He hooked his arms around her thighs and spread her legs to rest comfortably on his broad shoulders.

His mouth settled at her navel and trailed downward, moving wantonly in a loose pattern. Jensen's eyes held hers, refusing to break eye contact even as his nose brushed against the soft cropping of hair a shade darker than Daisy's blonde tresses.

Jensen's arms tightened around her thighs and bent Daisy's legs wider, seeing her pretty pussy. His tongue flicked over Daisy's clit, causing the sharp arch of her back off the bed.

A single taste was all it took for Jensen to be hit by the sweetness of Daisy against his tongue. Part of him wanted to bury his face into her legs until he suffocated; Daisy would probably like that outcome since she'd have an orgasm and the CEO position uncontested.

He swirled around her clit slower than the first time, applying pressure with the flat of his tongue. Jensen couldn't tear his eyes away from Daisy's as she watched him lap at her pussy, teasing instead of diving into her.

"Jensen," Daisy's voice weakly stammered. Her eyes fought valiantly to stay open while his tongue continued teasing the sensitive nub. Her hand threaded into his hair and gripped hard, tugging a little. "I'm not into edging."

"Well, then hold on tight, Your Highness," Jensen chuckled. Then, he wrapped his lips around her pussy. Suckling hard, his mouth went to work. The loud, sloppy noises from eating Daisy out filled his ears, but her moaning eclipsed them and the thundering of his heart.

Jensen's tongue slid from her clit to her entrance, dripping with her sweet arousal. From agonizingly slow, his pace intensified whenever Daisy's hands gripped tighter into his hair and pushed his face deeper into her pussy.

Fuck yes.

Jensen's gaze trailed upward to watch Daisy's pink cheeks darken while he lapped at her slick-covered folds. He moved his mouth back a little, greeted by a protesting huff. But he waited for Daisy's eyes to open before he dropped a stream of spit against her clit.

"Jensen." Daisy's thighs trembled when Jensen's spit dripped to mix with her slick, sliding into her entrance.

Jensen leaned in and, with his tongue, he cleaned his spit out of her. He swallowed the taste of them together with a quiet groan before wrapping his mouth around her pussy again. He ate in renewed vigor, losing himself in Daisy's moans and the quivering of her body.

Time could've passed quickly or slowly, yet the gradual tension of Daisy's body and the shrill edge to her moaning announced the arrival of her orgasm. Jensen cracked one eye open, taking Daisy in.

Her back arched off the bed, and her hands held his face close, but her lips moved in incoherent pleading. She begged for the release, praying at the altar of his mercy. She was on her best behavior when she wanted him to make her come.

Jensen kept his eyes open while he sucked and licked until her climax hit. Daisy's body trembled, racked with her orgasm, but Jensen continued to tend to her. His tongue swirled over her clit, and each lap cleaned Daisy up from her messy arousal.

Finishing once Daisy's body stilled, Jensen lifted his head from between her legs. He leaned forward, sitting Daisy up. "Lady's choice. Want me from behind or face-to-face?"

"What a gentleman." Daisy rolled onto her stomach, grabbing one of his pillows to tuck underneath her chin. "From behind."

"I didn't want you getting all impatient with me again," Jensen whistled, discarding his pants and boxers at the foot of the bed. The mattress dipped under his weight as he climbed onto the bed.

He leaned over to the bedside table, grabbing a foil from inside. He tore open the packaging with his teeth, rolling the rubber over his throbbing cock to the smear of pre-cum.

As he rubbed himself along her entrance, Daisy's head popped up. "Impatient? More like I was rescuing you from Delaney before she started with the waterworks. I heard her entire apology. It sucked."

"Funny." Jensen entered her to her muffled moan, buried into the pillow she grabbed. He grasped at her hips until he bottomed out, filling her tight pussy with his cock. "I tuned her out after a while because of your little photo stunt. So, should this be a punishment or a reward?"

"Do your worst," Daisy said.

Jensen's hands gently turned her face, tilting her to look at their naked bodies in the mirror instead of letting Daisy hide her face in the pillow. He chuckled and rolled his hips, thrusting hard and rough.

"Then, you should enjoy the mess I'm about to make of you... again."

Chapter 9

Daisy

IF SOMEONE PUT A gun to her head and told her to play golf if she wanted to live another day, Daisy would seriously consider the merits of dying. Yet she stood tall, carrying a nine iron in her gloved hands, on the Ridge's famed eighteen-hole golf course.

When she woke up that morning, Daisy intended to spend her day poolside. She enjoyed breakfast with the others—Nelson, Iris, Miranda, and Jensen—fully ready to hit the deck chairs until Harrison approached with shareholders trailing behind him.

The gaggle included Kenneth Malone, who vocally opposed her campaign for CEO. According to Sandra and Kagami, her name stayed in his mouth at every turn with nothing nice to say behind it. For lack of a better word, they told her he was "hellbent" on seeing her lose.

Daisy refused to lose.

She listened as Kenneth spoke, inviting Jensen to play a few holes of golf with some friends. The offer sounded innocent enough to the untrained ear, but every moment counted to win over the hearts and minds of stubborn shareholders.

So, when Harrison offered her a chance to join them and an out to reject in the same breath, Daisy shocked everyone by agreeing to accompany them. Her dislike of golf wasn't exactly a secret—given how much she complained during last year's charity golf tournament—but true winners never quit.

Kenneth wanted to make her look stupid? Then he better try harder.

"Daisy's up!" Harrison whistled from the final stretch of green, pointing toward the hole with its red flag fluttering in the breeze. After hours under the sun and wearing a tennis skirt a half-size too small on her, Daisy considered throwing her clubs into the nearest body of water.

But, with the grace of a princess, she plastered on a smile while trotting down the hill toward where her bright blue ball sat. She passed Harrison on his way up, sharing a look with the person she trusted most.

"You'll make it in next time, sir!"

"Ah, I'm out of my prime. Take home a win for me."

Daisy chewed on her lip, fighting a chuckle while she jogged to her ball. Despite her vehement hatred of golf, her skills with a club exceeded expectations—seeing as she sat atop the scoreboard.

She didn't play golf before working at the company, but she paid for some lessons and a couple dozen hours at the driving range in preparation for any more charity tournaments.

Daisy angled herself several times, examining the distance between her and the hole. She lined up her club, glanced behind her at the spectators peering from the top of the hill, and swung.

The soft *thwack* of iron meeting the golf ball echoed as her ball rolled across the green. Lucky for her, the swing generated enough force to knock the ball into the hole, eliciting applause or mumbling from the crowd.

"That's a bogey for hole sixteen!" Daisy shouted while collecting her ball from the hole.

As she bounded up the hill, Jensen descended it with his club. His turn landed directly after hers for several holes; the jabs had been flying for the last four hours while in between rounds. Jensen fixed the brim of his hat while passing, causing Daisy to roll her eyes. *Fucking jerk made tan shorts and a visor hat look attractive.*

She climbed onto the back of the golf cart Harrison rented for him, Daisy, and Jensen, swapping her golf club for her ice-cold water. She doused her throat while listening to the crowd murmur about Jensen, followed closely by his swing.

Upon their whistles and cheers, Daisy scowled. As good as she was, Jensen had years of practice and more appreciation for the game—making him her biggest competition once again.

"That's par for me!" Jensen shouted before he appeared over the hill, smiling wide. Someone wrote the score down and cleared their throat, lost in the crowd.

"That moves Jensen up in the scoreboard to second place. Daisy's still in first with a one-point lead. Others can still catch up if they wish on a star and hope for a miracle."

Daisy faced away in the cart and slumped back, hearing scattered laughter among some grumbles. The gap between Jensen and third place ballooned, leaving Daisy and Jensen vying for first place. As *usual*.

After a moment, Jensen slid into the back of the golf cart with her while Harrison took the wheel. The putter of the engine groaned to life as the three veered down the road, leaving the others behind.

"I don't know about you two," Harrison started. Daisy spotted his eyes in the rearview mirror, looking between her and Jensen. "But I think I'm all golfed out."

"Agreed," Jensen groaned.

"Yeah, me too," Daisy added, arms crossing over her chest until her golf bag jostled over a bump in the road.

Harrison chuckled. "I have a wager for you two then. How about we skip past seventeen and go straight to number eighteen? Let the old-timers enjoy their golf and conversations, and you two can compete for a small prize."

"A prize?" Jensen and Daisy perked up.

Daisy's grip on her bag tightened with every glance she threw Jensen's way or each one he returned. *Nothing like a competition to kick them into a second wind, huh?*

"Yeah, a friendly wager. Whoever wins the last hole gets the prize." Harrison passed the entrance to hole seventeen, guiding them around the small lake. No turning back.

"Sounds good to me," Jensen spoke first, tipping his head toward Daisy. "Is that suggestion amenable to you, Your Highness?"

"It is, and I can't wait to win," Daisy replied, snidely smiling when Jensen's smug look fell as he registered what she said.

Harrison didn't interject to espouse a plea for peace from the driver's seat, leaving Daisy and Jensen to glare at one another. He drove them further down the greens until reaching the marker for hole eighteen.

While Harrison hopped out of the golf cart and beelined for the starting tee, Jensen and Daisy lingered. Jensen scoffed, sliding his bag over his shoulder.

"Considering which of us has the better golf record, I'll be the only winner today."

"All I need is to keep my lead over you. I've been doing that since hole one."

"You're one point ahead. I can't wait for you to whine about me winning because I will never let you live it down," said Jensen.

Daisy cupped his chin, holding him still, and smirked. "I wasn't the one whining this morning, begging on my knees for attention. Remember that, or did you suddenly get amnesia from how good my head is?"

Jensen's jaw dropped, face painted pink with shock at her comeback. Daisy hadn't planned her response but couldn't be disappointed with the result. *Point Daisy.*

Daisy lightly tapped Jensen's cheek and jumped from her side of the golf cart, hearing Harrison's whistle. "Jensen! Daisy! Let's go!"

"Coming!" Jensen's bag caught on the seat, but Daisy raced down the green without a second thought. She arrived first, observing Harrison load up the tee and practice a few swings.

Jensen caught up quickly and stood beside Daisy. The two watched Harrison line up and swing, laughing as his ball traveled further down the green. "Looks like I can get a par if I'm lucky. Daisy, you go."

"Yes, sir." Daisy set up her shot. The final hole had a par of three, so if she scored par or above, she should come out on top. Standing behind the tee with a precise angle, the rest of the world vanished until she swung.

Daisy grinned, spinning around to face Jensen as her swing landed her right in the final green, seemingly inches short of the hole. Almost a hole-in-one for a not-so-avid golfer... *Beat that.*

Jensen brushed past her without a snarky comment. His face schooled into a concentrated frown—eyebrows knit together while his stormy eyes darted between the tee and the hole.

He slid up to the tee, audibly exhaling as he swung. A high-pitched whistle sounded off as Jensen's ball soared across the greens, rolling into the final stretch. Horrified, Daisy watched as the ball rolled into the hole, plunging her heart into her stomach.

Jensen laughed incredulously. "Hole in one! Looks like the prize is mine."

"Don't count Daisy out yet, son," Harrison warned. The sentiment hardly felt applicable to just their game of golf. Daisy's fingers curled tighter around her club, swallowing hard when trailing behind Harrison.

As Harrison prepped for his second swing, Jensen's presence materialized by Daisy's. She barely heard his quiet inhale before stopping him. "Don't even think about it."

"I won fair and square, or are you going to accuse the wind of favoring me due to nepotism?"

"You haven't won yet."

"Daisy," Jensen paused, almost sounding concerned for her. "You can't win."

"But that doesn't mean I lose, you dimwit." Daisy marched ahead after Harrison's ball landed shy of the green, ready for her turn. She jogged over to her ball and smacked it gently enough to roll in, scoring the hole in two. "A birdie from me ties our scores. It's a draw."

Harrison leaned down, picking up his ball without a third swing. "She's right. Both of you won... or lost, depending on your view. So, will we repeat this hole until one of you breaks the tie?"

"No!" Daisy gasped, ready for golf to be over. As much as she liked to fight Jensen, no prize was worth extra rounds of golf. Much to her surprise, Jensen shook his head hard. He looked more exhausted than she felt.

"Then, will you two agree to split the prize?"

"Yes, of course."

"Yeah, Dad."

"I want to see you two shake on it." Harrison gestured between them. Under his expectant gaze, Jensen reached out his hand first. Daisy met him halfway, avoiding any comments as they shook on it.

They glanced at Harrison, who reached into the pocket of his cargo shorts. He pulled out an envelope and handed it to Daisy. She peeled the sticker off, recognizing Oceanview Spa's wave-themed logo.

"It says a spa package for two at Oceanview. A massage and another service of each person's choice." Daisy heard Jensen choke, but she couldn't blame him. Oh, Harrison set them up—hook, line, and sinker.

Jensen and Daisy's gazes met, watching each other for any signs of revoking the offer. Neither moved nor spoke, stuck between chickening out of their handshake or sucking it up.

"Alright," Jensen mumbled.

"I'll set up the appointment back at our... the suite." Daisy tried to avoid Harrison and Jensen's eyes, walking to grab the golf balls from the hole. *Fantastic.*

Daisy took several days to recover from the golf course events. However, she gathered her courage and booked her and Jensen's spa appointment. Picking the earliest date on their final week at the Ridge, she considered it merciful to end their misery sooner rather than later.

But the heady blend of jasmine and mango oil floating through the dim hallways washed away Daisy's lingering agitation. Her heavy, insulated robe with 'Oceanview' monogrammed on the chest kept her warm. Her whole body buzzed, cleansed from the facial and algae body wrap she booked solo.

She needed the extra hour in her happy place before sharing with Jensen.

Daisy combed her hair into a loose ponytail as she approached the massage room assigned to her. She downed the last of her fruit-infused water before knocking on the door.

Immediately, the door swung open to the heavy aroma of eucalyptus spray, and a familiar grin greeted her. "Hi, stranger. You're long overdue for a massage."

"I was waiting for you." Daisy grinned, accepting the bear hug from Paloma, her favorite masseuse at Oceanview. "No one does it quite like you."

Compared to Daisy's corporate vibe, Paloma embodied an earthy, free-spirited personality. She never went anywhere without her favorite crystals on a leather cord around her neck. She always glowed with a warm aura and spoke softly. Dark, coiled curls framed her soft, round face while her smile stretched from ear to ear.

Paloma held the door for Daisy, guiding her into the darkened room. Beyond a few lit candles, blackout curtains cut off all light from entering the room. Two massage tables sat in the center of the cramped room, draped in fresh sheets.

At one of the tables, a blond surfer-looking guy in the same all-black uniform Paloma wore smoothed over the pillow tucked underneath the sheets. He pulled his hair back into a low bun, smiling.

He glanced up, mid-crack of his knuckles. "Good afternoon, ma'am. The room is ready for you and your companion. Paloma and I will be assisting you today."

"Daisy, this is Lars. Lars, meet Daisy Riggs. She and her companion work with the Ridge's parent company, Hidden Oasis," Paloma introduced.

"Welcome! You'll be more than satisfied!" Lars grasped Daisy's hands in his larger ones, shaking eagerly. "I'll give you two some space. We need a refill for our heat rub ointment."

Paloma waved to Lars as he exited the room, gesturing to one of the massage tables. "Anything I should know about you and your mystery man before he shows up?"

Daisy froze, quickly remembering that Easton was her boyfriend the last time she and Paloma spoke.

She shook her head. "About that. It's not who you think."

"Oh? That's... ominous."

"Two words: he cheated. So, I've brought someone else today because we promised to split the voucher for the massage. We're not together."

"That's too bad about your ex. What an idiot for stepping out on you because, well, has he seen you?" Paloma rubbed Daisy's shoulders, clicking her tongue disapprovingly. None of Daisy's girlfriends hesitated to drag Easton's name through the mud, soothing over whatever wounds remained.

"You're the best," Daisy chuckled.

"I'll head out for a moment so you can strip and get comfortable on your table. We're going to expel all that negative energy caused by that man. You'll be a new woman leaving my table," Paloma promised before stepping out of the room.

Daisy shed her robe, hanging it on the hook mounted to the wall. She shivered at the cool air against her bare skin, quickly climbing under the warmed sheets of the heated massage table. She laid her face on the padded headrest and slumped, groaning into the sheets.

Two minutes barely passed before a knock pulled Daisy's head out of the headrest. She watched the door swing open to reveal Paloma, arms full of labeled bottles like 'lotion' and 'scalp oil.'

"Hey, there's a man out there asking for you," Paloma whispered, but her teasing smile raised Daisy's brows. "He said his name is Jensen and that he's due for a massage. Is he the Jensen I've heard so much about?"

Daisy groaned, "Yes, he's *that* Jensen."

Paloma giggled, ignoring Daisy's narrowed eyes while stacking the materials on her table. "You never mentioned he was so dreamy. How do you ever get any work done with him in the office across from you?"

"I run on spite, caffeine, and more spite. Besides, he's annoying," Daisy grumbled. "Tell him to get in here."

"Sure thing. I'll give you both space." Still giggling, Paloma opened the door and waved Jensen into the room. She shut the door behind him, leaving Jensen and Daisy alone.

Daisy propped onto her forearms, examining Jensen bundled up in the fuzzy spa robe. "You should probably lose the robe and get comfortable."

"Okay." Jensen coughed, eyes averted from her. "Don't look at me."

"Unless your body changed drastically since last night, it's nothing I haven't seen before," Daisy snorted, burying her face into the headrest. She listened to the rumple of a robe and the creak of the massage table beside her, keeping her head down.

Silence washed over the room as Daisy lay there with Jensen to her right, feeling the hovering presence of his hand draped off the massage table next to hers. The door creaked, announcing Paloma and Lars' return.

Ambient river noises filled the room shortly before the massages began. Hands covered in hot oil glided down Daisy's back, and tension melted out of her with each touch, dripping to the floor. Paloma's hands applied pressure to elicit embarrassingly loud cracking from Daisy's body.

Daisy winced, greeted by the familiar strain of knots in her shoulders and back. She clenched her jaw hard while Paloma ran her hands over Daisy's neck, trying her best not to whimper or cry.

"Daisy?" Jensen's voice, softer than she'd ever heard, called from her side. "Are you okay?"

"I'm fine," Daisy lied, but the painful cracking of a knot finally undone interrupted her thought. *Fuck, she needed to increase her frequency of visits again.*

"Hon, your back has never been this bad. Did you injure yourself?" Paloma whispered, pausing before pressing between Daisy's shoulder blades, untangling another knot.

"No, but I think my chair at the office is to blame. It doesn't have a firm back support anymore," Daisy admitted through the aching in her jaw from clenching so hard. She relaxed when Paloma loosened the pressure for a second.

"Please tell me you've already replaced it." Jensen didn't skip a beat, not letting the conversation go.

"Not yet. I don't want to use company funds for my personal problems. I can afford to buy it, but it fell toward the bottom of my priorities because of everything happening." Daisy braced on the table as Paloma's hands circled back to her shoulder blades.

As much as she hated the pain, it would hurt more if she allowed the knots to stay.

Paloma's hands doubled the pressure against one of the tighter knots. Daisy cried out when the muscle finally loosened after enough weight from Paloma's body pushed down on hers.

Stuck in the haze of the pain, Daisy almost missed the feel of fingertips grazing against her hand draped over the side of the table. Yet she gasped when a hand grasped hers, lacing their fingers together.

She angled her head to the right, finding Jensen's hand holding hers, hanging between the tables. Although she couldn't see his face, she felt his touch and the soft squeezes of her hands.

Daisy held her tongue and squeezed Jensen's hand whenever Paloma rolled out another knot. She gripped him hard like her lifeline, fading in and out between each spike of pain, followed by a twinge of relief.

Fuzzy thoughts swirled around her head. Yet Jensen's hand remained her anchor to consciousness.

"This normally is later, but let's get the pain out of the way," Paloma whispered while helping Daisy move. She released Jensen's hand as Paloma rolled her onto her back, sitting up with help. "I can help fix your alignment."

Paloma gripped her under her shoulders and rolled her in a small circle, counting her down. Before Daisy blinked, Paloma had her bent over and rolled her spine to the raucous cracking of her spine.

A soft, breathy moan escaped her as the pressure in her back alleviated. The sudden release of tension screamed in pure bliss. Daisy slumped forward, letting Paloma bend her in a different direction to more popping and cracks.

Her gaze darted to the side, finding Jensen's head turned out of the headrest and his eyes watching her. Even through the darkness, his eyes glittered darkly like the ocean beyond the spa's walls. Their eyes linked, but the moment was fleeting.

Daisy gripped the edge of the table while Paloma rolled her spine out until the pain finally abated. She rolled to her stomach with Paloma's gentle guidance.

She placed her head above the headrest. She managed to face Jensen, struggling to hold his gaze while melting into the sheets from the oil and hot rub cream smoothed into her skin. Paloma murmured, "After this session, the spa offers a complimentary hot bath in our indoor bathhouse for you two. Would you be interested in that?"

Jensen's head lifted, exchanging silent glances with Daisy. Raised brows and pursed lips preceded the quiet hum from Jensen. "Sure thing."

"No peeking," Daisy teased before tucking her face into the headrest again. Jensen's quiet laugh reached her before she drifted off, slipping through the darkness for a while.

Chapter 10
Jensen

Pouring his second cup of coffee in the last hour, Jensen's tired eyes scanned the faces sitting around the breakfast table. Everyone else's lively conversations overpowered his stoic silence and Daisy's resting scowl into her coffee.

That morning marked the end of the retreat. Tomorrow, he and the others around the table would return to work, opening a can of worms that Jensen would rather fling into the ocean than acknowledge.

He and Daisy stayed up all night, searching for distraction between the sheets. However, even after they parted ways, Jensen struggled to sleep. From the quiet noises across the suite, Daisy didn't find rest either.

Pretending only worked while out of the office, away from regular life. The two stewed in their silence while strong-arming coffee. None of their coworkers appeared to notice anything amiss, wrapped up in their conversations and full plates.

Something brushing against his ankle under the table drew Jensen's eyes away from his coffee. He found Daisy staring at him; understanding passed between their linked gazes, riding on the same wavelength.

He and Daisy being on the same page still surprised him.

Jensen slid the coffee pot across the table, noticing fast how Daisy snatched it up. She sighed, "So, does anyone know what we're supposed to be doing this morning?"

"Not a clue. I thought you or Jensen would know since you're close with the boss," Miranda replied, mid-bite of her loaded waffle drowning in fruit syrup.

"Same here," Holden and Iris snorted in unison.

"We've had a suspicious lack of team-building events this year," Nelson mused while pushing around his over-easy eggs. "I expected a bonfire where we're expected to hold hands and sing kumbaya."

Jensen shuddered at the thought. Nelson had a point; past retreats emphasized team building and cohesion even while away from the office. The group had a few gatherings which felt fleeting compared to years prior.

Part of him assumed that the current retreat's loose structure reflected the uncertainty around the future. Hidden Oasis had always been his dad's great pride; it would be someone else's in a few short months.

Hopefully his, but still.

Jensen pushed back his plate, haunted by his half-finished eggs and the crumbs of his sourdough toast sprinkled over them. "I wouldn't be surprised by a team exercise or something last-minute. I'm sure my dad will say something."

"Speak of the devil," Daisy coughed, but her gaze sauntered past Jensen's shoulder. Along with the rest of the table, he turned to spot his dad standing at the C-Suite table.

Beside him, two smiling women eagerly shook his hand. Despite their visibly bright demeanors, the hollowness of their eyes always unnerved Jensen to no end.

Virgina and Leyla Flowers owned a "corporate synergy company" where they hosted team-building and other relevant training. Hidden Oasis hired them during the inaugural retreat and each one since. Everyone in the company knew Virginia and Leyla well.

"Great. Pass me the coffee," Easton remarked, but Daisy didn't move. The silence lingered until Iris leaned over and handed

Easton the coffee pot. All that HR training oozed from even the smallest of her behaviors.

Jensen shifted in his chair, downing the rest of his coffee until his throat ached from the heat. The caffeine needed to hit fast, or whatever the Flowers had planned would drive him to unmentionable boredom.

The squeak of sneakers over the tiles of the outdoor patio grew louder as Leyla approached; Leyla always chose to work with the V-Suite, so it had to be her.

"Look at all those lovely, familiar faces!" Leyla exclaimed. Daisy once said that Leyla had 'youth pastor energy.' Jensen never forgot that comment; she wasn't wrong. "If you're having a fantastic day, can I get a heck yeah?"

Jensen watched the members of the table eye one another, but Miranda and Iris crumbled. They lifted their hands and chorused a quieter "heck yeah" than Leyla.

Leyla bounded around the table with the colorful highlights in her mousy brown hair catching the light. That morning, her chosen color was bubblegum pink to match her cropped top.

She paused behind Easton, hands clasped together. "I don't see nearly enough smiles on those faces. Come on! We're about to have a great activity today!"

Leyla circled a finger around her mouth until everyone plastered a smile onto their faces. Well, everyone but Daisy. She sipped her coffee and stared into the distance, looking like she needed a rescue. *Once again, she had a point.*

But, as if she sensed his thoughts, Leyla's head snapped toward him. She bounced around the table and jammed herself into the small crevice between his and Holden's chairs, forcing Holden to scoot toward the others.

"Hello, Leyla," Jensen greeted, stuck under her attention like a deer in headlights. His coworkers busied themselves with their breakfast.

"Jensen! It's so good to see you again!" Leyla gushed. Her hand grasped the back of his chair as she leaned closer to him, hair falling over her eyes. "So, there's seven of you at the table. Our activity today needs even pairs. One of you can join the C-Suite table since they have a vacancy over there."

The table members looked at one another until Holden cleared his throat. "Jensen could probably go. He'd pair off with his dad. The rest of us could figure out our partnerships."

"If you don't want to leave the group, I'm more than happy to join and pair off with someone," Leyla added. Everyone turned to Jensen again, some of them curious and others expectant.

But Jensen counted his moves behind a slow sip of water, buying himself more time to decide. Leaving to spend time with his dad would be an easy solution and less likely to get him stuck with Leyla for the activity.

He witnessed how fast his colleagues began to form silent partnerships. Iris and Miranda already had their arms linked over each other's shoulders. Holden reached toward Nelson, who decided to return to his breakfast.

That left Easton... and Daisy as his only option. Easton's eyes fixated on Daisy, but her focus went everywhere but him. Her shoulders tensed as one of her hands gripped her fork so hard the metal looked on the verge of bending. Her features darkened while she turned away, even when Easton touched her shoulder.

Get off her.

"Actually, I'm good. Nelson, you should go chat with the CFO. I've heard he's been interested in consulting you on a project," Jensen remarked. Everyone stopped, turning to him with their gawking expressions.

But Nelson, like the intelligent man he was, rose from his chair. He grabbed his sunglasses from his pocket, saluting. "You're the best, man."

"No problem," Jensen chuckled, fist-bumping him before Nelson left for the other table. He pointed to Daisy across from him. "If we're picking partners, I call dibs on Daisy."

If the table hadn't been shocked before, the prior reaction felt tame compared to when Jensen said Daisy's name. Poor Iris spit out her orange juice, coughing hard and rubbing her nose.

The fork in Daisy's hand dropped, clattering harmlessly onto the tablecloth, but relief slipped past her defenses as her mouth twitched at the corners, fighting a smile.

She covered it up fast, aware of all the eyes on them. She scrunched her nose, humming loudly. "Fine. You're the lesser of two evils."

Although she spoke to him, Jensen watched Daisy's eyes slide toward Easton. If he noticed, then the rest of the table probably had.

"Says Satan," Jensen replied, refusing to miss a beat. They covered up their tracks with a few snarky comments, washing away the shock on the faces of their colleagues like how the ocean erased messages in the sand.

"You're going to wish I was Satan after that little comment."

"In your dreams."

"My dreams always involve me hitting you with my c—"

"Okay! Everyone else has a partner picked out?" Leyla interjected, voice cracking underneath the overzealous pep. Despite the smile on her face, the look failed to meet her eyes. Iris and Miranda held onto each other. So, as the last man standing, Holden offered his hand to Easton.

"Yes," the group chorused.

Leyla pointed to the nearby hiking trail. "Alright, everyone needs to get up for this activity. We'll be heading down to the beach. I'll explain more before we hit the trail."

Several groans erupted from the group. However, no one protested as they vacated their seats from the patio along the

Shore Building. Leyla weaved in between the six, pushing them into their chosen pairings.

Daisy kept an arm's length distance between them, letting Jensen follow her lead. Compared to the others, their closeness would invite more questions than answers.

Hate her or love her, it didn't matter. Daisy's presence was magnetizing yet loud, commanding attention from every direction. Wherever she went, all eyes fell on her with an unspoken reverence.

No matter how hard he tried, figuring Daisy out remained an untouchable puzzle with several pieces missing. Jensen knew the scent of her favorite perfume and how sultry his name sounded on her cherry-red lips, but so much remained a mystery.

A light jab of Daisy's elbow into his ribs jostled Jensen from his thoughts, finding them the first in line at the hiking trail. Leyla looked them over, rifling blindly through her bag.

"Okay, friends. Today's activity will be somewhat unconventional, but we will try it out! We've had great success with our trial runs of this activity," Leyla said. "As you know, being on teams requires a certain level of trust. Pick one person from your partnership."

Jensen exchanged a heavy stare with Daisy, who pointed at herself within seconds. He, with little choice otherwise, also pointed at her until Leyla acknowledged them.

"That makes Daisy, Iris, and Easton our first brave volunteers. The three of you will allow your partner to lead you on a trust walk down to the beach! Your eyes will be closed as you—"

"I'm sorry?" Daisy choked. Jensen's head snapped toward her, so sure he could hear her pulse quicken. Dilated pupils darkened her eyes from their glittering whiskey shade under the sunshine. "He's responsible for me walking down the cliff?"

"There's a paved path with ropes and wooden railings," Jensen remarked, but his commentary earned a glare from Daisy.

"What's to stop him from pushing me off the side of the cliff and claiming I accidentally tripped?"

"You've got to be kidding. I wouldn't risk jail time for you!" Leyla's smile dimmed. "No one will push anyone, and there's no jail time. This exercise is all about trust. You'll be trusted to help Jensen back up the trail after our excursion to the beach."

Daisy narrowed her eyes, arms crossed. "Alright, but you're all witnesses in case Jensen decides he wouldn't look god-awful in orange."

As Leyla pulled something dark from her backpack, Jensen rolled his eyes, saying nothing else. Leyla handed it to Jensen, weakly smiling. "It's not too late to switch."

"I'll pass," Jensen replied, trying not to sound frightened by her proposition. He'd take Daisy and her biting commentary over Leyla any day. He stared at the dark fabric, long and thin, draped over his hand. "Daisy and I can behave."

He lifted the item up. In the daylight, he finally realized what it was. *A blindfold.*

Jensen struggled to swallow around the lump in his throat while he dangled the blindfold between his fingers. He scooted closer to Daisy, lowering his voice, "I have to blindfold you."

"Are you asking my permission?" Daisy asked.

"You know I am."

"Mmm, I consent. You're quite the gentleman."

Jensen snorted softly. He and Daisy knew damn well that his being a gentleman went as far as the threshold of their hotel room.

Jensen slid behind Daisy, still careful to leave space between their bodies for the benefit of their coworkers. He trailed the blindfold over her shoulder, peeking out from her sundress, quickly pulling the fabric over her eyes.

As he tied the ends of the blindfold under her ponytail, he heard Daisy whisper, "Kinky."

"The last thing we need is to blow our cover because you can't stop from being a tease," Jensen murmured, a little rougher than he first intended. Daisy could readily point out his hypocrisy—considering that he pulled the sunscreen incident weeks earlier.

Daisy laughed at him, keeping her voice soft, "Oh please... You could do so much worse for a rebound. Look at who you dated for years."

Jensen bit his tongue when Leyla raced past them, burying his response to Daisy's smartass comment. Leyla gestured for the pairs to link hands, clasping hers together. So, Jensen reached around to take Daisy's hands in his.

"Here we go." Jensen stepped toward the trail, taking the outside edge of the path. If anyone would accidentally trip and fall off the clip, it would be him. The late morning's heat left his fingers lightly sweaty, but he held onto Daisy tighter. "I'll tell you every move I make if you'll feel safer."

"I'd prefer you didn't. Just... talk to me about literally anything else," Daisy said. If he didn't know better, Jensen swore he overheard a quiver in her voice while they descended on the trail.

"Okay. This is embarrassing, but Piper and Hayley ambushed me the other night and talked me into letting them wax my legs."

"No way. You're messing with me."

"I'm as serious as can be. They wanted to do my armpits and chest too, but I barely survived them ripping off my leg hairs."

"Hah, you're such a baby. I've fallen asleep mid-wax appointment, and I get the bikini line done."

Jensen's face burned, torn between pivoting away from his sisters' torture by wax and thoughts of Daisy and bikinis... or Daisy *in* bikinis.

As the two reached the midway point of the trail, known for being the steepest part, some loose sand shifted underneath

Daisy's feet. She gasped as her body slid a little, releasing her grip on Jensen.

But Jensen's hands snapped to catch her before she slipped, coiling around her waist. His arms yanked her close, safely cradled to his side with a firm grip.

Daisy yelped. Jensen could almost hear her heart jump in her chest. "This stupid trust exercise is going to get me killed."

"Are you two alright?" Miranda's voice echoed distantly from behind them, but Jensen kept his eyes on Daisy.

"We're fine. Be careful of sand or gravel on the road!" Jensen exclaimed, trying to move forward with Daisy wrapped around his side. But her hands dug into his shirt, clinging like a lifeline.

"Can't Jensen carry me down the rest of the way? I doubt that twisting my ankle will make me trust people!" Daisy shouted.

"Of course you want me to carry you, Your Highness. I'll bet you also want me to become your human footstool," Jensen grumbled. Daisy said nothing beyond a few mumbles while the two descended the remaining stretch of trail.

Daisy tore off the blindfold as soon as their feet hit the dry sand. Relief softened her features when she handed the blindfold to Jensen. "We didn't kill one another."

"That's a miracle," Jensen agreed, watching Leyla come down with the other pairs. "Now, what are we in for?"

Leyla pointed to the empty beach, occupied by a few seagulls on the prowl for their next meal. Otherwise, the early hour promised total privacy.

"Alright, so today's activity is about trust and vulnerability. Each pair will take turns recalling a time of struggle, but your partner will recite the same experience back to you, reframing it positively," Leyla explained, arms open like she expected a cheer or applause.

Instead, Daisy coughed, "So... it's essentially couple's therapy?"

Leyla ignored Daisy's remark, even though its accuracy threatened to pull a laugh out of Jensen. She waved the group off. "Find a spot with your partner, and let the vulnerability commence! Go on!"

Jensen grasped Daisy's hand without even thinking, linking their fingers together. He tugged Daisy behind him as they moved away from the others, who dispersed as ordered.

The two marched down the beach, parallel to the low tide swaying between the edge of the damp sand and the gentle waves cresting over the tide pools by the cliffs.

Jensen plopped onto the sand. Daisy sat next to him, still maintaining a small gap between them. She tucked her knees to her chest, sighing, "So, you packed already, right?"

"Yeah, this morning," Jensen agreed. "I didn't want to rush for tomorrow's early checkout."

"That's fair. I can't believe it's July already." Daisy shook her head. When her gaze settled on the water, Jensen finally noticed the slow crumble of her guard. It started with her shoulders sliding down, then her face relaxed, losing the tension in her jaw like she clamped everything she wanted to say between grit teeth. She curled into herself, resting on her kneecaps with a quiet exhale.

Jensen leaned back on his hands, sinking a little into the sand. "I've never told anyone this," he whispered, feeling Daisy's eyes on his face. "But there was a time when I almost failed the Intro to Business course back at UCLA, and I thought I was going to tell my dad I wasn't cut out for working at the company."

"What happened?" Daisy whispered.

"During that time, Delaney and I had been on shaky ground; our relationship hit a rough patch. I took it to heart, shifting my focus to her instead of keeping up with my studies. I bombed the midterm hard. So, the professor called me into his office and explained that he thought I should transfer majors. He mentioned that I was trying too hard to be my dad."

"What a jackass."

"He wasn't wrong, but I learned my lesson. I worked harder, took extra credit, and studied for the final exam weeks before the study period began. I managed to pull myself up to a B, which stayed at my lowest grade throughout my studies. So, what does that say about me?"

Jensen turned to Daisy, finding her staring at him with her head cocked. Her lips pursed, but she smiled faintly. "That you persevered. Your ego took a hit, which isn't hard because it's massive, but you didn't give up. You accepted a wake-up call and didn't let hurt feelings stop you from being better. Sound accurate?"

"More like surprisingly nice," Jensen joked, earning a quiet scoff from Daisy. He nudged her with his shoulder. "Alright. Your turn to share."

Daisy paused, still holding his gaze with hers. Something dark and unrecognizable flashed across her eyes, gone as fast as it came. She wrapped her arms over her chest.

"Before Hidden Oasis, I struggled to hold down a job. I worked odd gigs as soon as possible, even before legal age in California. For one reason or another, I'd find myself being let go and needing another job. I considered myself a loser because other kids my age had little worries besides dating, school, and their extracurriculars," Daisy spoke, but her voice lost all the piercing confidence Jensen associated with her. Instead, she tripped over her words. For the first time since they'd met, Daisy Riggs appeared small.

"What kinds of jobs?" Jensen asked.

"You name it, I did it. Secretary, babysitting, fast food service, retail, and lifeguard are a few I can remember." Daisy's dry laugh startled a poor seagull approaching them on the sand. "Alright, I'm done. Feel free to lie."

"Did you lie to me?"

"No."

"Then, I'm not lying to you." Jensen scooted a little closer, reaching for her hand. Daisy eyed him, bristling, but she eventually let him take her hand. "As a teenager, you had the drive to go and find jobs. Nothing stopped you from putting yourself out there, not even rejection. That shows discipline and bravery."

Silence fell between them, allowing the ocean's quiet gurgling and seagulls' far-off cry to fill space. Their hands and gazes kept them tethered to the moment, on the verge of drifting away.

"Bravery, huh?" Daisy swallowed. "Well, let's continue that trend. What will we do about our habit of falling into each other's beds when we head home tomorrow?"

"I should've expected we'd talk about this," Jensen mused. "We have two choices, really. Pierce the bubble and let this bleed into our regular lives, or pretend it never happened and leave it as a side effect of being in paradise."

"Yeah, that sounds about right. It's a corporate retreat, after all. Lines were bound to get blurry, especially with the room sharing."

"Right. But our circumstances haven't magically faded because of a small vacation. Easton and Delaney will probably still be together back home."

Daisy nodded. "They seem determined to stick it out and prove how happy their choice made them, but we're different kinds of people."

"We are," Jensen replied, finding them circling the point. "How about we play it by ear? Things are casual."

"I can live with that. We'll play it by ear." Daisy squeezed his hand, meeting his ambiguity with contentment. Jensen could live with that, too.

Chapter 11

Daisy

After one week back at the office, Daisy longed for days of the pool, ice-cold cocktails, and sunshine caressing her skin. She loved her job, but part of her remained at the Ridge, stuck in the soft duvet covers and the tall walls of her suite.

Although back in the heart of Beverly Hills, the July heat persisted. It seeped through the windows and walls, stroking a thin layer of sweat between Daisy's skin and her pantyhose.

Exhaustion tap danced in Daisy's chest as she walked down the hallway from her office. She had half a dozen copies to make, a handful of emails to answer, and the unshakable boredom pushing her head under. Everything screamed for her attention, but Daisy needed a will to live.

Coffee made life better.

When she reached the break room, she pulled her hair from its loose bun, hoping for a private audience with the espresso machine. One foot barely crossed the threshold before she paused, caught off-guard by the sight of Jensen.

The crisp charcoal of his favorite suit blended him into the break room's stainless-steel fridge. Daisy almost missed him at first, but he stood taller instead of casually leaning against the fridge when spotting her.

"Hey," Jensen greeted. Since their return from the Ridge, they hadn't spoken one-on-one at all. Even in group settings, their conversations revolved solely around work matters. No one paid any mind to them avoiding one another. "I'll get out of your way."

"It's fine. I'm here for some coffee," Daisy assured him before he could run out of the room. Their eyes locked as Daisy crossed the spacious break room for the espresso machine.

While there had been a lack of conversation, the silent glances across the hallway during working hours spoke volumes. What was there to say?

"I'm hiding from Delaney," Jensen mumbled, hands jammed into his pockets. His eyes followed Daisy, even as she rifled through the cabinets beside him for a mug. "She's been calling my office line all morning."

"Did you block her cell phone?"

"I blocked her number, email, all social media, and any of her friends or family she might use to reach me. She's been insistent on talking more. I'm not sure what she wants now."

"I wonder what's going on with her and Easton because I saw the two of them sucking faces the other night at one of my favorite restaurants."

"Great."

Daisy sighed, fiddling with the settings on the espresso machine. She needed the strongest available option to drown in. "I swear they've started a campaign to ruin all of my spots. Now, where will I get authentic Italian on this side of Los Angeles County?"

The hissing of the espresso machine grated against her festering bitterness, recalling another thing stolen from her by the exes. Daisy leaned against the counter, catching sight of Jensen's eyes dropped toward the floor, crestfallen.

Daisy couldn't blame him; no one liked hearing that someone they once loved moved on with their affair partner.

In the long run, she got off easier. She and Easton were never meant to be forever; he always wanted her a little more than she wanted him. Leaving him came easy with one foot already out of the door. Sometimes, not being the dating type worked in her favor.

Daisy reached for Jensen, stopping herself at the twitch of her fingers. Instead, she scooted down the counter, closing the gap between them. She shook her head as she said, "Jensen."

Jensen's head lifted, face unreadable. He shrugged. "Every time I think I've gotten past it, she finds a new way to disrupt my peace."

"There's not much you can do about that," Daisy murmured. "Does it bother you because you're still in love with her?"

"No. The cheating killed any feelings I might've had. Whenever I see her, I don't see the girl I went to prom with or the one who cheered from the audience as I accepted my diploma. I see her and Easton on that roof."

"It's anger. You're angry with Delaney, rightfully so. I was, too, but I realized that wasting my energy on them wouldn't make it worthwhile. Doing better without Easton in my life would."

Daisy watched Jensen's eyes flash curiously, but the slow roll of his gaze over her kept her still. Giving her dark, fitted work dress and her kitten heel pumps a once-over spelled trouble for them if anyone walked in.

"And how are you doing that?" Jensen asked.

"Throwing myself into my work and under someone else is a great starting point. You should consider it," said Daisy.

"Maybe I should." Jensen's rasp sent several flashbacks of rumpled sheets and the thump of the headboard against the wall racing through Daisy's head. She reached back for her coffee mug. In her distraction, she nearly burned her palm when missing the handle. "Any suggestions on where to start?"

Minding her manners enough not to suggest a secluded closet to blow off steam, Daisy hummed, "Well, we're supposed to get news on the contractor bids today."

"Right." Jensen cleared his throat. "Isn't legal finishing up the contracts soon?" His eyes jumped to the furthest point from hers while Daisy searched for something interesting in her coffee.

"Yeah, your dad wanted to make the announcement before lunchtime. It isn't his job, but he's eager to be involved... with December four months from now."

The mention of December struck hard and fast, needling beneath Daisy's skin. On the retreat, it was easier to dodge the subject and not let it linger, especially while she and Jensen explored their boundaries. But now, being back at work, neither could ignore the glaring reminders that they were at odds.

"I can't blame him. He loves this company."

Daisy carried her coffee toward the door, but Jensen followed behind her. He gestured for her to go first, letting Daisy slide back into the hallway. He matched her careful strides in two large ones of his own, slowing his pace down to match hers.

"I know he does. Which is why he's going to green-light the deal for Steelbird Structures to be our newest contractor," Daisy remarked.

"I don't know. My dad seemed more impressed with the presentation of Urbanite Developments' proposal," Jensen said, brows knit together in confusion.

"What makes you say that?"

"I know my dad, and I've heard from some of our investors about their personal preference for Urbanite."

"So, you think your dad will bend the knee for some of our investors? Be realistic, Jensen. The benefit of the company comes first. As charismatic as Urbanite's people are, the numbers don't lie. Steelbird wins in almost every scenario."

Daisy paused outside of her office, finding Jensen's mouth taut and his eyes narrowed into slits. Ah, she managed to push him back into competition mode... right where she liked him.

"Uh-huh. How sure are you exactly?" Jensen questioned. The disbelief dripping off his words told Daisy how little he'd believe a word out of her mouth. He might consider himself the Harrison Ramsey "expert", but she knew the numbers by heart.

"Absolutely certain." Daisy backed into her office, smirking before the door swung closed. "It's okay to be wrong, Jensen. You are a lot, but I'm used to it by now."

Jensen's face flashed a heated shade of pink. He spun around on his heel, ducking into his office, so unlike his usual penchant for a snarky comment in response. *Maybe he was learning not to challenge her.*

Daisy snickered, knowing he heard every word. She slid behind her cramped desk, burdened by small towers of reports and different schematics from their architects sprawled across the space.

Crashing to sit in her not-yet-replaced desk chair, Daisy planned for a morning of corporate triage. Urgent things would be handled before lunch, and everything else would be completed before the workday ended. However, with her schedule packed, the search for a new chair fell to the bottom of that list.

She had barely cleared the reports and schematics off her when her office phone rang. The shrill beeping demanded her full attention, not giving her a second to enjoy her coffee.

Daisy accepted the call, cradling the phone against her shoulder while she thumbed through the schematics. "Daisy Riggs speaking. May I ask who's calling?"

"I wasn't done with our conversation yet, Your Highness." Jensen's voice on the other line caught Daisy's focus. She moved her laptop to the side, revealing Jensen at his desk with a smirk. He waved the phone at her. "You're not usually one to run from a good debate."

"First of all, I didn't run, you did. Second of all, there's no debate. I'm right about this. Now, I suspect you have a kink for me humiliating you," Daisy said, keeping her tone dry.

"Hilarious." Jensen rolled his eyes, feet kicked up on his desk like such a douchebag. Only Jensen Ramsey could get away with the carefree bullshit act. "But if you're sure, how about we run a little wager? You versus me, like old times."

Daisy sat tall in her chair, rigid from the horrible back support. She grabbed the waistline of her work dress and straightened it, watching Jensen's face. The neckline of her dress dipped, revealing more cleavage. Jensen's gaze trailed after it. *Predictable.*

She laughed into the phone, making it extra sultry for Jensen. "I love a good wager. State your terms and prepare to be crushed."

Jensen's Adam's apple bobbed hard enough for Daisy to see. He slid his feet from his desk. Instead, his hand gripped it tight like he needed to hold himself from pouncing on her.

So close, yet so far.

"You and I guess who wins the contract. Simple as that," Jensen said.

"Sounds like a plan. When I win, you'll be my personal assistant for the day."

"Oh? When I win, you'll do all my reports for the rest of the week."

"I can't wait to wipe the floor with you." Daisy grinned. Jensen matched her with confidence palpable through several layers of glass. "My money's on Steelbird, and I'm guessing the contract will be around 3.5 million for the award."

"That high? I sure hope you're right or be prepared to be my ghostwriter for the rest of the week," said Jensen.

"Oh, please. It's Wednesday, and we never work too long on the weekends. Now stop stalling and announce your bet, pretty boy." Daisy slid her laptop back in front of her, refreshing her inbox.

"Fine. I say it's going to Urbanite and—" Jensen paused mid-sentence, messing with his laptop. His eyes widened, breathing a little harder. "Did this email just hit our inboxes?"

"It sure did. Open it." Sitting at the top of her unread email pile, Harrison's announcement email arrived with divine timing. She heard Jensen's mouse click. She did the same, opening the email to skim through the brief pleasantries. Harrison always included them, too nice for his own good sometimes.

Jensen's voice started out strong, fading by the end. "'I am proud to announce Hidden Oasis's newest partnership with Steelbird Structures. They will provide contracting and construction for the Alpine Project in Vermont, headed by our Project Development department, for an estimated cost of $3.65 million.'"

Victory tasted so sweet.

"Told you so," Daisy broke the silence following, not fighting her smile anymore. She raked her eyes over Jensen's newly pale face. He was so fucked.

"That's not funny. How the hell did you almost get the number right? The company was a fifty-fifty shot!"

"It's my job to know. But it's time to saddle up for the rest of the day, my new assistant. I need you for an extended lunch hour, so push back any meetings until after two today. Thank you."

Daisy winked, hanging up the phone with her orders laid out. *Man, it felt good to be a winner.*

"I'm torn. Should I go with the white or the nude?" Daisy held two perfectly dazzling heels—white slingbacks with a kitten heel and nude-toned ankle strap heel.

She spun around and lifted each heel for the opinion of her captive audience. Jensen stood behind her and, from the expression on his face, looked anything but thrilled to be there.

Buried underneath at least ten shopping bags, she barely saw his narrowed eyes from behind the designer brand haul.

His lunch hour as her personal assistant started with him buying her lunch. Then, she enlisted his services of bag carrying and funding an afternoon on Rodeo Drive. She conveniently "forgot" her wallet in the car.

Daisy raised her brow, waving the heels in front of Jensen for a response. He huffed, blowing a loose hair out of his eyes. "Whichever hurts my credit card more. That's your goal, right?"

"These are about equal price, so that doesn't help." Daisy clicked her tongue, maneuvering around him to the bench. She propped her right foot onto the bench, sliding off her work heels. "Guess I should try them on."

She heard Jensen's defeated sigh but no further protests. First, she slid on the nude heel, underwhelmed by its fit. So, she slipped on the white in its place. As luck would have it, the shoe fit like a glove.

She grabbed the box for the white slingbacks, marching toward the counter without waiting for Jensen to follow. She was a busy woman with things to do.

"Hi there!" The elegant woman behind the counter beamed at Daisy's approach. Her face gleamed brighter than the shiny pearl earrings she wore, framed nicely against her dark blouse and warm blonde hair. "Did you find everything you wanted today?"

"Absolutely. Thank you." Daisy slid the shoe box across the counter. She glanced over her shoulder at the rustling of shopping bags, finding Jensen. Her Rodeo haul hung on both of his arms instead of piled up into an unwieldy tower of clothes, shoes, jewelry, and a cute new purse.

"If this is everything? Cash or card?"

"Card, please."

Daisy hadn't stopped looking at Jensen and outstretched her hand wordlessly. Jensen dug into his pocket, revealing his shimmery black credit card.

He handed it to her, not looking at the price. After the second store, Jensen learned better, but Daisy wouldn't tell him she applied sales discounts to everything.

She liked making him sweat a little—it was character-building.

Daisy turned to pay for her brand-new slingbacks, noticing the impressed face of the store clerk. The clerk's eyes darted between Daisy and Jensen, too busy gawking to finish bagging Daisy's shoes.

Daisy swiped Jensen's card and gracefully plucked the shoebox off the counter. "I'll be alright without a bag. Thank you."

"Of course, ma'am. Have an excellent day, and thank you for shopping with us!" The clerk nodded.

Daisy tipped her head graciously before heading out the double doors. She inhaled the July sunshine, head rolling back to bask in the warm day. Her arms stretched out and brushed against Jensen, materializing by her side again.

"This was fun! I'm done shopping but need one more stop before we return to the office," Daisy said.

"Lead the way," Jensen sighed, despite sounding ready to ask what else she had up her sleeve. "We're in the Brighton parking garage."

"I remember." Daisy and Jensen strode across the sidewalk through Rodeo, moving through the sparse crowds for the afternoon hour. They caught a crosswalk right outside the parking structure at the perfect time.

Daisy waited for Jensen to fetch his car, enjoying every moment of his suffering. In the grand scheme of things, her demands were harmless and funny.

"Hey there, gorgeous." To her left, a gaggle of guys no older than their early twenties whistled, swaggering toward the valet. Several lowered their glasses to ogle her openly. One even licked his lips.

"Keep walking. Not interested," Daisy barked. At the first hint of aggression, the guys scurried away. *Good riddance.*

Jensen's car rolled up to her with all her bags in the backseat and him leaning over from the driver's side. He flipped down his sunglasses, brows arched. "Where are we going?"

"Obelisk Hotel. It's right before the intersection on Beverly Boulevard and La Cienega." Daisy tossed her shoes into the pile of shopping bags in the backseat before sliding into the passenger seat.

"I know where it is. That's one of ours, right?" Jensen cocked his head. He pulled away from the curb and sped out of the parking garage. Wind wildly threaded through Daisy's hair, blowing her sandy tresses around her face. "Is there a reason we need to stop by?"

In the passenger seat, Daisy slumped a little into the upholstery. She quietly picked at her newly manicured nails, painted in classic French tips.

It wasn't any of Jensen's business. Yet, Daisy swore a thin thread of concern danced in his question.

She sighed. "My apartment had a burst pipe in one of the upstairs rooms, but it caused water damage to my place. They're repairing it now, but I needed a place to stay."

Daisy caught the subtle twitch of his jaw, and his lips parted to speak. However, Jensen said nothing in the middle of turning onto Beverly Boulevard.

He cleared his throat once he completed the turn, zipping down the left-hand lane. "Let's see if the company can reimburse your stay."

"Jensen, it's fine. I can afford the room for a day or two since the pipes should be fixed by then. I needed extra clothes since the pipe burst at three in the morning, and I didn't grab any before being ushered out of my apartment."

"So *that's* why you took my credit card and me hostage."

"That, and they were having some killer sales today. Don't sweat the bill too hard, Mr. Moneybags."

Jensen chuckled beside her. He maneuvered them through the streets until the intersection approached. Off to their left, Obelisk towered over the nearby buildings. Its name suited the hotel due to the obsidian-tinted glass lining the side of the building, catching the light to shine.

The two entered the parking lot, picking a guest spot close to the entrance. Jensen and Daisy turned simultaneously and froze, both leaning toward the backseat.

"I'll get the bags. That's still my job," Jensen remarked while he cut the ignition. Before Daisy could protest, he scooped up the bags into his arms. Jensen stacked many smaller ones into the larger bags, cutting down the sheer volume of things to carry.

"I won't tell you no." Daisy climbed from his gorgeous convertible, slinking around the back with Jensen falling into step with her. The jostling of the shopping bags stacked on Jensen's arms announced their presence, encouraging people to clear their path.

The two skirted past the front desk of the opulent lobby—decked out with looming pillars and golden chandeliers strung overhead—for the elevators. For an accommodation made on such short notice, the Obelisk Hotel promised its guests luxury. Daisy participated in many of its renovations last year.

Daisy caught an empty elevator before the doors shut, dragging Jensen inside before anyone else could join them. As the doors rolled closed for the fifteenth floor, she turned to Jensen.

After the lunch hour, his hair sported that perfectly wind-tousled messiness that would drive a girl crazy. He lost the tie at the office, leaving his shirt with the top two buttons undone for a peek of his toned chest.

"You're kind of good at this personal assistant gig," Daisy complimented, catching Jensen's eye. The two had chosen to stand beside one another instead of their usual lean against opposite walls. "I almost want to reward you."

"Oh yeah? How exactly would you do that?" The rasp from earlier returned, turning Jensen's voice heavy with innuendo. The elevator walls felt much closer than Daisy remembered.

"That depends. Are you interested?" Daisy questioned, playing coy. She reached out, brushing her finger down the lapel of his suit, right along the edge of touching his exposed chest.

Jensen's eyes focused on her finger until she stopped alongside the fastened button. Then, his eyes wandered back up and settled on her lips. *Looks like she got her answer.*

Jensen's arms opened wider, and Daisy yanked him into a kiss. Her hands cupped the sides of his face while their mouths moved in perfect sync.

After a week of avoidance and small talk, their bodies decided to speak instead.

The elevator chimed before the doors opened, but Daisy and Jensen continued to kiss while stumbling out of the carriage. Daisy reached into one of the bags—her purse—and pulled out a small white card.

Her hotel room key.

"Come on." Daisy dragged Jensen down the hall. He followed without hesitation as they raced to the end of the hallway, and she let them into her room, moving frantically.

The two abandoned the shopping bags and all decorum at the door when it clicked shut. Jensen's mouth crashed back to Daisy's, ravenously tugging her lower lip between his teeth. *Oh fuck.*

Daisy threaded her hands into his hair, pulling him further into her room. She opted for a solo room with a king-sized bed, but it worked for her. The two maneuvered through the cozy room to the foot of the bed.

Between kisses, frenzied hands tugged at clothes. Layers were shed quickly, flung to the side with little remorse from either party. The slight chill from the running air conditioner spread goosebumps over Daisy's skin, exposed with every layer of clothing Jensen eased off her body.

Despite his rush, he never went too hard or rough. His touch treated her with utter worship, but his mouth promised a world of debauchery awaiting her.

"Still bossing me around, or can I make a request?" Jensen asked. His mouth skimmed the column of her neck, pressing hot breath against her as he sucked a mark right above her pulse.

"I'm open to suggestions." Daisy's hands fumbled with Jensen's belt blindly, hearing the clatter after a few tries. Her fingers moved into the button and zipper close to the end. The last piece of clothing between them kept her busy, flustered with each fumble.

"I'd been thinking about our time at the Ridge," Jensen panted while his roving hands slid over her naked breasts, but he didn't stop there. He grabbed at her hips and slid his thumbs down the hipbone. "I think about it while I work, when I'm at home, and when I try to sleep... I dream about how I never got you to sit on my face."

His words sent a flare of heat like a supernova between Daisy's thighs. Jensen's knees knocked against the edge of the mattress, sending him crashing into the plush duvet with a nudge from Daisy.

Jensen scooted further onto the bed when Daisy joined him. She inched closer, crawling to him on her hands and knees, her hair curling around her face. Her hand slid up his thigh, raking her nails lightly to Jensen's heavier breaths.

"You should get comfortable, then. I'm about to make your dreams come true," Daisy whispered. Jensen slumped back into the duvet and pillows, letting her take over.

She straddled above his face, hovering with her thighs on either side of Jensen's head, one hand preemptively reaching for the headboard.

"Why the fuck are you hovering?" Jensen's arms snaked underneath her thighs. The next thing Daisy knew, he yanked her down to fully sit on his face. The flat of his tongue pressed hot and firm against her clit.

Daisy yelped, startled. She gripped the headboard with both hands when his hands grabbed her ass. His fingers squeezed hard and spread her open nice and wide, running his tongue along her pussy.

Jensen's eyes, which were the only part of his face visible, blinked slowly as a haze settled over them. His hands tightened their grip on her ass and moved her to ride his tongue.

Daisy moaned. Her hold on the headboard tightened while she rocked her hips to Jensen's rhythm. Hot spit swirled in with the dampness of her arousal, teased by Jensen sliding his tongue into her entrance.

As she rode Jensen's face, every flick of his tongue against her clit or the wrap of his mouth around her pussy elicited an incoherent plea from her lips. She begged him for pleasure. Each response was met by the sloppy sounds made by Jensen eating her out or his muffled praise whispered against her skin.

Still, Jensen's eyes stayed open despite the haze swirling around his irises. His pupils dilated so much that his blue eyes darkened to navy. His gaze locked onto Daisy, who couldn't hold her composure.

She panted and squirmed, wiggling her hips whenever his tongue slid just right against her clit. He lapped at her like a man deprived of water, and she became his oasis in the desert.

Spit and her slick smeared against her inner thighs from the messiness of Jensen's mouth. His eagerness turned the arousal gathering in her lower abdomen into an unignorable tension, drawing tighter with every caress of his tongue.

"Please don't stop—" Daisy's voice cracked, teeming with pleasure. Beneath her, Jensen winked and shook his head, tearing another moan from her lips. "Jensen!"

A hand dropped from the headboard so Daisy could rake her fingers through his hair. Grabbing a fistful, she angled Jensen's head and ground her hips down onto his tongue, lost in the pleasure of his mouth.

Daisy's fingers went from a grab to a light scraping against his scalp, watching Jensen's eyes flutter closed. He moaned, the sound muffled between her thighs, dropping one of his hands from her ass.

Daisy paused. Part of her braced for the palm of his hand to smack against her ass, shooting a small jolt of pleasure straight to her throbbing and sensitive clit. But Jensen's quiet moaning grew louder, followed by more sloppy sounds.

She glanced over her shoulder, finding Jensen's rogue hand wrapped around his cock. His length glistened with a pretty red flush, leaking tiny beads of pre-cum from neglect.

Jensen's hand rapidly bobbed up and down his cock, timed to the muffled moans cried into Daisy's pussy. His thighs shook as he jerked himself off and ate Daisy out at the same time.

Despite the tightness in her stomach growing heavier with every passing second, Daisy let go of the headboard. She leaned back a little and wrapped her free hand around Jensen's, matching the pace of his strokes.

She continued to grind her hips against his face, chasing the pleasure found on Jensen's tongue. Jensen's hand sped up its pace, but even in a race, it wouldn't beat his tongue to the climax.

Daisy screamed his name as a final stroke against her clit brought her orgasm crashing around her. She paused, feeling Jensen do the same. Her body quivered with finality and exhaustion, stalling out while Jensen cleaned her up with gentle strokes of his tongue.

His hands eased her off his face, but Daisy couldn't protest as he rolled them over. She lay on the bed with Jensen kneeling between her legs, looming over her.

Jensen's hand wrapped around his cock, slick and smeared with pre-cum, and gave himself a few quick strokes. He came with a groan of Daisy's name as a thick trail of cum splattered onto Daisy's stomach, breasts, and hips. Daisy took it all, laying on the rumpled sheets and panting.

"I know we said we'd play it by ear, but I missed the perks of this little arrangement," Jensen mumbled, also short of breath. He swallowed hard when his eyes sought hers.

"Me too. I think we should resume it, same rules and everything." Daisy dragged one of her fingers through Jensen's cum, bringing it to her lips. She licked the digit clean with a curl of her tongue and smiled, seeing his wide-eyed nod. "Give me ten for a shower, and we'll return to the office?"

Jensen slumped beside her on the bed. "Make it fifteen. I need to borrow some of the hot water."

"Deal. Also, you're off the hook for the personal assistant thing for the rest of the day. I'm feeling generous." Daisy laughed, stretching out across the sheets. She needed a good fuck and some clothes more than help with spreadsheets and emails.

Chapter 12
Jensen

"C'mon. Hurry up!" Jensen's throat tightened while he jabbed the button for the doors to close. The last rider vacated the elevator, turning the once-packed carriage into a ghost town.

The last thing he needed was to be late for his meeting, especially one called so suddenly before work hours.

Jensen lost the middle weeks of July amid paperwork in the post-retreat catch-up. His focus on the business filled every hour with emails, calls, and endless questions about the future of Hidden Oasis. Even when he left the office each day, he couldn't escape work unless he opened himself up to a much-needed distraction. His favorite one at the moment happened to be blonde with a penchant for bickering as foreplay.

Jensen's hands ran down the length of his shirt, pressing out any wrinkles his fingertips grazed. He had enough wits about him to smooth over his rough, slightly disheveled appearance.

He overslept that morning.

The tap of his foot impatiently counted each floor he passed without incident. Yet, Jensen held his breath, waiting for someone to get on the elevator and slow him down. With less than a minute until Kenneth expected him, his nerves shot through the roof.

What could be so urgent to call him in so abruptly? Something had to be wrong.

Jensen's luck hadn't run out yet, reaching his floor without further interruptions or stops. He sped through the doors before they fully opened, making a beeline to the conference room.

The conference room sat closest to the elevator, right before the start of the narrow hallway. Jensen vaguely recalled the reasoning being "increased productivity in the office composition." He suspected it was actually more out of convenience.

And its location was convenient for him today.

Jensen ducked into the conference room, greeted by an empty table and chairs undisturbed since the last department meeting. Relief replaced the dull headache stretched tight between his temples.

He earned himself an extra-large coffee for his suffering and an hour where he avoided calls like the plague.

Jensen leaned against the windows overlooking the Beverly Hills streets, arm propped against the glass with a perfect view of his watch. The slow ticking of the hands passed the stated meeting time from Kenneth, interrupted only when Jensen's eyes dropped to the morning traffic starting to gather below.

Sighing to himself, Jensen's eyes fought against his exhaustion. "The meeting couldn't be that important if Kenneth isn't on time. I'll give him five minutes."

The moment he mumbled those fateful words, the door swung open. Jensen snapped to attention as all exhaustion exited his body as if someone had injected caffeine directly into his veins.

Jensen cleared his throat, "Good morning, Kenneth... and gentleman." Mid-turn, Jensen noticed several pairs of footsteps shuffled into the room. He stared into the expectant faces of Kenneth and two more shareholders, known to all as the Clements Brothers.

No one knew their first names, not even Daisy, since the two brothers rarely spoke. At all. Jensen would never say it aloud, but the Clements gave him the creeps.

"Good. You're here." Kenneth hobbled forward. Despite the heat already brewing outside the office, he brought out his favorite brown suit—one in a worn taupe and made from the style of an era long forgotten. "We'll get started right away."

"Forgive me if I sound uninformed, but I don't know why I'm here. Your message was a little vague, Ken." Jensen tried to keep it light as Kenneth shuffled toward the chairs.

Instead of sitting down, Kenneth grasped the back of a chair and remained standing. His usually affable demeanor appeared in short supply, exchanged for a stern and hardened frown.

"We need to talk about the future of this company. The CEO race has me concerned."

"Shouldn't Daisy be here, then?"

"What?"

"If we're discussing an issue regarding the CEO position, shouldn't Daisy be here?"

Kenneth's eyes met Jensen's, and the anger within them knocked the breath out of him. In all the years Kenneth knew Jensen and his family, Jensen couldn't recall a single time where the old man raised his voice or demonstrated such ire.

Kenneth spat, "She's the problem we need to discuss, along with your failure to contain her."

"I'm sorry?" Jensen stepped forward, finding no glint of humor in the stony expressions between Kenneth and the Clements Brothers. With every second passing in the tense silence, the gathering felt less like a meeting among allies and more like an ambush. "Elaborate for me what exactly the problem is."

"This company will not continue to succeed if we allow that *girl* to win enough votes. You cannot lose your father's legacy because you held back." Kenneth waved his hand, but his casual venom weaseled under Jensen's skin.

"Don't you think you're being presumptuous? It's only been a month. Besides, I'm finding opportunities to bend backward for every shareholder I can. Between meetings, I'm writing emails and calling in favors for votes. I'm pulling my weight," Jensen snapped.

"That may not be good enough," Kenneth said. Those words zapped all of the fight from Jensen's body, stunning him into silence. The room dropped ten degrees when the heat once dominating the space rushed out the conference room door, fleeing from the scene.

"What are you not telling me?"

"At the start of the summer, you had a considerable lead over Daisy in the number of votes. The directors leaned toward your side with no questions. But some have begun to waver in their commitment to you, finding Daisy an actively better choice."

"Shit."

"You could've crushed her like a bug under your heel ages ago. Instead, she's made you weak," Kenneth remarked. Jensen's entire body went rigid. The coldness pressing down on his skin prickled like pins and needles. *There's no way Kenneth knew about him and Daisy.* "If you lose your lead, you lose this company to her. Will you fail your father so spectacularly?"

Jensen's jaw clenched, expression hardened. "Is this supposed to be my wake-up call?"

"I'm looking out for you. I have the Clements Brothers and others ready to crown you as the king, but new allegiances are forming daily. You may not be dating my granddaughter anymore, but I won't let your family lose their hard work and pride. I will do whatever I need to help you win." Kenneth reached over to clap his shoulder, but Jensen brushed him off.

"Then, what do I need to do?" Jensen asked.

"You need to take the kid gloves off. I'll handle convincing my fellow shareholders to do the right thing, but you can't fuck up again. Destroy Daisy Riggs," Kenneth said, interrupted by the chime from the elevator.

Jensen's eyes leaped past Kenneth as the elevator doors slid open. Out stepped Daisy, draped in a navy skirt suit that turned her hair into spun gold waves while her skin glowed, dewy smooth under the harsh fluorescent lights.

She walked forward, but her eyes caught Jensen's from across the room. He watched realization dawn on her with how the soft curve of her lips vanished into a scathing frown. Daisy marched closer in thunderous, echoing strides from the slam of her heels.

Kenneth turned around, clearing his throat. "That'll be all. We'll see ourselves out, but remember what I told you, Jensen."

He hobbled toward the Clements, who flanked the open doorway, and all three ran into Daisy hovering in the hall. She stepped back with enough space to let them out but not far enough for them to escape her scathing glare. Oh, she was *pissed*.

"Mr. Malone, what a surprise to see you here," Daisy greeted. The sweetness of her voice teetered along the edge of suffocating while she glared at him. "Same for you, Mr. Clements *and* Mr. Clements."

"Miss Riggs, a pleasure to see you," Kenneth replied. Unlike Daisy, however, Kenneth couldn't mask the annoyance in his tone; he addressed her like a pesky gnat buzzing around his head. The coolness of Daisy's gaze rolled past Kenneth to hold Jensen hostage.

Daisy allowed Kenneth and the Clements Brothers to pass, but her body intercepted Jensen's in the doorway. Jensen could've moved around her, but he sensed a fight brewing. The anger lingering in his mouth festered, ready to claw its way out.

Daisy crossed her arms, stepping forward to push Jensen back into the conference room. She hissed, voice barely above a whisper, "Call another shareholder meeting without me?"

In one question, Daisy lost the thin veneer of composure she wore for Kenneth and the Clements. Rage tainted her face red, but Jensen imagined his face looked the same.

"I didn't do anything. Kenneth called me to speak, not the other way around," Jensen snapped. After that morning's emotional whiplash, he needed an hour of solitude to calm the fuck down.

Yet Daisy loved to push his buttons.

"Do you honestly expect me to believe that?"

"It's the truth. Get off my back, Daisy!"

Daisy yanked the door closed, shutting them into the conference room. "Look me in the eyes and tell me what exactly you and Kenneth were conspiring about."

"Like you, Kagami, and Sandra? It's none of your business what I discuss with shareholders." Jensen shook his head. The woman before him hardly resembled the girl in his bed that morning. "If you miss meetings and information about work, that's not my fault. It's on you."

"I was wondering when the selfish jackass side of you went, but I see he's returned in full." Daisy's laugh sliced him open with its serrated sarcasm, turning on her heel. She reached for the door, pausing when Jensen stepped closer to her.

She bristled, scowling over her shoulder at him. Her eyes narrowed at him, probably matching his.

Jensen scoffed, "Fuck you."

"You already did today. And you've reached your quota for the week." Daisy shrugged him off before stalking out of the conference room. She stormed down the hallway toward their offices, leaving Jensen alone.

Jensen's shoulders slumped as the anger drained from his body, falling from that morning's highs. Guilt cropped up in the back of his mind, but Jensen waved its quiet musing away.

He could overthink about it later; he had work to do.

Ambient lighting and the polite dinner conversations of strangers accompanied Jensen's entry into the main dining room of Lumina, the trendiest new Mediterranean restaurant in the heart of Beverly Hills.

Fixing the collar of his turtleneck, Jensen considered himself a brand-new man compared to the one who woke up that morning.

Ever since meeting with Kenneth days ago, Jensen's life derailed off the right track. His focus on work fractured between the CEO position and his daily duties, further blurring the lines between working hours and his home life. He didn't have time for anyone or anything that wasn't work.

Stuck in desperation to win, Jensen had begun to drown until his dad swung by and ordered him to take the day off. They argued about it for a while, luckily hidden from prying eyes by lunch hour, but Jensen caved.

His dad smoothed everything over with the offer of dinner at Lumina after work.

Jensen's eyes roamed across the wooden tables, scattered Grecian-style columns, and walls painted cerulean blue and crisp white with murals of Santorini. His gaze jumped from table to table until he spotted his dad in the middle of the hubbub.

He weaved in between the tables of other diners, enjoying their Saturday. As he reached his dad, the brightening of his dad's smile hit him right in the chest. Somehow, his dad's good mood made everything else feel less important.

"Hey there, stranger." Harrison rose from his chair. He yanked Jensen into a hug, not letting him escape without a tight squeeze. "You clean up nicely, just like your old man."

"I hope that's a compliment," Jensen chuckled, accepting the firm slaps of his dad's hand along his back. Eventually, he noticed a third chair at the cozy table. "I didn't realize we had company tonight. I thought it was us two."

"She'll be here momentarily. She texted me right after you did." Harrison gestured for Jensen to take his seat, but the click of heels approaching stopped him in his tracks.

Jensen turned over his shoulder as his eyes landed on Daisy. She sighed, gaze buried in her mini purse. "So sorry I'm late. I had an extended phone call with Steelbird about some information regarding the Alpine—oh, Jensen."

Daisy's "oh, Jensen" rattled around in his brain, undeniably startled. He took it that she didn't know he'd be there either.

In the silence, Jensen examined her. She changed from that day's work attire—swapping her sensible suit for a curve-hugging black dress—and pinned her hair out of her face.

Jensen stepped away from his chair, pulling it out for her with a tip of his head.

"Evening, Daisy."

"Thank you." Daisy inched past him, but the full view of her back drew Jensen's eyes along the zipper stretching across the dress. Daisy had the zipper pulled down to the small of her back, essentially turning the dress backless. "I appreciate the dinner invite."

Holy fuck. The sight of Daisy's bare skin went straight to his head, bringing him to slump into the other chair like a fool.

Jensen clawed his thighs hard under the table when his dad chuckled, "Don't sweat it. I wanted to celebrate the two of you tonight for all the hard work you invested in Hidden Oasis. You two are my most dedicated workers, and I'm honored to be your boss... and your dad, Jensen."

"Harrison, I love you, but you're a sap." Daisy laughed to Jensen's left, forcing him to push past the lump in his throat after an eyeful of her back. *He needed to see it with his marks littered all over.*

Jensen coughed, raising his water glass. "She's right, Dad. You're a sap."

"I can't help it. Over the last decade or so, I've watched you two grow into two fine, extremely capable people. I'm proud of both of you." Harrison smiled, only breaking his focus on them when the waiter swung by to hand over the drink menu.

Jensen reached for his water, nursing it close to his chest like a cocktail. No alcohol tonight, not with him behind the wheel. "Tonight is purely celebratory, right?"

"Yes, at least until dessert. I have one small update about CEO stuff, but that can wait. You two deserve one night that's not about business; I don't think either of you know the definition of 'time off,'" Harrison said.

Instantly, Jensen perked up... and so did Daisy. *Big mistake.*

Daisy reached for her place setting. "I don't know about Jensen, but I'd prefer to have the information upfront. It'll keep me from worrying." She pursed her lips, smudging her shimmery dark berry lip gloss.

Jensen almost missed the red.

Daisy and Harrison's eyes flitted over to Jensen, awaiting his response. So, he, trying to be fearless, nodded until the words decided to work.

"I can handle it, Dad. Tell us," Jensen promised, forcing himself to look ahead. Although his dad might know if he lied, Daisy would sniff out his fear better than any feral wolf.

Harrison sighed. "Very well. Some directors voiced their thoughts about needing more information to help their decision. After some counsel, I've decided to implement a small task for you two. You'll create a policy proposal for the Board to hypothetically vote on if you become CEO and present it to the company."

If Jensen were honest, he expected worse news. Still, the added layer of a policy proposal and the thought of the entire company judging his ideas cemented the concept of "being CEO" a little more.

His eyes darted toward Daisy. The unshakeable calmness on her face never betrayed her thoughts, yet her eyes screamed her inner monologue through a megaphone.

She looked either pleased or unsurprised, meaning someone told her about the proposal before his dad had. *That's how she stayed ahead; a spy was feeding her information.*

Jensen watched her politely nod and grin, sparkling like a diamond under the light. "I'm down for the challenge. One moment, I need to take a call."

Daisy flashed her screen to the table, not long enough for Jensen to see the caller ID, before she rose. She elegantly dodged between diners in a hurried jog across the room.

Once she ducked into the hallway with 'restrooms' painted over the archway, Jensen lounged back in his chair. He leaned forward, winking at his dad. "Any suggestions on what I should do?"

"Nice try. I'm not playing favorites in this one either." His dad shook his head, smile holding firm despite his fatherly chiding.

"She won't know!"

"But you won't feel like you've won it. I know you, Jensen. You want people to take you seriously without using our family's reputation as a crutch. The idea will be more authentic from you and your desire to do right by the company."

"Why do you have to be so wise or whatever?" Jensen sighed, prompting good-natured laughter from across the table.

"It comes in the parenting manual," his dad remarked between sips of water. "You'll understand if you choose to become a dad one day."

Jensen's eyes wandered toward the bathrooms, counting the time since Daisy left the room before making his getaway. He cleared his throat, "I'll be right back. Need the bathroom."

Jensen excused himself from the table without waiting for permission, too old for that. He sped through the packed dining room with quick pardons thrown out at each opportunity.

On the hunt for Daisy, he ambled into the hallway, darker than Lumina's main room. It didn't take long to find her leaning against the wall with her phone in hand.

She glanced up, brows arched. "Looking for me?"

"You know I am." Jensen's hands pushed up the sleeves of his turtleneck while sidling closer to Daisy. "Who told you about the policy proposal?"

"You're not the only one who gets allies, Jensen. Don't take it so personally that I'm playing your game. I never took you for a hypocrite," Daisy replied coolly, stepping closer to him.

"I'm not a hypocrite."

"Could've fooled me. First, it was Delaney, and now Kenneth? The Malone family has you under their thumb. How often have you and he conspired to keep me out of the loop?"

"None. Every time I knew of something that I thought you should know, I said so. You failing to come isn't on me."

Daisy said nothing, leaving the two to stare one another down, chest-to-chest. She raked her eyes down his face, shaking her head.

Jensen's jaw tensed. "You're holding back. What is it?"

"I'm—nothing—" Daisy sighed, a heavy and tired echo falling from her lips. Jensen leaned forward, but she moved back. "I'm not in a fighting mood. Not tonight and not with you."

"Why not? You love fighting with me and sticking it to the man." Jensen cocked his head, inching forward with every step Daisy took back. She would move first, whereas he followed, driven to match her.

Daisy's back eventually bumped into the wall, and Jensen stood in front of her, gazing into her whiskey eyes. The tension still crackled with its electricity, but not with an angry tongue. Instead, it whispered a quiet seduction.

They were alone, heated after a quick and snappy exchange, so prone to the temptations best shared in the dark.

"I should be angry at you right now since we're back to competing, but you bought my chair," Daisy whispered, not breaking eye contact.

Jensen froze. His heartbeat quickened in his ears, thundering away in a nervous frenzy. He swallowed. "I don't know what you're talking about—"

"Cut the crap. I left around lunchtime with that shitty old chair I kept pushing down my list of priorities and returned to a brand new one with a massage voucher to Oceanview. There was no one else who knew *but* you."

"Okay, so what if I did it?"

"You did do it, and I want to thank you," Daisy said.

Jensen's hand reached out, tipping her chin back to stare right into her eyes. "Well, I should be mad at you, but you wore this dress tonight."

The words curled off his lips as dark and hushed as smoke, filling the space of the hallway with their big promises. Unspoken tension needled at the tiny gap between his and Daisy's mouths until Jensen's thoughts imagined smearing her lip gloss against his neck.

Neither moved as the quiet shuffle of footsteps preceded an older woman entering the hallway. Jensen backed away from Daisy as he turned his face away from her, too embarrassed to look.

He should head back before he lost his damn mind... if he hadn't already. Kenneth saw weakness in him when Daisy got involved. Maybe he was right; Daisy Riggs had him bent around her finger, compromising every instinct in him determined to win.

Chapter 13
Daisy

Nothing screamed "fun weekend plans" like drowning in paperwork, yet Daisy dove headfirst into the papers scattered across her mom's dining room table.

Her fingers sifted through the stacks while 90s pop blared into her thick headphones. Alanis Morissette's woes and Mariah Carey's love songs became the perfect soundtrack for her evening.

In her peripheral, Daisy caught the occasional flash of the television. She came over to spend time with her family since her free time remained in short supply. Mom and Dex always understood, though.

Dinner the other night with Jensen and Harrison put her straight into work mode, even with a vague deadline attached to the policy proposal. Daisy couldn't afford to waste a moment—her proposal *needed* to be perfect for when she chose to launch it. She wasn't the type to loiter around when she had the chance to strike.

Daisy pulled every piece of information relevant to her inquiry. She gathered the corporate bylaws in print form, the articles of incorporation of Hidden Oasis, current policies on the books, retired proposals phased out over time, and proposals that met a grisly demise during the annual shareholder meeting. Within those papers and files, Daisy should find her answer.

It wasn't the first time she made suggestions to the higher-ups, but it would be the first one where those stubborn old men had to hear her out. Daisy had petitioned the Board for policy changes more times than she could count.

Despite a dull thud pulsing against her temples, Daisy committed to the work instead of the more fun suggestion of watching a cheesy action movie with her family. She followed the different thoughts, unspooling them further while doing research.

Daisy's gaze wandered away from her open laptop and the different papers. It landed at the end of the table where a dark box with blocky handwriting on its label sat. That was her secret weapon.

After some pleading, bargaining, and stellar persuasion, Daisy obtained last year's exit interviews and corporate culture surveys. For smuggling the files out of HR, she owed Iris a box of gourmet chocolates and her favorite bottle of white wine. With input from former and current employees, Daisy would create a policy to keep the workforce happy and incentivize newcomers to join.

As a young CEO, she would solve the high turnover of the under-twenty-five demographic and look so hot while doing it. She represented the employees and the shareholders, not just the latter.

So focused on her work, Daisy nearly jumped out of her skin at a tap against her shoulder. She pushed her headphones off one ear, turning to find Dex.

"Hey." Daisy slid her headphones off, ignoring the music continuing to play. "How's my favorite guy doing?"

From the day he was born fifteen years ago, Dexter Riggs changed Daisy's world for the better. Daisy watched as her brother grew from the adorable, red-nosed cornball who liked frogs more than anything else and who hid from his shadow into the brilliant young man he was now.

He stood tall for his age, around six feet even. With his shaggy blond hair he let grow out, Daisy always swore he looked like a palm tree turned human. His lanky frame made him a natural for sports, but he spent lunch hours in his school's science labs to help tutor his classmates.

Dex managed a tired smile as he draped himself over her and looped his arms around her waist. "M'sleepy. Wanted to tell you goodnight before I left."

"Okay. Promise me you'll have a great day at school tomorrow."

"I'll try. I have a chemistry test during second period and Academic Decathlon practice after school."

Daisy squeezed her brother in a tight hug, careful not to accidentally hit his glucose monitor while pulling him closer. She kissed his forehead, feeling his brows scrunch. "Alright. Love you, bub. Sleep well."

Dex mumbled his 'I love you' back and shuffled toward the other room, backlit by the flashes from the television. With her mom's salary and all the extra cash Daisy chipped in, they managed to afford a modest, two-bedroom apartment in Los Angeles and tuition for Dex's private school. It was because of her hard work that her family pulled themselves up in the world.

He'd never go without, not on Daisy's watch. She would provide and never needed to rely on people who turned their backs on her. *They struggled enough.*

A nearby chair creaked, and Daisy noticed her mom holding a steaming mug. A tea bag hung over the pink ceramic rim, smelling like warm honey and earthiness.

"Thank you," Daisy gasped, filled with warmth when the mug touched her palms. Heat radiated through the ceramic to stretch past her fingers. "I shouldn't have another coffee, or I'll be up all night."

"Tea won't stop you. All-nighters have always been your thing, especially when you're determined to finish a project." Beyond the few streaks of gray scattered through her hair and dark bags underneath her brown eyes, Belinda Benton was Daisy's clone.

If someone were to ask Daisy who she looked up to most in the world, her mom would be her immediate answer. No competition. Yes, she adored Harrison and her other mentors, but she defended her mom's honor with every breath. Her mom modeled the kind of woman she aspired to be.

Daisy shrugged. "I'm not steamrolling through this one, so I might need a couple of days to mull it over."

"Want to talk it through?"

"And bore you with corporate nonsense and legalese? I'll pass."

"I appreciate the thought, but I can handle a few big words," her mom teased while grabbing one of the pages off the table. An almost mischievous twinkle in her eye elicited a smile from Daisy, one that hadn't been seen for the last forty-eight hours.

"Alright. It's for that promotion... the CEO one," said Daisy. Her legs bounced underneath the table, suddenly at a loss for words. "The directors want me to create an original policy proposal and present it to show that we're capable of innovating ideas. I'm scouring for some inspiration."

"I see. Sounds like you've got a solid plan figured out, my shining star." Her mom nodded, scanning her with that thoughtful look.

"The plan's set. If inspiration would like to show up, I'd appreciate it." Daisy set the mug somewhere safe after a sip, hit by the strong taste of peppermint and honey.

"I might not be a corporate genius, but I'm not worried about your success. You're the hardest worker in that company, and you always have a knack for figuring out what works best for everyone," her mom mused, brushing Daisy's hair off of her face.

"If only it was as easy as being a hard worker," Daisy mumbled but softened her approach at the slightest change in her mom's expression. "We've been through tougher situations, so I'm not worried."

"Of course not. You grew up far faster than you deserved, blossoming into the fierce, intelligent woman I see. I only wish I could've—"

"I don't blame you for the past, Mom. I get up every day and work to keep you proud of me."

"And I will be proud of you as long as you're honest and continue to fight for those who can't defend themselves. You, Daisy girl, are the future... and what a beautiful future it is," her mom whispered.

The moment ended with the abrupt buzzing of Daisy's phone, which she forgot to switch into silence for the night. Her screen lit up, and she peered at the notification. *Jensen texted her.*

Daisy closed the screen with a click of the button, tempted to see what Jensen needed so late in the evening. But she turned, seeing her mom's curious expression. Oh, she definitely saw Jensen's name.

"Who's that?" her mom asked.

Daisy smiled, but the look probably didn't meet her eyes. "A coworker. They can wait until the morning." *Work rival turned frequent hook-up* would be more accurate, but her mom didn't need to know that Daisy cruised in the casual lane like her life depended on it. If she so much as mentioned "not the dating type," her mom might smother her... lovingly, of course.

"Ah, Mondays." Her mom let the conversation go without much fuss, shrouding Daisy in her optimism. "Any chance I can convince you to stay?"

"I'd love to, but I need to be at the office early for some meetings. I'll take you and Dex out to dinner tomorrow, celebrate the chemistry test or something silly," Daisy murmured, leaning in for her mom's cheek kiss.

She listened to the creak of her mom's chair as she stood up, eyes firm on the files. She knew the answer was somewhere in there.

Stifling a yawn behind her hand, Daisy entered the Hidden Oasis headquarters feeling like death. The August morning let up on the heat sitting over the Los Angeles area for several weeks, yet Daisy couldn't sweat out the feverish warmth stuck under her skin.

Time slipped through her fingers while Daisy spent every break between working hours and well into the evening researching. July became August in the blink of an eye, but she intended to use every moment to her advantage. No matter how long she took, her proposal would be perfect.

That morning, however, Daisy wasn't at her best. The last time she remembered sleeping for more than twenty minutes was two days ago. She ran strictly on adrenaline, but the concerning amounts of coffee she consumed helped.

Daisy's strides across the lobby quickened after the tentative sip of her third coffee that morning. The taste of black coffee left her with a side of the jitters, twitching every so often.

She should have taken the day off to rest and recover after typing the final period on her policy proposal, but the thought of Jensen beating her to the podium forced her to hit the ground running, sleep-deprived and all.

Daisy juggled her coffee, the pressed leather portfolio with her prepared remarks, and headphones. While driving into the office, she blasted her guilty pleasure playlist—hits from the infamous boy bands of the '90s.

Slipping her headphones on while she shotgunned her coffee, Daisy fell into the energizing synth. The fog over her thoughts faded when she cranked up the volume. After her announcement, she'd take a power nap in a file closet or her office and consider it another successful day.

The chair Jensen bought her was as soft as a cloud. She should thank him again, but work had kept them apart.

Daisy jogged up to the elevator, pressing the up button until her ride arrived. She stepped inside, ready to head to what the employees colloquially called "The Ballroom."

With plush emerald rugs over ivory marble floors and spacious, high walls, The Ballroom hosted any important mixers not suited for the lobby or when an outside venue couldn't be secured on short notice.

The doors began to close, preparing to take her to her make-or-break moment on the fifth floor. Yet, a hand catching the elevator pushed the doors open, revealing Easton in a disheveled state.

He slid into the carriage without making eye contact with Daisy, jamming the close button until he sealed them away from the world.

Daisy's eyes flicked over him, taken by the unkempt rumples in his suit. She imagined if she leaned in close enough, the pungent odor of stale beer might waft off him. He seemingly forgot how to shave from the weeks' worth of stubble lining his jaw, and the dark hickeys littering his neck peeked out from the uneven collar of his shirt.

The sour twist of his lips and rigid posture betrayed the appearance of a man escaping from a quickie with his life. The image pulled a laugh out of her, loud enough to eclipse her music.

Once the first laugh fell, the rest came flooding out of her to the irritated twitch of Easton's jaw. Daisy tried to stop herself, but being sleep deprived and a deliciously vindictive bitch kept her cackling.

Her head rolled back enough for her headphones to slide off, catching around her neck. She reached to fix them, but the cackles soon turned into wheezing.

"Shut up," Easton snapped. "What's so funny over there?"

"Oh, nothing. How's sleeping on the couch been for your poor back? Did Delaney banish you there after you made her mad?"

Daisy asked, but the mocking tone elicited a hiss from Easton. Busted.

"You don't know what you're talking about."

"I don't? So, you haven't fallen back into your awful habit of being charming for a few days, starting a fight with your girl where she puts you on time out, and then crawling back when you get horny again? Answer carefully. I tolerated your bullshit once upon a time."

Easton's face paled, admitting everything without a word. He bared his teeth into a sneer. "You're a bitch."

"Don't I know it," Daisy replied, nowhere near bothered. If she had a nickel for every time a man called her a bitch, she'd retire tomorrow; he'd need to get more creative than elementary playground insults. "Grass isn't greener on the other side, right?" she said with as much smugness as she could muster so early in the morning. Daisy was running purely on spite, bitchiness, and a splash of coffee.

"And you're still fucking bitter." Easton's retort flew off his tongue like a shot, matched by the malice in his eyes. He loathed her, but Daisy hoped he liked her loathing in return.

"I have every right to be. You cheated on me with the girl and are pretending this relationship will last more than a few months. Besides, I'm not bitter. I've recently picked up a new bed warmer, and I love it." Daisy observed the swift jolt of shock kicking Easton straight in the chest from how fast he wrangled his expression into stillness.

"Who? Who is it?"

"None of your business."

"Stop playing with me right now—"

"No games. But I hope you enjoy the highs and lows with your new girl when you start missing me. I'm better off without your lack of ambition and otherwise unremarkable presence dragging me down."

The elevator doors chimed before opening. Daisy took her cue to leave, strutting out of the elevator and through the narrow space between her and The Ballroom.

Smiling politely to coworkers she recognized, Daisy entered the double doors to The Ballroom. Rows of chairs were occupied by a sea of faces—general staff, executive officers, the Board of Directors, and various shareholders—waiting for her address. She had the proposal done but needed to stick the landing by nailing the speech.

Everyone faced the stage, where Harrison fiddled with the microphone attached to the podium. The poor woman from the IT department assigned to that day's announcement looked frazzled while she adjusted the microphone's cable, tapping it to gauge the sound.

Daisy climbed the stage while some stragglers rushed to take their seats. Her eyes jumped between the people whose gazes held hers briefly, ending up squarely on Jensen in the front row.

Under her gaze, he sat taller in his chair, but his arms crossed over his chest. Ripples formed in the fabric of his navy turtleneck, drawing Daisy's eyes down his chest. *No intimidation? He was going soft on her.*

"Can everyone hear me?" Harrison's voice boomed throughout the room, preceded by sharp feedback from the microphone. A few murmurs of assent rose up from the crowd. Harrison flashed a thumbs-up, beaming. "Great! Thank you all for being here and waiting patiently. Would you join me in warmly welcoming Daisy Riggs, Vice President of Project Development, for her policy proposal?"

Applause filled the room with the resounding echo when Daisy stepped forward, trading places with Harrison after a handshake.

Daisy set down her coffee and tucked her other items in the hollow podium. She brushed the frontmost strands of hair away from her face, taking a moment to breathe. Since her confrontation with Easton in the elevator, her heart began to skip every other beat. *That could also be the caffeine.*

"Good morning, everyone. Thank you for coming," Daisy spoke into the microphone, wincing at the distorted echo of her words. "Normally, we'd have an itinerary of what to expect, detailing when to snooze or shop online. But in the interest of going paperless, I emailed the thirty-six-page policy proposal I will be covering this morning."

Several laughs erupted from the crowd as people grabbed their laptops, tablets, or phones. While going paperless was a noble goal, people's eyes on their devices meant less of them on her—a win for everyone involved.

Daisy cleared her throat and opened her portfolio. "We at Hidden Oasis pride ourselves on being a welcoming and adapting work environment for all our employees. However, there's been a significant issue in worker turnover rates among the under twenty-five crowd. After research, I've determined a significant issue to be conflicts with college education, which is why I am here to propose a comprehensive reshaping of our current scholarship program."

She paused, letting the audience ponder over her words. "Currently, we fund one to two scholarships annually for a local student who applies to our program. A better use of the program would be to redirect that energy toward pre-existing workers to help cover a significant portion of their studies, plus a stipend for travel expenses. Additionally, the program would develop a part-time work program to have more hands-on and viable promotional tracks for these workers if they commit full-time after graduation. Everyone deserves access to quality education, and our workers shouldn't be forced to pick between this company and developing themselves. Thank you."

Applause took over the room again, but some faces of the crowd brightened with enthusiasm. Daisy's colleagues rose from their chairs, joining the standing ovation, comprised of the executive officers and general members of the office. Many directors and shareholders in attendance followed their lead.

Daisy smiled. In those pleased faces, a shining glimmer of loyalty rose out of the crowd. She had a fair chance to win in December's election, so she should double her efforts. Whatever she needed to do, it would be done.

Daisy dismounted from the stage with her arms full. She beelined for her coworkers, who chose the front two rows for their seats, as the audience stood up. Everyone else would head to their daily duties as the Hidden Oasis offices opened for business.

"Daisy, you are a genius!" Iris gushed, reaching over to shake her shoulders.

Daisy laughed, shaking her off. "I've been one of the lucky few whose education was assisted by the company. It's only right to pay it forward."

"That's noble of you. I don't know how many people would do the same in your position," Nelson said, eliciting nods from Miranda and Holden.

"Like I said, it's the right thing to do." Daisy tucked the portfolio into her chest, still hearing the faint music from her headphones. She forgot about those.

The moment died a little when Easton scoffed, breaking the silence before Jensen did. "You can't be serious. Are you trying to tank the company with your bleeding-heart bullshit?"

"Easton, dude... stop." Holden cleared his throat while wary eyes glanced at the others. None looked pleased with his comment, but everyone else held their tongues.

Daisy planned to say something back, equally bitchy as her commentary in the elevator, but Jensen beat her to the punch. "You might work in the finances department, but you aren't the only expert on fiscal responsibility. If you read Daisy's proposal, she details the allocation of funds. I read a quarter of it, but it's a great plan."

Those words slammed into Daisy like a freight train, left utterly speechless. After that, no one added their two cents, treating Jensen's word as the final one.

Easton stalked away from the group, taking his second unsuccessful confrontation with Daisy in a pissy mood. With him, the others faded away with their incoherent excuses. Daisy didn't hear a single one, too focused on Jensen.

Jensen reached into his briefcase, pulling out an unopened plastic water bottle. He handed it to her. "I meant it. Your proposal was great."

"Thanks. I appreciate that. And how you dealt with Easton." Daisy attempted the awkward shuffle of the items in her arms. Jensen leaned over, plucking the portfolio and her coffee from her arms before she dropped them.

Jensen hummed. "I'll admit, I didn't know you were such a softie."

"Oh please," Daisy scoffed, fidgeting with the water until the lid cracked open. She met Jensen's eyes while she brought the water to her lips. "There's a lot you don't know about me."

Chapter 14
Jensen

The splash of sunrise stretched across the skies, becoming a painted backdrop to the darkened skyscrapers and palm trees. Mid-sip of his coffee, Jensen admired the still-sleeping city, softened without the rush of morning traffic.

Jensen would never be at work before seven on a given day, but sleeplessness pushed him out of bed in search of a distraction. He hit the gym for some cardio and weights, showered, and made breakfast with too much time left to waste at home.

So, he headed into the office, beating the rush hour traffic.

Jensen walked past the conference room, leaving the August sunrise behind for his office. His reflection rippled across the darkened glass, contrasted against the sickly glow from the fluorescent lights, all loose, damp hair and a crisp woolen suit.

His body ached from that morning's run, but he yearned for the peaceful hush over his thoughts while his feet hit the speeding treadmill. Air conditioning and cable news had occupied him, leaving the countdown between him and December at the gym doors.

As he reached his office, the sight of Daisy's office stopped him in his tracks. When Jensen went to make his coffee and watch the sunrise, he was alone on the floor. But now, Daisy sat behind her office desk, basking in the subtle light.

Wearing her favorite pair of headphones, Daisy swayed in her chair to whatever she listened to. Jensen always pegged her as an indie girl or classic rock based on how his dad recounted their conversations about beloved rock bands.

Her sandy blonde waves framed her face while she typed away at her laptop, intensely focused on her screen. She hadn't spotted Jensen staring at her, so he turned into his office, intending to keep it that way.

Jensen settled behind his desk, cluttered with paperwork and his laptop. In his restlessness, he shafted some of his big-picture assignments while trying to brainstorm his policy proposal. Unlike Daisy, who had around thirty pages of the right answer, nothing came to Jensen.

He considered soliciting the opinions of trusted colleagues. However, no one seemed willing to disclose what they hated about work to the boss's son. Therefore, Jensen was on his own, barely treading water.

Jensen's eyes jumped up at the movement, seeing Daisy rising from her desk. His gaze dropped down her flowy cream blouse, tucked into the waistband of pressed navy slacks. When she bent over for a pen on the floor, the pants molded around her perky ass and soft hips like a second pair of skin.

"Oh, Christ," Jensen whispered, head slumping back into the padded chair. His eyes squeezed shut, gripping the edge of the desk and breathing hard through his nose. Popping a boner from one look at Daisy in tight pants wouldn't be his proudest moment.

He needed to stop acting like a horny teenager who'd never seen a pretty girl before. Have some decorum.

Jensen cracked open an eye, daring to search for Daisy. Luckily, he witnessed her gorgeous ass striding toward the break room. His eyes trailed her until she vanished from his angle, able to breathe with her out of view.

Ever since returning from the retreat, neither of them managed to stay away. What should've become a momentary distraction spiraled into a full-fledged affair behind the scenes.

Their sharp-tongued exchanges in the break room turned into heated make-outs in the back of Jensen's convertible. Daisy's scoffs and snide remarks became moans of his name and pleading for more while her nails raked down his back.

She had him hooked on her.

Despite the flush under his collar, Jensen scooted closer to his desk, already behind on his work. He opened his email and checklist for the week; with enough focus, he could finish all his assignments and then fling himself back into his relatively unsuccessful policy proposal.

Fingers raced over the keys faster than he'd thought possible, churning emails and setting up investor meetings. Under Daisy's supervision, the Alpine project began to garner some buzz among their loyal investors, and as a result, the questions came rolling to his desk.

"Who knew ski chalets would be such a hit? Usually, the old guys like the tropics for the golf and sun," Jensen clicked his tongue while sifting through all the unread emails from his inbox. Before his eyes, his list of priorities sorted itself out, making the day a little easier to swallow.

Midway through his tenth email, the door to his office creaked open. Jensen didn't look up from the computer while finishing his sentence. "Our meeting isn't for several hours, so I assume it's urgent."

He and Daisy stumbled into using codewords for their little encounters. Neither ventured too far out of the box when choosing "meeting" as their signal for a quick rendezvous.

No one suspected anything when he or Daisy uttered the word aloud, not while in the office's four walls.

At the silence, Jensen's eyes lifted from his computer screen while sending his last email. However, the sight of Delaney standing there, wearing oversized clothes belonging to a man, paralyzed him.

Immediate questions of why she was there and how she got into the offices bounced around his head with such velocity. Delaney's eyes stared at him expectantly, arms folded over her chest like she had any right to be upset.

During their entire relationship, Delaney never came to the office before a certain hour. She always cited her disdain for leaving bed before nine AM, but it only took several months with Easton to change that habit.

"Who did you think I was?" Delaney asked.

"You're not welcome here," Jensen sighed, finding it too early for a fight, even if it was Delaney. For weeks, he managed to avoid thoughts of her, finally appearing like his life got back on track. He found better people to keep his mind occupied. "You're lucky Daisy hasn't seen you yet. I'm sure she's still itching to give you an earful."

Delaney's face contorted, twisting her normally doe-like eyes into a cutting glare. She leaned forward, fists pressed into his desk. "Didn't realize you and Daisy were close these days."

"What can I say? She and I realized we had plenty in common. We both love the company and want to be CEO, among other things," Jensen remarked, hoping he sounded half as harsh as Delaney did.

Delaney's eyes widened for a split second, regaining her coldness. "That's low."

"Yeah, I don't care. Why are you here?" Jensen closed his laptop, folding his hands on top of the computer. He watched his ex-girlfriend fidget with the pockets of her borrowed clothes, hanging off her frame like a child playing dress-up.

"I let myself in. I borrowed Easton's card," Delaney admitted. All Hidden Oasis members received a key card to swipe in during off-hours, having access to all entrances and exits. "I came because you've been avoiding me."

"Gee, I wonder why."

"I get it. You hate me. But I have some information you need to hear. It's about Daisy, and it'll make you think twice about becoming friendly with her."

"You have two minutes. So, keep this brief. If you step over the line once, you're done."

Jensen flashed his watch to Delaney, tapping its face. The moment he suspected her of wasting his time, his last shred of grace would be walking into the elevator.

Delaney sighed, "Easton and I had been talking about Daisy last night. He had been ranting about her proposal, whatever that meant, and about how she didn't deserve her position in the company. He told me that, while they were together, Daisy got super drunk one night at his place and confessed that she'd been arrested before. Jensen, she has a juvenile record—"

Jensen's breath hitched in his throat, but denial flashed through his head. There was no way Delaney's allegations were true. "Alright, that's enough. You're done."

"I'm telling the truth! That girl is a criminal! A fraud!" Delaney pointed accusingly at Daisy's empty office.

"Which you're basing on the word of her asshole ex-boyfriend. That's hardly convincing," Jensen hissed, watching Delaney shrink back from him. His voice raised, words spewing past his lips too fast to stop, "I know Daisy. The company wouldn't have hired her if that were true."

"How well do you know Daisy outside of the front she puts on at work? I remember all your venting sessions about her. I haven't forgotten the space she took in our relationship," Delaney said, breaking Jensen's patience.

"Get out."

"Fine. But I warned you. If Daisy wins, you'll be upset you didn't stop her by whatever means possible. I know my grandpa warned you about this."

Delaney stormed out of his office, striding down the hallway toward the elevator. Jensen braced for the sounds of a scuffle if she and Daisy ran into one another, but the quiet call of the elevator filled the silence.

He slumped into his chair, head buried into his hands. In the heat of the moment, Jensen rushed to Daisy's defense. But, when confronted by the silence, he wondered.

What *did* he know about Daisy?

Jensen fumbled for his office phone. He punched in Iris' personal line, knowing she wasn't in yet. He'd leave a message because Iris owed him a *huge* favor, one he planned to collect.

He cradled the phone to his ear, whispering after the answering machine message, "Iris, it's Jensen. Call me back as soon as you get this message. It's an emergency."

Jensen spent the workday pacing around his office in between meetings, calls, and answering emails. Close to twelve hours passed between him leaving the message on Iris' machine, but he caught her earlier in the day.

At first, Iris balked at his suggestion. His request—pulling Daisy's original job application and requisite background check—went against company policy. He gambled with both of their jobs simply by asking.

However, the nagging worry about what Delaney said ate away at him all day.

Jensen saw two outcomes for him, both win-win if played right. If Delaney and Easton were correct, he stumbled upon the best possible ammunition to secure his future. If they were lying, then Daisy's file should prove her innocence. The truth would fix everything.

Jensen pushed away from his desk to pace some more. He half-expected to find scorched impressions in the shape of his boots burned into the floor. God, he'd never been so knocked off-kilter when seeing Daisy before.

She haunted him, staring at him with a confused look to stir the faint twinge of guilt lingering in his chest. When he acknowledged its presence, it grew. If he ignored it, the sensation ate away at his resistance.

He needed answers, but at what cost?

Darkened offices filled the hallway outside his door, emptied hours before when the workday ended. Jensen stayed behind, waiting for the call to come at any moment. He couldn't imagine finding sleep without knowing, tossing and turning in his bed instead of pacing.

The shrill ring of the office phone interrupted his thoughts. Jensen nearly sailed over the desk, answering the phone with it gripped tight in hand. "Hello?"

"Jensen," Iris greeted, but her voice rattled over one word. "There's something you need to see. I don't want to take these files out of HR. What's your personal fax?"

"+424-85-0034." Jensen spun around, squinting hard to recite the numbers printed on the side of his fax machine. He rarely used it, leaving it to gather dust in his office. "Maybe I should come to you."

"No. I'll delete the fax. You can shred the papers when you're done," Iris remarked, voice still shaky as papers began to slide out of the fax machine. "Have they shown up yet?"

"They're coming."

"Let me know when it's all printed."

"Okay."

Jensen watched the papers slide into the tray, recognizing the familiar questions from the new hire application. Neat handwriting filled the open spaces, but the last page had a grainy headshot of none other than a younger Daisy.

He grabbed the papers from the fax machine, running his thumb along the long edge. Jensen mumbled, "All the papers came through. What do I need to see?"

"You'll need to look at page three for any information about the background check," Iris said. Jensen flipped to the third page, eyes sweeping over the information. "The files indicate that something flagged in her background check, but there's a note from the interviewer at the time."

"What exactly flagged the background check?"

"I couldn't bring myself to read it. It's wrong to invade Daisy's privacy, Jensen."

"I'll read it myself," Jensen assured, even while his stomach turned into a knotted mess. He scanned the page until he reached the section on criminal history, finding more than the standard not applicable. His heart fell through his stomach, heavier than lead. "Give me a second."

"Of course," Iris' voice echoed distantly while Jensen read through the file.

PER THE APPLICANT'S ADMISSION, A JUVENILE CRIMINAL RECORD WAS FLAGGED DURING THE BACKGROUND CHECK. THE MINOR WAS CHARGED WITH THREE COUNTS OF SHOPLIFTING AND ONE COUNT OF CRIMINAL TRESPASSING, HANDLED BY THE DEPENDENCY COURTS. AFTER INTERVENTION FROM UPSTANDING COMMUNITY MEMBERS, THEY RECEIVED A SENTENCE OF 'TIME SERVED'.

SPECIAL ORDERS: CRIMINAL HISTORY WILL NOT AFFECT THE APPLICANTS' ADMISSION OR REJECTION. INFORMATION WILL BE KEPT PRIVATE

"... Iris, has there ever been an exception to a failed background check?" Jensen asked, finding it hard to speak through the lump in his throat.

"In the seven years I've been here, no. Company policy forbids it with no exceptions. None of the HR managers who trained me allowed for exceptions either," Iris replied.

"Then, who has the authority to approve a special circumstance? Who would break the rules so blatantly?"

"I don't know."

"Thank you, Iris. I'll dig into everything further myself." Lost in the rush, Jensen missed the quiet creak of the door, but his body turned enough to catch sight of someone in his doorway. *Daisy.*

Her eyes dropped from his face to his hands, noticing the application with her writing all over it. "I have to go."

Jensen barely hung up the phone on poor Iris before Daisy pointed at the papers. "Where did you get those?"

"Daisy..."

"You went snooping through my files? Accessing personnel records from HR is against company policy!"

"You know what else is against company policy? Hiring people who fail the background check, especially those with criminal records."

"You don't know what you're talking about." The color drained from Daisy's face while her eyes flicked between Jensen's and her file. She pushed the door to his office closed, cutting their conversation off from the otherwise empty hallway.

"I don't? Does shoplifting and criminal trespassing ring a bell? What I still haven't figured out is who covered this up because it's all over the files," said Jensen.

"You've crossed a line," Daisy mumbled. Jensen wasn't in the mood for her games.

"Is that right?"

"Yeah, it is."

"Well, you sure like keeping your secrets. If Delaney hadn't—"

"If Delaney hadn't, what? Go on, Jensen, enlighten me about what fucking *Delaney* said to encourage your out-of-line fishing expedition."

Jensen met Daisy's eyes, finding her face revived with bursts of red in her cheeks. Those damn whiskey eyes glinted angrily in the dim office, darkened with a warning. *Tread lightly, or else.*

His jaw twitched. "Delaney ambushed me this morning. She told me that Easton confided in her about you having a criminal record, disclosed while you were drunk. I didn't believe her at first, but I thought checking your files would put my worries to rest. Look how wrong I was."

"Don't act like you're a victim here. Neither you, Delaney, or Easton had your privacy invaded, and your deepest shame revealed without your consent!" Daisy snapped. Her hands balled up into fists by her head, but she dropped her hands. She spun away from him, flashing him her profile. Shadows stretched across her face, plunging her anger into the spotlight.

"Oh, so that makes you the victim?" Jensen scoffed. Somehow, the thought of Daisy getting a corporate job with a salary more than most people make in five years, a world-class education at UCLA, and plenty of material things didn't paint her as a hapless victim.

He tossed the file onto his desk, but the slap of the papers against the counter snapped the mounting tension. The room felt hot, warmer than the sticky, late-August heat outside. Jensen's heart rattled around in his chest, watching Daisy scowl at the wall.

Daisy leaned around, snatching up the file from Jensen's desk before he could. She thumbed through the pages until she reached the front. Jensen noticed the slightest hesitation of her hand, grazing over the photocopied headshot.

Her throat bobbed as she whispered, "You're lucky, you know that? You grew up in Beverly Hills with a loving family unit, never wanting for anything because your dad's filthy rich. I'm surprised you can feign empathy with that silver spoon shoved so far down your throat. Be thankful you've never needed to debase your reputation and do things you weren't proud of in the name of survival. Even after the record's been sealed for years, I'm still paying for my indiscretions, and you're just as bad as Delaney and Easton."

Jensen froze. Normally, a snappy comeback would pop up, ready to fire back. Yet he stumbled, at a loss for words. "Daisy."

"Forget it. To think I started respecting you a little more since the retreat, but I made a mistake there. Feel free to tell everyone about my past so they can also judge me. You win," Daisy scoffed, but she almost sounded worn down.

A wince escaped him when Daisy slapped the files back onto his desk. The awkward smile of her photo faced him, feeling more like a stab between the ribs than a rush of validation. Earlier, he considered finding dirt on Daisy a win. Now, the idea felt hollow and wrong in all the worst ways.

The heated conversation boiled over when a knock put the room on ice. Jensen's eyes widened when he spotted his dad hovering outside the office. As he opened the door, Daisy bolted.

She mumbled her greeting to him and strode down the hall. Yet, she didn't move fast enough to hide how her hands wiped at her eyes. Jensen watched her go, picking up the file from the desk.

"Come in." Jensen waved his dad into the room. "We need to talk."

"Sounds serious. What's going on?" his dad asked, stepping inside the office as Jensen requested. Although he spoke, his eyes drifted to the file held in Jensen's arms.

Jensen exhaled, "I might've broken a rule about HR files, but I think someone covered up a massive red flag in Daisy's application. Dad, she has a criminal record. The file said there were special orders to overlook it—"

"A criminal record that has not only been sealed but expunged," his dad remarked, seemingly unfazed by Jensen's discovery. "I gave the order."

"What?"

"I also petitioned the court on Daisy's behalf, being her support and part of her rehabilitation plan."

The ground beneath him shifted, forcing Jensen to lean against his desk before his legs failed him. All at once, his thoughts screamed for clarity, and the foundation of what he 'knew' cracked under the pressure. Instead of answers, he discovered more questions to the mystery of Daisy Riggs.

"Why?" Jensen questioned, but the words felt like a borderline interrogation of his dad.

His dad sighed, abstaining from the frown so evident in his eyes. "Do you remember when you were fifteen, and we had that argument about you taking over the company one day?"

"Of course I do," Jensen whispered, remembering the night too well. At fifteen, he fell into an identity crisis, one he thought would be cured by abandoning his family's plan for him to inherit Hidden Oasis.

"We went to an event that same night for the office. Investors and colleagues gushed to me about what a fine young man you were becoming and how the company would be perfect in your hands. I followed the conversations, even when I thought I was lying to my colleagues. But then, security pulled me aside and demanded a private audience. They'd caught a young, frightened thief attempting to break into the car for a roll of cash that fell out of my pocket."

Jensen stood there, caught up in the story as his dad told it. The memory resurfaced in perfect detail, but the gaps filled themselves in the more his dad spoke.

"Security brought me to confront her before they handed her off to the police. But I looked into her eyes, a kid no older than you with such desperation, and asked her why she tried to break in."

Jensen swallowed. "Did she tell you why? I assume you didn't call the police, right?"

"I didn't. Daisy had a good reason, and it isn't my story to tell. But she doesn't owe you an explanation," Harrison said. His tone bordered on an accusation, making Jensen's chest sting. "We were in a position to uplift someone in need. So, I opted not to press charges for that night and helped her get the prior incidents expunged. I gave her the money on the sole condition that she would come to the office and interview for a legitimate job."

"Looks like she did," Jensen whispered, seeing the misty glaze settling over his dad's eyes when recalling that night.

"She did. At the time, she didn't know a thing about hospitality, but I promised her she could learn. Meeting Daisy that night felt like a sign from the universe, handing me the perfect fail-safe in the wake of you not wanting the company," Harrison remarked.

Those words landed harder than the rest, crashing into him. He let his dad down all those years ago, but Daisy rescued him in uncertainty, fixing Jensen's messes since before he even knew her name.

For a moment, the room went still. Jensen sat in the discomfort of the silence, stammering over his words, "On a scale of one to ten, how badly have I fucked up this time?"

"Eleven." Harrison eased the papers from his hand. "I'll handle these, but you should consider how to apologize. I don't want to get too involved in you two's rivalry or whatever you call it, but this deserves an apology."

"You're right. I'll—I'll figure something out," Jensen agreed, reaching for his phone before stopping. Calling her wouldn't fix his mess.

"Before you rush into it and make another mistake, consider looking into the company's healthcare policy. Trust me on this one. Daisy always took a special interest in reforms during elections," Harrison suggested, tipping his hand to Jensen one last time before he dismissed himself.

In those words, Jensen planned to find the first step of an apology.

Chapter 15
Daisy

As a young woman in the telltale red vest of the catering staff waltzed by, Daisy snatched a tall flute of champagne from her tray. She nursed the drink close to her chest, ready to down it in one fell swoop if she weren't in polite company.

Daisy couldn't go too far without finding a pair of eyes or several staring at her. When she noticed them, the attention scurried away; some were bashful about getting caught, and others were fearful, like they had attracted the notice of the apex predator.

Then again, she stood out as a splash of vibrant green among the crowd.

That September evening, she trotted out a customized dress. Emerald green made a loud statement, especially when paired with a sleek silhouette and an open back with twin strings of pearls hanging over the bare skin. The pearls clacked against her body whenever she moved, attracting attention her way.

Harrison suggested everyone come in style to celebrate Hidden Oasis' legacy. Daisy couldn't deny his wish. However, everyone else's attention made her wish she had.

Since her argument with Jensen, Daisy shut the world out. Beyond handling her duties, she went home and left no room for anyone. Although her mom and Dex voiced their concerns, they witnessed her rebuilding her old walls brick by brick.

She hadn't asked around while waiting for the other shoe to drop. At any moment, her career might implode in a spectacular crash and burn whenever Jensen decided he was tired of her presence around the office. Not even the two of them fooling around could save her from that trainwreck.

Even then, the eyes of her coworkers watching her could know all about her past, and her fiercest glower couldn't fend off their silent judgment.

The champagne on Daisy's tongue dragged her from the hopeless thoughts swirling around, replacing the fearful haze with a lighter, more reckless one. She moved the flute away from her lips, confronted by the lipstick smeared onto the rim and the golden liquid halfway gone.

Nothing short of expensive whiskey would soothe her jagged edges if she needed to flirt, charm, and entertain the audience at that evening's events. Yet, the open bar wouldn't start until after the first hour of mingling.

The crowd in The Ballroom chattered in small clusters—all dressed to the nines—while Daisy set herself adrift among them. She sifted through the gaps, squeezing past people and offering polite smiles to those who acknowledged her. She never stayed long enough to be roped into conversation.

At least everyone else seemed thrilled to be present at the annual autumn fundraiser, Funding the Oasis, ready to enjoy the hors d'oeuvres and watch as investors poured funds into the company's developing projects. *Her* projects.

Daisy headed for the back of the room, content to sulk in the corner until the people she needed to perform for arrived, but before she reached the back wall, a hush fell over the space.

Her gaze darted toward the podium at the front, seeing Harrison stepping onto the stage. His wife, Eileen, clung to his arm, radiating warmth in navy blue and moissanite jewelry.

Harrison stared at her so lovingly that it almost caused Daisy's ribs to ache. He looked at Eileen like she was Helen of Troy and that each second they shared the same air promised a devotion befitting her. He kissed her softly before approaching the microphone, keeping his wife close.

"Good evening, everyone. Thank you for coming to the annual Funding the Oasis gala." Harrison smiled, receiving applause that followed everything he said. "I want to take this moment to admire how good everyone looks before I open the doors to our guests. Wow, this could be the Met Gala instead of a corporate shindig."

Laughter accompanied the smattering of applause the second time, filling The Ballroom with an energy not unlike the champagne in Daisy's hand. She raised the flute to her lips and downed the rest against her better judgment.

An effervescent, bubbling sensation slid down her throat as Harrison continued his remarks, smiling wide. "One last and hopefully short announcement before we get the party started. My son, Jensen, will announce his policy proposal for your consideration."

Jensen's name inspired something sharp and cutting in Daisy's chest, causing the champagne flute to nearly slip through her fingers. Of course, he chose a better time to speak than her, holding an already amiable crowd for his proposal.

Daisy set her empty champagne onto a tray passing her and watched as Jensen jogged up to the stage. In a sleek, pitch-black suit, Jensen channeled the image of a CEO in spades. Even the black bow tie he added to his suit made him suave instead of dorky.

Shit, he looked good.

Like Daisy had, Jensen carried a leather portfolio tucked under his arm, probably with a prepared speech. Somewhere in the crowd, a noisy shutter of a camera or two went off while Jensen ran his hand over his gelled hair.

From her spot toward the back, Daisy noticed the subtle scan of his eyes over the room. She waited for him to speak or flip open his prepared remarks. Instead, his eyes landed on her.

Under Jensen's rapt attention, Daisy tried to avert her gaze to the nearby wall, but she couldn't. She stood still, trapped by

Jensen's eyes, which flickered softly over her dress, pinning her down. From his place on the podium, he undressed her with his eyes as if the crowd weren't there.

What had gotten into him?

Jensen's hands opened the leather portfolio but didn't take his eyes off Daisy. "Good evening, all. I won't monopolize your time while the night is still young. I've spent the last few weeks considering how to improve our company beyond its already stellar benefits. But it was the ambitious vision of one of our own who gave me the breakthrough I needed."

A few murmurs rolled off the crowd, buzzing around the curiosity in the air.

"Our company prides itself on inclusivity, but our healthcare policy hardly adheres to that promise. Our coverage is limited to certain pre-existing conditions and not much else. Additionally, who we invite into the fold doesn't represent how diverse the family situation of our workers might be," Jensen said, still holding Daisy captive with his eyes. He spoke to her—not the crowd—and she felt every word. "This is why I emailed out a seventy-five-page proposal restructuring our current healthcare coverage to encompass conditions like pregnancy, diabetes, asthma, and others while expanding the policy for family dependents such as parents or siblings."

Daisy swore she stopped breathing, her heart going silent, but she could not look away from Jensen. And, from the soft furrow of his brows and the gentle gleam in his eyes, he knew it, too.

Dex flashed in Daisy's mind. How many years had she petitioned for additional medical coverage for him, only to be shot down by jaded businessmen with no clue about the cost of medicine on a paycheck-to-paycheck family?

Her throat bobbed when applause erupted from the crowd, raining praise and appreciation onto Jensen. Despite having every reason to soak it in, Jensen gave her one last once-over before excusing himself from the stage.

Daisy couldn't decipher the tightness tumbling around her stomach. Left with more questions than answers, the urge to drink flared back up like a bad itch.

She spun around, searching for more champagne, only to come face-to-face with Delaney. The dark red of her silken sheath dress barely rivaled by the flush angrily overtaking her face. Daisy might've attributed the redness to a bad blush job if not for the harsh scrunch of her brows.

"Daisy, just the girl I was looking for," Delaney said, tone snappy like a child who lost their toy privileges.

"Delaney," Daisy greeted, flicking her eyes over her. "Where's your date? I know he's lurking around here somewhere. You should watch him closely in case he decides to sneak off with another girl. Work parties are his weakness."

Daisy knew Delaney accompanied Easton, hearing all about it from Miranda during that morning's elevator ride. The whole encounter happened suddenly, the words falling from poor Miranda like well-timed word vomit while Daisy suffered through it.

"I saw how Jensen was looking at you while he spoke tonight—" Delaney hissed, voice pitching a little too loud.

Daisy hesitated when some of her coworkers glanced at them, but the doors opening for the evening's guests diverted their attention away from her and Delaney; they didn't need an audience for this.

Daisy scoffed, pretending not to know what she meant. She set her hands on her hips, and her brow quirked. "Like what?"

"Like there was no one else in the room. Don't play dumb blonde with me."

"You're delusional."

"I know something's going on!" Delaney shouted when Daisy stepped away from her. "Since when have you two been so friendly?"

The sheer absurdity of the moment put Daisy's thoughts on pause. Did Delaney seriously think she had any sway over Jensen or her? Hadn't she already done enough to insert herself into Daisy's personal life for no damn reason other than her selfishness?

A bitter laugh escaped Daisy as she sauntered closer, getting in Delaney's face. "You lost the right to be concerned with my business when I caught you screwing my boyfriend. Regardless of how you feel about me, Jensen doesn't need to cater to your feelings anymore and can associate with whomever he wants. So, why don't you march those overpriced monstrosities you call heels to anywhere else in the damn room."

Delaney's face leaped from flushed to pale, opening her mouth to yell when a hand grasped her shoulder. Easton appeared at her side, bug-eyed and chest heaving like he sprinted through the crowd to find her.

"Delaney, let's go," he remarked, refusing to meet Daisy's eyes. Her gaze swept over his suit, searching for any sign of infidelity. Men like Easton never stopped with one.

Delaney gasped, pushing back against his chest. "I'm not done!"

But Easton didn't back down, flashing a scowl at his girlfriend. "I said let's go."

"Easton!" Delaney snapped as Easton dragged her away from Daisy, making a beeline for the other side of the room. Their conversation nosedived straight into tension and sharp hand gestures.

Daisy leaned back, content to watch the lovers' heated quarrel while snagging another glass of champagne. *Oh, how the mighty have already fallen.*

Sauntering through the crowd much looser than at the start of the night, Daisy only had one thing to say. She *loved* champagne.

After a second drink and some hors d'oeuvres, Daisy managed to take the edge off. That, and the number of compliments on her dress from other women and some men throughout the night fueled an upturn in her mood.

"Excuse me?" a voice beside her brought Daisy's attention to a man she didn't recognize as she approached the open bar. "I swear I've seen you before."

"I don't think we've met," Daisy hummed. She raked her eyes over the man, dressed in a fine Italian suit. He loomed over her, easily six-two, and flashed perfect pearly whites from his thin smile. He gave the All-American vibe with his blond hair and square jawline, ripped straight from the runway.

The man wasn't deterred, beaming from ear to ear. "Huh, must've been in my dreams then. I'm Brooks Holloway."

He held his hand to Daisy, still smiling, so a chuckle escaped her. Apparently, Brooks didn't know the meaning of subtle when it came to flirting. He wasn't her usual type, but Daisy would allow it for the night. If someone wanted to give her attention, she wouldn't brush them off because someone else had her tied up in knots.

"Daisy Riggs," she replied, shaking Brooks' hand. "Nice to meet you, Mr. Holloway. I hope you're enjoying the evening."

"Oh, I am. Especially because I have the hottest woman in the entire room's undivided attention."

"Hmm, you're big on flattery. Is there something I can do for you?"

"Actually, yes. How about you and I schedule a lunch sometime? I'm in the tech business, but I am looking to diversify my investments." Brooks fished out a business card and slid it into Daisy's hand. "It has my number in case you're desperate to reach me."

"A word of advice?" Daisy mused but laid heavy on the playful lilt of her voice. "Me and desperate are never in the same sentence." She slotted the business card between her fingers, but someone plucked it out of her hand in the blink of an eye.

Daisy's head snapped to her left, greeted by a familiar pair of stormy blue eyes and the dark suit haunting the back of her thoughts.

Jensen examined the card for a second before sliding it into his pocket. His expression straddled the line between disinterested and annoyed, but he aimed for Brooks instead of Daisy. "Thank you for your interest in Hidden Oasis. If you have any questions about becoming a client or investor, I'll happily speak with you further."

"I'm sorry, you are?" Brooks glanced at Jensen in confusion but looked at Daisy as if he wanted her to shoo Jensen away.

"Jensen Ramsey and I need to borrow Daisy for a moment," Jensen said with a tone equally calm and dismissive. Brooks gave Daisy one lingering look before he took the hint, leaving.

Jensen stepped into the spot where Brooks stood in front of her, forcing Daisy to meet his eyes. His face shifted into that softened expression he wore at the podium. "We should go to our office."

"Yeah, that would be best," Daisy agreed. She fell in step with him, striding for the double doors. The fundraiser raged on without them as they caught an empty elevator up several floors.

Neither Jensen nor Daisy spoke while the elevator ascended from The Ballroom, silence filling the cramped space. Daisy hadn't been alone with Jensen since their argument all those weeks ago.

Yet the wounds bled as good as new; she didn't trust herself around him.

When the elevator doors chimed, Jensen stepped out first and reached a hand toward her. Daisy stepped out on her own, watching how his hand dropped to his side.

She stared at him, waiting for him to speak. Jensen wanted the space to talk, not her. She said nothing as Jensen swallowed but held her gaze. "Daisy, I'm sorry."

"Sorry for what?" The words flew out of her, and Daisy clapped a hand over her mouth. Her knee-jerk urge to snap back at Jensen moved faster than her rationality ever could.

However, Jensen stayed calm and unwavering.

"I'm sorry for overstepping and digging into your personnel files. I'm sorry for accusing you of the awful things I said. I'm sorry for believing Delaney and using my weakness as an excuse." Jensen reached for her hand again, and that time, Daisy allowed him to take it. "I know nice words won't smooth over my stupidity, but I hope my proposal is a good first step in me doing better by you."

"So, you did it for me?" asked Daisy. She almost cringed at how desperate and vulnerable she sounded, with hope tinging her voice.

Jensen nodded. "No matter how long it takes, I will ensure that policy gets its votes. The ideas are yours, so I call it the Riggs Amendment." His mouth twitched into the ghost of a smile, a tad bashful but wholly honest.

From how fast her thoughts crashed, Daisy thought she might keel over and throw up. Her hand gripped Jensen's tighter.

"An apology would've been fine."

"Maybe, but I don't think 'fine' is enough."

"Yeah, but I would've investigated the rumor if I was in your shoes. If someone promised me an advantage to secure the CEO position, part of me would consider it. I appreciate your apology. But it's water under the bridge, so you don't have to pretend to care."

"It's not pretend, Daisy. I read every single proposal you wrote to the Board. If I had known they shut you down so many times before, I would've backed you up." Jensen's hand squeezed hers while guiding her away from the elevators.

"I learned long ago that the world isn't filled with people I can rely on. So, I pick and choose who to trust," Daisy replied, walking down the glass hallway. Her fingers knotted with Jensen's while the lights flipped on in their wake. "Honestly, this is the second nicest thing a Ramsey has done for me."

"My dad's still first?"

"Yeah."

"I need to up my game. The old man will never let me hear the end of it."

Jensen and Daisy caught each other's gaze, bursting into laughter. Jensen grabbed the door to his office, escorting Daisy in. She let go of him before trailing over to his neat desk.

Daisy leaned against the desk as Jensen took to his chair, admiring the peacefulness overtaking his once nervous eyes. She sighed, "I have a brother. His name is Dexter, but everyone calls him Dex. When he was four, the doctors diagnosed him with Type 1 Diabetes."

"How old were you?" Jensen asked.

"Fourteen. My mom already worked two jobs, and we were barely scraping by on bills. Medication and hospital bills would've wiped us out. I got a job immediately, but holding onto those jobs became difficult," Daisy mumbled, forcing herself to meet his eyes.

She wanted Jensen to know she was telling the truth. Unlike what the past might suggest, she wasn't some royal fuck-up; she left that version of herself when Harrison gave her a second chance.

"What about your dad?"

Daisy shook her head. That man deserved to stay a footnote in her history. "It's just my mom, Dex, and I. My mom talked about getting a third job, but I knew she couldn't take another one without everything falling apart. So, I started shoplifting. It was wrong, but going hungry wouldn't keep Dex healthy or my mom going. I mostly took food or things I could resell for cash to pay off our debts until I got caught. The charges on the file were from a prior incident before your dad took pity on me."

"I'm so sorry." Jensen's hands froze, unable to tear his gaze away from hers. He looked startled, lips parted breathlessly when the apology came out. Remorse weighed those three words heavier than Daisy had ever heard them before.

"I figured since you know about the record, you should know the whole story. I did bad things, yes. But I did it out of love." Daisy shrugged.

The softness of Jensen's eyes startled Daisy, observing him as he climbed out of his chair and took her hands with his. His thumb stroked along the back of her palm and said, "And it's a secret I'll keep. No one else knows, and they won't."

"Jensen," Daisy breathed.

He smiled faintly. "What's one more secret between rivals?"

A watery laugh escaped her. "If you tell anyone this, I'll deny it, but I almost missed your annoying face. Work without your antics isn't as enjoyable."

"Oh, so I add spice to your life? You might as well tell me that you want to kiss me," Jensen teased, his smile widening in undeniable amusement.

Daisy rolled her eyes, pushing Jensen back with a gentle hand. He rocked on his heels, playing along, so she hummed, "And why's that?"

"Because I've been thinking about kissing you since I saw you in the crowd, wearing this dress," Jensen replied, not missing a beat. His eyes searched her face, circling around her lips. *Oh fuck.*

Daisy's breath hitched, but any coherent response died when Jensen's hands slid up her hips. A shiver slithered down her spine when he stepped closer, lips parted in invitation.

And Daisy? She caved.

Their lips collided as weeks of tension unraveled from the skillful brush of Jensen's tongue against hers. The kiss screamed to be let out, clawing at the walls. Jensen kissed her like a plea for mercy, and Daisy's response was his sweetest damnation.

They could be caught then and there, but neither slowed to worry about such things.

Jensen's hands squeezed her hips tight before he lifted Daisy onto his desk, seating her right at the edge. Between their hungry mouths, he panted out, "As much as I want this dress on the floor, we don't have time."

"Push it up, but be careful," Daisy gasped, head tipping back when Jensen's mouth wandered down the column of her neck. "It's a custom."

"I could buy you a new one, but you'd kill me."

"Yes, I would."

"Lift your hips, and let me do the rest."

Daisy obeyed his request, lifting her hips to his breathy countdown. Jensen's hands pushed the silken emerald fabric of her dress above her hips to reveal the thin panties underneath. She should've left them at home.

Jensen dropped his hands from the puddle of fabric pooling around Daisy's waist, eyes fixated on her thighs. Wordlessly, he grabbed the elastic of her panties and slid them off her thighs without any assistance.

Daisy watched as Jensen shoved them into his pocket like a souvenir, bending her legs wide open and pressing his mouth right above her clit. She moaned, gripping the edge of Jensen's desk for support, spread out across it.

"Jensen, you—" Daisy's eyes rolled when Jensen's mouth wrapped around her clit. He sucked hard and kept his eyes on her while eating her out. Jensen sat in his office chair like he intended to do paperwork, wholly focused on running his tongue against her entrance. "Fuck me."

A rumbling hum against her pussy sent a shockwave of pleasure to crash over Daisy as her head rolled back. Her fingers threaded through his hair; she raked her nails down his scalp, eliciting a moan from him. Jensen always made the prettiest noises.

Jensen's tongue lapped at her like he wanted to make up for lost time. Although Daisy's eyes fluttered close, she heard all of Jensen's moans and the clattering of his belt over the sloppy noises from him eating her out.

She cracked her eyes open long enough to see Jensen's pants puddled around his mid-thigh and one hand stroking his erect cock. But his mouth stayed buried into her pussy, sliding his tongue through her arousal with hums.

Daisy's thighs shook from the sight of Jensen debased before her, but his tongue helped her along. He pulled his lips back for a second but moved up to Daisy's clit, eyes sparkling in mischief.

As his lips sucked her clit, the hand not occupied by his cock slid a single finger into her. Daisy gasped, bucking her hips wildly while she tightened her grip on his hair.

"Jensen. Oh god." Daisy couldn't bring herself to admit how close she was because of his tongue and its eager hunger alone, but the sensation of a finger stretching her pussy open and thrusting into her at a much faster pace than his tongue accelerated the arousal mounting in her stomach.

It was all too much. Jensen overwhelmed her senses until the brink of orgasm, there to catch her when she fell.

Jensen added a second finger, not slowing down his pace. His fingers, tongue, and the greedy look in his eyes pushed Daisy straight over the edge. She hit her climax with a broken cry of his name, riding out her finish on Jensen's fingers.

He nudged her through the euphoria enveloping her, snapping the tension throughout her body like a rubber band. The ripples of exhaustion followed in hot pursuit while Jensen's fingers continued to thrust.

Jensen's head pulled back, gasping for air and showing the smear of slick and spit glistening on his chin. He grinned. "You should see your face right now, Your Highness."

"Don't make fun of me," Daisy panted.

"Oh, I wasn't making fun." Jensen's fingers began to thrust a little faster, having slowed when Daisy's orgasm completed. "If you keep looking so pretty, I might do it again."

"Please," the moan escaped Daisy, mouth dropped open at his boldness. Jensen didn't hesitate, bringing his mouth back to her clit and sucking hard. His two fingers rocked her shit when he nearly pulled them out, only to push them back in. Sensitive from her first orgasm, Daisy's thoughts unraveled.

Her hips shallowly rocked for more friction. When Jensen shook his head roughly, pleasure spiked in her chest. She might finish again, embarrassingly fast.

Daisy gripped Jensen's hair tighter as her arousal grew, mounting and mounting until her second climax was about to hit. But then, he stopped.

Daisy pulled his head away from her clit, gasping, "Jensen, what the fuck?"

"I want you to come on my cock," Jensen replied, almost purring against her inner thigh as he laid a kiss along her hipbone. He smeared his slick-covered fingers against Daisy's thigh before he stood. "C'mere."

Jensen's hands gently flipped her over, now bending her over his desk. Daisy faced the hallway with her hands flat against his desk. Jensen propped one of her knees against the edge.

"Do you have a—"

"A condom? Yeah. I stocked a few in the desk."

Daisy heard a drawer open, but her attention faltered when Jensen's hand cheekily squeezed her ass. He leaned in close, mouth grazing the shell of her ear.

"Imagine if someone walked in on us right now," Jensen murmured while rubbing the head of his cock against Daisy. Her sensitive pussy ached from the friction, knowing she'd fall apart when he pounded into her. "They'd see how fucking gorgeous you look while taking my cock."

Jensen pushed in, followed by Daisy's pleasured cries. He groaned a quiet murmur of Daisy's name against her neck while he made her take every inch until bottoming out. Jensen's hands grabbed her right hip, helping keep her leg propped up on the desk. The other held her close as he thrust into her.

The slap of skin filled the room, interjected by moaning and panting from both Jensen and Daisy. Their bodies moved in sync while he fucked her from behind. Bent over his desk, Daisy braced herself, already on the verge of orgasming.

"Jensen," Daisy warned, sounding more like a whimper than a threat.

"It's okay. Be as loud as you want. Tell me how good it feels," Jensen praised her. The sensation of his words shot straight to her head. "I sit in this office every day, seeing you across from me. Sometimes, your outfit choice has me rock-hard for hours on end. My favorite is when you wear one of those pencil skirts because of how it clings to your thighs. On those days, I sneak off to the bathroom and jerk off if we don't have plans to meet."

Daisy's fingers tightened against the desk, envisioning Jensen locked up in some bathroom stall with his cock in his hand. She imagined the muffled moans and panting of her name while he tried to stay quiet.

Daisy cried out after a rougher thrust. Her head lolled backward as one of Jensen's hands slipped up her chest. When his fingers lightly collared around her neck, his thrusts became wild and rough. Jensen pulled her close, molding his body against Daisy's.

Fuck if this was part of his apology, she'd let him use her like this.

Jensen continued to pound into her like she belonged to him. Daisy's nails scraped against the desk when her second orgasm crashed into her, unraveling in Jensen's arms. Her balance wobbled, struggling to stay upright while he held her close.

"There we go, Your Highness. I've got you. You're good," Jensen's voice pitched while his hips stuttered, pressing a quiet groan into her neck. Daisy weakly panted as something hot and slick ran down her thigh.

"I think that was the best one yet," Daisy laughed breathlessly as Jensen pulled out. His arms lightly turned her around and helped her off his desk. "We should head back."

"We should," Jensen agreed, but neither made a move to leave.

Daisy raked her eyes over him, lips tugging into a smirk a second before pushing him into his chair. Jensen let out a quiet "oomph," staring up at her with unbridled arousal flashing among the stormy blue. "But I don't want to leave."

Jensen's hands grabbed her hips. He guided her to straddle his lap, chest heaving but smirking wolfishly. "Then, take your throne. I'm all yours."

Chapter 16
Jensen

As he watched cars zoom past him on the Sunset Boulevard sidewalk, Jensen checked the time like his anxious gaze would summon Daisy out of thin air. *If only it were that easy.*

For a Friday night in the middle of September, Jensen planned to kick off his weekend with some takeout and tackle his backlist of Food Network shows. But those plans crumbled when his parents called, asking for a huge favor.

They were supposed to attend some award function honoring upstanding members of the community and their contributions to the Los Angeles social scene. Supposed to became the operative words there as his dad and mom caught a nasty strain of the flu.

Piper and Hayley offered to check in on them, bringing them soup or whatever else they needed. However, someone needed to accept the award for their dad since he couldn't stop throwing up for more than ten minutes.

Even after his dad called Daisy and asked her to cover for him, Jensen offered to go on his behalf. So, Jensen waited for Daisy to arrive, standing outside in the light of the golden hour.

Jensen's foot tapped against the plush red carpet outside the restaurant, apparently rented out for the night by the organization hosting the awards. The modern exterior exuded the swanky, high-society vibe promised by these events. A regular snooze-fest of people patting each other on the back and making painful small talk over expensive snacks. After the first few, the rest lost their mystique.

His gaze wandered away from the busy intersection when a dark car rolled up to the curb. The back door flung open, revealing Daisy, dressed for the occasion.

The black, floor-length gown she wore billowed in the breeze when Daisy emerged from the backseat, quick to smooth over any flyaway hairs. The fabric clung to her from her dress's twisted, high neckline until the slight poof around her knees, but the simple bun and elegant dress bore a striking contrast to dark eyes and a red lip so bold it felt like a punch to the throat.

The sunset gathered like a halo around the back of her head, framing her in a shower of gold, orange, and a touch of pink. Daisy glowed in the colors of the fading sky, glittering brighter than a diamond or the sunlight catching on the skyscrapers of the Los Angeles skyline. Radiant, the best word to describe her, reached Jensen's tongue, but he held the thought close to his chest.

Daisy had always been beautiful, untouchably so. Yet, in that moment, she touched a new plane of ethereality, standing right within his grasp.

"Thanks. Expect 20%, okay?" Daisy shouted over the nearby rush of traffic before slamming the door shut. She rushed onto the curb as the car peeled away, tires screeching against the asphalt.

She inhaled sharply, finally noticing Jensen from how fast her face pulled into a resting smirk.

"Daisy," Jensen greeted, offering her his hand. "Did my poor, very sick dad interrupt something important? Was it a date?"

"Your dad was throwing his guts up between every sentence. I wasn't about to deny him a favor." Daisy shook her head to several strands loosening from her bun, framing her face. "And no, I wasn't on a date."

"So, what got you so dressed up tonight?"

"I like to go out and have a nice dinner sometimes. No special occasion, no companion. Just me, some nice wine, a candlelit dinner for one, and a slice of cheesecake to go."

"That sounds really nice, actually."

"It is. I've only enjoyed life's finer things in the last few years. Plus, when the opportunity arises, I will never deny myself a slice of strawberry cheesecake."

The mention of cheesecake inspired a quiet grumble in Jensen's stomach, reminding him about the abandoned takeout order on his laptop. Daisy raised her brow at him but said nothing.

Her hand reached toward him, held out for a handshake, and Jensen grasped her hand. The gesture quickly melted into something entirely different when Daisy's hand slid up his arm, hooking into the crook of his elbow.

"We should head inside. We're a little behind," said Jensen.

"Right. I assume Harrison called the organizer to inform them we're arriving on his behalf," Daisy agreed, heading inside with Jensen.

The two crossed into a gorgeous foyer—all spiral staircases with a balcony overhead and polished marble floors so bright they could see their reflections—when a harried stranger raced over.

The guy grabbed the bright blue pocket square from the breast of his luxury suit, dabbing his sweaty forehead. "You must be Harrison Ramsey's representatives, yes?"

"Yeah, I'm his son, Jensen. This is Daisy, one of my colleagues at the company. We came as soon as we could. Sorry for any delay this might have caused."

"It's no trouble. We wish Harrison and Mrs. Ramsey a swift recovery. You two have only missed a few awards; we placed your seats at the back of the room by Mr. Ramsey's request to not disturb the ceremony."

"When will we be called up?"

"It should be any moment now. If you'd like to stay for the rest of the ceremony, we can provide dinner and two drink tickets for the bar."

"We'll think about it." Daisy smiled, tight crinkles forming around the corners of her eyes. Jensen watched the organizer nod mutely, noticing how his eyes boldly ran over Daisy's figure.

Her hand on his elbow squeezed tighter, scooting closer to him when Jensen's arm snaked around her waist.

"Thank you." Jensen guided Daisy through the double doors as a lucky award recipient wiped at their eyes mid-speech. Jensen brought him and Daisy closer to the back wall, whispering, "Hopefully, we're up soon."

"Same here. It's not that I'm not happy for your dad, but I could've been sliding into a food coma right about now." Daisy's voice rose slightly when the room erupted in applause, awarding the recipient on stage one last time.

Jensen clapped politely as the stage cleared. Right then, the Mayor of Los Angeles, Emilio Canales, sauntered onto the stage. His pearly white smile gleamed almost as bright as the pomade slicking back his dark curls.

He waved, garnering vigorous applause and whistles from the crowd when he reached the podium with a glittering award. Emilio adjusted the microphone, pausing for the cameras to snap some photos. That man never met a camera he didn't love, apparently.

"Evening, everyone. I'm honored to be here with you tonight. We're celebrating the movers and shakers of this city, and our night wouldn't be complete without honoring a man whose track record with success shines like a star on the Walk of Fame. I've been honored to host events on his properties and take my family to The Ridge every summer. Not only does he give this community opportunities for high-end experiences, but his generosity and dedication to giving back to those who welcome him speak volumes. Would Harrison Ramsey please come to the stage?"

Whistles and clapping filled the room again as people looked for his dad, bringing Jensen forward. Daisy nudged his arm off her waist, looping their arms together instead. In a crowd of strangers, holding her like that might raise a few questions.

Jensen led Daisy through the crowd, weaving through the applause. Some faces flashed in recognition as he passed; he knew some of these strangers, mostly as vague memories from work events of the past.

So, Jensen smiled while helping Daisy onto the stage, aware of the cameras on them. Daisy strode over to Mayor Canales, who brightened and shook her hand, speaking to Daisy too softly for Jensen to hear.

Daisy beamed at whatever Mayor Canales said, accepting the award from the mayor. She glanced over her shoulder—award cradled to her chest—and Jensen bridged the gap in two strides.

"It's a little sharp, so be careful," she whispered before passing the award into his arms. Jensen leaned in to properly hold the trophy. Daisy failed to mention how heavy it was for a tiny little thing.

Jensen cleared his throat. "Thanks. I've got it." He maneuvered enough to shake the mayor's hand, who lingered off to the side. Daisy paused, standing short of the microphone's range.

"Do you want to say something, or should I?"

"We can both say something short."

"Okay." Daisy cleared her throat a few times until a hush fell over the crowd, giving the spotlight to them. "Good evening. Jensen and I are here on Harrison's behalf to accept this award. I have been privileged to know Harrison as a boss and mentor for the last ten years. The first thing anyone will tell you about him is his commitment to Hidden Oasis. However, everyone should know that he wouldn't be half the success story he is without his humility. That comes from how close he keeps good people around him, like his family."

Daisy's eyes flickered to him as she spoke, leaving Jensen to fight a stupid grin stretching across his face. Someone should capture the moment on film because Daisy saying nice things about him didn't happen often.

Jensen sidled up to the microphone. "My dad started Hidden Oasis with a simple mission: create enjoyment and entertainment. He continues that mission when he shows up to work, bringing the same enthusiasm to every task crossing his desk. As his son and a proud company employee, I can confidently say we all look to the future and know he'll lead us to a better tomorrow. He will cherish this honor once he recovers from the flu. Thank you."

A few laughs mingled with applause signaled their cue to leave the stage and let the ceremony continue. Jensen secured the award in his arms as he walked. Daisy's hands slipped down his sides as she trailed behind him.

Jensen turned to her, leaning his mouth to graze her ear. "I think we should get out of here. The split pea soup doesn't look all that appetizing."

He eyed the bowls of murky, green soup at the nearest table and the small portion sizes of the other entrees. Yeah, none of that looked more appetizing than the promise of greasy takeout. Jensen wasn't sticking around.

Daisy paused, but her mouth twitched. "You have a place in mind? I'm still thinking about my cheesecake."

"I know just the place. I'll drive."

Cruising down Franklin Ave, Jensen watched the light above the intersection as his car sped through, catching the last few seconds of yellow. He sailed across the crosswalk on the opposite end before the yellow switched to red.

The road ahead appeared sparse with other drivers, so Jensen brought his car to a smooth drive along the Los Angeles roads.

To his right, the flutter of Daisy's sandy blonde waves on the wind caught his attention. Jensen glanced over, finding her curled against the passenger side door while basking in the dusk. The sun dropped below the horizon, so the pinks and purples drained into the nighttime.

Daisy stared straight ahead as the wind continued to swirl around them, carrying the distant taste of cigar smoke and car exhaust into the distance.

In her lap, she balanced a grease-stained paper bag with their dinner—picked up from a mom-and-pop burger joint Jensen liked. While checking out with their sloppy cheeseburgers and French fries, they agreed that a good burger defeated a fancy meal every time.

Daisy's slender fingers hovered over the dial to the radio, hesitating to change the song from the pop station she chose at the start of their drive.

Jensen remembered how his brows arched when the cheesy pop throwbacks from the nineties spilled out from his radio, but Daisy shrugged noncommittally. The music provided a nice layer to their aimless cruise, filling the space instead of silence as their backseat passenger.

The fresh air and the promise of food gave them every excuse to leave the award ceremony, not sparing split pea soup a second thought when sprinting from the restaurant.

"Jensen," Daisy whispered when the radio hit a commercial break, lowering the volume. Their dinner rustled on her knees when she leaned toward him. "Griffith Park is coming up in a block."

"Yeah?"

"The observatory has a parking space with a good view. Want to stop there so we can eat for a little while?"

Jensen thought about it, already hitting the turn signal. The left-hand turn onto the winding side roads into the park approached. "Sounds like a plan. Have you been there before?"

"Once, on a field trip in the fifth grade." The mistiness in Daisy's voice wasn't lost on Jensen, who rarely heard her speak with such fondness about anything. Daisy laughed. "I remember how excited I was to visit the telescope even though it was daytime. I got lost in the gift shop for half an hour, trying to find something cheap to take home if I skipped lunch at the food court. I regret never catching a planetarium show since we left early."

"You never came back?" asked Jensen, thoroughly invested in the tales of ten-year-old Daisy running amok in the observatory. Somehow, he imagined a little girl with blonde pigtails and as much attitude as her adult self, peering at the planet-shaped dioramas or wandering the gift shop with stars in her eyes.

"Never, but I always wanted to visit." Daisy shrugged. In the dying light of dusk, Jensen almost swore her cheeks darkened from the rosy kiss of the cold. But he kept his eyes firmly fixed on the road.

The two lapsed into silence as Jensen drove through the winding path around the Hollywood hiking trails, heading for the observatory at the top of the hill. At that hour, Jensen only anticipated a few people milling around the observatory, free from the rush of school buses and families.

Jensen's convertible sped into the parking lot. As expected, the empty spots outnumbered those filled with cars, but as Daisy guessed, the view from Griffith knocked the breath clear of Jensen's lungs.

The city skyline glittered darkly against the final touches of sunset as building lights began to flicker on. Traffic roared past in blurs of light like little rockets, turning into a steady trickle of light spilling from the streets.

Jensen chose a spot overlooking the city, one in the front row by the observatory's manicured lawn. He cut the engine, beckoning Daisy for his burger.

The rustle of the paper bags echoed through the quiet air shortly before Jensen sank his teeth into a juicy, everything-on-it burger. He moaned through the first bite when the patty melted on his tongue like butter.

Beside him, Daisy snorted while devouring a handful of fries. Her eyes fluttered shut, humming delightedly. "No offense to the chef, but I'm taking the burger over roasted quail every time."

"I feel like the chef would understand," Jensen chuckled, wiping at his mouth when burger sauce trickled out from the corner of his lips. He wolfed down half the burger in several quick bites, starving. "Those events are nice sometimes, but do you ever feel like the small talk grows..."

"Tiresome?" Daisy finished his thought, lips downturned while she held her burger.

"Exactly. It's usually the same conversations recycled by people you vaguely recognize unless you're close. Even then, there are so many layers of pleasantries to dance around. It's exhausting."

"You're telling me. At least you have it a little easier."

"And how's that?"

Daisy raised her brow in the middle of a bite into her burger. But she chewed fast, covering her mouth. "As a guy, the expectations of you aren't as high. You could wear the same suit to every event, and no one would bat an eye. If I want to represent the company in a good light, people expect me to show up in a perfect outfit, all done up. There can't be a hair out of place. My makeup must look acceptable, not too much or too little. The outfit I choose needs to be not too frumpy but not too sexy, just right to show off my body. I need to be attractive enough to make me eye candy for the men who dangle their checkbooks over my head."

Jensen's throat dried, and his appetite wavered with it. He put the burger back into its bag, sampling a few fries. The salt hit his tongue, but the bitterness edged the taste right out.

He sighed. "Do you think about how different your life could've been?"

"All the time," Daisy whispered to the sky, tipping her head back to study the faint view of the stars through the light pollution. Jensen's eyes traced down the edge of her jaw as her profile bathed in the first touches of moonlight. The graceful silver softened the woman he knew most for her fierceness. "But I try not to. I've been given a chance to make my life mean something, at least something more than being a girl whose potential outweighed the rest of her."

"I don't know. I feel like your sheer stubbornness would have driven you to be great at whatever you did," Jensen murmured, but his levity was lost on Daisy.

She shook her head, voice shaking. "No, you could've done anything you set your heart on. The world should aspire to be so lucky."

"Yeah, but for a long time, I wandered aimlessly. I liked life, but I didn't love it, not like how I do now. I had everything I could ever want, but money couldn't buy ambition, purpose, or happiness."

"That's why you stay in the business? It gives you purpose?"

"That... and it helps me feel like I'm making my dad proud. I don't know. I get up every morning, and while work sometimes gets on my nerves, I can't imagine doing anything else with my life."

Jensen's gaze wandered back to Daisy when her breathing quieted, following the line of her vision. Her wistful eyes, back to that damn shade of whiskey he'd become so attached to, stared at the observatory.

No more what-ifs.

Jensen clicked the button for the convertible's roof. The mechanical sounds snapped Daisy straight from her trance. She jolted, eyes darting between Jensen and the roof sliding back on.

"Jensen, what?" Daisy stammered.

"Griffith doesn't close for another few hours." Jensen unbuckled himself and grabbed the burgers. He tossed the bags into the backseat beside the trophy and pulled one of his discarded coats to cover it. "We should go inside and catch a planetarium show."

Daisy's face flustered in a dark shade of pink, stretching across her cheeks and nose. She opened her mouth to say something until Jensen's hand clicked her seatbelt for her.

Instead, her mouth pulled out the prettiest smile Jensen had ever seen, and she grasped his hand. "Okay, and if the gift shop's open, I want one of those Newton's cradles for my desk."

"I have no idea what a Newton's cradle is, but I'll take your word for it!" Jensen breathlessly exclaimed while he and Daisy scrambled out of their seats. The car doors chirped behind them while he and Daisy raced toward the observatory.

Despite her low heels and dress, Daisy's strides looked more like those of an Olympic track athlete. Jensen fought to keep up with her while the few people they passed stopped and stared at them, racing down the pavement in black tie attire.

However, neither stopped running until they burst through the double doors of the Griffith Observatory. Jensen's hand grasped Daisy's while he dragged her toward the short staircase, taking her through the hallowed halls of scientific discoveries memorialized and enshrined for curious young minds.

The two stumbled outside the planetarium's doors, where a ticket machine blinked at the ready. Jensen's credit card emerged from his pocket faster than Daisy could fumble for her clutch. Within a minute, two tickets to the final show of the planetarium fell into his grasp.

Jensen presented them to the worker at the door, who waved them along. He and Daisy plunged into the dim planetarium room, staring into the ceiling with celestial bodies painted around its circumference.

"Grab seats at the front!" Daisy whispered, but her voice pitched slightly when she nudged Jensen toward the front row. Most of the chairs were empty, but Jensen liked the front.

He and Daisy crashed into two seats in the first row, muffling their laughs when sinking into the plush chairs. And, in the dimly-lit room underneath the painted stars, Jensen's eyes met Daisy's shining ones.

Somehow, the look in her eyes put the rest of the universe to shame.

Chapter 17
Daisy

The smell of browned butter and freshly baked bread greeted Daisy as she flung open the door to Le Vue de Pavilion, an upscale French café several blocks from the office. Although she had back-to-back meetings bookending her lunch break, an urgent phone conversation summoned her for fresh pastries and wine.

Daisy smoothed over her skirt, pushed her purse higher on her arm, and tightened the coat she grabbed before leaving the office. The weather for a late September afternoon ended up warmer than expected, dry without winds from the north sweeping in.

She missed the coast and sea breeze more than ever.

"Daisy, over here!" a voice called to her from one of the tables. Daisy's eyes scanned the room until she found the faces of several investors seated in the back. Her stomach hardened into a pit, leaving her breathless.

Daisy's hand waved while she strolled over, feeling her pace drag harder than usual. Meetings with investors usually didn't scare her, not with enough time to prepare. However, she walked into the café blind to their intentions, sidling along the tightrope with her reputation perched as extra weight on her shoulders.

Fixing on a megawatt smile, Daisy stopped at the investors' table, charm dialed to ten. "Good afternoon, ladies and gentlemen. It's lovely to see you on this fine afternoon."

"That it is," the domineering voice of Edna Bullocks, one of the more influential shareholders for the company alongside her husband, eclipsed the other greetings from the crowd. "Please join us. This lunch is for you, after all."

"At the risk of sounding unlike myself, I'm not sure if we're celebrating or if this is an intervention," Daisy replied.

Luckily, her voice treaded along the thin line between informality and closeness carefully enough to invoke rich, amused laughter from those gathered around the table. Although she held her smile hostage—drawn taut across her face—Daisy's chest clenched until the breath dried up.

But Edna gestured for her to take one of the spare chairs around the table. "When it comes to you, Daisy, I never have to worry. This is a celebration of you, my dear."

Knowing better than to protest, Daisy sat herself among the investors. She crossed her ankles under the table, cutting off the urge to bounce her legs. Daisy couldn't help the restless energy spreading through her limbs, crackling and waiting for a tiny mistake to set it off. The expectant eyes of the investors followed her every move; when she unfurled the napkin with her place settings or brushed her loose waves out of her face, their eyes pinned her down.

Daisy cleared her throat. "I never turn down a celebration, especially with such distinguished company."

"Good," Edna hummed, her voice so overwhelmingly saccharine, as she swirled her glass of red. "See, we've all been discussing what a great CEO you'll make in a few months. All of us here see what Harrison sees in you. If you believe the whispers around the office, others see it too."

"Really?"

"Oh, yes. We've conducted some inquiries and found that your prospective tenure as CEO promises higher employee morale, increasing our social status in local circles. You have a reputation for being undeniably professional and highly competent. People are thrilled with you or Jensen, but a woman CEO gets buzz."

Daisy's tongue slid over the back of her teeth, chewing on a response to that. *So, people liked the idea of a female CEO, but did that mean people wanted her to be in charge? Or would any woman be good for optics?*

"I'm honored by their faith in me. I won't let their confidence be misplaced." Demure wasn't her style, but Daisy still treaded carefully. She settled on something polite, appropriate for the company she held around the table of red wine and half-eaten pastries. No matter the occasion, she always knew how to play the game.

Energetic chatter erupted from the investors, followed by the raise of wine glasses or other cocktails despite the early hour. Daisy's hands folded over her lap, signaling for a waitress so she could join them in enjoying some wine. It had to be five o'clock somewhere.

A nearby waitress caught sight of her hand, sidling over with wine from behind the bar. She topped off Daisy's glass until the bottle of red ran empty.

Daisy took her wine, finding a smile easier than before. "Could I get a menu, please? Oh, and a cup of beef bourguignon with a baguette to start. Thanks."

"Of course, Miss."

Daisy and her wine leaned backward in her chair, slipping into the moment. No longer did anxiety bear down on her chest, breathing a little easier without the suspense hanging over her head.

But her peace crumbled at the pointed cough from someone around the table, yanking Daisy back into the game. Her eyes landed on the wry smile of Spencer Fitzgerald, another prominent investor with a penchant for getting a little too sloppy at the company's black-tie events. After instances of graphic lamenting about literal war stories, the people who sought his company grew small each year.

Another small thing to note about Mr. Fitzgerald: he often flitted around Kenneth Malone and his cronies like a lap dog. Yet, he always seemed to attend gatherings meant for her supporters. *He made for a terrible spy.*

The smug twist of his mouth preceded a quiet, brisk laugh. "So, does the beginning of this new era signal the end of the Ramsey dynasty before it even begins? I'd admit, you're a woman who knows how to fight her battles."

Immediate but awkward reactions flashed across the faces of the investors around him. The others stayed so still that Daisy wondered if they heard at all. Mr. Fitzgerald's clumsy attempt at a trap came with neon, flashing red flags attached, screaming for her to run as far away from the statement as possible.

Daisy let the air simmer with the anticipation, held like a bated breath, while she sipped her wine. Courage pooled into her throat as the wine went down easy, stealing her resolve to pull the trigger on the sharp-witted response she turned on her tongue.

"Truthfully, I am a Ramsey. Harrison molded me in his generous, accomplished image when he took me under his wing. I may not have his last name, but as his protégé, I'm like him in every other way that counts. I shall continue his vision as he intended... so the Ramsey dynasty will live on, no matter what anyone else might assume. Every other speculation is made in the absence of knowledge."

The words sank in, letting their double meaning flourish in the silence around the table. *Anyone who doubted Daisy's loyalty to Harrison was a fucking fool, speaking out of ignorance so lethal it might sign the death of their careers.*

No one rushed to contradict her words. Daisy sipped her wine again while letting the conversation recover from the reality check, enjoying the flustered sight of Mr. Fitzgerald squirming in his seat.

Besides, her loyalty to the Ramsey name would outlast any external force hellbent on destroying her, like the Malones. She imagined their heads might burst into flames if they knew how their perfect 'savior' in Jensen routinely got on his knees for her.

She wouldn't spill their business, but the knowledge she held over their heads would ruin their day.

Edna raised her wine glass into the air as if she sensed the chance to recover the conversation from the awkwardness. "That's a proclamation deserving of a toast. To Daisy and continuing the great work."

Daisy lifted her glass, ready to chime in something good-humored with the mood back on track. However, the outburst of forced giggling stole her attention from the table.

She watched as two people to her right—a tall man in a dark suit and the very young woman on his arm—scooted past their table for a cozy, intimate booth in the corner of the room. Their table fell right into Daisy's line of sight.

She studied the girl in quiet, quick glances. She wore a dark dress stretched across her body with no room to breathe, and expensive jewelry glittered around her neck and forearms. But her youthful gleam and the softer curve of her cheeks stopped Daisy cold; the girl hardly looked legal, dripped out in designer clothing and grasping at her male companion for his attention.

He could be her father, an uncle, or a brother, but the latter sounded too far-fetched from how the young girl batted her eyes at him. Daisy moved in circles where younger wives or flings with twenty-somethings by older men existed as an unfortunate, uncomfortable reality. So, she watched, unable to pull her gaze away from the scene as the world faded into background noise.

"Ooh, everything here looks so good. Can we get some macarons to go?" The girl giggled while sliding into the booth, her back facing Daisy. Yet, her voice carried over the quiet conversations between the booth and her table.

"Of course, sweetheart," the girl's companion remarked. Three simple words, but Daisy's whole body froze. Her muscles stiffened up, barely registering the feeling of her wine glass leaving her fingers. She hoped she settled the glass on the table instead of spilling it everywhere. "Whatever you want, it's yours."

The girl giggled while the man headed for his side of the booth, but neither noticed the horrified observer watching their interaction. Daisy's eyes refused to break away while her body went cold.

Turn around. Turn around. Don't be him.

Yet, her silent plea withered when the man's face came into view, cementing the recognition with a choking certainty. Of course she did; she'd never forget the face of the man who abandoned her.

Lawrence Riggs. *Her father.*

Daisy couldn't breathe while staring at his neatly trimmed sandy brown hair and the dark brown eyes as detached as she remembered them. Twelve years later, the hateful glint when he had declared his intention to leave haunted Daisy's childhood like a specter, casting its shadow over those memories.

The night her father left their family to struggle, her mother ushered Dex and Daisy into their shared bedroom and closed the door behind them. She told them not to come out until she got them, but the walls hadn't been thick enough to muffle the screaming of Lawrence while he cursed at her mom, blaming her for their poverty and ruining his life. She "ruined" his life when she chose to bring two kids into the world, and Daisy never forgot those words.

She had clamped her shaking hands over Dex's ears, only three at the time to her thirteen, so she heard it all. Every word stuck to her skin, stinging harder than bullets. Lawrence vanished from their lives for good when he slammed the front door to their house.

He never made contact and left them to struggle until Daisy yanked them out of debt by the skin of her teeth. But there the useless bastard stood, less than ten feet away from Daisy, with a girl decked in designer and doting on her like a loving man. *Like an honorable one.*

How old was that girl? She couldn't be older than Daisy. Oh, God.

The buzzing in Daisy's ears morphed violently from a low hum into something agonizing, clattering against her head with screamed instructions about how to proceed. *Confront him. Leave the shop. Cry. Get angry and throw the wine. Lose the composure and scream. Drag the girl away.*

Each scenario played before her eyes, worse than the one that preceded it, but Daisy balked all the same. The hot churning of bile crawled up her throat—no matter how hard she swallowed, the sensation spread across her skin in a flush. An empty stomach of red wine boiled until her chest burned hot.

She was going to be sick.

"Daisy? Earth to Daisy?" Edna's voice pierced through the chaos, unraveling Daisy's composure faster than she could catch it. The call of her name broke the paralyzing trance Lawrence and his 'sweetheart' forced on her, bringing Daisy back to the table.

Her eyes scanned the faces of the investors, but none of them appeared aware of her panic or the walls closing in. Even with her attention shifted from her father in the booth with his barely legal girl, bile pressed against the back of her mouth in a warning.

"If you'll excuse me for a moment. I'll be back." Daisy climbed from her chair and smiled politely despite her rush for the bathroom. Her legs wobbled after every unsteady stride, threatening to take her down.

Humiliation blistered hot behind her eyes while Daisy choked on the vomit racing up her throat. Red wine never felt better coming up than going down.

She crashed into the bathroom, not caring to check under the other stalls and confirm she was alone. Daisy scrambled into the nearest stall, slamming the door shut. Her fingers fumbled with the lock twice, distracted by pained, dry heaves.

She clawed at her coat in desperation until the fabric loosened from around her chest, tearing the buttons out of their fastenings. A cough interrupted her as she leaned forward, coat pushed away from her mouth.

Daisy shrugged off her coat while heaving hard. She managed to strip and toss it over the door behind her. Her hands dragged her dress to puddle around her thighs as Daisy kneeled on the tile.

She wore tights as a thin layer of separation between her and the bathroom floor, no less shameful than her bare skin. Daisy gripped the toilet and buried her face into the rim as she lost the battle to nausea.

Time passed unbearably slow while Daisy listened to her dry heaving, interrupted frequently by the squelch of vomit or the quiet splash when the bile hit the toilet water. Her nails scraped against the porcelain underbelly, echoing off the walls harshly.

Daisy gave in until her stomach hit empty. She fumbled for the handle with her eyes screwed shut—too afraid to see the mess she made. She slumped back onto her knees, screaming from the indent of the tiles through her tights.

She opened her eyes, stuck in her shame. The taste of red wine and regret stained her mouth while Daisy caught her breath on the bathroom floor. Her shallow pants filled the silence with their desperation; she wobbled onto her feet, ready to flee from the scene.

Daisy tugged on her coat and rushed to the sink. Cold water ran into the bowl as Daisy switched the faucet on high, bending down to invite the cleanse into her mouth. She spit into the sink until her hands stopped shaking, too unsteady to hold water.

With a paper towel, Daisy cleaned away any water on her face. She reached into her coat's pocket for the small tube of lipstick stashed away for a touch-up after lunch when the bathroom door swung open.

Standing in the doorframe, the girl flounced into the bathroom to the metallic chimes from her jewelry. Twinkling noise invaded Daisy's skull as the girl chose the sink right beside her despite the three other perfectly good sinks down the row.

Daisy observed the girl in her peripheral view, noting how the girl stared unabashedly at her. She braced, half-expecting to have been caught watching the interactions between this stranger and her estranged father.

The girl, however, sucked in a breath and smiled so innocently that the sweetness carved Daisy's heart out through her ribs. "Sorry to bother you, but I love your dress. Where'd you get it?"

"Oh, I ordered it online from Rose & Luxe. It's 'Goddess' from their office attire line," Daisy stumbled over her words, more awkward than she intended. But the girl's face brightened, blissfully unaware of the tension.

"Thank you! It's so nice to find someone who doesn't gatekeep all the cute clothes and trendy spots in town. Granted, I haven't met too many people since I'm new," the girl rambled, twisting the knife a little deeper between Daisy's ribs.

"New, huh? You don't look older than college age."

"I'm twenty! I transferred to a college downtown to attend auditions and stuff."

"Like movie auditions?"

"Exactly! The industry is cutthroat, but my boyfriend thinks I'm made for stardom."

'Boyfriend' reminded Daisy of her father sitting in the cramped booth, stirring the queasy feelings up. She grabbed the sink, chewing hard on her cheek to slow the nausea.

"Oh? I'm sure he's very proud," Daisy said, finding her tongue heavier than lead while forcing the words out. "Is he waiting for you or something?"

"Yeah, I got a callback, so we're celebrating with some pastries. He's the best," the girl giggled.

Daisy catapulted somewhere between shame, disgust, and fear. How could this girl not see his intentions to use her? *Did she honestly believe a man twice her age—who had a daughter older than her—would see her as an equal?*

But she swallowed those questions, far too aware of the delusions a young mind would bend to believe. She hummed, "I wish you luck on your stardom journey. But could I give you some advice?"

"Sure," the girl replied, eyes wide and earnest.

"Be careful around older men. They might seem invested in you or your successes, but there's a reason they don't go for women their own age. Innocence is like currency, so keep it close," Daisy remarked and bolted for the door, not interested in sticking around for the protests and the 'he would never' schtick.

She had been naïve once, young and full of hopes, chasing after men who had no business in her life. But she never gave them her heart, too headstrong and unpredictable for them. *Never the dating type.*

Daisy barely cleared the bathroom door before she collided with a body. Her hands instinctively shot out to steady herself, and the stranger grasped her wrists to help.

"Are you alright?" Her father's voice calling out to her sent a jolt straight through Daisy, paralyzing her to her core. Yet, her body recoiled, shrinking away from him. The venom of his final words of regret and hatred toward her mom echoed in her head. *He meant those words to Daisy, too.*

Daisy said nothing. Instead, she lifted her head to meet his eyes, challenging him with her stare. Beyond a few wrinkles, he looked identical to the day he left while her mom aged from the stress of raising two kids and narrowly avoiding homelessness.

She, however, looked like a carbon copy of her mom.

Daisy stood firm, waiting for the recognition to sink in. He allegedly loved her mom once, so her face should haunt him, but whatever reaction she hoped for, it never came.

Her father stared blankly at her, letting the silence fester until the bathroom door opened behind her. Daisy stepped around him without a word, even as the heat of his gaze bore holes in her back.

She needed a drink.

Chapter 18
Jensen

Beyond the flashes of commercials and stray light from the kitchen, Jensen sat deep in thought in the dark of his townhouse. With the television on mute, silence lurked in the spacious home.

Some might argue that a townhouse was too big for a bachelor, but Jensen liked to entertain. He factored those details in when he invested in the property years ago, using a small chunk of his trust fund to buy his home instead of funding a lavish eighteenth birthday.

He hadn't regretted the decision once.

Jensen clicked through a few of the work reports, knowing he'd earn some lecturing from his sisters about bringing work home. His habit of prioritizing his job led to many fights in the past, mainly with Delaney. He promised to better separate work and home life for his own sanity.

Just not *that* evening.

The evening news made good background noise while he worked, keeping him from falling asleep in the middle of a spreadsheet. His informational emails weren't about to write themselves.

Between every few emails, Jensen glanced at the television to catch the newest headlines flashing onto the screen. Except for President Spencer's planned address in the morning, nothing new grabbed his attention off the spreadsheets clogging his laptop.

"And that should be a good place to end for the night," Jensen said to himself. He let out a yawn while hitting the last email address on his list. He cracked his spine while stretching over the back of his sectional, ready to crash. "What a wonderful start to my weekend. I should've accepted Cal's invitation to go out."

Although he lamented about the hypothetical night he could've spent in a loud, dimly-lit club with some friends, Jensen knew he'd choose to be home nine times out of ten. Somewhere between graduating college and then, he lost interest in wild nights out and boozy adventures.

It had everything to do with his impending responsibilities as a potential CEO in less than two months. For Hidden Oasis, their leader's actions helped the company's reputation shine or caused it to crumble. Jensen needed positive press if he wanted the job to be his.

As his eyes drooped a little, a knock at the door spurred him wide awake. *He hadn't been expecting any company.*

Jensen climbed off the couch, leaving his laptop to sink into one of the cushions. He jogged over, opening the door without checking the peephole, but when his eyes landed on sandy blonde hair, he froze.

"Daisy?" he whispered.

The sight of her bordered on unrecognizable. Her hair fell out of a sloppy bun, framing her red, puffy face. Watery mascara streaks darkened her cheeks in the tell-tale shape of runny tears. Her work clothes looked disheveled as she swayed on her feet, nowhere close to the confident woman he knew.

"Jensen," Daisy's words slurred, hard. If Jensen leaned in, he expected to smell alcohol wafting off her. She staggered forward into Jensen's arms—more of a stumble than a lunge.

Jensen's eyes scanned the street for Daisy's car. "Daisy, please don't tell me you drove here."

"No... Took a taxi... You're pretty," Daisy giggled. Her hands slid over his white tank top, looping around his neck, and she leaned into him. When Jensen looked down, her mouth crashed against him with a fierce, albeit clumsy, kiss.

Jensen almost recoiled from the sharp taste of tequila and lime in his mouth. *Shit, she was drunk out of her mind.*

His nonresponse elicited a whine from Daisy, who tried to pull Jensen back to her when he turned his face. Her hands played with the hair at the nape of his neck, batting her lashes at him with a pout.

"Daisy, no," Jensen spoke softly, not wanting to hurt her. His hands grabbed her waist and held her steady when her legs wobbled. "How much did you have to drink tonight?"

Daisy didn't give him a clear response, giggling while she tried to grind against him over his sweatpants. Her head lolled back. "I don't know... Now, take me to bed. You can rip my clothes off and put me in my place."

"I'm not going to do that."

"Why not? Am I not pretty anymore?"

"Daisy, you know that's nowhere close to true."

Jensen listened to her groans of disappointment when she buried her face into his neck, gripping him tighter. Her touch pleaded for attention, pawing at his clothes and pressing herself against his body.

He guided her into his house, shutting the door behind them. Jensen sighed when Daisy giggled and kissed his neck, clearly thinking she'd be getting laid. He had no clue why she gave the taxi his address instead of hers, but she'd be safer here than trying to go home—too drunk to get inside without additional help.

Jensen eased off her shoes and dropped them by the front door with her purse. He locked the front door, earning a few more giggles and noises from Daisy.

"Come on, Your Highness." Jensen scooped under Daisy's thighs and hoisted her into his arms, slightly bending her over his shoulders. "You'll thank me later when your head is pounding after all that tequila, and you've become well-acquainted with my toilet."

Daisy continued to play with his hair as Jensen climbed the stairs, heading toward his bedroom. Despite her drunkenness, Daisy wiggled in his arms and squeezed him tighter like the excitement kicked her wide awake.

"Bedroom... I like your bedroom...." said Daisy.

"Yeah? What do you like about my bedroom?" Jensen asked.

He pushed the door open with his shoulder and took in the neat bedroom, except for the rumpled sheets of his bed. Jensen set Daisy onto the edge of the bed, but she flopped backward with a laugh, writhing on the sheets.

"I like your bed because it's where you like to fuck me." Daisy arched her back off the bed, striking a seductive pose. She rolled around, yet all her attempts to convince Jensen firmly solidified his resolve to gently let her down.

Something wasn't right.

"Yeah, but we've also defiled my couch and my kitchen table and the patio out back." Jensen sat her up, holding her when she swayed a little too hard. "Stay here, okay?"

"Okay," Daisy sighed while Jensen darted into the ensuite bathroom. He pulled several drawers open and rummaged through them, hunting for something in the dark.

He fumbled around until he grabbed the crinkly package of makeup wipes. Either Hayley or Piper saved his ass with their pesky habit of rearranging his bathroom drawers, stuffing them with their things for when they stayed over.

Jensen slipped back into the bedroom, finding Daisy stuck in her dress pulled halfway over her head. He kneeled before her and eased the dress back down. Daisy's bewildered face came into view while he pulled open the makeup wipes.

"You can't fuck me with my clothes still on," Daisy whispered when Jensen brought the makeup wipe to her cheeks. He cleaned her cheeks free of damp mascara and the rest of her smudged makeup. "Don't you... You want me, right?"

"I want you when you're sober and able to consent," Jensen hummed while wiping away the eyeliner and mascara, softening her face. He moved to her lips to fix the smeared, cherry-red lipstick she loved. "I like you when you're feisty and constantly talking shit, even when I've got you pinned."

Daisy didn't respond while Jensen tenderly wiped the last of her makeup away, leaving her skin dewy and flushed from the crying she'd obviously been doing. Tears and the alcohol made for a rough pairing.

Jensen rose off the floor and dimmed the bathroom lights before turning on the shower. A hiss filled the air before steam rose from the warm water, not scalding hot.

"You can take as long as you need in the shower and use my stuff for shampoo or soap. I'll wash your clothes and give you something from my drawers to wear," Jensen murmured, helping her off the bed.

But Daisy gripped onto him, sensing his intention to give her space. She shook her head, burying her face in his shoulder. Her voice wavered, "Please don't go. Don't leave me."

Jensen froze. In the years that he knew her, Daisy never begged him like that for anything, let alone for him not to leave her. He could count on one hand the number of times he saw her cry. The vulnerability struck him straight through the heart.

"I won't go, okay?" Jensen promised. His eyes met Daisy's glassy, red-rimmed ones for a split second until she nodded, acknowledging him. She grabbed at her clothes until Jensen helped her out of them, dropping them into a puddle on the floor.

He guided her into the shower, standing in the open doorway while Daisy basked in the warm torrent of water. She blinked hard as she lingered under the water, no longer swaying as much.

Jensen grabbed the shampoo from its bottle in the carved alcove. He squeezed some of it into his hands, lathered them up, and ran his fingers through Daisy's damp hair. He scraped his fingers along her scalp, humming quietly as Daisy let him wash her hair.

She turned her face out of the water to stare at him. Jensen watched tears well up in Daisy's eyes. Her lips trembled a little as her face darkened, unable to hide the quiet drop of her gaze. She was ashamed.

"I'm sorry," Daisy hiccupped. "I'm so, so sorry for—"

"You don't have to apologize to me for anything. I've got you," Jensen shushed her, holding her face in his soapy hands. Maybe she'd talk when she sobered up, but he knew something drove her to his door. It *haunted* her.

Daisy sucked in a shaky breath as Jensen's hands returned to her hair, sliding through the heavy tresses. Her gaze focused on the wall, letting a glassy, far-off look paint over the whisky-colored irises.

Jensen's eyes stayed on her face while he washed her from the night's indiscretions before she showed up at his doorstep. She needed sleep; his room would be her safe place to crash, free to stay even after the sun rose in the sky.

Whatever she needed, Jensen would give.

From his spot on the sectional, Jensen scrolled through the channels of the muted television. Sleep abandoned him somewhere in the rush of the night. However, he didn't seek its embrace, distracting himself with something mindless.

Two hours passed since the unexpected arrival of Daisy on his doorstep, stumbling drunk and in a bad way. After the shower, he had put one of his buttoned work shirts on her before tucking her into bed. Daisy went without a fuss, curled up on his side of the bed.

Since then, he checked on her a few times. He always left after seeing her chest's peaceful rise and fall, buried under the weighty duvet.

Jensen's eyes jumped to the clock for the time, ready to do another pass by his room, until the stairs creaked. He sat straight up and turned toward the staircase, spotting the rumple of his white dress shirt.

Daisy stepped into view with hands rubbing her bleary eyes. The shirt hung heavy on her, barely grazing the middle of her thighs with its hem. Her hair dried during her sleep and framed her face in waves. The grimace of her hangover painted her face in its discomfort.

She wandered down the steps, almost skittish with how she hesitated at every step until she saw Jensen. Her eyes locked with his across the room. She stilled, hands tucked behind her back.

"Hey," Daisy whispered. The greeting carried over the space as Jensen pushed off the couch. From the coffee table, he snatched up the hangover cure he grabbed as soon as Daisy fell asleep.

"Here, I grabbed these for you." Jensen met her at the stairs, holding out his hand with the meds. In his other one, he offered a chilled bottle of water. "You should start with this."

"Thank you."

"Sure thing. But you can't go on an empty stomach."

"Jensen, you don't have to feed me. I already interrupted your night by being a nuisance."

"Well, too bad. You're already here and can't drive home at this hour. I know you've got this attachment to being independent and not needing help, but it wouldn't kill you to let me."

Daisy's mouth opened to argue, but she stopped herself. Jensen assumed the quiet staring contest they fell into might've sold his point. She sighed. "Okay. Do you have anything here?"

"I have leftover Chinese." Jensen grinned, offering his arm to Daisy like a gentleman. "I'll make you the best stir fry known to mankind."

"I'll be the judge of that." Daisy sniffed, but she accepted his arm. She plodded alongside him into the kitchen, backlit with the lights around the stove. She let go of him long enough to jump on the kitchen counter, sitting beside the stove.

Jensen watched Daisy take her meds and chug half the water bottle. When her eyes jumped toward him, he busied himself with the paper boxes of Chinese takeout from the other day. *Noodles, chicken, broccoli and assorted veggies... Perfect.*

Grabbing the ingredients out, Jensen stationed himself on the opposite side of the stove from Daisy. The sizzle of oil drizzled into a warming pan echoed throughout the kitchen while he got to cooking.

Beside him, Daisy shifted on her countertop perch. Her bare legs dangled off the side while Jensen's shirt rode higher on her thighs when she leaned back.

"So, I don't remember much," Daisy mumbled. "Showing up here is blurry, thanks to the shots I took."

"Exactly how much tequila did you drink?" Jensen pushed the leftovers around the pan, confronted with the mouth-watering smell of the ginger chicken. His tongue swept over his lower lip when meeting Daisy's eyes.

Daisy's cheeks flushed pink. "Uh... at least four shots of tequila, and I had some wine around lunchtime. But that number might be off because I stopped officially counting after three. I might've been too mad to eat an actual meal today."

"Daisy..."

"In my defense, I had an absolutely awful day deserving of several drinks."

"What happened?" Jensen asked, more than a little curious. Sloppy drunk and Daisy weren't two things he considered in the same sentence until earlier that evening. She always held herself together, even when buzzed in the past.

"Can we talk about what happened between me pounding back my second shot of tequila and me waking up in your bed with your clothes on, smelling like your soap? Please?" Daisy mumbled.

Avoidance... Something else not like Daisy.

"Alright. But don't think I won't circle back to this conversation," Jensen replied, pointing his spoon at her. The comment earned a slight nod from Daisy, almost sporting the ghost of a smile. He pushed the noodles and chicken around a little more. "You showed up at quarter past nine in a bad way. You were mostly coherent when asking me to sleep with you. You couldn't even stand still when you tried to initiate. I stopped you, wiped off the smeared makeup, and helped you shower before letting you sleep the alcohol off in my clothes."

Daisy listened to his brief recount, eyes wide in horror, before burying her face into her hands. "Fuck."

"I didn't want to send you home in the state you were in. I figured you'd be safe here, and I expected to fall asleep on the couch."

"Well, thanks. I wouldn't have been as unscathed if I went home alone."

"Daisy, you don't need to thank me. It was the right thing to do."

"Well, most guys would've either turned me away into the night instead of helping me sober up... or brought me to bed anyway."

Jensen's chest seized when those words left Daisy's lips, leaving him short of breath. He tried to say something—anything really—but he couldn't get past the mental image. No matter how adamantly Daisy pushed him to take her to bed in that state, the slur of her words and the vacant look in her eyes would kill the thought every time.

He shook his head, finding it hard to swallow around the lump in his throat. "So, what happened?"

"Why do you think something happened?"

"Because I know you. Daisy. As much as you talk a big game, you're never the person to drink for the fun of it. You drink when you're upset, pushed to the edge of your patience... like at the Ridge."

Daisy's tongue swept nervously over her lower lip. "I saw my father today. I went to lunch with some investors, and there he was, looking exactly the same as when he left. Before then, I hadn't seen him in twelve years. He left me, Dex, and my mom when I was thirteen, which caused a dozen other problems in my life besides quintessential daddy issues."

"Shit. Daisy, I'm so—" Jensen nearly dropped the wooden spoon he used to poke at the stir fry. *Holy fuck, that was a valid excuse to drink until blackout.*

"Please don't say you're sorry. You didn't do anything," Daisy interjected, voice strained with agitation while she shifted on the counter. "It would've been bad enough to see my father after all these years, point blank. But today, he was on a date with a twenty-year-old girl who was basically his glorified sugar baby. The poor thing is wrapped around his finger because he has money. I should be more worried about her or grossed out, yet all I've been able to think about is how he ruined my life and my mom's life only to walk away and date someone younger than me."

Daisy's chest heaved hard, drinking the rest of her water to calm down. Jensen couldn't blame her; the thought of his dad ever leaving his mom felt too unfathomable to conceive, let alone abandon her to date girls barely older than Piper.

Jensen watched as Daisy shook her head. "Before I was born, my mom had greatness ahead of her. She had been a Ph.D.

student, one of the only women in her program to be studying astrophysics. But then she met my dad, who laid it on sweet and thick until she got pregnant with me. Then, he became the bitter jackass I knew growing up."

"What happened with the Ph.D. program?" Jensen asked.

"They wouldn't let her continue when she was pregnant with me. So, she dropped out to raise me. When she started to think about going back, she fell pregnant with Dex," Daisy said, bitterness flickering to life in her voice. "She never managed to go back before he left us. Her credentials weren't enough to be hired as a single mom in that field. Her dream died with me."

"It wasn't your fault. Don't blame yourself for what your bastard of a father did."

"I used to think I played a role in my mom's unhappiness. It's my fault she dropped out in the first place, after all. I spent years watching her struggle to keep a roof over our heads until I could chip in, wondering how much better her life would've been if I'd never been born."

Jensen's jaw clenched when thinking about this guy wandering out there. All the pieces of Daisy's past shuffled around, fitting into place to perfectly assemble the woman perched on the counter beside him. Despite it all, she rose above the shitty hand life dealt her, presenting a royal flush for the world to gawk at.

"And now?" Jensen asked.

Daisy's face softened. "I know Lawrence is the one to blame. My mom asked me to forgive myself a long time ago. For her, I did. It didn't alleviate my guilt completely, but it helped."

"Your mom's a wise woman." Jensen turned down the heat on the stove, giving space to the silence between him and Daisy. "She sounds like a great lady who raised a smart, stubborn daughter."

"She'd actually agree with you there," Daisy chuckled. "My mom was able to find a job she loves once I started working at

Hidden Oasis full-time. I'm glad I can help provide for her and Dex, even though I wonder what might've been."

Jensen perked up. "What might've been if what?"

"If I had chosen astrophysics too." Daisy's faint smile dropped; she couldn't hide the crestfallen glint in her eyes from Jensen. Her hands fidgeted while he grabbed two bowls for the stir fry. "I took some prerequisites at UCLA that were part of the major—astronomy, math, and physics. I realized quickly that the love for space runs in the blood."

"The observatory," Jensen trailed off when meeting Daisy's eyes, forgetting the stir fry and the earlier events of the evening. He fell back into the memory of Daisy's wonderstruck eyes the night they ran for the planetarium show.

"I think a small part of me always knew how much I loved the universe. I never pursued it further because I owed your dad for taking a chance on me. I couldn't juggle a double major while working because of my scholarship. I refused to ask him to switch majors, so I stayed with business."

"Daisy, I don't know how you did it."

"Did what?"

"Let your dreams go."

"I grew up, Jensen. Dreams come and go, especially when you don't have the illusion of choice blinding you from reality," Daisy whispered. Jensen searched her face for any sign of regret, but a mask of indifference pulled over her features.

He might never know how badly she still ached for what *should've* been.

Daisy stared at him, head cocked and brows furrowed like she wanted to pluck his thoughts out of his head and study them. The almost scientific inquisitiveness had always been there, hadn't it?

She approached the world with the rationality of a woman who ran the odds before she gambled them—so sure and confident of where she'd land. Behind that exterior, did the frightened girl who had no clue what came next hide?

Jensen set the wooden spoon into the hot pan, not caring if he burned dinner. He could order a damn pizza.

His arms pulled Daisy to his chest and crushed her into a hug. He waited for her to squirm or push away, but she didn't. Daisy laid her chin on his shoulder and held him close. "Jensen."

"Enjoy the moment, okay? I'll let you choose what we watch on TV with our dinner," Jensen mumbled, hearing a slight snort pressed against his ear. The thought of sitting up with Daisy on the couch, sharing dinner, and watching television struck a painfully domestic chord. Except for hook-ups, Jensen couldn't recall a time when he and Daisy spent time together outside of work. He didn't mind it though, not tonight.

Daisy's mouth skimmed against his earlobe. "And what if I want to watch cheesy reality television dating shows?"

"Bring on the roses, Your Highness."

Chapter 19

Daisy

A cool October breeze rustled through the palm fronds to run along Daisy's cheeks and bare shoulders. Her hands tugged the thin spaghetti strap of her sundress, tempted to change into something else.

But her lunchtime appointment was strictly casual, with an emphasis on strict.

After a helpful second opinion text from Giselle, both agreed that the creamy white and soft floral pattern of her sundress fit with the hot sun, bright Pacific waters, and the gorgeous buildings of the Ridge.

Daisy piled her hair into a simple updo and left most of the makeup on the bathroom counter of her suite. She and her partner booked the room on the company dime since it was company business.

The company didn't need to know that only one of those beds had been used.

A hand grazed against her ass, causing Daisy to stumble forward. However, two strong hands caught her waist before she crashed to the pavement—hands she knew all too well. She glared over her shoulder at Jensen's smirking face, finding those stormy blues alit with amusement.

"Jumpy, are we?" Jensen hummed, righting Daisy onto her feet as his hands lingered around her waist for a split second too long. He dropped the touch when some strangers passed by the Bluff Building, but one hand hovered over the small of her back at their departure. Heat radiated off his palm, rivaling the sun overhead.

"Shut up," Daisy mumbled, face turned away from Jensen's smirk while heat stung her cheeks. "Are you done being a menace today?"

"Me? Being a menace?" Jensen scoffed, almost like the suggestion offended him if the glint in his eyes didn't scream how thoroughly he enjoyed pushing her buttons. His hand splayed across the small of her back, causing Daisy's spine to straighten.

Her body went rigid under his touch, primed and ready for things to escalate. They were in public, yet a pitiful clench of her thighs at the slight scrape of his nails down her back undermined any chastising from her brain.

Everyone had moments of weakness; hers came in the form of a brunet, blue-eyed hunk whom she debated between strangling with her bare hands or suffocating between her thighs.

Daisy rolled her eyes while she headed down the stairs, strolling onto the Ridge's busy walkways with Jensen. Her voice dropped to a whisper while she leaned toward Jensen, walking beside her.

"You say that, but the hand-shaped prints on my ass tell a different story. How did those happen then?" she grumbled.

Thankfully, Daisy chose a longer sundress for that day. Its flowing, slim skirt covered any accidental marks left behind from the last hour.

Jensen chuckled. With a flex of his arm, he shifted their balance, causing Daisy to wobble into his chest. He clicked his tongue. "Oh, those? Those were your doing."

"Excuse me? How exactly is this my fault?"

"I didn't say fault, but if you didn't want me to bend you over the couch, then putting that perfume on your ankles was a dangerous decision. Sundresses on you are already tempting enough to deal with, Your Highness."

Jensen's feral expression when he had backed her against the couch and pushed her dress around her hips flashed through her head, awakening the electrified buzz from all the places he had touched her.

Daisy's mouth dropped open as heat pooled between her thighs, spreading into her sore hips. She stammered, "You're an asshole."

"You made sure to remind me of that between the moans and the cries for me to push you harder against the couch." Jensen sighed teasingly, not giving her any space for denial.

Moans and screams had been muffled into one of the throw pillows Daisy grabbed, so the creaking of the couch shaking with every thrust of Jensen's hips permanently imprinted into her memories. It echoed along with the cheeky mocking Jensen had lavished onto her in the cockiest drawl known to man.

"This'll be the last time I mess around with you," Daisy scoffed. She avoided the knowing twinkle in Jensen's eyes and deepening smirk. Even as she spoke, she didn't believe a damn word she said. "You get on my nerves."

"Right back at you. I'll let you get me back after lunch if it makes you feel better." Jensen's hand returned to hovering over the small of her back while the two passed the pools, robbing her of the warmth from his touch. The two continued down the path until they ended up outside the Palm Building for their reservation at Bayside.

Seated on the patio deck, Daisy spotted Brooks Holloway—the potential investor from the company's gala—conversing with a stranger at a table. The similar facial features and the nearly identical way they lounged in their chairs caught Daisy's notice.

Daisy's posture straightened. "You reviewed the pitch materials, right?"

"Daisy, you know I did," Jensen replied while they reached the stairs, letting her up first. "I won't embarrass you in front of your boyfriend."

"Brooks isn't my boyfriend. He's a potential investor, him and his friend." When Jensen told her Brooks scheduled a lunch meeting with him, he asked for two things. First, he demanded Daisy join them. Second, he requested the meeting at the Ridge.

Nothing in his email mentioned a potential plus-one, which worried Daisy. She'd never tell Jensen about the unease tumbling around her stomach, turning the thought of lunch into something dread-worthy.

Hiking her skirt between her hands, Daisy beelined for the table. As she approached the table, Brooks and his companion, who glanced up from his phone, rose from their seats.

"Nice to see you again, Brooks. Thank you for meeting with us," Daisy greeted him first, shaking his hand with a smile. "You remember Jensen, my colleague?"

"Sure do. Nice to see you both. May I introduce my older brother, Hayden? He asked to join us since he'd also like to get into investing." Brooks gestured to the stranger. Yeah, they looked like brothers.

"Pleasure to meet you." Daisy grasped Hayden's hand first with her firmest handshake. "I'm Daisy Riggs. And this is Jensen Ramsey."

She stepped to the side as Jensen materialized by her side, shaking Brooks's hands. He then turned to Hayden, who had yet to speak but nodded. "Gentlemen."

"Thank you for meeting us today." Hayden shook Jensen's hand quickly, yet his face never moved from a stoic, almost scowling expression. "Let's get started."

"Agreed." Daisy reached for her chair behind her but watched Jensen get there first. He pulled out her chair for her, eyeing her with quiet expectancy. "Have you two ordered already?"

"Not yet," said Hayden, sounding almost bored.

"We wouldn't get started without you," Brooks added. The roam of his eyes over her sundress laced his words with an undertone Daisy knew all too well. *She suspected Jensen was her unwanted tag-along.* "I told Hayden we would be idiots to miss our chance on the Vermont project."

Daisy's stomach loosened at the mention of the Alpine project, her proudest achievement yet. Since its announcement, people's interest drove investors into her open arms. It earned her a fair share of arguments with Jensen, who wasn't fond of her getting in his business.

But he, like a rational man, could be persuaded to let the argument go for the sake of the game. The push and pull of their professional rivalry promised nothing short of a thrill and the prize to end all promotions for the victor. Daisy lived for the chase, and so did Jensen.

"We'd be happy to discuss the project," Jensen remarked while taking his chair, mirroring the Holloway brothers. "Daisy can give the best explanation of the vision and all its amenities."

Daisy's brow arched, gazing at Jensen for any sign of doubt. However, she found Jensen's eyes already on her when he tilted his head. *Go on*, his gesture spoke without words or much beyond the calm hum when he reached for his ice water.

So, Daisy scooted closer to the table, grabbing her water. "The Alpine Project—its official name still undecided—will be a new winter resort. Our company has focused on hotels and resorts in warmer climates, but we've overlooked the winter market for too long. The base plan is for around 350 rooms, broken down by habitation for a single guest, two guests splitting a room, or family suites for three or more people. Our resort goers can access plenty of snow for skiing in the chosen area. We've got plans to make snowboarding areas, ice rinks, and man-made hot spring saunas."

Brooks held onto her every word, leaning on the table with elbows propped around his plate. His smile should've reassured her to keep going, but her attention landed squarely on Hayden.

He returned to his phone sometime between Jensen's comments and her explanation of the Alpine project. His fingers flew across the keyboard, illuminating his scowl. That irked her.

"Do you have any questions, gentlemen? We're also happy to pass along some brochures or revisit the topic later." Daisy cleared her throat while slipping on the most pleasant voice in her arsenal, sweet and dripping with deference like honey.

She spoke to both men across from her, but Hayden didn't glance up from his phone screen. He sat there, looking utterly annoyed, and continued to text in her face. *Fucking rude.*

Finally, he stopped texting, sighing, "Mr. Ramsey, is it?"

"Jensen is fine." Jensen cleared his throat and leaned into Daisy's full view, no longer lounging back with his water and the unreadable purse of his lips.

"This project sounds a tad extensive," he said to Jensen as if Daisy wasn't the one who was just talking to him. "How can we be sure our money won't go to waste? Development projects routinely fail or never finish, leaving the investors shortchanged. I'm not interested in being duped."

"Mr. Holloway, I assure you this won't be an issue. Hidden Oasis has an uncontested record in our developments. We know the viability of a project before any concept is approved. Daisy can further break down the industry standard practice of how resorts are built and where the Alpine project stands."

Daisy almost choked but managed a graceful swallow of the freezing water with a rogue ice cube floating inside it. She cleared her throat, prepared to speak until Hayden hummed.

"How long will construction take?"

"Daisy? You know the estimates better than me," Jensen said, not even pretending to think about the answer.

"Our current plan for the resort is to be conscientious and set our construction timeline at around 30 months, giving space for any pushbacks or unexpected delays. If everything goes according to plan, we'll finish in 24 months."

"And where exactly is your company in the process, Mr. Ramsey?"

Jensen's eyes darted warily between Hayden and Brooks, who stayed silent throughout the exchange. Daisy witnessed it all despite his attempt to remain calm. He hummed, "I believe we're in the process of approving the designs with our team of engineers and architects. Daisy can correct me if I'm wrong. It's her favorite thing to do."

"Someone has to keep you on your toes," Daisy replied sweetly—avoiding the sarcasm while in the company of clients—to Jensen's quiet snort. "He is correct this time. We've gotten through a round of revisions on the design and hope to start our landscaping analysis soon."

For the first time since the pleasantries, Brooks made his presence known with the clap of his hands. He beamed at his brother. "I told you that she's impressive."

"You did. Miss Riggs is clearly well-versed on the project," Hayden agreed. The praise went straight to Daisy's head, as sweet and welcomed as the summer day. A smile tugged at her lips, thoroughly pleased.

Daisy laced her hands over her lap, sneaking a glance at Jensen beside her. "Thank you."

But instead of her, Hayden's attention turned to Jensen. His lips twitched, almost framed in a cold smile. "Though, I've never experienced a businessman who discloses so many details with his secretary. I understand why you trust her with such matters, Mr. Ramsey."

The once pleasant air around the table vanished as Daisy's body stiffened. *Did he just... call her a secretary?*

Her gaze jumped at the men around the table—Hayden, Brooks, and then Jensen—wondering where the idea that she was a secretary came from. That was one hell of a demotion.

Daisy's eyes lingered on Jensen briefly, but it was long enough to see his shocked expression. *He didn't expect it either.*

However, the shock melted into narrowed eyes, with Jensen's lip curling in disgust. Anger tainted his face with its presence, darkening the mood around the rest of the table.

"Daisy isn't a secretary," Jensen snapped at Hayden. Under the table, Daisy's eyes drifted to his balled fists, matching the hardened clench of his jaw.

"Apologies. I assumed," Hayden remarked stiffly, but three words were all Jensen gave him before cutting him off.

"Mistakenly. Nothing against secretaries, but Daisy didn't spend four years at UCLA's business school and almost a decade in the industry to be called one. You won't even address her directly with your questions, and she's the Vice President of Project Development. I'm only here because it's my job to make clients happy, but I don't tolerate disrespect."

"Like I said, I'm sorry—"

"Are you? If you took one look at any of the promotional materials I forwarded to you, you'd see her name on all of them. Daisy is one of our office's best executives; she's why her department runs as smoothly as it does. She deserves your respect and nothing less."

Jensen's tone was almost venomous when he spat at Hayden, who stilled in his chair. His expression ran the gamut of emotions while nearby tables looked their way, drawn into the conversation.

Brooks sprung up from his seat, hands thrown out to stop the fight. "I apologize as well. My brother made an honest mistake. I think we should start over."

Jensen scoffed. "No. You knew Daisy's position in the company. You didn't bother to tell your brother before he ran his mouth like a moron?"

Watching Jensen unravel from angry to downright livid should've moved Daisy out of her chair to say something or intervene. She could accept the apology and smooth things over. But Jensen had her spellbound, stuck on his every word.

God, the angry, defensive act did something for her.

"That's it." Hayden rose from his chair, sneering hard with teeth bared while he towered over the table. "You can't talk to me that way. Is this how you do business with respectable clients?"

Daisy's eyes flicked to Jensen, who rose from his chair. Although Hayden stood taller than him, Jensen didn't flinch away from his gaze. His hands quietly rolled up the sleeves of his buttoned shirt, cuffing them at his elbows.

"Yes, when you speak with contempt toward one of our future CEOs and dismissively toward the other." Despite the sunny day, the air around Daisy dropped at least ten degrees. "Unless you want this to be your first and last venture in this industry, I suggest you pivot fast."

Daisy froze. Underneath Jensen's words, a threat swung wildly into play; she knew it, and Brooks and Hayden sensed it too, from the pallor crossing their features.

"Give us a moment," Brooks yelped before Hayden could stutter out a pleading apology, dragging him away from the table. The two locked into a hushed conversation as they left.

Daisy pushed out of her chair, lost for words. Her tongue grew heavy when meeting Jensen's eyes, which softened as he turned away from the Holloways. "Are you okay?"

"Me? Jensen, I'm fine," Daisy stammered. "You didn't have to go scorched earth to defend my honor."

"It was the right thing to do."

"Right thing, my ass. If I didn't know better, I would say you did it because you like me. You don't have to blow up a good deal because a man was rude to me. I'm used to it."

Jensen said nothing to that, but he reached for his water. His eyes never broke from hers, even as he drank. His throat bobbed when he swallowed. "Don't stress about the deal. Those two will come back and grovel to be involved in the project. If not, I'll owe you dinner and whatever else you want for wasting your time."

Daisy's lips parted, but she clammed up as soon as the Holloways entered her vision. They walked back toward her and Jensen, shame etched into their features. *She stood corrected.*

Sleep eluded Daisy again despite the bundle of blankets wrapped around her, cocooning her in warmth and pressure. She lay in her bed, tucked under several blankets and a heating pad for the cold October night, hopelessly awake for hours.

She should've gone out. Halloween weekend came with dozens of offers for partying, club hopping, and endless fun.

But after several days of endless work and time spent in the company of one Jensen Ramsey, Daisy declined the fun. Instead of breaking out the iconic Cher Horowitz costume she had been planning since last year, she went to the gym, made herself dinner, and headed to bed early.

Daisy rolled over, wiggling one arm around her blanket cocoon to snatch her phone off the edge of her dresser. The screen's brightness filled the otherwise darkened room in its blinding light. Daisy fumbled to dim the screen, but it was too late to salvage her exhaustion. Any prospect of sleep fled into the dark of Daisy's apartment, rushing away from the light.

THE GAMES WE PLAY

Once the brightness died down, she cracked open an eye to read all the notifications cluttering the home screen. A text from Giselle victoriously sat atop the pile, boasting its sweet offer for Daisy to change her mind and crash the costume-friendly spooky dinner party at her and her boyfriend, Jude's, apartment.

Beneath it, dozens of unread notifications from the rarely used V-Suite group chat from Miranda and Iris. They asked Daisy to go clubbing with them, but she declined. So, the two began sending drunken photo updates into the chat, all blurry from the fun.

Daisy's fingers opened her messages app, clearing the notifications one by one. Beyond the few people she regularly spoke with, her contacts could be counted on two hands—including Jensen.

His conversation thread sat third on the list, still fresh compared to everything beneath it. Daisy clicked it, reading through the chat—her last message to him had a timestamp for the night before, obscenely late into the night.

> **DAISY: Have a nice night, asshole.**

> **JENSEN: You too, Your Highness.**

Quiet laughter slipped from her, spilling onto the silken pillowcase as she scrolled further into their texts. Her and Jensen's texting for the last few months modeled after their in-person conversations—a mixture of rapid-fire insults, sexually pent-up flirting, and the occasional comment about work or other professional plans.

If anyone picked up either of their phones, they'd be in for quite a surprise. Daisy and Jensen managed to hide the change well, still receiving the same comments from colleagues as those when the two strictly detested each other.

These days, however, it was competitiveness and sexual tension with a sprinkle of annoyance somewhere in there.

Daisy went to close out the conversation, but her finger slid too fast across the screen. The screen changed to an outgoing call with Jensen's name at the top.

"Shit!" Daisy never moved faster than to end the call. Panic and relief flooded her chest within seconds of one another, seeing the screen return to the text chat. *Close call.*

She reached to set her phone back on the charger until it began to buzz with an incoming call: *Jensen Ramsey calling*

Daisy winced while the phone's vibrations echoed in the darkened room, torn. Her thumb hovered over the 'accept' button, ready to blurt out a quick apology and be done with it.

She answered the call, but Jensen's voice beat her to the punch. "Daisy? Is everything okay?"

"Yeah, I'm fine," Daisy replied, brows furrowing at the soft, almost muffled sigh from the other side. "What made you think otherwise?"

"You never call me, at least not after hours or without a heads-up beforehand. I figured it might've been an emergency or that you needed me. Stupid, I see that now." Jensen coughed.

A tightness filled Daisy's chest; she never realized that about their conversations. She shifted around in her blanket bundle. "It's not. But everything is okay. I accidentally hit the call button. Sorry for disturbing your night."

"Oh, okay. And you didn't disturb my night."

"You sounded a little out of breath there, Jensen. Lying isn't your strong suit, buddy."

"I never said you didn't startle me."

"Yeah... So how's your Halloween weekend?" Daisy asked, joined by a quiet hum in her chest while waiting for Jensen's voice. She lay alone in her bedroom while the rest of the world enjoyed the night. Somewhere in the silence, its heaviness encompassed her so wholly that she felt less alone.

After a moment, Jensen laughed. "Honestly, I'm not doing much. My sisters were supposed to come over for our annual tradition of not-so-spooky Halloween movies. Piper isn't big on horror, so we work around her. But the two got invited to some college party at the last minute and decided to go. So, I'm stuck with paperwork and the sugar cookies I tossed into the oven."

"I'm trying to imagine you baking, but somehow, I can't. Do you have a cute little apron and oven mitts?" Daisy bit her lower lip, fighting against a cackle at the mental image.

"Oh yeah," Jensen snorted. "I have one patterned with bright pink rose buds. It makes me look so manly."

Daisy buried her laughter into her elbow. *What was he wearing under that apron then?* "Since you have me on call, did you need me to stick around? I can keep you company while you do paperwork. You know, talk you through it."

"Usually, that's my job," Jensen hummed. "But I'll actually take the company. Thanks."

"No problem," Daisy murmured, scrunching further into her bed. The warmth enveloped her again, even as she closed her eyes while listening to Jensen's faint scribbling. "Besides, annoying each other is what we do best."

"I wouldn't call you whispering into my ear with that sleepy voice of yours all that annoying."

"If you tell me it turns you on, I might find the energy to crawl out of bed and show up at your house so I can tire myself out."

"Don't threaten me with a good time. I'll dramatically shove all my paperwork off my desk for you before we desecrate it. It's one of the few places we haven't touched at my place."

Daisy had a sharp quip at the ready when she heard a loud crash in the background, followed by some drunken giggling and a second voice yelling something incoherent. "Except you have company. . ."

"Hold on—Piper, how much did Hayley have to drink and—" Jensen hesitated, audibly confused. Daisy imagined his brows knit together while his eyes darted around. "Where's her other shoe?"

"Too much, and she lost it on the way to the car. I didn't realize it until we were a block away," Piper squeaked out, stone-cold sober and so over it.

"Can I have some cookies? Puh-leaseeeeee?" Hayley shouted loud enough for Daisy to hear on the other line.

"Yes, you can. Piper, please put her on the couch."

"Sure. Who were you talking to when we got in?"

"It's work," Jensen lied swiftly, voice softening when Piper and Hayley's voices faded in the background. "Hey, I'm so sorry."

"Go spend time with your sisters. Hayley will need someone to hold back her hair and feed her consolation cookies for the lost shoe. You're kind of good at that or whatever," Daisy whispered. The smell of stir fry tickled at her nose, couched between the memories of Jensen becoming invested in reality dating shows and the two almost falling asleep while cuddling on his sectional.

"I'll make it up to you."

"I'll hold it to you."

"Have a good night, Daisy." Jensen hung up his end of the line, voice soft around her name. Daisy sank further under the covers. She plugged her phone onto the end table by her bed, and when she tried to close her eyes, that time stuck.

Chapter 20
Jensen

AFTER THE THRILLING SAGA of Halloween weekend, Jensen promised himself to stay away from situations involving drunk people. Hayley did a number on him and Piper, sobbing about a situationship—*whatever that meant*—through mouthfuls of cookies, almost choking twice.

However, his luck barely lasted a week when a call from a friend decided to cash in a huge favor he owed. The favor? Being a designated driver for his friend's bar-hopping birthday through Los Angeles.

That landed Jensen sitting shotgun in a van, cruising through the packed Los Angeles streets with the windows rolled down. Rock music blared from the stereo, booming over the November wind, the surrounding traffic, and the hollering from the Virginia Beach Foxhounds in the backseat.

"Turn right at the next light. We'll be at the club," Cal's voice rumbled from the backseat. Through the rearview mirror, Jensen spied the cheesy cowboy hat with 'BIRTHDAY BOY' embroidered in blue yarn on black felt. "We can skip the line, too."

"You're the best, man!" Mason, one of Cal's teammates, hooted while recording the passengers of the van on his phone. The flash of his camera brightened the dark interior of the vehicle.

Cal chuckled, tipping his hat, and clicked his tongue for the crowd. The hat sat low on his medium brown hair, casting shadows over his more oblong features. But with enough light, cool green eyes emerged from the dark. "Anything for my team."

Jensen met Callum Lambert, the Foxhounds' star center fielder, at a charity event some years ago. Five years ago, the Foxhounds were established as the first major league sports team in Virginia; their record proved stellar as they made the playoffs every year and won one series championship.

The two became good friends after Hidden Oasis provided sponsorship funds to renovate the Foxhounds' Virginia Beach stadium. The Hounds, as Jensen affectionately referred to them, were good people.

"You happy to be back in Los Angeles for the night?" Jensen switched the station when a commercial break interrupted the steady flow of guitar solos and heavy drumming. Gage, another Foxhound, made the right hand turn mentioned by Cal, fighting for space on the crowded road.

"You know, I am. I miss LA, but Virginia Beach is my life now. Visiting the city helps keep the homesickness away. Nowhere does beaches quite like California." Cal scooted forward, leaning over the center console.

He cut that thought off when he pointed through the windshield. "There it is! Cobalt & Neon. Try to find a spot closest to the club."

"Aye, aye," Gage whistled, guiding them through the hectic flurry of cars. Street parking in Los Angeles was another beast entirely, so Jensen witnessed a borderline miracle with how smoothly Gage slid their van between two gleaming sports cars.

As he climbed out of his passenger side, Jensen spotted bangles made of glowsticks and an ungodly number of chromatic outfits from the line of eager clubgoers.

Lost in thought, Cal almost knocked him over when tossing a casual arm over Jensen's shoulder. He grinned when several people in the crowd murmured at his arrival. "Thanks for coming out tonight, man. You need some fun before you're the big boss of your own company."

"I'm a man of my word." Jensen nudged him with a laugh. "Besides, someone needs to ensure no drunk or disorderly charges are obtained. I remember your last birthday party in Vegas."

"I promise that no one is going to jailbreak a tiger this time," Cal snorted as the other guys joined them, huddling up on the curb. "Alright, Gage and Jensen are the DDs on standby tonight. Additionally, I'm not date hunting either, so I'm your wingman."

Mason and the other guys exchanged fist bumps, but Jensen shook his head. Even off-limits, Cal would have women clawing at his arms for attention. Lucky for Jensen, he wasn't interested in finding someone at the club.

Together, the group of guys swaggered up to the bouncers at the door. One of them glanced at a tablet in his hands, returning to them with a flat stare. "Name?"

"Callum Lambert. I called your boss ahead of time for me and my guys." Cal's smile didn't falter, even when the security guard consulted his VIP list. Quickly, he undid the rope stretched across the doorway.

"Go ahead, gentlemen."

"Thanks. Have a good night." Cal clapped his hands together, offering the onlookers a charming smile and wink.

Jensen fell to the back of the group while Cal and the others rushed forward into the darkness. But that was for the tunnel inside. Eventually, every color visible to the human eye illuminated the club's walls. The bass cranked to an almost headache-inducing volume by the technicolor dance floor. Bodies packed on top of the shifting floor, illuminating the silhouettes in the rainbow as they danced. The dance floor and bar occupied polar opposite sides of the room stuffed to the brim with people.

"Drinks first! We need one shot to get the party started!" Mason bellowed over the music, playing some EDM mash-up of pop hits that Jensen vaguely recognized.

"Agreed!" Cal threw his hands into the air as his friends carried him to the bar. Jensen followed behind them, hands tucked into his pockets. He probably stuck out like a sore thumb without all the sparkly attire or glow sticks. But he rocked the dress shirt and the dark pants everywhere.

Cal's group crowded in an empty space at the bar. As Jensen stepped behind them, he overheard loud whispering from Cal and Gage.

"Do you see her? In the red?" Gage's voice pitched a little higher than its usual baritone, following the tense line drawn by his pushed-back shoulders.

"The blonde?"

"That's the one."

"I can see why you like her. Those legs look a mile long."

Jensen inserted himself between Cal and Mason, who leaned over the bar for some shots. His eyes scoured the crowd until he landed on a blonde with her back facing them. Red ruched fabric kissed every inch of her body before abruptly stopping before the middle of her thighs in a tight, short skirt.

But while he watched her, Jensen's head buzzed like he took a couple of shots. *Why did she feel familiar?*

Before either Cal or Gage said anything, she spun around, revealing none other than Daisy Riggs.

Daisy, wearing the sexiest dress Jensen had ever seen her in, nursed a sparkly cocktail with a quiet frown. Her eyes scanned the dance floor before she hoisted herself onto the nearest stool, stretching out her legs.

"Oh, Jesus," Gage panted, reminding Jensen that he wasn't the only one with his eyes on Daisy. Something hot prickled inside his chest, jamming up against his lungs and stomach. Each breath he took came with a sharp, painful sensation like someone decided to shove needles into his skin. "I'm going to be such an idiot talking to her."

"No way, man!" Mason shook his head. A tray of neon green shots sloshed in his hands when he stood up too fast from leaning against the bar's counter. "You're a catch, and girls dig athletes! You don't have to work too hard for it!"

"Don't listen to Mason. He's chronically single. You want me to hype you up?" Cal slapped Gage's chest while Mason scowled.

"I'll get you back for that one, Lambert."

"I'd like to see you try."

"You two can finish your pissing contest later," Gage interrupted. But Jensen almost opened his mouth to suggest otherwise. *Let them get distracted, squabbling amongst each other instead of eye fucking Daisy from across the bar.* "I'll talk to her, but I need a good opener."

Mason clapped his hands. "Atta boy! Alright, how about—?"

The Foxhounds huddled up again, forgetting about Jensen while they brainstormed Gage's plan of attack. However, with their attention off Daisy, Jensen broke from the group.

He strode past the stares of strangers until he reached Daisy, still lounging at the bar with her crisp white Louboutins and her fucking scarlet dress like sin personified. He leaned a hand against the edge of the bar. "Starting to think I can't let you out of my sight."

Daisy's eyes jolted away from the dance floor, but they softened when seeing him standing there. She laughed, head rolling back. "I can never get a break from you, can I?"

"Nope," Jensen grinned. "You're stuck with me for another month until one of us gets promoted."

"One month too long. Anyways, what are you doing here? Clubbing doesn't seem like your thing."

"Oh, and why's that?"

"You have the personality of a wet noodle. You look like you just came from the office with that outfit. Oh, and you've mentioned how you're not one for clubbing."

Jensen sighed. "You could've started with that instead of insulting me."

"Where's the fun in that?" Daisy smirked while she brought the straw of her drink against those sultry red lips, sipping slowly. "You and I aren't us without a few insults thrown at one another."

"Clubbing isn't my thing, but I owed a favor to my friend, Cal, who brought all his teammates to celebrate his birthday. One of them thinks you're hot, by the way." Jensen coughed. He felt the eyes of Cal and his friends piercing holes into his back without even looking at them.

"Oh? Which one?" Daisy's brow arched, somehow treading the line between amused, elegant, and shocked.

Jensen pointed over his shoulder. "Tall, black curls, and the bomber jacket."

Daisy peered around him at the guys, giving a slightly flirty wave to them. Or at least, the soft wiggling of her fingers screamed flirty to Jensen.

When she leaned back, Daisy laughed. "He's a cutie but not my type. I don't go out with athletes."

"Dare I ask what your type is, then?" Jensen asked, unable to stop himself. His face heated when Daisy caught his eyes before he could avert his gaze, and he was stuck without the alcohol excuse to save him.

"That's confidential." Daisy's lips twitched. Yet her eyes flicked over him with confidence, like when she negotiated with contractors on muted phone conversations that Jensen watched from his office. "Maybe I'll spill with a little incentive."

"How about we start with something easier then? What brings you here tonight? I didn't peg you as the clubbing type either."

"I'm not. But one of my friends, Giselle, is celebrating her engagement. She and her fiancé were surprised by some of their college friends with an impromptu outing."

"So, you're here as a favor, too?"

"Yes. Giselle is normally more introverted, so I worried the club might be too much for her. But she took a shot of Pink Whitney and should be with Jude in the crowd. Maybe they're dancing or making out in some dark corner, but they're celebrating."

Jensen's eyes dropped to the glass in her hand, sporting something ridiculously blue and glowing under the light. "What number are you on?"

"One. My one and only for the night," Daisy promised, holding her glass out to him. Jensen shook his head, knowing better than to let himself try whatever heinous concoction someone cooked up behind the bar. He might start tasting colors. "I'm taking all drinking easy after last time."

"Smart choice."

"Not that this conversation isn't enthralling, but it looks like your friends are coming over."

Jensen almost did a double take when seeing Cal and the others striding toward them, all curiously glancing between him and Daisy. Jensen stepped around to stand at her side, facing them.

"Gentlemen, this is Daisy. She and I work together," Jensen remarked as Cal's mouth opened to say something. The guys immediately shifted their posture.

"Oh! Nice to meet you," Cal chuckled, grasping Daisy's hand to shake. "We didn't want to interrupt your conversation."

"It's alright. I had been pestering Jensen for a dance," Daisy lied between sips of her drink, batting her lashes to sell it.

Jensen gripped onto his poker face for dear life as a nervous chuckle escaped him. "I told her that I have two left feet, but she's very persuasive."

"It's wrong to deny a dance from a beautiful woman," Mason remarked, stone-faced. Even Gage, who had been debating the best method to score Daisy's affection mere minutes before, nodded solemnly. "If you don't, one of us will take her to the floor."

"I hear you, loud and clear." Jensen snaked an arm around Daisy's waist as she slid from the stool. She rested her hands on his shoulder and nudged him with her hip, prompting a quiet stutter from Jensen. "Be right back."

He guided Daisy into the throng of bodies—grinding and rocking to the beat of a slower song—as the lights dimmed. The dance floor switched to a deep magenta pink, illuminating the shadows with a seductive undertone.

Once they vanished far enough from the eyes of the Foxhounds, Jensen's arm around Daisy's waist became two hands gripping her hips. He pulled her close, bringing her chest-to-chest to a gasp.

"If you wanted to get me alone, there are easier ways," Jensen murmured into her ear as they began to sway to the music. Their bodies melded together, pushed closer by the people surrounding them, lost in the rhythm.

"Maybe," Daisy panted, running her hands along his spine to shivers. "But I saved us both the trouble of letting your friend flirt with me and the awkward denial I planned."

"Yeah, I wasn't looking forward to that."

"I noticed."

Daisy grinding up against him sent Jensen's mind into a tizzy, spinning to the thumping bass while searching for her eyes in the dark. He found whiskey irises drinking him in while the magenta of the floor deepened, painting her features in its shade of desire.

"Keep looking at me like that, and we might start making out on the dance floor," Daisy whispered, but she inched closer.

"You say that like you're not pushing me into you with your hands on my back," Jensen murmured, feeling the run of his tongue over his lower lip. Daisy's eyes followed its movements, which was all the confirmation Jensen needed.

But as he went to lean in, the sudden flash of copper curls and a giant, albeit drunken smile right next to them preceded an excited shout of, "Daisy!"

Daisy scrambled backward while Jensen witnessed everything happen in slow motion. The jostle backward knocked Daisy off-kilter, and when she tried to right herself, one of her legs twisted hard.

She slipped with a cry, but Jensen didn't stand around. His arms shot out and caught Daisy by the waist, holding her off the ground. He looked down, seeing the frantic rising of her chest in shallow breaths.

"You okay?" he asked.

"Yeah, I should be," Daisy stammered but struggled to stand up. Jensen's hands stayed close when righting her, but his eyes landed on the way she hovered her left leg off the floor. "I think I messed up my ankle."

"Daisy, I'm so sorry!" The girl hiccupped, covering her mouth. The poor thing looked devastated, swaying a little drunkenly and wearing a sparkly sash with 'Just Engaged' on it. That must be Giselle. "Thank goodness for... Jensen?"

"Uh, hello." Jensen cleared his throat, aware of the shocked stare from Giselle.

"I don't believe we've officially met."

"Giselle, it's not your fault. I made a bad footwear choice for the club. And yes, this is Jensen. Jensen, this is Giselle."

"Congrats on your engagement." Jensen went to offer Giselle a hand to shake but stopped when he remembered his arms remained the one thing between Daisy and the ground.

"Thank you." Giselle chewed her lip, and her eyes darted to Daisy. Unlike Daisy, who has a refined poker face, poor

Giselle wore everything on her tipsy sleeve. "You should get that checked out."

"I will," Daisy promised.

Jensen nodded. "She will. I'll take her right now since she's in no shape to be driving. I can stay with her at urgent care."

Giselle glanced into the crowd as a tall guy strode toward them with a fiercely stoic look. *Ah, the fiancé.* She reached for him, prompting a rumbling voice out of Jude. "What's going on?"

"Daisy slipped. Her coworker is taking her to the hospital." Giselle turned from Jude to Jensen in a split second, pleading with her eyes. "Take care of her?" Her lip trembled, and the guilty doe eyes she flashed almost made Jensen feel bad.

"I've got her. Try to enjoy the rest of your night," Jensen remarked. He leaned into Daisy. With a hand under her thighs, he scooped her into his arms. Well, at least urgent care would be quiet.

"On the count of three, I'm going to pick you up, okay?" Jensen opened the passenger side door of Daisy's car, greeted by the exhausted flutter of Daisy's eyes. After three hours spent at urgent care and one diagnosis of a sprained ankle later, Jensen expected Daisy to fall asleep sooner. "One... two... *three*."

Jensen scooped her from her seat, careful with her head and the top of the door. Daisy clung to him, her arms wound around his shoulders and her non-injured leg wrapping around his waist.

"Mmph," Daisy mumbled into his shoulder. Jensen stopped by the hospital gift shop while waiting for the doctor, purchasing an oversized sweater to swap with her dress and some make-up wipes. "Sorry if I'm heavy."

"Daisy, I could carry you all day. I do lift sometimes," Jensen murmured, leaning down to grab the crutches off the floor. He had already stuffed her phone, wallet, and keys into his pocket.

No response from Daisy, but the slight tightening of her arms around his shoulders told Jensen she heard him.

With a light kick, Jensen shut the door to Daisy's car before heading into the apartment building. He marched across the threshold with Daisy in his arms, dragging the crutches along the carpet.

Jensen tipped his head to the doorman, whose agape mouth and startled eyes almost made him laugh. "Evening."

"Good evening, sir."

"You know which floor is mine, right?"

Jensen glanced at Daisy in his arms, humming, "Yes. I know what floor your apartment is. We'll take an elevator up."

"Good call." Daisy yawned while Jensen strode toward the elevator. "I can't believe I sprained my ankle. This is why I avoid wearing heels taller than two inches."

"Happens to the best of us," Jensen promised. He tapped the button for the elevator a couple of times, watching it glow bright orange. The doors opened, revealing a semi-packed carriage of people.

They all gawked as Jensen stepped onto the elevator with Daisy and her crutches balanced in his grip. He tapped the fourth floor with his elbow before pushing Daisy higher into his arms.

A quiet hiss buried into his shoulders brought his attention to her. "You okay?"

"Yeah, accidentally grazed someone. My ankle hurts," Daisy whispered while the elevator doors closed.

The elevator reached the first stop on the second floor, causing a flood of people to rush to the front. Jensen narrowly dodged a few collisions from the careless strangers itching to get off the elevator.

Jensen backed him and Daisy into the corner of the less full elevator, watching the doors close. The elevator's ascent was short-lived, stopping on the third floor for another person. He kept himself calm with a quiet count under his breath.

One more floor. Only one more floor.

Once the elevator doors closed, its ascent crawled up to the fourth floor. Jensen beelined out of there with Daisy. The rattle of the crutches echoed off the ground, muffled in the carpeting as Jensen marched down the hallway.

He knew Daisy's apartment number from the last time he visited, staying long enough to remember the deep cerulean carpeting and the perfectly white walls lined with warm wooden doors and golden brass knockers. However, the inside of her apartment existed as a vague blur in his memories.

He remembered the matching purple set she wore to the door when greeting him, though. *He still needed to replace it for her after he got eager with his hands.*

Jensen leaned the crutches up against the wall when outside Daisy's door, using his newly freed hand to rifle around his pockets. He found her keys and let them into her apartment, taking it all in.

White walls to match the exterior sported a few rogue paintings to throw the room together, all soft grays and tans. The apartment didn't have much life beyond the woman who lived there, a copy and paste of the units around it.

Jensen set her down on the couch, propping her ankle up. "Let me grab your crutches and some ice. The doctor suggested icing it for a little while."

"I don't want to," Daisy groaned, slumping back into her throw pillows shoved to one side of the long loveseat. "Do we have to?"

"At least give me five minutes instead of twenty?"

"Fine. Five minutes only."

Jensen jogged back to the door, gathering Daisy's crutches and locking the deadbolt. He set the crutches against the kitchen counter and swapped them for a bag of frozen veggies in the freezer. *Those would work.*

He yanked a dish towel from the stove, wrapping up the frozen bag in the cloth, and knelt down at Daisy's feet. Careful not to harm her more, Jensen lifted her ankle and slid the ice underneath.

Daisy's face screwed up when her bare skin met the wrapped ice pack. She squirmed a little, but Jensen held her ankle still. "Shit, this sucks."

"Yeah, you're going to be out of commission for a while," Jensen murmured, rubbing a feather-light touch over her ankle. He hovered over the skin, too worried to even touch. "How are you feeling otherwise?"

"Tired. So tired."

"I bet. I'll get you to bed. Then, I'll crash on the couch. Do you have some extra pillows or a blanket I could borrow?"

"Jensen, you don't have to sleep on the couch."

"Right, but you shouldn't worry about locking up behind me. That would be counterproductive to me helping you to bed."

Daisy sat up, scowling at him. But the harshness of her expression faltered around her eyes. She sighed, "I'm saying that the couch won't be comfortable for you. My bed is big enough for two people."

"Oh." Jensen's throat dried while confronted with Daisy's quiet stare, head cocked to the side and brows knit—from pain, expectation, or both. "Are you sure you're comfortable with that? We've never done that."

"Jensen, *sleeping* in the same bed as me for one night isn't a big deal. You've seen me naked more times than I can count and have done things to my body that would scandalize our entire workplace," Daisy deadpanned.

"Fair point. Any chance you have something I can wear for sleep?" Jensen asked.

"You want to borrow the red lace number?" Daisy's lips twitched, fighting off an evil smirk from how fast Jensen's nose scrunched up.

"You know what I mean."

"I do. I have some leftover clothes of yours in my bathroom drawer. Now, let's put the ice away so I can sleep."

Jensen lifted the ice from Daisy's reddened skin, which was cold to the touch even with the insulation of the dishcloth. He moved between the kitchen and the couch, tidying up along the way.

Daisy's arms held out for him when he returned, prepared as Jensen scooped her off the couch. The two limped into the bedroom. Much like the living room, there was little personality on display with pre-arranged furniture.

But if Daisy liked it, Jensen would keep his thoughts to himself.

He brought them to the bathroom, where he seated Daisy on the closed toilet and passed her a toothbrush. Before he could ask for a spare brush or some clothes, she pointed to the bottom drawer of the sink.

Jensen opened the drawer and found spare toiletries like deodorant, a toothbrush, and soap, alongside a pair of his sweatpants and his favorite gray henley shirt. *So that's where it went.*

Daisy leaned over to brush her teeth, flashing Jensen a quiet thumbs-up. "I'm not completely useless. Look at that."

Jensen didn't reply, midway through stripping off his club clothes. Somehow, he failed to notice the tiny specks of glitter from Cobalt & Neon stuck to him, feeling like ages ago instead of a few measly hours. He should probably text Cal in the morning and promise to repay the favor another time.

He tossed his clothes into the laundry basket resting against the nearby wall, sinking into the comfort of the sweatpants.

Soon, the bathroom filled with the quiet scraping of the toothbrushes and the gargling of mouthwash.

Neither he nor Daisy said a single word while they hobbled back to the bedroom, lights still off beyond the moonlight filtering through the window. Jensen set her into bed first, easing Daisy to lay on her side.

As he pulled the duvet over her, he sighed, "So, for the next few weeks, the doctor said that you can't put too much pressure on your foot. That includes driving."

"I remember. I'll call a car for the mornings and evenings. There are plenty around," Daisy mumbled through a heavy yawn, struggling to keep her eyes open.

Jensen stepped back toward the window, drawing the curtains shut. In the dark, he felt for the edge of Daisy's bed while heading to the other side.

"Yeah, that's not feasible," he remarked when finding the open spot across from her. Jensen climbed into the bed, ignoring his stomach drop harder than the mattress dipping under his added weight. "I'll come get you every morning and take you home. It'll save money."

"Jensen, I don't need—"

"Yeah, we're not debating about this. You do need help, and it's okay to ask for help. No one will think less of you if you do."

"That's not what this is about!" Daisy's voice huffed indignantly in the dark, but Jensen wouldn't back down no matter how hard she protested. Not tonight.

"Maybe so. But I'm going to help you, Daisy. Let me be helpful," Jensen murmured in the dark, rustling deeper into her duvet. Warmth inched up his legs with a slow, welcoming weight pressing down on him.

There was silence for a while after Jensen spoke. He waited for a response from Daisy, torn between calling her name and letting her drift off to sleep. But, as he went to close his eyes, noise from her side of the bed startled him.

"You need to say something mean to me," said Daisy.

"And why's that?"

"You being so nice without a snarky comment is throwing me off."

Jensen blinked, thrown for a loop. Daisy knew how to keep him on his toes. "Alright, then. Goodnight, asshole."

"You too, asshole," Daisy murmured, not missing a beat of their favorite sign-off for their texts.

"No, you're supposed to call me something else. It always starts with goodnight asshole from you and a sarcastic 'Your Highness' from me." Jensen clutched his pillow tighter under his head.

From somewhere in the darkness, Daisy giggled while burrowing in her spot. "If you say so, Princess."

"I hate you."

"Good. It'll help when I'm your boss in a month."

"Yeah, right."

Chapter 21
Daisy

Daisy hadn't expected to end up in the cramped, plastic chair in a hospital pediatrics wing the day before Thanksgiving break. But there she sat, curled up without her crutches bogging her down, on edge with every noise from the door.

Her doctor cleared her to drive two days ago after two weeks of healing, so Jensen finally stopped driving her around. His constant presence—as a chauffeur, coworker, and hook-up partner—left his imprint on her daily routine.

When the frantic call from her mother came as she intended to leave for work, Daisy turned to look for him in the kitchen of her apartment. However, she quickly remembered that he had gone home the night before.

Despite the bright colors painted into murals on the waiting room walls, a sterile hum of the fluorescent lights washed them out. The stilted heartbeat of the hospital buzzed louder than the anxiety in Daisy's ears; the unsettling quiet lorded over everyone scattered in the rows of chairs, undeterred by the distant calls from other wings and the ancient television playing some kid's movie.

Daisy shifted in her chair, rolling over to face the double doors leading to the patients. Her eyes refused to leave the door, willing a nurse to walk through it and call her name.

So, as the room crawled to a standstill around her, Daisy waited, trapped in the unforgiving clutches of time. Even when leaning onto her side, her leg bounced to the soft rumpling of her pantsuit.

At first, the dull ring of a phone melded with the other mildly distracting noises throughout the waiting room. She ignored its persistence until the buzz grew louder.

Her hip pushed against her purse perched on the seat, making the ringing even louder. Daisy's head whipped toward the purse, and the glow of her phone screen illuminated the inside pockets. Oh, that would be *her* phone ringing.

As she answered the call, she offered the rest of the room an apologetic look—greeted by flat or otherwise annoyed expressions. She didn't check before pressing the phone to her ear. "Daisy Riggs speaking."

"Daisy, where are you?" Jensen's voice intersected with hers, cutting her off. His breathlessness collided with Daisy's thin composure, bringing it crashing down. "We've got a V-Suite thing in ten minutes, and no one's seen you all morning. Security says you didn't swipe in today."

Daisy froze. She racked her thoughts for any mention of a meeting in the last week, knowing she'd never forget something so important. Her hands dove into her purse for her handwritten calendar, shaking while she dug through all the chaos.

No. Not again.

The abrupt push of pressure bearing down on her chest cracked her in two, leaving her short of breath. Her stubborn tongue refused to move until she pulled out her planner and flipped to that day's date. Underneath the numbers, she didn't have a damn thing.

"Jensen, I wasn't told about a meeting."

"The email came in last night. Everyone's email was listed on the recipient list."

"I double-check my inbox every night and every day before I leave for work. I'm telling you, no one told me."

Daisy tasted the ire on her tongue—metallic and sharp—standing before an unspoken accusation. In all her years on the job, she never missed a meeting or skipped a day because she could. Should she chalk the sudden occurrences of forgotten meeting invitations and last-minute rushes to coincidence?

Jensen quieted on the other line, the subject of her scolding despite the fault not being his burden to bear. He sighed, "Look, it's probably a misunderstanding, okay? I'll see if I can stall until you get to the office."

Daisy grimaced hard. "I won't be able to make it in time."

"How far are you from the office? I can try to stall for as long as possible or make up some excuse like traffic. It'll be fine," Jensen remarked.

Daisy's eyes jumped to the clock on the opposite wall, staring at the little hand ticking away. Even if she could jump in her car and rush to the office, Jensen couldn't stall long enough to conceal her arrival.

Her voice wavered as she tried to speak, scrunching her eyes shut. Shame ran over her, and the weight of it bent her harder than the back of the chair she sat in. Daisy knew she couldn't lie, not to Jensen.

"You won't be able to hold them off for over thirty minutes, okay? I'm not making it in time. I can't leave the hospital right now—"

"The hospital?! Did something happen?"

"Jensen—"

"Daisy, I'm serious. Please tell me you're okay," Jensen panted out. "Fuck, I knew I shouldn't have left early last night."

Daisy shushed him, trying to quiet her voice before she earned more glares from the others in the waiting room. "I'm fine! I got a call from my mom about my brother—something about him being rushed to the hospital during a school field trip at the California Science Center. I'm waiting to see him."

Silence broke the conversation for a moment. Daisy heard the rustling noise in Jensen's background, like the rumple of fabric and the click of a door. Finally, he asked, "Which hospital?"

"It's New Horizons Medical Center on Wilshire—"

"Don't leave. I'll be right there."

Daisy choked on her tongue, rendering her speechless. She gripped her phone tighter. "But the meeting. There's no reason you should miss it because of this."

"Screw the meeting," Jensen said. Daisy felt every ounce of sincerity through the phone, tied to Jensen's urgency by a thread. "I'll reschedule it. If Easton wants to complain, he can come to me."

A comment about Easton swirled along the tip of her tongue, prepared to lighten the mood when the doors swung open. A curvy nurse in pink scrubs and a bouncy ponytail entered the waiting room, holding a chart. She became a notable bright spot in the room, all strawberry ginger hair and round cheeks.

"Dexter Riggs? Anyone here for Dexter Riggs?" the nurse called in a voice as sweet as a peach, scanning the room with warm eyes.

"I've got to go. The nurses are calling me back," Daisy mumbled to Jensen, throwing her hand in the air for the nurse while she grabbed her bag.

"Okay. I'm on my way," Jensen replied. The phone cut out, hung up by both at the same time. Daisy tossed her phone into her purse once she clicked off the ringer.

"Follow me, miss!" The nurse waved her over and grabbed the door. Daisy ducked inside, greeted by the vaguely depressing odor of cleaning supplies.

"Can I see my brother now?" Daisy asked.

"Yes, of course. Dexter is lucid and asking for you. I'm his nurse for the afternoon shift, Madison."

"Thank you, Madison. What happened to him?"

"Well, from the reports of the teacher who rode in the ambulance, your brother showed concerning signs. He had been throwing up, splitting off from the group for frequent bathroom breaks, having issues with his breathing, and disorientation. We got him here and ran some tests, identifying his glucose as dangerously high." Madison pulled Daisy to a stop outside one of the rooms.

Her gentle frown further stoked Daisy's worries. "How high are we talking?"

"We're fortunate that the teacher didn't send him home. The doctors identified the issue as diabetic ketoacidosis. Ketoacidosis can be dangerous if left undiagnosed, but we've already implemented the treatment. He'll be able to leave the hospital by this afternoon and make a full recovery," Madison assured.

Daisy could see why she worked in pediatrics. Her voice stayed calm, even while explaining how close Dex had come to being seriously ill.

"Thank you. Can I see Dex now?" Daisy asked. Madison nodded, leading Daisy to the end of the hall. Spotting her brother in a hospital bed with a paperback in his hands, Daisy didn't wait for permission.

She ran into the room and crashed into her little brother, pulling Dex close to his quiet groan. He mumbled, "Daisy, please—"

"Shhhhh." Daisy held the back of his head, finding her breath. "You scared the hell out of me, bub. Let me have my hug."

Dex hugged her back. "I didn't mean to. The doctors said I might've missed one or more insulin shots. I can't remember when I took them last since I fell asleep early last night."

"It's in the past now. We'll set up alarms and reminders on everyone's phone. Problem solved." Daisy glanced up as Madison re-entered the room with their mom, still in her work clothes.

"Daisy! Thank goodness you made it!" Her mom dropped her purse by the table. Daisy jumped into her arms, leaving poor Dex to breathe. Her mom's arms snaked around her waist and held her close.

"I wouldn't let anything stop me from being here."

"I know. I didn't want to bother you at work, but I knew you'd be upset if I didn't call you."

"It's okay. Did you talk to the doctors already about what happened?" Daisy murmured while she watched Madison check Dex's IV. She offered him a thumbs-up, and Dex flashed one back, managing to smile.

"They told me everything. Thank goodness for Mr. Garland's quick thinking. I'll bring him some muffins or something as a thank you." Her mom stepped back enough to let Daisy go. She bit her nail, eyes focused on Dex. "I planned to stay, so you don't need to take the day off."

"Forget about it. I'm staying until Dex is discharged with a clean bill of health," Daisy scoffed, grabbing one of the spare chairs in the corner of the room. She dragged it to the table and lounged back, ready to wait for a while.

"If you two ladies want to stay, would you like me to change the television?" Madison cleared her throat, holding up the television remote.

"Yes, please. News or some cheesy soap opera is preferable." Her mom laughed when picking up her tablet from her purse.

Madison laughed, "I hear you. Sorry to the Foxhounds, but I'm sure their score lead isn't going anywhere. I've never been much of a sports enjoyer."

"Me neither," Daisy hummed. The score between the two baseball teams flashed on the tiny television screen before Madison switched the channels to the morning news.

Daisy got comfortable in her chair. While she had nothing but time to kill, she might as well prepare for her return to the office; the missing meeting from her calendar deserved answers.

Sometime between Madison leaving the room and their mom stepping out to take a work call, Daisy scooted her chair next to Dexter's bed. Apparently, he took a small gap between all the vomiting while at the Science Center to buy a book on space shuttle designs.

"Maybe you're destined to be the first Riggs to become an astronaut. I hear NASA's hiring," Daisy murmured when he flipped the page, reading over his shoulder.

"Maybe," Dex replied, but Daisy saw the twitch of his lips like a smile trying to poke out. "I'll have to think about using my science powers for good."

Daisy snorted. "As opposed to evil? We all know you're too much of a goody-two-shoes to ever do anything bad. You cried when you pulled a prank on your middle school science teacher with a dead frog."

"Hey, that was ages ago!" Dex whined, swatting at her with the space shuttle book. Daisy dodged but caught the pages between two pinched fingers, smiling hard.

"And I remember having to pick you up from the principal's office and take you to my evening class like it was yesterday. Nice try, though." She fluffed his hair, which had grown enough to cover his eyes.

Dex sighed, flopping back into the bed. He ran his fingers over the cannula inserted into his palm, closing his eyes. As the frown overtook his face, Daisy's lips parted to speak until a familiar voice sounded from the hallway.

"She's in here. Is there anything else I can do for you, sir?" Madison asked, appearing in view. But Daisy's eyes focused solely on the man beside her.

"No, thank you." Jensen nodded and rushed past the window. He stepped into the doorway, dressed in one of his more expensive suits with a winter coat draped over his arm for the colder California morning. His eyes met Daisy's halfway. From his lips, a relieved sigh fell. "Hi."

"Hi," Daisy whispered. "You came."

Jensen strode forward from the doorway, arms outstretched for a hug. Yet he stopped short of Daisy and dropped his hands to her shoulders, holding her at arm's length. "I promised I would. Is everything okay?"

"Yeah. My brother's condition stabilized. They've gotten him caught up on insulin and some of the fluids he needed." Daisy nodded. She laid her hand over one of his, letting her thumb slide over his knuckles.

Jensen's throat bobbed while taking her in. "And are you okay?"

"I'm getting there." The words fumbled out of her mouth before Daisy could think, coaxed by a gentle look from Jensen. "My heart's stopped racing, and I'm not anxious that some awful fate has befallen my little brother in my absence."

"That's good. I'm glad you're okay and that everything's okay."

"Thank you."

Dex's pointed cough interjected from behind her, reminding her of his presence. Heat seeped into Daisy's face as she watched Jensen's gaze jump over her shoulder. *Nice going, Dex.*

"You must be Dex." Jensen dropped his hands from Daisy's shoulders and stepped up to the hospital bed, hand outstretched. "I'm Jensen. Your sister and I work together."

"Yeah, I think I've heard your name before," Dex remarked with a sly glance tossed Daisy's way. She spotted the subtle arch of his brow and the light flashing over his eyes, bristling under his gaze.

"Is that so?" Jensen glanced at her from over his shoulder.

"Don't even start," Daisy warned, but her voice faltered when footsteps creaked behind her. She turned around, finding her mom having returned. "Hey."

"Who's this?" her mom asked, locked on Jensen at Dex's bedside. Her gaze darted between him and Daisy, slender brows arched with curiosity. *Not her too.*

Jensen strolled past Daisy, offering his handshake to her mom. A polite smile grazed his features when her mom grasped his hand. "And you must be Daisy's mom."

"Call me Belinda."

"I'm Jensen Ramsey. Your daughter and I work together."

Daisy watched her mom's eyes snap wide while her lips parted, painted pale from the shock. "The Jensen?"

"I'm the only one I know of in Daisy's life. I'm sure she's mentioned me once or twice," Jensen chuckled, but Daisy wasn't feeling as eager to hear the answer.

She stepped forward, slotting between her mom and Jensen. "Okay, you two have met—"

"Oh, you have no idea, young man. Your name is familiar to this household." Her mom winked at Jensen. Daisy's heart decided to dive into her stomach, dropping harder than a ton of lead.

"Mom."

"What? It's true."

"She's not lying. You only mention three work-related topics around us—your projects, boss, and Jensen," Dex chimed in from his hospital bed. Daisy whirled around and flashed him the nastiest glare possible, met by her brother's cheeky grin.

When she turned back, Jensen's shining eyes raked over her. However, it was the shit-eating smirk threatening to cave her ego in two. He chuckled. "How many people do you talk to about me?"

"Enough." Daisy crossed her arms. "They all know about how much I loathe you."

"I'm touched." Jensen didn't miss a beat. He tucked his hands into his pockets, leaning forward with a smirk.

Daisy intended to grab the last word while she had a chance, but her mom's face entered her vision. She and Jensen turned, forgetting their little conversation in front of her whole family.

"Since you're here, Jensen, could you please convince my

stubborn daughter to head back to work? The doctors plan to release Dex in the next hour once his vitals are back to normal. I don't want her to miss anything."

"Mom, no," Daisy replied.

"Yes. Dex and I are okay here. We would feel bad if you missed more work than necessary." Her mom shook her head. She gestured to Jensen, pleading eyes and all.

Jensen contemplated for a moment, a pensive gaze torn between Daisy and her mom before he smiled. "I'll escort Daisy to her car, ma'am. Don't worry about her."

"Jensen," Daisy protested while Dex and her mom waved. She dragged her feet a little as Jensen guided her from the room. "I can't believe you teamed up on me with my mom."

"I'm sure it's payback for all the times you and my dad have ganged up on me together. Now, we should probably talk about this morning," Jensen lowered his voice while the two passed the other rooms curtained off, walking her past the nurse's station.

Daisy noticed a few eyes from some of the nurses following them, or rather following Jensen until they exited the pediatric ward. The door spat them out at the elevators, and they waited for one to open.

"What about this morning?" asked Daisy shortly before the elevator doors opened.

"I double-checked the email on the way here and noticed your email was misspelled. It seems like an accident," Jensen remarked, holding the door open for Daisy to get on first. "I postponed the meeting to this afternoon, so you'll have enough time to prepare. Also, I scheduled a visit from IT for the V-Suite computers. They'll ensure no one's emails are getting forgotten or blocked."

"Are you sure the mistake wasn't intentional? Easton was the one who sent the email." Daisy held the doors while Jensen got onto the elevator. The doors closed them in, beginning their leisurely descent.

Jensen went quiet, jaw twitching, but his voice stayed soft, "We'll never be one hundred percent sure, but let me handle it. I would never let Easton get his grubby fingers on this competition."

"Even if it would make you look better?"

"I deserve to win fair and square. You deserve the same chance."

Daisy met Jensen's eyes, locked in a staring contest until the elevator's doors opened to the busy hospital lobby. She stepped to leave first, but the familiar presence of Jensen's hand hovering over the small of her back stopped her mid-step.

She hummed, "So, are you going to actually walk me to my car, supervising me the whole way?"

"How about we grab some food that isn't from the hospital cafeteria first?" Jensen replied. "After this morning, I think you need something to eat."

"I'm not going to argue with you there. I left my half-eaten breakfast on the kitchen counter," Daisy sighed, letting Jensen usher her across the crowded lobby. He reached for the glass doors first, holding them open. *The gentleman act worked well, but something about him acting a little cockier suited him best.*

Stepping into the fresh air of the overcast November day, all Daisy's worries shed from her shoulders. She moved to the side when Jensen joined her, holding the door open for others.

An elderly woman wheeled by a younger girl beamed at them, sporting a gummy smile without teeth. "Why thank you, young man!"

"Anything for a distinguished lady," Jensen offered while leaning against the door. To that, the stranger gave a hearty laugh, the kind from deep within the belly.

She pointed to Daisy and remarked, "You're such a sweetheart. I can see why you have such a gorgeous girlfriend." She said it loudly, at least enough to catch the attention of several people near the doors.

"Oh, we're not—"

"She and I work together."

"A shame. You'd have beautiful babies." The woman cackled as her caretaker pushed her inside the hospital, quietly chiding her. Jensen's face adopted a bright shade of pink, but Daisy knew hers wasn't any better.

As she watched Jensen shake the comment off and turn to her expectantly, the flip in her stomach caused her to hesitate. She offered her hand to him and pushed the unease down.

Right, she wasn't the dating type.

Chapter 22
Jensen

As the lid of the apple cider clinked into the sink, Jensen raised the chilled bottle into the air to a round of cheers from his family. Gathered around the dinner table of his townhouse, the smiling faces of his parents and sisters filled the space with more warmth than the heater running.

"Here you go!" Jensen poured cider into the crystal champagne flute in Piper's hand, grinning when he topped her glass off. "First drink for the birthday girl."

The cheesy paper crown constructed with a glitter glue gun and bright pink construction paper slipped down Piper's forehead. She fixed it with a gentle push. "Thank you."

"Chug, chug, chug," Hayley chanted from her seat at the table, pumping her fist in the air while she hollered.

Piper rolled her eyes while flouncing back to her seat. She nursed her drink like it was aged whiskey and prodded at her chicken parmesan on top of a bed of marinara and penne.

Jensen filled the rest of the glasses for him and the others. Many years ago, on a cold December night, Piper Delilah Ramsey brightened the world with her presence. So, it was Piper's night to do whatever her heart desired.

Every year, without fail, she demanded board games, Italian food, and family time. This year, however, marked Jensen's turn to host. He considered the "turns" a friendly competition between him, the parents, and Hayley.

"Drinks for everyone else." Jensen handed off the cider while staring at the empty table. "Have we decided on the game of choice?"

"Hayley and I suggest Monopoly," his mom started, but matching groans from him and his dad interrupted.

"No way. I'd like to leave property acquisition at work, please." His dad shook his head, talking between bites of his plate. A small flake of parmesan sat on his lower lip until his mom's hand gently thumbed it away.

"I agree." Jensen cleared his throat. "I'm avoiding discussing work after five o'clock for the next few weeks. That's a rule."

That month marked the impending annual shareholder meeting, better known as when a group of businessmen would decide his and Daisy's futures at Hidden Oasis. Despite his self-imposed limits on thinking about work, the prospect haunted him, lurking in every corner of his life.

Late at night, he stared at the dark ceiling while his phone sat on the end table, begging him to call her. There was only one person in the world who knew how he felt, yet no matter how close he was to picking up her number, Jensen held himself back.

So close to the end, he and Daisy sat in the dark with a mile of space between them.

"Oh, come on! It's Piper's birthday!" Hayley jumped out of her chair. She pointed at Piper, caught mid-bite of her chicken parm with cheeks puffed. "We need to pick something fun."

"So, ask her what she wants to play," Jensen retorted dryly.

Piper swallowed. "Whatever the majority picks. When I picked last year, Mom and Dad almost divorced over Uno," she said, albeit heavy with the teasing in her voice. The infamous Uno debacle of Piper's eighteenth birthday still inspired a thousand jokes and a collection of memes Hayley curated for the family group chat.

"We're split down the middle, it seems," his mom mused between sips of her cider, but a second call for a vote never came. A loud knock at the door ceased all conversation, not urgent yet bold.

"Stay here. I'll see who it is," said Jensen, leaving his cider at the table. He jogged from the table and left the quiet whispering in the other room. He tossed open the door to the sight of a tan trench coat.

"Hi." Daisy shouldered the oversized purse higher on her shoulder. When she opened one of the straps, the plastic-wrapped head of a champagne bottle poked from the rim of the purse. "You look surprised to see me."

"I am." Jensen's arms posted against the top of the door, leaning against the frame with a smirk. "But I'm not upset."

"Mmm, you won't be when I show you the surprise I've brought."

"Surprise? I can see the champagne in your purse."

"That's not what I meant." Daisy's eyes pinned him under her seductive stare while her hand tugged at the belt of her trench coat. The coat fell open, revealing the red lace of the teddy clinging to her body.

Jensen stood there, sucker-punched by the sight of Daisy in nothing more than an oversized coat and lingerie on his doorstep. *Oh yeah, he liked his surprise.*

His hands abandoned the door frame for a more comfortable position, holding her hips. Jensen dragged Daisy closer, one heeled foot in the door and the other lifted off the doorstep.

His mouth hovered over hers while his fingers traced the distinct line between the red lace and Daisy's skin, letting Jensen admire her under the distant light of the street lamps.

Easing her close, Jensen murmured into her mouth, "Red? Fuck, you know exactly how to push all my buttons."

"That's what you tolerate about me, isn't it?" Daisy replied softly. Her voice rose over the rapid thrum of his pulse in his throat. "Now, are you going to invite me in?"

"Definitely."

As Jensen's thumbs dipped underneath the lace bordering Daisy's hips, a sharp clang from the dining room sliced through the tension. Daisy staggered backward, dodging around Jensen's hands to be two feet firmly on the doorstep.

"You have people over?" Daisy hissed, fumbling around her purse as she grabbed her coat. Jensen moved his body in front of hers to block the view from the kitchen doorway.

"Yeah, my family," Jensen swallowed hard. His eyes dropped to his pants, and he inhaled shakily. "It's Piper's birthday. That's why I'm surprised—"

Daisy's face darkened. "I wouldn't have shown up if I knew that! You made it seem like you had a free evening and wanted me to come over."

"When? I don't remember that."

"When we ditched the fire safety seminar that hasn't been changed in twenty years and made out in one of the empty conference rooms. You said you'll think about it and how you needed me all night."

A vague memory of that statement flashed across Jensen's mind, lost in the haze of his hands hiking Daisy's dress higher on her thighs and his mouth leaving a little mark beneath her neckline. *Right. Shit.*

"I'm still thinking about it," Jensen mumbled, earning a sharp and swift raise of Daisy's brow. "Sorry. I don't know what came over me," he croaked, but Daisy shook her head.

"I didn't mind the make-out instead of listening to the fire marshal drone about his arson horror stories. I am disappointed, however, that I exfoliated and opened my brand-new lipstick for this," said Daisy, sighing while she tied the belt closed.

"Jensen, who's at the door?" his mom's voice called, accompanied by the shuffle of several pairs of feet quickly approaching.

"It's um—" he started, stranded between Daisy in the doorway and seeing his family peering around the wall. No excuse came to Jensen's rescue. His mouth flapped—much like a fish out of water—while he gestured toward Daisy. "Daisy."

"I promise not to interrupt any longer." Daisy reached into her purse, producing a folder. Jensen blinked twice when Daisy pushed the folder into his hands. "Jensen needed some numbers before tomorrow. The clients in question aren't fond of going paperless."

"She really goes above and beyond, doesn't she?" His dad grinned with the same prideful smile reserved for one of the kids.

"It was no trouble. I was passing by," Daisy replied, smiling big despite the lie passing through those pretty red lips. Jensen knew her apartment building was on the other side of town from the office and his place. "Anyways, I should go."

But as Daisy stepped back, his mom flitted forward. "No! Please stay for dinner! We have chicken parmesan or plain pasta if you have dietary restrictions."

"I agree. I'm not going to pass up an opportunity where you're not busy or have other plans," his dad added. "After years of trying, Eileen and I finally got you to join us for dinner."

Jensen nearly gave himself whiplash from how fast his head snapped around, eyeing the matching smiles on his parents' faces. His dad's eyes crinkled in the corners while his mom's shoulders shook with barely suppressed laughter.

He glanced at Daisy, who cleared her throat. "I really shouldn't. I didn't plan to stay long. Besides, I hear it's someone's birthday—"

"It's mine." Piper raised her hand shyly. "We have extra pasta, apple cider, and cake. If Jensen says it's okay, would you stay?"

Daisy's voice faltered, looking at Jensen silently for help. But he didn't feel like much help, not when trapped under Piper's puppy dog eyes. So, he stepped out of the doorway with nothing left to lose.

"Come on," Jensen grasped Daisy's hands and guided her into the townhouse. "We're not going to win. You might as well grab a slice of cake and watch how fast we descend into Lord of the Flies over cards."

"Well, it'll be more interesting than doing chores like I planned." Daisy shut the door behind her. Her smile warmed when Piper cheered, bouncing with her pink paper crown. As his family headed back for the kitchen, Daisy stopped him.

Jensen raked his eyes over the coat she wore, swearing he felt his dad's eyes through the wall. "If you go to my bedroom, I should have something you can borrow."

"Thanks," Daisy whispered, striding for the staircase to his bedroom. She moved through his home, a little too confidently for her 'first time' there.

Jensen returned to the dining room to find Hayley adding an extra place setting to the table. One last plate completed the table, but someone had a sense of humor to sit Daisy next to him instead of trading places.

Jensen eyed his family while taking his seat, searching for the culprit. No one moved an inch or strayed from the grins on their faces, endlessly amused. *Yeah, laugh at his suffering.*

A stab of his chicken parm kept the mood light until Daisy's head popped into the kitchen, sans trench coat. Instead, a dark dress with long sleeves covered any trace of the lingerie she brought to his doorstep. Her sandy hair curtained around her face, free from the loose hair tie hanging on her wrist.

"Dinner looks lovely," Daisy remarked, picking up her dish. When his mom and Piper protested, she made them stay seated with a silent yet firm gesture. "So, what are we playing?"

THE GAMES WE PLAY

"What are your thoughts on Monopoly?" asked Piper, leaning on her folded hands. Her quizzical stare followed Daisy around the kitchen as she loaded her plate.

"I love Monopoly." A laugh sweeter than summer fruit escaped Daisy while she joined the table. She slid her plate to the side and reached for the cider bottle. "Is that what we're playing?"

"Yes. It's a 4 to 2 vote," Piper hummed. Her eyes flitted toward Jensen and their dad, daring them to appeal the decision of the women gathered around the table.

Jensen held up his hands in surrender. His dad shrugged, taking another bite of his chicken parm. With no disagreements, the box for Monopoly was dropped into the center of the table.

A flurry of hands pried open the box in a crash of brightly colored 'money,' the Board, and the little player pieces. Hayley snatched up the cash to hold over her head. "Dibs on being the banker!"

"I will allow it." Piper pursed her lips while Hayley rifled through the cash. She sorted everything into piles while smirking at Jensen. *His sisters were weird.*

When Piper uncovered the silver player pieces, he reached immediately for the battleship—his favorite piece since childhood. However, his fingers brushed against Daisy's, forcing them to recoil away from the battleship.

"I always play as the battleship." Jensen's nose scrunched up while his fingers inched toward the silver battleship again. But as he curled a finger around it, Daisy's hand knocked it from his reach.

"And? I'll be playing as the battleship tonight," Daisy hummed.

Jensen plucked the piece up and set it to the side, watching Daisy's brows furrow. He held his hands out with a fist on a flat hand. "Rock, paper, scissors?"

"What are we? Children?"

"Is that a no, then?"

Daisy matched his hands for rock, paper, scissors, and their eyes met halfway. They did the silent countdown until they flashed their hands. Jensen pulled out scissors... and Daisy chose rock.

"Hah! Suck it!" Daisy cheered, taking back the battleship piece.

"I'm still going to take you down," Jensen replied, scoffing while he grabbed the wheelbarrow. He maneuvered the piece through his fingers and set it at GO.

"In your dreams."

"You say that now, but you won't be so smug when I'm rolling in Monopoly money."

Jensen smirked at Daisy, who rolled her eyes. Although her face turned from him, Daisy pushed him back with a feather-light flick to his chest. Jensen leaned away, eyes landing on his family observing the exchange.

His gaze jumped from the curiosity of his parents to Piper and Hayley's quiet giggling behind their hands. *Right, they had company.*

Everyone got tired of Monopoly around the two-hour mark, with the pasta long gone and the cake half-eaten.

Within the first hour, Jensen's parents folded and became spectators to the fierce competition. Daisy might not have been a Ramsey by blood, but she played with the competitive spirit of one.

She fit right in at their table.

"Alright, the birthday girl is falling asleep," Jensen murmured while he raked his fingers over Piper's hair. His baby sister still had some viable properties but was fighting for third place. "Time to call it a night."

"Agreed." Hayley yawned. She gathered the money scattered in her pot as the rest of the table shuffled to clean up the table.

Piper's head stirred with everyone moving around her, blinking all bleary-eyed when she looked up. "Is Monopoly over?"

"Yeah, we're cleaning up now," said Jensen.

"Mmm, did I win?"

Jensen paused for a second but heard a quiet hum from Daisy beside him. She folded the Board into the box. "You did. Congrats, birthday girl."

"Yay." Piper yawned, climbing out of her chair. She collided with Hayley's side, gripping onto her like a koala. "Are we going home now?"

"Yes," the rest of the table chorused—in one way or another—while they cleaned the table. Between five hands, fixing Jensen's table went smoothly and quickly.

As his mom packed up the last few slices of birthday cake, Jensen rounded the table and pulled Piper from around Hayley's waist. Her arms curled around his shoulders, and her face squished into his chest, smiling wide.

"Thanks for making my birthday the best night of the year," Piper whispered, peering up at him.

"Of course. Happy birthday, Pipes. I love you." Jensen squeezed her tighter, knowing the years with his sisters would start slipping by. Right then, they were twenty-five, twenty-two, and nineteen, but life changed quicker than anyone could stop.

"Love you, too."

"Okay, let's get you in the car and back to the apartment. You've got classes tomorrow morning," Hayley remarked from the sidelines, already shouldering her purse.

"Mmm. . ." Piper let him go, stretching with a yawn. She started toward the door, stopping herself to race around the table. Jensen stilled when Piper threw her arms around Daisy's shoulders, burying herself into Daisy's arms for a hug. "Thank you for staying!"

Daisy froze in the embrace. Her hands hovered at her side, fingers flexed wide. Jensen couldn't miss the roughness of her swallow, even if he tried to turn a blind eye, but he witnessed the softening of her features as Daisy hugged Piper back.

"Thanks for having me. I know I don't always see eye-to-eye with your brother, but I think you're pretty awesome. Maybe we can be friends," Daisy murmured, loud enough for Jensen to hear, whether intentional or incidental.

"I'd like that," Piper agreed with a giggle. Jensen had never felt so breathless in his life. "See you, Daisy."

"Keep your chin up, kid. A princess never lets her crown fall." Daisy relinquished her hold on Piper, turning to watch her skip toward her and Jensen's parents.

The lump in Jensen's throat burned warm as he tucked in his chair. "Let me walk you all out. Come on."

Jensen's family headed for the door, exchanging quiet hugs and sweet goodnight messages whispered to one another. His hug with his mom lasted the longest, and he was almost reluctant to let go.

He watched his family file through the front door, lingering in the doorway until their cars drove away from the curb. In the late hour, silence settled over the neighborhood. Somehow, this dazzling and perfect place existed in the heart of Los Angeles, busy at all hours of the day.

Jensen closed the door behind him, locking up in the dark. Silently, he returned to the kitchen, where Daisy stood by the counter with her bottle of champagne smuggled in.

"I like your family a lot. They're nice, and they like me, even though you hate my guts," Daisy remarked, but the soft lilt of teasing lightened her words. She held up the champagne.

Jensen sidled to her, hands tracing the counter as he approached. "Piper likes you. Hayley likes you. My mom likes you, and we know how my dad feels about you. I guess I'm the hold-out."

"Maybe I could change your mind with champagne?" asked Daisy.

But she backed against the counter when Jensen's hand dipped underneath the hem of her dress. He fisted the fabric and raised it over her hips, revealing the red lace from before. *Perfect.*

"Forget the champagne," Jensen murmured. His hands lifted her off the ground to a shocked gasp, squeezing hard while sliding his fingers down the back of her thighs. "I want you instead."

"I like the sound of that." Daisy licked her lips before she pulled Jensen to her with a fistful of his dark henley. Their mouths moved in a clash of heat, interrupted by the occasional tug of Daisy's lower lip between Jensen's teeth and her pretty moans. "Bedroom?"

"Bedroom," Jensen agreed, breaking the kiss long enough to rush out of his kitchen. Daisy clung to him with a flex of her thighs around his hips, ankles locked together. Daisy didn't need instructions anymore.

Crashing into the bedroom, neither stopped to do anything beyond running their lips over one another. And fuck if Jensen didn't love it.

He brought Daisy to the edge of his bed, tossing her onto the mattress. She gasped, losing the sound somewhere among the rumpling of the duvet. Jensen leaned forward, pushing his knuckles into the bed as Daisy sat up.

"Let's get this off," Jensen remarked, hands halfway tucked into the hemline of his shirt and pulling it from his body. "Need help with your dress, Your Highness?"

"I've got it." Daisy's hands reached back to pull for her zipper, arching her back and twisting to grab it. By the time Daisy got the zipper halfway down, Jensen's hands slid his boxers off.

Jensen snagged the zipper between two fingers with a chuckle, tilting Daisy's chin to meet his eyes with his other hand. "You know you can ask for help, right? After how good you were at dinner, I'd give you any you wanted."

"Good? We were playing footsie under the table half the time while your parents debated the greatest Shakespeare rom-com adaptation," Daisy panted while Jensen's eager hands removed her dress, running rogue fingers over the sight of red lace splayed across her body.

"I meant about how you interacted with them and what you said to Piper before she left," Jensen murmured while his hands continued their delicate trace along the lingerie. "Don't think I didn't notice."

"Well, I know how to be polite."

"When you want to be."

"Getting mouthy, are we?" Daisy replied dryly. Her deadpan stare made the tiny glint of arousal streaking in those whiskey-colored eyes when Jensen dipped his hand right between her parted thighs even better.

Her lips quivered, pushing through a shaky exhale as Jensen ran his fingers along the seam of her panties. Jensen slowed while circling her clit through the already damp fabric of her lingerie. He smirked when Daisy's hips ground against his hand, seeking more friction.

"You love it when I give you a hard time," Jensen tsked, applying more pressure with his fingers against her clit. Daisy's hips rocked roughly, riding his fingers despite the clothes in the way. Jensen grinned, encouraging the response, "Look at you. You're a soaking mess. I've barely touched you."

"Are you going to do what you promised, or will I need to do the heavy lifting myself?" Daisy whined, grasping his wrist when he tried to pull his hand back. She clamped her thighs around him hard, trapping his hand so she could grind.

Jensen rubbed harder and faster over the fabric, feeling the wet patch grow with the dull throb of Daisy's clit. He pressed their foreheads together, whispering, "How attached are you to this cute little outfit?"

"Not at all. I bought it to be torn."

"You know just what I like."

Jensen retracted his hand and grasped two fistfuls of the red lace between his fingers. Starting around her breasts, he tore outward to the rips of fabric. He panted while he tore apart Daisy's lingerie in three tugs.

Writhing in his sheets, Daisy's back arched off the bed. She stretched out for him but squealed when Jensen yanked her toward the edge of the bed. His hands gripped her thighs wide, keeping them spread open.

Jensen sank onto one knee at the edge of his bed, running his mouth around the red lace as he marked her skin. His lips did all the talking, sucking hickeys into her smooth skin. The bittersweet aroma of her cherry liquor perfume submerged him when he swiped his tongue over the marks, drowning him in his own need.

Daisy's moans filled his bedroom while her hands clawed at his sheets, too lost in the pleasure of his mouth on her. Those sweet noises became more desperate the closer his mouth came to her pussy, hovering around her navel to protests and impatient huffing.

"Look at me," Jensen commanded from the comfortable spot between her spread legs. He stopped his ministrations until Daisy's head lifted off the sheets to smirk up and pushed a thick bead of spit off his tongue. The spit slid down her clit, and he waited for it to drip into her entrance, thrusting it into her with two fingers. "You take orders so well."

"Jensen," Daisy's voice quivered harder than Jensen had ever heard before, stalling his fingers for a second. His eyes met hers, but she gasped. "Don't stop!"

"Just checking. Now, be a good girl, and don't look away."

Jensen's mouth wrapped around her, swirling his tongue against Daisy's clit while his fingers pumped in and out of her pussy. He pushed them in as far as they could go, finding his digits coated with her slick arousal.

Daisy's thighs clamped around his head while Jensen's mouth and fingers turned her into a soaking wet mess. She chewed hard on her lower lip, crying his name loud enough for him to hear through her thighs.

He didn't stop, not when she rode his face or fingers and squeezed her thighs tighter. Jensen wanted to get lost in Daisy, finding himself utterly helpless when the aroma of her perfume and the salty tinge of sweat mixed together.

But when Daisy's head slumped back into the pillows, Jensen's mouth leaned away from her clit, stopping his fingers. Daisy's head snapped up, swallowing hard with shocked eyes. "Why'd you stop?"

"You stopped watching. Keep those beautiful eyes open for me and watch the show," Jensen remarked, waiting for Daisy to nod before he resumed. His fingers adopted a new frenzy while his tongue lapped at her clit, all while Daisy kept her eyes on him.

Fuck, she had no idea how sexy she looked.

Daisy, with those slightly swollen red lips, heavy-lidded eyes, and her legs spread nice and wide, would be the death of him.

Jensen's fingers curled while buried inside Daisy, prompting a rushed buck of her hips from the motion. She cried out, "I'm close!"

He lifted his head and pushed her thighs back, panting, "I hear you. Stay here and get comfortable."

Daisy didn't argue while she shifted in the duvet, giving Jensen enough time to snag a condom from his nearby drawer. He tore the wrapper open, watching as Daisy hesitated at the edge of his bed.

Jensen cocked his head. "Everything alright?"

"Yeah, it's good. I want to watch you while you're on top," Daisy coughed out. Jensen's hand almost fumbled the condom, snagging it between two fingers with a vice grip. "Is that okay?"

"Yeah, whatever you want."

Jensen slid the latex along his length before approaching the bed, almost shy. Daisy laid back down for him to climb over her. Jensen joined her on the bed, gently angling her legs to hook around his hips while lining his cock to her entrance.

Their eyes met momentarily, holding a breath together until Daisy nodded.

Jensen pushed into her pussy with a quiet groan, feeling how Daisy took every inch of him. As he bottomed out, Jensen's eyes dropped to Daisy beneath him, causing warmth to blossom hard in his stomach.

Shaking his head, Jensen pinned her wrists to the bed, short of the pillows. He took the first thrust extra slow, giving Daisy ample time to change her mind. Yet, she didn't.

Jensen's eyes examined the sight of Daisy sprawled beneath him. Even through the darkened bedroom, moonlight painted her in a silvery glow that took his breath away. Her hair fanned out like a halo while she softly panted with each gentle thrust of Jensen's hips.

Her hands twitched until Jensen slid his fingers and laced them with Daisy's, abandoning the domineering pin of her wrists. Daisy gasped, but her grip tightened. Jensen became her anchor while his thrusts sped a little, still focused on depth rather than roughness.

"You're beautiful," Jensen remarked. "I know this probably sounds so sappy, so feel free to ignore me, but fuck, you're so gorgeous."

He braced for Daisy to roll her eyes or say something back with snark laced in between each word. However, a quiet hiccup escaped her, "Say it again."

"That you're beautiful?" A nod from Daisy. "You're so fucking beautiful, Daisy. You literally are the most breath-taking woman I know, even when you're a pain in my ass."

Jensen swallowed the rest of the ramble before he let himself go too far, focusing on the thrusting of his hips. Daisy's legs tightened around him, but her eyes stared up at him with such vulnerability.

Daisy's body tensed when Jensen's hips started to speed up more, face scrunching up with a quiet whimper, "I'm almost there... Please."

"I've got you," Jensen promised between soft panting, holding Daisy's gaze. Her eyes raked over him while he slowly fucked her to the finish line, shuddering and clenching around his cock. "I've got you, Daisy."

Jensen went to pull out, but Daisy's legs locked around his hips, shaking her head. Her body jolted with small aftershocks, but she met his eyes. "Finish."

"Yes, ma'am," Jensen breathed out. Caution left the room as he pulled her to his chest, fucking into her tightness until his climax hit him hard. Jensen groaned into Daisy's neck, greeted by her perfume, and sweat as he came. "Fuck."

"Thank you," Daisy murmured when their bodies slumped into Jensen's duvet, sinking into the cold sheets with their bodies.

Jensen's felt her arms slide up his spine, breathing hard. "For what."

"I don't know... Everything, I guess." Daisy's eyes averted to the window, but her fingers traced absentminded shapes over his skin. Their bodies stayed pressed together as the silence ticked by, too comfortable to move.

Chapter 23
Daisy

For the millionth time that morning, Daisy hit the backspace button with a groan, watching her latest attempt at an acceptance speech being erased behind the blinking cursor. She might cobble together great speeches on a dime, but the tension in the office left her head foggy.

After months of agonizing waiting, the second week of December finally arrived. The days standing between her, Jensen and the annual shareholder meeting could be counted on one hand—two days to go.

Nervous hardly began to describe the festering, growing bundle of stress in the pit of her stomach. All the anxiety sitting under her skin burned hot like an itch out of reach. With it, her thoughts ran her into the ground before sprinting away from the scene of the crime.

Either she was CEO material or spent the last few months campaigning for humiliation. While the latter might sting her ego for a while, Daisy understood that she met her match.

Jensen, despite everything she expected from him, played fair. Every move he made fit within the rules of the game, honorable. He refused to stoop low like Kenneth, earning respect in Daisy's book. He proved her wrong, and she hated to admit it, but he had given her every reason to put her faith in him.

Harrison should be proud. He and Eileen raised a good potential CEO and an even better man.

"Okay, let's try this from the top," Daisy murmured, dragging her laptop across her desk. Her hands hovered over the keyboard, unsure of where to start. "It should be grateful and humble but pleased because they made the right choice. Where's a ghostwriter when you need one?"

She tested out a few openers, quick to jot them down and even quicker to delete them. The irony wasn't lost on Daisy that she couldn't write a winner's speech. Her "concession" speech came easier, at the expense of her pride. Its completion mocked her hopeful spirit.

After a minute of nothing, Daisy grabbed a notepad and pen instead of her laptop. The blinking cursor was swiftly replaced by the stain of black ink between the lines. With a pen in hand, the ideas trickled in slowly.

Daisy toyed with the pen, jotting down as much as she could before her current thread of inspiration unraveled. Her notes sprawled across the paper in messy scribbles, but the sentiment circled around legacy. Ten years marked one hell of a career at the same company, climbing from the bottom rung of power until the topmost one sat right within her grasp. The legacy of a mentor handing the reins over to his protégé, molded in his image, echoed in perfect parallel.

Daisy shifted in her chair as she closed her thoughts with a period, staring at the stream of consciousness written over the notepad. Although most of it didn't sit nicely in the lines, the ideas were there.

"It's a start," Daisy's voice trailed off when the shadows warped over the glass of her office windows. Dryness crawled up her throat at the sight of Delaney in the hallway. Hanging off Easton's arm, she stood outside Daisy and Jensen's offices, dressed in all-black like an absolute ghoul.

Almost as if Delaney sensed an audience, she faced Daisy through the glass. A smirk as sharp as knives stretched across her face while she stared at Daisy.

Daisy's eyes narrowed in response, sneering at her. *What did she want? Why was she loitering outside her office?* Delaney seriously needed a hobby besides being a nosy freak who minded everyone else's business besides hers.

Delaney's stare persisted, even as Easton led Delaney down the hall without glancing toward Daisy. The sight of them vanished from Daisy's view, leaving her with Jensen's empty office across the way. Yet, something about their lurking raised every sensible alarm in her head.

How often had Delaney tried to tear the promotion from her hands, interfering in a game she wasn't invited to play? Daisy failed to see how Delaney and Easton sleeping with each other to reassure their inflated egos wasn't already a cruel enough act to warrant leaving her and Jensen alone. Unlike Easton, who seemed mostly content to ride off into the sunset with his spoils of the affair, Delaney made it her personal mission to rain misery on Daisy.

Shaking off their presence, Daisy picked up her notepad and grabbed a different color pen. A knock on her door derailed her focus as she circled a few lines that didn't make her immediately scoff at how corny they were.

Daisy's eyes wandered toward the door, sitting taller when she spotted Sandra outside her office. She cleared her throat, gesturing for Sandra to join her. "Sandra. How are you?"

"I'm alright, thank you." Sandra swept inside her office and closed the door behind her, leaning against the glass walls. Daisy couldn't see her face at first but was soon met by an unreadable expression. "Can we talk? It's important."

"Of course. You know you can tell me anything," said Daisy.

She pushed her notepad and laptop to the side. Tension danced along the razor-thin edge in the air; Sandra hadn't given away much, but it didn't take a genius to notice all the signs of something big.

Sandra swallowed. "You need to resign. Immediately."

Daisy froze. Seconds passed her by while she stood there, *bewildered*. While most of her thoughts stilled, the little voice in her mind screamed at her to do anything. *Refuse. Get angry. Take a breath. Ask for more information. Do something—*

Shakily, Daisy rose from her chair to meet Sandra at eye level, standing taller than her friend. "Why?"

"The Board has become aware of some previously suppressed information about how you were hired at Hidden Oasis. It's caused some rumblings about our image and how the public might react if they found out."

"Is that what Easton and Delaney told you? They waltzed into your board meeting two days before the Board vote to share something so scandalous about my past that it calls into question everything I've worked for in the last ten years?"

"Unfortunately, yes. The Board is aware of your youthful indiscretions," Sandra whispered. Red-hot anger streaked through Daisy's veins harder than a pump of adrenaline straight to the heart. "Ms. Malone raised concerns about a cover-up and accused Jensen of helping you hide this from the company, but the Board didn't find such evidence. Therefore, he's not on the hook for this oversight."

But she was.

The sharp pricks of heat dancing along the back of her eyes warned Daisy about the tears ready to rush out of her. But she clenched her hands around the edge of her desk when her knees threatened to cave from underneath her. She refused to cry in front of Sandra.

"So, did you come to rake me over the coals and tell me how badly I destroyed my career?" asked Daisy.

"No. I don't think your past should disqualify your promotion after ten years of changed behavior. You aren't involved in that life anymore. We've all made mistakes," Sandra sighed. "However, the rest of the Board doesn't share my sentiment. Harrison abstained from voting long before this incident, so he wasn't there to mitigate. People have professed their intention to vote for Jensen, including the new directors from this election cycle."

"How bad is it?"

"Daisy..."

"The least you can do for me is to tell me. How bad?"

"It'll be a slaughter—a unanimous vote for Jensen," Sandra whispered. The entire conversation balanced on the world's thinnest tightrope. 'Unanimous' swung at Daisy like a sucker punch to the stomach, threatening to topple her over the edge. "Which is why you shouldn't be there. The Malones want to see you humiliated; they will gleefully relish in your suffering. You won't give them that victory if you resign gracefully and quietly."

Daisy's head spun, but she managed to stay upright at her desk. "You said the vote is unanimous. If you don't think I should be punished for ten years ago, then why is your husband voting for Jensen and not me?"

Guilt flashed across Sandra's face, darkening her elegant features. Sandra's husband, Blaine, had sat as a member of the Board of Directors since Daisy first started at the company, and his seat would be one of the few up for election in next year's election.

Sandra told him to vote for Jensen.

"You, of all people, should understand survival. The Malones are closing ranks, and anyone who dissents will be met with opposition. Kenneth threatened to target those who opposed a clean, unanimous sweep with hand-selected candidates next year. Our hands were tied," Sandra stammered.

"So, you protected your pockets instead of your promise?" Daisy spat back. "All that talk about breaking barriers with you, Kagami, Edna, and whoever, what was that? Did you throw together feel-good buzzwords until you realized that change could cost you money?"

"Daisy, you have to look at the bigger picture. Your life isn't over because you aren't the CEO of this company."

"Yeah? Well, it sure feels like it's over to me."

"You can take this setback for what it is and make something good out of it. If you resign, you'll get a tidy severance package, and several of us will write you good references to help you find a new job. Once your non-compete ends, the world is yours!"

The thought should've sounded reassuring, but Sandra had never been the best of liars with an even worse poker face. Daisy studied her through narrowed eyes until her aching fingers distracted her. She kept saying "resign" instead of advising Daisy to remove her name from CEO consideration.

"You're holding out on me," said Daisy, voice barely above a whisper but laced with an accusation so venomous, Sandra flinched. "Why are you suggesting I resign instead of trying to fight for my place in this company?"

When Sandra's shoulders hunched and her normally statuesque posture vanished into something timid, Daisy dug her heels in. Leaning over her desk, her mouth fought against a mean snarl. Maybe she was comfortable being a bitch, but control slipped through her fingers.

Eventually, Sandra spoke, "If you decided to stay, Kenneth wouldn't stop until your career was a pile of flaming ashes. I heard him and Delaney speaking. He promised her that you would never see another promotion or a raise. Your career is done from here on out."

Silence blanketed the room in its oppressive, heady presence. Sandra watched her face, but Daisy reached the bitter end of her resolve. Defeat flooded her mouth with its pungent taste, drowning her tongue underneath exhaustion.

Fine. Daisy gave up.

"I think you should go. I need to be alone," Daisy remarked. The thin shred of her dignity burned at the edges while the inferno raging in her chest spread into her stomach. If she didn't already have a blackened heart, then it would've burned up then and there.

Sandra made no protest while she backed toward the doors, never taking her eyes off Daisy. As she fled from the office, Daisy waited until the sight of her disappeared before she grabbed her laptop and purse.

With her things in hand, she nearly left the office until her eyes landed on the pitiful attempts at a victory speech. Daisy flung the entire notepad into the trash without hesitation.

She wouldn't need it anymore. Speeches were for winners or gracious losers, and she felt like neither.

After the third round of knocking at her door, Daisy seriously contemplated the ethics of hitting someone with a chair.

She restlessly shifted under the mound of blankets strewn over her couch that she aptly dubbed her 'pity cocoon' while the knocking raged on. Her hands clamped over her ears like it would shut out the insistent asshole in her apartment hallway.

Daisy hadn't been doing well since Sandra broke the news; she called off work, using all her sick days in advance. The Board meeting would be tomorrow morning, bright and early, but Daisy refused to spend another moment in that office.

Even at home, she mourned her loss. Beyond managing a shower and changing into comfortable clothes, Daisy qualified as a bona fide wreck. She spent hours crying and throwing up every meal she tried to stomach in between reminders to write her letter of resignation, effective immediately.

Ten years dedicated to that company and for what? She lost her chance to do what she spent years dreaming about, sentenced to watch the wasted potential circle the drain.

But beyond the self-pity, worry crept in through all the questions swirling through her head. If she needed the money, how fast could she find another job to keep up with rent payments and her family's expenses?

She hadn't figured out how she planned to tell them she lost her job. Her mom and Dex didn't need to remember how bad of a fuck-up she was, not after she tried so hard to make up for her mistakes.

Daisy scrunched her eyes closed while trying to find sleep, waiting until the knocking at the door stopped, but it only grew louder until her temper finally boiled over, screaming.

"I'm fucking coming, okay!" Daisy exclaimed despite the scratchiness of her throat, making her sound like a chain smoker. In reality, she lost her voice from all the tears and constant vomiting.

She ambled for the door without her blankets—clad in an oversized hoodie and bleach-stained sweats—and yanked it open, prepared to hiss profanities at the idiot knocking on her door. But the sight of Jensen stopped Daisy cold, almost prepared to throw up again.

She blinked at him, dressed in his favorite navy suit to bring out the sharpness of his blue eyes. Then, she spotted the bottle of alcohol hanging from his hands. The gorgeous neon orange glittered against the backlighting from the hallway while held in Jensen's grip; Daisy would recognize the brand anywhere.

Although she probably looked like death, Daisy coughed, "That's my favorite bourbon. Where'd you get this?"

"I know a guy," Jensen murmured. "But if you're asking how I know this brand is one you like, I pay attention. You always order a drink with either whiskey or bourbon during every company event with an open bar. This is the one our catering company carries on staff."

"Oh. And you brought me a bottle because...?"

"Because I thought you and I should share a drink before tomorrow. We only have one more night of not knowing. Us not killing one another before we made it to tonight warrants celebration."

"Jensen," Daisy started. She should let him down gently and send him home to enjoy *his* last night of the unknown.

"I didn't see you at work today, and someone mentioned you left early yesterday." Jensen reached his hand out and cupped Daisy's cheek. His cool fingers slid against her burning skin like salvation, threatening to summon a new rush of tears. "You're not coming down with something, are you? Do you need anything?"

With the tender feel of Jensen's hand against her face and his gaze turned so attentive, Daisy's resolve to keep herself together crumbled. She sighed, "One drink. Come in."

"Thanks. Do you have glasses?"

"I do. You can make yourself comfortable. I'll grab the glasses."

Daisy turned her back to Jensen, letting a rogue tear on the tip of her lashes fall. Was drinking a bad idea? Probably. Yet, the prospect of numbing the pain inside her sounded like a good enough solution.

One drink only.

Daisy rifled through her cabinets for glasses. Even with Jensen hanging in the living room, her apartment stayed quiet, in a reprieve from the last thirty-something hours of emotions.

She turned around, two glasses gripped between her fingers. When her eyes landed on Jensen, however, all calm broke loose. He stood in front of her open laptop with an unreadable expression overtaking his features.

His eyes jumped up, unable to hide the betrayal from her. It cut deep to watch his gaze drop to her laptop again with her resignation letter still on the screen.

He knew.

"You're resigning?" Jensen whispered into the chasm between them, feeling like several miles of distance instead of a small apartment's length. He didn't wait for an offer to explain, jaw clenching. "I didn't think you were the type to run away."

Daisy bristled. His accusation stung, but he was right. Running away went against everything Daisy stood for as a person. Could she call it running when the world ripped the rug from underneath her, and she needed to land safely?

She swallowed. "You don't understand."

"Try me." Jensen stepped away from the laptop, setting the bottle of bourbon on her coffee table. Daisy watched him walking toward her, perfectly still. Jensen stopped a few inches from her to preserve some space between them. "Don't underestimate how much I can meet you in the middle, Daisy."

"You really want to know?"

"Yes!"

"Fine! It's over. I know how the Board is voting for the election, and there's no reason for me to stay."

Confusion pulled Jensen's brows into a tight furrow while his mouth moved around the words he wanted to say. Instead, his stormy blue eyes peered into Daisy's for something more.

Daisy crossed her arms over her chest. "It's unanimously in your favor, Jensen. My career is finished, and you're the new CEO. I'd like to tell you congratulations, but I can't stomach it after the lengths they went through to make me lose. They wanted you to win so badly."

Her voice broke, making Daisy sound pathetic as she struggled to choke the words out. She never stood a chance, but she refused to leave without dignity.

Jensen stepped closer. "Who's they?"

"Kenneth... and Delaney. That whole family is comprised of demons," Daisy hiccupped. "Delaney and Easton told the Board about my past and turned them all against me. They tried to get you in trouble, but no one believed them that you knew about what I did and hid it from the company. They fucked me over for you to win."

From confusion, anger bloomed on Jensen's face. His eyes darkened until they no longer looked blue in the light while his mouth fought against a furious scowl. "Fuck. I will raze their reputations to the ground until there's nothing left."

"No, you won't," Daisy interjected, grasping Jensen's wrists until his fists loosened. The ripple of tension down his wrists prompted a quiet shiver to curl along her spine, wanting him to be mad. He meant to protect her, but it was her turn to protect Jensen. You're going to attend the Board vote and graciously accept your win. You earned your promotion with all the bells and whistles attached."

"That's not fair."

"Life isn't fair, Jensen. I, of all people, know how it plays favorites, and the rest of us get shafted. I'm taking my raw deal and playing it out."

Jensen's mouth opened in protest. "I can't let this happen. What they did was wrong and cruel—"

"I'm used to it," Daisy shushed him, finally letting go of his wrists. "Look, I don't think we should drink tonight. You should prepare for your crowning moment tomorrow, and I need to finish my resignation letter. Get home safely, Jensen."

Jensen said nothing. He merely stared at her, shrouded in his palpable disappointment curling off him in waves. Daisy drowned under them, trying to keep her head above the fray.

He stepped back from her and nodded, still not saying a word. Jensen headed toward the door, pausing to spare her one last sidelong glance. Then, he left her and the bottle of bourbon behind in the apartment.

A shudder crawled from Daisy's lips while her knees collapsed inward, crashing her into the nearby kitchen counter. Her arms scrambled to hold herself up until they burned too much to stand.

Daisy slid to the kitchen floor, ungraceful, unseemly, and unlike herself. Tears welled in her eyes when she glanced toward the door, and she held her breath, hoping Jensen would walk back in. She knew he wouldn't, though.

She let him down. Her final failure.

In the haze of it all, she forgot to broach the subject in the back of her mind. Them. What happened to them with her gone and Jensen moving on to better things in the company they loved so much?

Daisy swallowed, knees tucking into her chest. It didn't matter anyway. Time would pass, and maybe one day, it would stop hurting.

Chapter 24
Jensen

As Jensen stormed into the lobby of Hidden Oasis headquarters, the memories from the prior evening followed in lockstep behind him. The defeated look in Daisy's eyes when she told him everything haunted him until sleep became impossible. He lay there, staring at the ceiling while fuming in the dark.

So, on the morning meant to be his greatest triumph, Jensen walked into the office, out for revenge.

He strode through the packed lobby, surrounded by strangers, while his pulse roared in his ears. Jensen felt his mouth move around the words but didn't hear them over the rush. Yet, people parted from his path, scrambling to move when their attention landed on him.

His anger must've shown on his face, or maybe the world finally started to sense how pissed he was at it.

Faces blurred together from the quickness in Jensen's steps, but he slowed down when one of the last people he wanted to see appeared in his peripheral vision. Delaney scurried to stand in front of him, blocking his path to the elevators.

Being in people's way was Delaney's favorite place to be.

"Delaney, get back here!" Easton hissed nearby, but Delaney's eyes raked over Jensen. Her lips pulled into a thin, tight smile, yet the glint shining in her eyes betrayed her feigned innocence.

"Jensen," she greeted coyly, spoken like she hadn't set all the dominoes in motion to fall in his favor. "Good luck with the vote today. I'm sure you'll make the best CEO for this company."

"Don't talk to me," Jensen hissed, watching as Delaney stumbled backward from his response. Shock registered on her face while her arms raised up, ready to gesture wildly during whatever defense she strung together. Hindsight removed the blinders from his eyes, and Jensen saw Delaney for who and what she truly was: a liar.

"The least you could do is thank me! I saved your future as CEO because you were too trusting not to report Daisy's past. I gave you that information freely!"

"Get out of my way. Now."

"Delaney, what are you doing?" Easton materialized by Delaney's side, gripping her shoulders to drag her away from Jensen. He refused to meet Jensen's eyes, even while Delaney squirmed out of his grip.

"I already gave you a fair warning that I'm not in the mood for your bullshit. Either you two clowns get out of my way, or I'll find it worth my while to give everyone a show," Jensen remarked, not easing up on the ire for a second.

That time, however, he didn't wait for the two lovers to step to the side before pushing past them. Jensen shoulder-checked Easton as he beelined for the elevators, back on the warpath.

He mustered a nod to security flanking the elevators before catching the next ride up, alone in the carriage when hitting the button for the tenth floor. The metallic hum trickled into his head, pushing through his angry pulse until all the noise subsided.

The doors opened, announcing his presence to the otherwise empty clusters of cubicles standing between Jensen and the conference room reserved for the vote. Across the room, he spotted the directors gathered behind the glass, renewing the anger washing over him. Everyone but his dad stood there, ready to crown him as king, while he questioned everything.

His anger deepened into a rage when his gaze landed on the man who orchestrated everything, pulling the strings like the gleeful puppet master. Kenneth's grin cranked the heat under Jensen's skin to the boiling point, burning over until he marched into the conference room.

Jensen threw the door open. All eyes fell on him, prompting a few stray "congratulations" from the Board. Their mouths shut quickly after noticing the less-than-pleasant twist to his demeanor. He probably didn't seem in a good mood for a new CEO.

Despite the hush falling over his puppets masquerading as Jensen's colleagues, Kenneth hobbled closer, his face brightening. "There he is! Congratulations to you, Mr. Ramsey, on your promotion."

"Shut up," Jensen demanded, barely allowing Kenneth to finish his congratulations. In him, he spotted the tiny cracks in Kenneth's façade. The similarities to Delaney were overwhelming. Guess he knew where she picked up her lying habit from. "Do you think I'm an idiot?"

"Son, what are you talking about—?"

"I am not your son. I know what you did to Daisy and how this vote is a sham. Don't pretend you're a good guy while you and the other cowards in this room smile in my face."

Kenneth's face steeled into something colder but much more natural compared to the smile he once wore. He replied, "We did what was best."

"For you, not the company," Jensen said, shaking his head. "You might as well have stuck the knife in my back, too, with how you manipulated everything. How do people like you sleep at night, putting your personal feelings about who should be in charge ahead of everything else?"

"You should be grateful to me, young man. I saved this company from a woman who would tarnish your family's legacy with her weakness. She wasn't worthy of this spot," Kenneth's voice rose, painting his face under the strain of his anger, but the malice in his eyes when avoiding Daisy's name grazed Jensen like a bullet.

"And I'm worthy? We'll never know for sure since you lied. You hurt Daisy and used me to do it," he corrected Kenneth, bringing as much malice to the table as he had. Jensen hoped the old man could stomach his hatred spewed back at him. "Don't act like you did this for anyone but yourself."

Jensen shot him one last lingering glare before turning on his heel, ready to be done with this farce of an election. He won the title but lost much more in the process.

"You're making a mistake talking to me like this," Kenneth shouted, following after him despite his slower pace and the cane.

Jensen paused, turning his face over his shoulder but not the rest of him. Kenneth might demand his respect, but that was earned by men far better than him, not a pathetic old bastard with a grudge.

He chewed on his words before he spat them at Kenneth's feet. "Then, punish me. You can threaten to tear this position from my hands or whatever else your imagination comes up with, but I'm the monster you made. You and all your lackeys will learn that I won't forgive you, not even when your heart gives out from all the poison you keep in there. You talk a big game for someone who won't last the next three years."

"Jensen," his dad's voice called from the elevators. The room froze, too stuck in the tension to interject. "My office?"

"Of course. I was just leaving," Jensen replied, abandoning the shocked stares from the Board of Directors. Neither said a word while they caught a lift to the top floor.

Between the elevator's narrow metal walls, Jensen stewed silently and waited for guilt to bite him with a stinging admonishment. Yet, he felt nothing of the sort while ascending to his new office.

The one he earned on a rigged vote.

His dad guided him past Kendall's empty desk as the elevator's doors opened. Jensen stepped through the double doors to his future office but stopped short at the sight of sandy blonde hair and a dark suit.

Daisy's hands dropped from her face before she looked over her shoulder at him and his dad. Her eyes—glassy and diluted by the tears—flicked over Jensen, unable to mask her shock at his presence.

Jensen stared at her too, taking her in. Dark circles underneath her eyes underscored pure exhaustion. Neither of them slept last night, had they?

Despite it all, her beauty radiated through. Those whiskey-colored eyes, pouty red lips, and the tiny flicker of that recognizable fire gathering in her features beckoned Jensen closer. Come home, they begged him.

But no matter how hard she pulled him in, the words felt stranded in his throat. Jensen choked on them, silenced. *Say something to her, idiot!*

"Have a seat, Jensen," his dad stated while stepping around his desk. He and Jensen took their seats together—like father, like son. His dad laced his hands on top of the desk. "We're long overdue for a talk. All three of us."

Jensen glanced toward Daisy, finding her eyes already on him. Something downright *electric* zapped through a single look shared between them. Somewhere deep within him, he wondered if they had been found out.

Harrison didn't wait to break the silence. "I can't say I expected today to turn out how it did. After Daisy showed up to my office this morning with her resignation and Sandra called to warn me as soon as the vote finished, I struggled with how to proceed. The vote should've been fair, and my rational side demands a redo."

"But?" Daisy whispered hoarsely while Jensen sat there, still choking on the taste of his inaction.

"But you spoke to me honestly about how this life isn't for you. I can't force you into a vote or to be unhappy," Harrison replied. "I never tell you enough, but you've made me incredibly proud, Daisy. As your mentor, I've spent the last ten years witnessing your greatness grow beyond my wildest imagination. So, I'm letting you go if you promise not to become a stranger."

A quiet hiccup escaped from Daisy, short of a sob. Jensen saw the smile pull at her lips, watery and fragile. Although her eyes watered, the softness eclipsing the sadness told the story of a woman who made peace with her decision.

Daisy shook her head. "I'd never forget you, not after everything you did for me. You know how to reach me."

"I'm glad I do. But I have a small confession while I have you and my son here. Since the retreat, you and Jensen have grown significantly over the last few months. So, I must admit that I may have been responsible for the fiasco that was your rooming assignment."

"What?" Jensen's voice finally lodged free of his throat, startling himself and Daisy from how she perked up. "Dad, are you serious?"

"I am."

"Why did you do that?"

"After years of you two fighting, I thought you'd be better off on the same side. And I was right."

Daisy said nothing while she shifted forward in her seat. Jensen observed her profile in his peripheral, bearing witness to the slight changes before the laughter started. Guttural, unbridled laughing poured off Daisy's lips, flowing with the honeyed smoothness of the wine.

Her head slumped into her hands as she laughed, filling the room with the resonance of the sound. *Jensen loved that sound.*

Daisy pushed out of her chair and grasped his dad's hands across the desk, smiling hard while tears streamed down her cheeks. "Thank you for everything, Harrison. Take care."

"Take care, Daisy," Harrison murmured, letting go of her hands. For a shining moment, Daisy gathered Jensen's attention with a gentle look. Her fingers twitched toward him, but she left the office with her wordless goodbye.

Jensen watched her leave while the world crumbled around him. His vision tunneled when the elevator doors opened to pull her in. He would've waited until they closed, but his dad's voice cut in.

"Jensen, look at me."

"Yes?" Jensen whispered, reluctant when facing his dad.

"Son, I'm about to say this with unconditional love, but you're terrible at being subtle. A girl like Daisy doesn't walk into your life every day and doesn't wait around for you to wise up. Don't let her walk away," Harrison said.

"What are you—"

"You're in love with her."

The clench of Jensen's chest around his heart would've hurt more, but he focused on how his dad's proclamation ripped the air straight out of his lungs. He had seen right through him.

Jensen nervously ran his tongue along his lips. "How long have you known about Daisy and me?"

"That you two have hooked up? Right now, watching how you two snuck glances at one another when you thought the other wasn't paying attention." His dad's smile quickly abandoned him, face crestfallen. "But I knew you would fall in love with her the night you met. Your mom and I listened to you rant about your first meeting for an hour, and we went to bed in agreement. You were already gone."

"That—why didn't you say anything?" Jensen asked. His voice begged, betraying a thin veneer of calm. The words came out cracked, splintered into small pockets of weakness in his soul.

He loved Daisy?

He loved Daisy... and he spent all his time lost instead?

What had he done?

"You weren't ready to see it yet, but you outgrew Delaney long ago. No one wanted to push you before you saw it on your own. Jensen, you're the type of man who needs an equal match—a partner in every sense of the word. Your love needs to grow alongside you and challenge you to be better. Deep down, you know who does that for you." Jensen didn't process a damn word before he found himself flung out of his seat, thrumming with energy.

He swallowed. "I have to go."

"If you intercept her before she leaves, you'll ensure that Piper wins the betting pool," his dad murmured, catching Jensen's eye. His dad almost glowed with an impish twinkle. "After Piper's birthday, your sisters joined the bet between your mom and me about when you'd realize."

"I'll be mad about it later or laugh. I can decide after I speak with Daisy," Jensen promised, bolting from the room. He sprinted for the elevator, jamming the button several times to watch the button glow.

The elevator would be too slow, letting Daisy slip through his fingers.

Jensen abandoned the elevator, in too much of a hurry to wait around and hinge his bets on a miracle. He wasn't letting Daisy slip from his hands, not when he had already wasted so much time.

He scrambled toward the door in the corner of the spacious room, yanking on the handle. Due to the size of the building, elevators became the default method of travel around the office. However, the stairwell ran through every floor.

No one used it... until today.

Jensen yanked with all his might until the door swung open, promptly dashing down the stairs. His hand skimmed the railing while skipping every few steps in his oxfords, but Jensen only had Daisy on his mind.

His legs burned in his slacks with each flight of stairs he rounded, sprinting regardless of the pain. The burn could encompass the rest of him with its stinging sensation while his legs threatened to collapse. Still, Jensen would run as long as he had adrenaline in him.

The number of stairs dwindled from the dozens to the single digits until the door to the lobby appeared. Jensen grasped the handle and yanked it open.

Jensen emerged into a lobby full of people, eyes scouring the crowd for Daisy. He looked high and low, spotting the dark suit and blonde hair heading directly for the revolving door. He lurched forward, propelling toward her.

"Daisy!" Jensen shouted, not caring how loud he was. People's heads swiveled toward him while he raced past them. He mustered another breath and begged, hoping she heard him. "Daisy, stop!"

That time, however, she halted while the rest of the room did. A hush fell over the lobby, truly silent after Jensen's plea. As Daisy turned around, Jensen felt the world fall away; he and she became the only people left.

He stepped forward on numb legs when Daisy sighed, "Jensen, if you've come to convince me to change my mind, I—"

She barely got through the words as Jensen reached her, passing by the faces of the strangers and the likes of Easton and Delaney. His hands grasped her face despite all the witnesses around them, cupping her cheeks to tenderly graze his thumb along her skin.

Then, he pulled her close and laid his lips onto hers, kissing her without remorse. Jensen's mouth moved on its own accord; he poured every unspoken feeling into the embrace while holding Daisy close to him, refusing to let her slip through his fingers.

Daisy didn't fight or pretend for their audience. Instead, she coiled her arms around Jensen's neck and kissed him back.

Their lips molded together like two perfect puzzle pieces, speaking in the language made for them alone.

A soft moan from Daisy stoked the burning in Jensen's chest, bringing her closer to him. Who gave a fuck if they had an audience? He didn't want to wait for privacy, not when he was done hiding from the world.

Shaky hands cupped Daisy's face when they pulled back, heaving for air while their lips stayed close together. Jensen's breathless laughter pooled onto Daisy's parted lips when he murmured, "Just listen, please. I didn't run down over a dozen flights of stairs for me to lose you."

"Okay, I'm listening." Daisy's head leaned back enough for him to meet her eyes. But staring into those whiskey-colored irises, drenched in enough longing to start a fire, only made Jensen want to kiss her until she deciphered the confession on the tip of his tongue.

"If you keep looking at me like that, I'm going to kiss you again," Jensen said loud enough for the world. The lobby stayed quiet enough to hear a pin drop while he paused, collecting his words into something presentable for Daisy. "You created this fire in me that I didn't realize I needed to keep going every day. But I need it as much as I need air. I love the way you laugh, the passion you carry for every project, or how you've never let a bad hand stop you from trying. I love your intelligence, loyalty, and kindness hidden behind your tough attitude. I love the way we bicker, how you put up with my endless shit, and how you keep me on my toes with that exacting tongue. But most importantly, I love you, Daisy Riggs. I don't know who I'd be without you, and I never want to find out."

Daisy's eyes widened, but speechlessness took hold of her like it had held Jensen hostage in his dad's office.

So, he stroked her hair with a gentle hand, pushing a strand back from her face. "I will walk away from this damn job if you ask me to, or I can march up there right now and demand a revote."

"Jensen, that's not necessary," Daisy shushed him before he descended into further plans to blow up his career. Jensen waited, quiet while she processed his words.

His voice shook, exhaling, "Please say something?"

Daisy looked him over, but then her mouth crashed back to his. Jensen's body melted into her embrace, eyes closed and hands tugging her close despite there being no space left between them.

The feel of her mouth on his felt right. She kissed him like they might uncover the universe's secrets in one frenzied embrace. Her tongue swept over his lips and asked for shelter, softer than when she prepared a barb for his ego. Fuck, she completed him when he never realized he was missing something.

Daisy's lips broke the kiss enough to whisper against Jensen's mouth, "Does that answer you?"

"It does."

"Good. Just for the record, I love you too, Jensen Ramsey. I want you when we're up, when we're fighting, and when the world seems stacked against us. After knowing you, I realize that our souls are cut from the same piece of the universe. I was always meant to find you."

Jensen's hands held Daisy's face, stricken by the heat of tears behind his eyes. Yeah, fuck their audience. "What's the plan now?"

"Honestly, I negotiated a nice severance package for my resignation. Your dad signed off on everything," Daisy remarked while her arms slid further down Jensen's shoulders. "I have a monetary settlement plus a full scholarship to continue my education. Your dad's writing me a letter of recommendation so I can work on that thing we discussed."

"The astrophysics thing?" Jensen asked, earning a nod from Daisy. He grinned hard; Dr. Daisy Riggs, PhD in astrophysics, rolled off the tongue quite nicely.

Daisy scrunched her nose. "What about you? Don't you have a meeting to proceed over?"

"Hah, no. I called everyone a coward and told Kenneth that I didn't see him living long enough to unseat me, so they could all fuck themselves." Jensen laughed when Daisy yanked him into another kiss, that one having more oomph behind the touch.

"Yeah, tell me more."

"Well, I'll use the winter break to move out of my old office and into the new one. I might miss you too much if I have to stare at your empty office."

"Oh my god, you're such a sap."

"My apologies, Your Highness."

Daisy shushed him with a chaste peck. "I don't care how sappy you get. I want all of it, you hear me?"

"Yes, ma'am," Jensen murmured while peppering her face with kisses to her laughter. "Can I take you back to my place, or will we go to yours? I want to spend quality time ignoring our phones and littering the floor with clothes."

"Yours. Your bed is softer." Daisy grasped one of her hands in his, and Jensen pulled her toward the door. Of all the arguments they waged over the little stuff, Jensen looked forward to loving Daisy.

That, he knew, was a game he'd *always* win.

Epilogue

ONE AND A HALF *years later—June*

Underneath the dimmed lights of the ballroom, the faces faded into the shadows at the edge of the dance floor. The rest of the world fell away while the chorus from *Iris* by The Goo Goo Dolls played overhead. Projected onto the ceiling, a glittering display of the night sky and all its stars set the mood for the perfect evening.

Daisy's head lifted off Jensen's shoulder, hearing his soft murmuring to the song's lyrics. The two stood in the middle of the dance floor, swaying with the spotlight beaming on them. That was standard for weddings, after all.

Jensen's voice quieted, but Daisy's gloved hand slid up the lapel of his suit jacket. "Keep going. Your voice is so beautiful."

"Oh, yeah?" Jensen chuckled, chin tilted down so their eyes would meet halfway. "That's not what you said in the shower last week."

"First of all, I said that you're not built to belt Whitney Houston, but most people don't have the skills for that! And second, please... for me?" Daisy scooted closer to Jensen, batting her lashes at him.

"Alright, alright." Jensen's hands dipped lower on her waist, leaning down until their lips brushed together. He fought a smile, sparing a glance toward the faces hidden in the darkness. "Anything for my wife."

Daisy's hold on Jensen—her *husband*—tightened while they circled around the ballroom. Between Jensen's whispering of the lyrics, the two collided into kisses, filled with enough passion to stretch across the four walls, helplessly falling into one another's gravity.

Nuzzling closer to Jensen, Daisy tucked her face into his neck, listening to the steady thump of his heart. It was the sound Daisy heard when she first woke up and the last thing she heard before she fell asleep. Its steadiness grounded her to the world, even when her head landed somewhere among the stars or the rings of Saturn.

A sniffle escaped her as the outro to the song echoed over the speakers, prompting a soft sigh from Jensen. "Honey, do you need a tissue?"

"I'm fine," Daisy huffed, albeit playfully, while fanning at her eyes. She didn't spend a pretty penny on her make-up for the photos to have mascara smeared down her cheeks or splotches of red. "I'm still recovering from the surprise our parents sprung on me."

When planning their wedding, Jensen and Daisy knew some traditions would need different executions. Chief among them was the father-daughter dance.

The two had brainstormed ideas, settling on making the dances for their families instead. Jensen shared the dance with his sisters and mom to an upbeat, crowd-pleaser. Daisy planned to dance to one of her favorite Billy Joel songs with her mom and brother.

During the dance, however, Daisy felt a tap on her shoulder, finding none other than Harrison and Eileen standing behind her. They offered their hands to her, asking for their turn to dance and welcome her to the family. She barely emerged from the dance with her make-up unscathed. That, and she heard enough camera clicks to have a photo album filled with her crying face taken mid-dance.

Jensen hummed, "I can't wait to see how those photos turned out. Even while on the verge of crying, you're still the most beautiful woman in this place."

"And you're such a sap." Daisy suppressed her laughter into Jensen's shoulder, feeling it shake underneath her with his own laughter.

"I can spout off Hidden Oasis' quarterly reports if you prefer instead of lavishing you in compliments about how divine you look tonight," Jensen said.

"You're annoying."

"I love you, too."

"I love you more."

Daisy's nose scrunched at him, smiling wide. The lights around the room raised, revealing all the faces of their friends, family, and former coworkers sitting at their assigned tables. Applause rolled from the audience, including whistles and hollering from the crowd.

Jensen and Daisy stepped apart when the emcee's voice echoed from the DJ stand, "Once again, let's hear it for Mr. and Mrs. Ramsey. What a lovely couple!"

"Not to be pedantic, but it's Mr. Ramsey and soon-to-be Dr. Riggs!" Jensen declared above all the cheering from the crowd, waving his hand toward the emcee. He said it with a cheesy smirk while Daisy rolled her eyes.

"Ignore him," she called out. "I don't have a PhD yet, so it's still Mrs., but when the time comes, it'll be Dr. Ramsey. Thank you."

Daisy twirled out of Jensen's arms, taking in the downright goofy smile on his face instead of the suave, composed smirk he wore before. Their marriage could still bring surprises to the table.

"With the first dances done, we will proceed to the bouquet toss! All the single ladies, get out of your chairs and line up!" the emcee shouted while Daisy raced to the sidelines, hiking the glittering skirt of her ivory sheath gown into her gloved hands.

She held her hand out to Giselle—her matron of honor—and accepted the bouquet of classic red roses. The spaghetti strap of her dress slipped down her shoulder while she raced back to Jensen on the floor.

As the music played, women from around the room rushed to the floor and packed into tight lines. Daisy turned her back to them, practicing her toss while she whispered to Jensen, "Hayley's girlfriend slipped me a $20 to toss it to her."

"Just shoot for the stars, honey," Jensen chuckled, hands tucked into his suit's pockets. Those stormy blue eyes sparkled while watching her. Daisy winked as she flung the bouquet behind her.

"Let's see where it landed," Daisy snorted, glancing over her shoulder with Jensen. The crowd of girls had parted and revealed the bouquet perfectly seated on the lap of one Callum Lambert.

Cal held up the bouquet, waving it in the air. "I'm off-duty and still catching flying objects. Any chance you want to pitch for the Foxhounds, Mrs. Ramsey?"

"I'm good, thanks! You're next on the marriage market, so good luck." Daisy smirked while the audience howled. Despite wrinkling his nose, Cal held the bouquet to his chest and swatted hands away from taking it.

A pair of arms slid around Daisy's waist. She gasped softly before Jensen's mouth found hers, crushing a loving kiss to her mouth. She, of course, reciprocated with a teasing nibble to his lower lip until Jensen pulled her closer.

"Is the garter toss next?"

"Your turn, Jensen!"

Several people in the crowd yelled—suspiciously at the Foxhound table—and Jensen waved them off, keeping Daisy close to his chest.

"None of you freaks get the garter toss. My wife, my eyes only!" Jensen exclaimed over the playful ribbing from the sidelines. He turned back to Daisy when she looped her hand into his lapels.

"I know that's right," she whispered, crushing their lips back together. Once, they might've been rivals at one another's throats, but in each other, they found the one person who would never let the other settle for less than the best. It was what Ramseys did.

The Story Continues

Daisy and Jensen played a game with an unexpected outcome, But what comes next, or rather who?

*Love can be hard enough, especially when fame gets involved so **keeping** it a **secret** sounds like the best idea possible.*

Afterword

Have you ever read a book that ended up being like a mirror?

When I sat down to start *The Games We Play*, part of me knew that Daisy and Jensen's story would be more than a story to me. Much like some of my past books, I examined pieces of myself and my life experiences through my characters' perspectives. Yet nothing could've prepared me for how much of myself I see in Daisy.

In short, Daisy represents the image I present to the world—tough, ambitious, sharp-tongued, and highly competent.

But in the same way, she mirrors the flaws and shortcomings I see. She's prickly. She pretends that she isn't hurt or that others can't hurt her. She shuts out the world and keeps people at arm's length, even those she loves. She's hyperindependent and almost allergic to depending on others. She scorns vulnerability.

Writing her love story became a lesson in patience, acceptance, and hope. She gives me hope to find a partner who treats me as his equal yet cares for me deeper than fathomable. She and Jensen are a fiery, passionate love story between two people who fight hard but desire even harder. She and Jensen are for those who always shoot for the stars and never settle for less than they think they deserve. They might not be everyone's cup of tea, but they're *mine*.

Yet, I wouldn't be sincere if I omitted how scared I was throughout the writing process. The thought of crashing and burning on another manuscript I felt deeply connected to haunted my waking moments. I lost so much sleep over this book and the worries about the audience's reception of the story. I shouldn't care so much about that, but I do.

If you're reading this, then thank you for being here. This book is a confessional of all my hopes, fears, and dreams that I needed to get off my chest. Thank you for letting me share.

Acknowledgements

Going into this book, I needed a lot of extra support. Baring my soul on the page through Jensen and Daisy, I leaned on my village more than ever for reassurance. They delivered every time. So today, I honor them and give them flowers. Without them, this book wouldn't be half as good or in your hands at all.

Thank you to Melody, my cover designer for the Royal Ridge romances, for creating another showstopping design. When I told Melody the vision of "hot pink" and "steamiest cover," she went above and beyond to deliver on *The Games We Play*. Her emails were the highlight of my day during the design process, and she continues to be a remarkable collaborator. Genuinely, I couldn't imagine a better designer for this project, bringing the sweetness to my spicy.

Thank you to my alpha reader, my new best friend, Evelyn Leigh, for tagging in. I needed an alpha reader, and she dove head-first into my story. The memes, inside jokes, and otherwise unhinged commentary that ensued made our friendship even stronger. Despite all my doubts and fears about their reception, Evelyn is the sole reason I never gave up on Jaisy. She's hilarious, and I can't wait for the world to know her before her fantastic book, *Elevator Pitch*, enters the world in a month.

Thank you to my beta readers, Katy, Olive, and Estelle, who provided feedback and reactions once I got all the messy parts onto the stage. They brought sincerity to all of their comments.

They reassured me when I thought the book was unsalvagable garbage and never let me get too into my head. You three rock!

Thanks to my editors, Sophie Fitzpatrick and Cassidy Hudspeth, my superstar editing team. These two ladies dove straight into the project and cleaned up all the jagged pieces. They continue to lift me when I'm struggling through the editing process. I love you two.

Thank you to all the early access readers—ARCs—who gave this story a chance and visibility in the market. Having people eager to read my stories helps me stay focused on what I have. They leave their mark on me, and I hope my books stay with them in the future.

Thank you to my family and friends. The support of those closest to me is pivotal to my successes and weathering through the storms and rough patches. The people in my inner circle understand how integral writing is to my life. Shoutout to my mom, Ari, Kit, Shan, Evelyn*, Holly, Fallon, Kayla, Hannah, and Bree. A special mention to Shanti, my baby girl, who provides reluctant cuddles and emotional support during the rough periods.

Finally, I give a shoutout to all the 90s music I played to get into Daisy's headspace and all the episodes of 9-1-1 I binged. Every writer needs small vices to get them through the day and reward themselves.

About the Author

Cassandra Diviak is a 9x-published indie author in fantasy and contemporary romance. As a lifelong bookworm, books are her best friend and her greatest joy. In her final year of law school, Diviak knows the importance of words and how people use the written word as self-expression. While not at classes, filled with legal theory and the insatiable urge to cry about why she signed up for academic torture, Diviak is a cat mom to two stinky house cats (Gray and Shanti), loves cooking, hosting book club with her internet friends, falling down internet rabbit holes out of sheer boredom, coaching other writers in how to find their unique story.

Diviak writes manuscripts at inhuman speeds, earning her the moniker of "Muse Cass." She's thankful to spend so much time doing what she loves and building a community.

<u>CONNECT WITH CASSANDRA:</u>
Insta: https://www.instagram.com/author.cassandradiviak/
Tiktok: @author.cassandradiviak

Website: https://cassandradiviakauthor.weebly.com/

Also By Cassandra Diviak

The Shadow and Soul Series

Shadow of the Beast (Book 1)
Soul of the Sorceress (Book 2)
Of Wild and Witchcraft (Book 3)
Of Death and Divination (Book 4)

The Laws of Love Duology

Love on the Docket (Book 1)
Love Thicker Than Blood (Book 2)

Love at Royal Ridge

The Lies We Tell (Book 1)

Standalone Romances

The Signature Move

Printed in the USA
CPSIA information can be obtained
at www.ICGtesting.com
CBHW022302210924
14613CB00046B/590